Edward Frederick Leveson-Gower

Letters of Harriet, Countess Granville, 1810-1845

Vol. II

Edward Frederick Leveson-Gower

Letters of Harriet, Countess Granville, 1810-1845
Vol. II

ISBN/EAN: 9783744715850

Printed in Europe, USA, Canada, Australia, Japan

Cover: Foto ©Andreas Hilbeck / pixelio.de

More available books at **www.hansebooks.com**

LETTERS

OF

HARRIET COUNTESS GRANVILLE

VOL. II.

LETTERS

OF

HARRIET COUNTESS GRANVILLE

1810—1845

EDITED BY HER SON

THE HON. F. LEVESON-GOWER

IN TWO VOLUMES—VOL. II.

LONDON

LONGMANS, GREEN, AND CO.

AND NEW YORK : 15 EAST 16th STREET

1894

LETTERS

OF

HARRIET COUNTESS GRANVILLE

1828

TO LADY CARLISLE.

Paris: January 7, 1828.

Dearest sister,—I know not what to think of politics. Parliament so near meeting. Events of such importance pending. How I wish there was another head to the body; something new, respected at the head! Lord Carlisle, or, if he would not, the Duke of Portland; and young Stanley, if used enough to business, Chancellor of the Exchequer. In the Government I want something to look to, to be admired for the present, and promising for the future. Whilst Goody remains, one can see nothing but ridicule justified, and failure apprehended.

I do not fear the Ultras, because you have all such an opinion of the King's stoutness. I fear nobody but Goody, and do not understand his imbecility.

Your letters are most amusing. I see Windsor. What for Lady Conyngham out of spirits? I am curious to know. I am quite convinced that sense and spirit will carry us through this new I don't know what.

God bless you, my very dearest sister.

VOL. II.   B

To Lady Carlisle.

Paris: January 11, 1828.

My dearest sister,—Let me first say that we have
heard of Lord Goderich being at Windsor, so here we
are again all curiosity and suspense. I wait for Sunday
with the utmost impatience in hopes of the fog clearing
up. I hope that the sun that will shine forth will not
be an Ultra-Tory. My answer is that the nerves of any
given man are stronger than Goody's, and that, as you
say, in some cases calmness and courage come with the
call for it, and that in every other respect Lord Carlisle
is so entirely fitted for the situation, so uniting understanding, high rank, unequalled integrity, and moral
worth and universal respect and consideration, that it
is impossible a wish should not incline that way. Not
to forget that the first is not the most arduous or
wearing *rôle*. But this will probably cease to be a
question when my letter reaches you, and I only wish
to state my opinion with its grounds. There is one
change in the *siècle*, remarkable everywhere. Greedi-
ness for place seems exchanged for a dread of it, and
the difficulty everywhere is to man the boat.

Monsieur de la Ferronnays,[1] and Madame de Martignac,[2] cry all day, and Ultras *partout* seem to be the
only creatures grasping at high situations.

I cannot say how anxious I am to hear what is
decided, and my dread is of hearing nothing on Sunday,
but that the King was not well enough to see the old
lady.

Miguel must have been better amused with you
than with us. I never go out, my cold is still enough

[1] The Comte de la Ferronnays became Minister for Foreign Affairs in
the Martigny Ministry, which had just been formed.

[2] It is sad to think that Madame de Martignac, the widow of the most
deserving Prime Minister during the Restoration, was reduced to accept
in 1853 a small pension kindly granted to her by Louis Napoleon.

for a pretext, and the *Carnaval* slides by me like the Seine.   I receive visits in the evening which amuse me, and the conversation of such men as Pozzo, Molé, etc., is historical, and gives me an interest in French politics which I never had before.   They talk here of the impossibility of going on without added strength, and where that is to be looked for is a speculation as in England.

The Normanbys were here for a few days.   She is good, amiable, and, above all, sweet-tempered and good-natured, and he is the best of creatures ; but there is something wanting in both to give dignity to their merits, and liking them both as much, one is surprised at not admiring them more ; often clever, often pretty, there is something wanting—the *ensemble* is not complete, not sufficiently supported, a want of interest in the story.

To the Duke of Devonshire.

Paris : January 11, 1828.

You do not know the pleasure it gives me to see your handwriting.   I thought it was political, and was almost relieved to see Chatsworth and to know you out of the way of the present worry and suspense.

I do hope that something decisive will now be settled ; anything is better than the sort of suspended rickety state we are now in.   It is the same here, and when all over the world questions of such interest are pending, it is sad that Governments should all be put in for repairs.

I had heard nothing of poor Baron Delmar.   I hope, if the report is true, that she will find herself well provided for ; and then it is not a calamity, for he can have enjoyed little happiness, and her attachment cannot have been more than duty and gratitude.   I have seen Miss Rumbold,[1] very nervous but very

---

[1] Madame de Delmar's sister.

happy. She has caught a Chevalier de St. Clair of a good family, *de quoi vivre,* one child of four years old, good-looking, the image she tells me of the Emperor Alexander, fond of reading, singing well, with a château in the south of France. He liked her twelve years ago, thought she liked another, married, lost his wife, down the middle and back again to her feet. They only wait for Sir William Rumbold's return, to marry. I have sent her your letter, and asked her to come and see me that I may *sonder* about her cachemire. I am quite disgusted with the ill-nature of French and English about it. Instead of a most natural feeling of pleasure at her being extricated from a miserable situation, nothing but sneers. All the old stories about Septeuil raked up, her age exaggerated—in short, spite and ill-nature in all its shapes ; and this the more odd, because there is nothing brilliant enough in her fate to excite envy. It makes me long for the ceremony, as, without knowing him, I have fears of his being a man to be influenced by somebody or something.

To Lady Carlisle.

Paris : January 18, 1828.

No courier from England. This is really a little trial of patience, coming as it does at a moment of such anxiety and suspense. Granville is just returned from La Ferronnays. Their mail is not arrived. The weather has been delicious and perfectly calm, and I begin to think Governments, posts, all the regular order of things, are at an end. It is impossible to do anything but watch and listen. To-day is dark and rainy. Nothing can be more cheerless than the aspect of things. I will, however, try to write, though physically and morally it is difficult.

The Government here are to meet the Chambers as they are, the difficulties of deriving strength from either party having been found insurmountable. I will keep my letter open in the hope of being able to finish it with our post from England arrived. I am sure you will pity us for this *contretemps*. The only courier that has failed since we first arrived on the Voorhout. Every moment it seems to me more extraordinary that the well-known rumble of the courier's *calèche ne se fait pas sentir*.

I begin to think there is to be no administration, king, lords, or ladies, and a stop to all foreign relations. I see nobody but the embassy and Lord Seaford, which is a comfort, as we are all in the same frame of mind.

Three o'clock.—Twenty-three hours in the fog was the wretched courier at sea, my adored sister. It is a disappointment to know nothing. Mr. Huskisson says nothing can be decided till next courier. He only writes a note to this effect, being unwell. No statement of the case, no detail of anything.

How kind you are to Sukey! Her heart and letters overflow with it.

I expect to hear that the Ultras are in on Sunday. The difficulties in any other arrangement are so immense, the mischief all in that—yet I see no alternative.

We are in Huskey's [1] boat. We have the greatest reliance on his integrity and honour.

To the Duke of Devonshire.

Paris : January 21, 1828.

My dearest brother,—You must be happy, for you [2] have acted perfectly. I do not yet know enough of the case to pronounce upon it in any other quarter. Was any offence given to Lord Lansdowne? Is it true that he excused himself from meeting Miguel at Windsor,

---

[1] Most of Mr. Canning's personal friends approved of Mr. Huskisson retaining office, but not so Lady Canning.

[2] He had resigned the Lord Chamberlainship.

and that the King was furious? What pledges are
given that Mr. Canning's policy will be pursued?

It has been a real pleasure to me to drive out for
the first time with Flora opposite, so like Spot that she
reminds me all day of you. Pray do not be offended at
the *rapprochement.*

Be as lenient as you can, dearest brother, to Mr.
Huskisson. If he were an aspiring, healthy man, you
might suspect him of many motives. Knowing that he
is neither makes one believe that he is solely prompted
by a strong sense of duty, and a certainty of being able
to carry all Mr. Canning's measures into effect.

The maiden Rumbold evidently sighs for a bracelet.

To Lady Carlisle.

Paris : January 25, 1828.

My dearest G.,—I read your letter with a great
deal of pain, though its contents do not surprise me.
I feel every sort of sympathy with your feelings about
Lord Lansdowne, and admiration and regret must be
the ruling ones with regard to him. I cannot enter
into the case. I hate the separation, but I cannot
condemn Mr. Huskisson.[1] I believe he has a security
upon every one object of Mr. Canning's policy, that
left him no alternative. It remains to be seen whether
promises are kept and pledges sacred; as long as they
are, I think it is his duty to remain. Will you read
the ' Observer ' of last Sunday? The defence of Mr.
Huskisson in it is so exactly my opinion. Here it is.
' The propriety of Mr. Huskisson joining the Ultras is a
question which at this moment we are not prepared to
discuss. All depends on the conditions he has made
with them. . . . He may not be disposed to give up
to party what was meant for mankind. He may be

---

[1] Lord Goderich's Government being dissolved, the Duke of Wellington
formed an Administration to which Mr. Huskisson adhered.

honourably anxious not to leave in the very stage of projection the great processes which he has been superintending, at a more formidable individual responsibility than was ever before incurred by any public man in this country. Provided he has the assurance that his laboratory will be undisturbed and uncontrolled, we can understand the powerful motives that fix him to office, even in conjunction with men whose opinions and qualifications he cannot but in his heart despise.'

Now, dearest sister, we must see his task will be difficult. He must be a Shylock, and weigh their concessions and promises with a severe, uncompromising scale. He must remain to effect, and not a moment after the doing so is made impossible.

I hear Lady Canning is very violent. Howard,[1] I am told, disapproved, till made acquainted with the terms. As to the former, I think her feelings quite natural, and I should not like her to be able to reason the case as the ' Examiner ' does.

God bless you, dearest sister. I am obliged to answer your letter politically, but it is a painful subject now, especially as you will daily see and hear those who will increase your hostile views.

I shall on the contrary think it right to work myself up in a contrary direction. No, I shall keep to my present opinion—right if he can maintain liberal principles—if, finding he cannot, he stays an hour, I am utterly mistaken in him as a man and a politician.

To Lady Carlisle.

Paris: January 28, 1828.

Dearest sister,—Politics are in a most unpleasant state. Whilst I think it the duty of Mr. Huskisson to remain, I wonder every moment he does. I do not

[1] De Walden.

think him a man to be humbugged. I do not think him greedy for place. I still, therefore, continue to rely and expect; but *en attendant* his position must be a most comfortless one. But at the end I think he will either have the only reward anybody seems to me ever to get in this *bas monde*, that of having done right, although in vain, or he will, at the expense of health and happiness, stand higher as a practical, useful politician than anybody ever yet has done. I long to have Lord Seaford back again, to hear him argol-bargle about it all.

We live in the Bois de Boulogne, where less intrepid people do not venture.

To LADY CARLISLE.

Paris: February 1, 1828.

Dearest sister,—You are all growing so calm that I am enchanted. Lord Carlisle and Lord Lansdowne are adorable. I am delighted that Mr. Huskisson is at Eartham. If to their reluctance to accept or remain in office the Whigs add uninfluenced support of principles they approve, they will become my *beau idéal* of politicians. I ask no more, for I mean to go out myself, if Ultra-Toryism carries a tittle.

We had an event here last night which agitated me very much. A robber got into the garden, rushed on the guard, and in the struggle was killed. I was alone, and heard the gun and the cries just under my window. It was terrible to be so near this work of death, and I had fears of the guard having been precipitate, and the man perhaps coming to the house for other purposes, as he was well-dressed, with books and verses signed with his name, and a letter to ' Caroline ' in his pocket, unarmed and no instruments for robbery. My relief was consequently great in finding that he has been recognised as a notorious robber by the police, *condamné à mort* four months ago, and searched for in vain ever since. God bless you, my beloved sis.

To Lady Carlisle.

I have no news to tell you. The present Ministry here are going on as they are. I do not at all object to the word 'shabby,' I approve. You know my letters to you at the time of the victory[1] were all deprecating the language talked and view taken of it in England.

Last night brought us a much better account of Mr. Huskisson's health from Mr. Wilmot, who was staying with him at Eartham.

I have just had a Miss Webster with me, who brought me a letter about Caroline William[2] from W. Ponsonby. This account of her patience and resignation interested me very much, and makes me feel how much to education and subsequent events the errors of her life must be attributed.

To Lady Carlisle.

My very dearest G.,—Poor Lord Seaford! I pity him from my heart, for never was so true a friend, so true a man, and it is in these points he is attacked.

I do not wonder at your feeling delighted and proud. Lord Carlisle is the only man in the present time above suspicion and beyond malice. I dread Lady Canning's violence and want of judgment at a time when both would be so entirely out of place. I could allow for any bitterness of feeling but not the demonstration of it by production of letters. Personal abuse and attack would destroy my sympathy—unfeminine, un-

---

[1] Of Navarino.   [2] Lady Caroline Lamb.

feeling, unchristian. There is something too sacred in grief to make me understand its descending to the practical hostility of shewing up letters and quoting conversations. I saw Leopold to-day, but had little conversation with him. Is it true that Mme. de Lieven and Lady Cowper are very personally bitter and angry with the Duke? It would surprise me in the latter.

Tell me if my dearest brother is in spirits. He has a good conscience and more liberty—two pleasant things.

Alava is here. He says the Duke writes in good spirits, but Lord Clanwilliam told me that he had said 'There is an end of health and happiness for me.'

TO LADY CARLISLE.

Paris : February 11, 1828.

A thousand thanks, my very dearest sister, for your kind and most interesting letter.

No—you will not be violent, you will not prepare such a pang for yourself.

Are you aware that we are now suffering great anxiety on account of Mr. Huskisson's health? We, Lord Seaford, all Mr. C.'s friends, are convinced of two things—that he has acted upon the purest principles, from the strongest sense of duty, and that personally the sacrifice he makes is to him a most painful one.

When I tell you that one of his friends writes 'the sacrifice of his health, aye of his life,' you will dread to add by one drop of bitterness or hostility to the agitation and worry of his present arduous career.

The Ultras are furious. Is this no argument in his favour?

I wish I was at liberty to quote his letters, but I trust he has written fully to Lord Carlisle.

Give my best love to dearest Hart. I hope it will not annoy him to have my girls for a day or two on their way here, but I conclude he is in correspondence with Sukey, and will stop her if it does not suit him to have them. God bless you, my very dearest, dear sister.

I think I love you better than ever.

To Lady Carlisle.

Paris: February 15, 1828.

My own dearest sister,—It was very true that I was frightened, but not in hysterics, when the wretched man was shot in the garden. I could have no fear of one sort, for we have three guards at night. My fear was that the man ought not to have been shot, but it all turned out right—killing no murder.

About politics I feel how altered everything is! Zest and pleasure are gone. I admire Lord Dudley's speeches; they have in them spirit and self-protection, which is what I think the *siècle* wants. What is supposed to have put papa Wortley into such a rage? They say he was white and shaking with passion. How magnificent Brougham's speech,[1] the seven-hour-power one!

Granville dines out. Roast turkey, Irish stew and hungry children are waiting for me. I had a delightful letter from Hart, which I must answer in the course of the evening, but domestic life is become so dissipated that I have scarcely a moment to myself.

To Lady Carlisle.

Paris: February 18, 1828.

Dearest sister,—Yesterday's post leaves little doubt how it will end. It is impossible to judge how far a certainty of carrying on Mr. Canning's system has been secured till we know more. I am grieved at the political separation between Mr. Huskisson and the Whigs more than I can express. Much annoyed at

[1] On a reform of the Common Law.

dearest Hart's conduct and natural displeasure, with a feeling of gratitude to Lord Carlisle for being so fair, so kind. This is no cut at you, D. and George. I wonder at nothing, but accept with joy anything that makes me look to a diminution of hostile and personal feeling. Excuse me from entering into the political question. There is so much of personal feeling mixed up in it, pulling all ways, that I cannot.

To Lady Carlisle.

Paris: February 22, 1828.

Dear, darling Mary, the only thing I envy in the world. My girls are in a state of health and happiness not to be described.

I have not read the debates. Pray forgive me; I have no zest at all in politics one way or the other, yet I do read all the papers, all the speeches, but it is upon principle.

The *Carnaval* is over. I must begin being at home on Fridays, the first of next month, but I am so happy I want a little grievance.

Mrs. Marcet[1] and her daughter dined here yesterday. She is very intelligent and the image of Pisaroni, and the girl good-looking. Lord Mahon dined here. He looks old, like Lady Stanhope's uncle. Lord William Hervey is here. I never have dared touch upon politics with him, as I think he may be against Mr. Huskisson.

God bless you, dearest. I dress at four, dine at a quarter before six, to go at eight to a lottery at the Duchesse de Berri's, where I hope to win six pretty prizes, and probably shall return with six blanks.

[1] The author of *Conversations on Political Economy.*

To Lady Carlisle.

Paris: February 25, 1828.

It is not to be told, my own very dearest sister, with what delight I think of yours and my brother's visit to Brighton.

I am glad to hear a favourable account of Mr. Huskisson's health. Lord Lansdowne is not quite the person, with all his great merits, to meet Mme. de Lieven's piercing, unbounded understanding. I see her longing to box his placid ears.

Lord Dudley is a treat, and deserves his cutlets for the admirable despatch he wrote the other day. Do not say so, for I believe I ought not to talk of despatches.

The good, that is, quiet news from Constantinople confirms every hope of ultimate good. The tone of all here—Government, French, and English—about the victory has been uniformly loudly triumphant. We shake hands with joy at having fought and conquered together. I say to my *intimes*, ' Avouez, nous sommes des *fine creatures*,' and they laugh and say, ' Et nous aussi, s'il vous plait.'

My last Friday was my first dancing one. It began, my house open, and as bright as candles and Baudouin's band playing ' Cherry Ripe,' could make it, by my sitting to receive at eight alone [1] and crying, for at this very time, to that very tune, my adorable and happy child was last year at my side. People came flocking in, and they said it was gay and pretty. Pauline de la Ferronnays,[2] Mme. Victor de Caraman, Mme. Sabouska, Mlle. Rozoumofski, and two others whom I forget, with half a dozen Poles and Russians (Walewski, the hero of the day, Buonaparte's little one, included) danced a lovely mazourka. Pray show this to Hart.

[1] Her two daughters were away at Brighton.

[2] Who became Mrs. Craven, the accomplished author of many popular books. She wrote the life of Lady Georgiana Fullerton.

To Lady Carlisle.

Paris: March 8, 1828.

Very dearest sister,—Lord Seaford's return has been most interesting. He dined here alone with us yesterday, and talked of everything and everybody. He says that, though strong in opinion, nothing can be kinder or fairer than you are, and for this I feel delighted and grateful pleasure.

Tell me what Hart does about his soirées; has he asked the enemy? I can hardly understand the result of the debates. I am with Lord John upon the question.[1] Angry with Lord Milton for being, one must say, so provoking. I see him, hear him, and could fly at him and pull his pink locks. I am quite indifferent as to whether Mr. Peel loses his temper or not.

Why did Hart tell Lord Seaford he would have betted anything Granville would not have remained? I own it made me feel, only for a minute, very angry, as he has held different language to me, independently of my thinking anything about it as matter of opinion. Do not repeat it. Lord Seaford is such an angel of a man that I should hate to give Hart any little feeling against him for repeating, and still more because my anger entirely subsided when I recollected that dearest brother must have been angry, and could not resist saying whatever gave force to his conversation.

To Lady Carlisle.

Paris: March 3, 1828.

My dearest sister,—We have a dinner to-day before the usual Friday soirée—Flahaults, Dawsons, Charles and Catty. Lord[2] and Lady George and Caroline will not stir, because they have got Titchfield here on his way to Nice, and till he goes they shut up with him.

[1] On the Repeal of the Test and Corporation Act.
[2] Lord George Cavendish, created Earl of Burlington in 1831.

Tell Hart that aunt and uncle and niece make their *début* at a small dinner and soirée here on Tuesday. Lady George in a *toque* with marabouts, copied from one of mine of Herbault's. I am sorry to say that Caroline looks deplorably. Yet I think they will persevere till they marry Titch.[1] *Malgré* his grief and *deuil* and their *retraite* with him, they went to see 'La Muette de Portici' one night, 'Don Giovanni' and Mlle. Sontag yesterday. I lent them my box, which holds five with difficulty; they sat it out seven. Lord George with a black stock was, I am told, taken by the French for a great naval commander. To-day I have sent them an order to see Soult's pictures—a sober joy. Catty a very great love. 'Lady George bought herself a very smart cap to go to the Opera. When we got into the lobby off it flew. I thought the people would have died of it.'

TO LADY CARLISLE.

Paris: March 9, 1828.

Dearest of all dear sisters,—I cannot describe my happiness. Here they are every day all day. Susy is as well as possible. We have begun a life that even the uncompromising, inflexible Verity smiles upon. They arrived on Thursday; on Friday and Saturday she took long rides with her papa in the Bois de Boulogne; to-day we walked nearly round it. There is no excitement, but great delight. She is in buoyant spirits, in perpetual sunshine. Verity leaves us with little Granville on Thursday. I have promised that Susy shall go to Dieppe as soon as the weather is fine. With such happiness and hope we can submit with good grace to one further separation. My own health and spirits have returned with a rebound.

---

[1] Lord Titchfield had just lost his sister, Lady Caroline Bentinck.

Georgy is a dear girl. Eward and I talk and cry, and cry and talk. Sister, you do not tell me that you are sixteen, that you look beautiful, and younger and gayer than your daughters.

I must go to bed to rest my happiness and wonderful activity during the day.

Monday.—I received your letter this morning, dearest of sisters. I think you very amiable and candid, and respect your lingering feelings of hostility. I do think you must be proud, elated about Lord Carlisle, and delighted with the universal admiration and respect felt for him by all people, by all parties. It was your own letter that had given me the impression of your having worries, and I am glad they are not weightier ones. Our children must plague in proportion as they bless one.

A snow-storm prevents the ride to-day, and walking in the conservatory or dancing is to be the substitute.

To Lady Carlisle.

Paris: March 1828.

Dearest of sisters,—Our life is one of unbounded gaiety without excitement. Our expeditions in the morning are delicious. To-day the girls and I were for three hours in the Bois de Boulogne, in the most romantic green paths, with a smell of country and the cones of the fir trees, gathering violets and sweet-briar. Oh, how we sigh for you and yours! As you own to the detrimental effects of London, will you, can you not just come and refresh yourselves and invigorate yourselves for six weeks of spring here? What hinders, what keeps you at that time, dearest? All the babies will be born, you have nobody to chaperon, no Cumberland, no Yorkshire. Think of it, dearest sister.

You cannot have been enamoured of young Peel at

the first blush. I see it was Spring Rice you had never seen—no more have I. I pity you for your royal ties, though I believe the Duchess of Gloucester is charming, and methinks Sophy the pleasantest girl I ever met. But it is always more or less *accablant* to be with them.

Does it not redeem Lieven's character with you all to see her so stout and Whiggish *envers et contre*—power and place? It cannot be her interest to hob-and-nob with Lord Fitzwilliam. I always knew her to be a busy but an honest woman.

I see your soirée, dearest, and you don't know how your letters amuse me. Do you see mine last night ?—- A round table. Gontaut very absent, drinking *eau de veau*, which has cured her of all her complaints. She was hypochondriac, bilious, languid. She is now gay, rosy, and as strong as a lion, and without a nerve. ' Une tasse de thé ou de café en me levant, une cinquantaine de huîtres à une heure, une aile de poulet a diner, et tout le jour de l'eau de veau.' French women *en déshabillé*, some making tea, all bawling.

I believe Harriet Caulfield is going to be married to a French Marquis, but I shall know more about it when Mrs. Caulfield has ' trespassed her ideas upon me,' which she wrote me a note to beg leave to do.

To the Duke of Devonshire.

Paris : March 21, 1828.

A thousand thanks for your kindness about my boys. Granville's holidays last a week, Freddy's a fortnight. Lodgings is all I ask for them, as they need not be troublesome to you in the day, G. having promised to harbour them. I have been writing to her a sketch of our plans. We begin to despair of you here, but Susy thinks you will come to Dieppe.

The Cavendishes are settled at Meurice's. They go to the *spectacles* almost every evening. On Friday they arrived all very well got up. Lady George wears modest Herbaults—Catty is a regular French beauty. Caroline well dressed, but I suppose it is an unhappy passion for Titch that makes her look thin, wretched, and the colour of a bruise. Lord George is a dear. He looks as I remember him when I was three. He rides in the Bois de Boulogne with his own set out every day—very jocose, and a little smitten with Mme. Rothschild.

Harriet Caulfield's marriage is off. He like a prudent spark went and peeped at her at the Opera, when she knew nothing about it. He saw her with half a dozen sparks, very happy. Next day his Mama came to say that there must be no more of Mme. de Courval, and Mons. de Mornays and Mons. de Chabots, and to propose matrimony shorn of all its beams. A château, a few of his friends, economy. Harriet was of course alarmed, and, as I told G., sent in her resignation.

We had a curious dinner at Rothschilds' the other day. Leopold, Kent's son Leiningen, old Talleyrand, Mme. de Vaudemont, Prince de Hohenlohe, Juste de Noailles, Dalbergs, De Labordes, Mme. la Baronne de Lemurra and Mlle. Sontag, Mme. Merlin, Mons. et Mme. Rossini—her first appearance in decent company, I believe.

'La Muette de Portici' is beautiful, a *barcarolle* sung by Nourrit *fils* so enchanting, the scenery and decorations so beautiful, that it would answer to you and Lady Wharncliffe to come over together on a Tuesday to see it and go home on Thursday. God bless you.

To LADY CARLISLE.

Paris: April 4, 1828.

Dearest sister,—You have no idea how I see you at Chiswick, all you are, all you do, and Freddy in the midst of you.

Lady Londonderry is better than I expected, she is quieter, but I have only seen her once. They put out their airs a little, I am told. She would not dine at a great dinner given her by Talleyrand yesterday, but sent word she was tired with shopping. They go to soirées taking Sir Roger Gresley with them, as Prince Leopold does Sir Henry Seton.

To Lady Carlisle.

Paris : April 1828.

Dearest of sisters,—The banker [1] was an honest man, and had he delayed his act of insanity three or four hours later, a letter from Turin would have set all right. The Dalbergs have left Paris. They have lost immensely, but it is said that what made them most unhappy was a letter the banker wrote to the Duke, talking of the happiness he had enjoyed before he was over-persuaded by him to come to Paris, that he had urged him on to persevere and carry on what could only end in ruin and desperation. This is only an *on dit*.

Talleyrand's loss was equal, but he has hobbled about just the same ever since. He is beyond blows of all kind ! An upright creature !

To Lady Carlisle.

Paris: April 1828.

Dearest sister,—All you say of obstacles are daggers, but I understand your difficulties. I now pin my hopes on a meeting at Dieppe, arranged when the time comes. Methinks nothing would be easier than to meet like Henry the 8th and Francis the 1st on the edge of the Continent, suiting our time to our respective duties.

[1] An agent of the Duke de Dalberg, whom he defrauded, and who committed suicide. Many years afterwards his descendants restored some of the money to the Duke's family.

c 2

I wish I knew something of French politics, or understood English. Leopold is, I think, against the Government,[1] but do not say I say so, for perhaps he is not, he not being very clear, I not very attentive; but he shakes his head and wags his tail very significantly whenever he mentions Abercromby, on whom he doats.

To Lady Carlisle.

Paris : June 1, 1828.

I have a thousand things to say to you. I shall be very sorry if Mr. Huskisson goes out upon such a subject,[2] a mere squabble, or pet. Any great question would have been more creditable to him. What will the others do ? If all but Ultra-Tories leave the Government, how will the Duke ever be able to patch up an efficient one ? for Lord Grey I think will never do. By-the-by, whilst upon politics let me tell you that Lord John Russell delighted me about Morpeth. He says he never speaks without rising in estimation, that nothing can be more promising than his progressive excellence as a speaker.

To the Duke of Devonshire.

Paris: June 2, 1828.

My very dearest, kindest brother,—Your letter last night gave me the greatest satisfaction. I need not tell you what Granville's intention is, but I beg you not to mention it till his official letters upon the subject have been received. Of our plans we have of course scarcely had time to think. The *mappemonde* floats before my eyes. Your kindest of kind offers is an immense comfort to us, as, whatever we do, the possibility

---

[1] In England.

[2] He resigned owing to a misunderstanding between himself and the Duke of Wellington. Lord Palmerston and Mr. Charles Grant went out with him.

of seeing you and G. for a moment is invaluable. My girls go to Dieppe on the 15th. We have our house at Caudecote till October, and during the summer no place can be so good for Susy.

I beseech you to write and tell me what is thought and said: if the Whigs and Huskissonians meditate strong opposition, and how opinion in general inclines. There is an Ultra-Tory member here, indignant because of military Government barracks, etc. There is a letter from Lord Jersey, saying he cannot see how such a Government is to last. There are reports of Peel going out. Write, pray write.

I am glad that the moment of hurry and bustle is one of *relâche* as to fashionable life, that Paris is beginning to empty and will soon be quite deserted by French and English. We meet at Flahault's, Juste's, and here two or three times a week, and that is all.

I am glad the Hardy girls[1] are liked. Louisa is a very charming, clever, nice girl, and they are both quite free from coquetry. It is their spirits make them familiar, like birds who peck rather too hard when quite tame. I am sorry for your opinion of ——. I wish we were all like Madame Appony, who thinks every son and daughter of Eve divine, and said of her to me, ' Charmante! Douce et angélique nature.'

To Lady Carlisle.

Paris: June 9, 1828.

Dearest sister,—Lady Keith has just been here with numbers of letters she has received. Even courtiers and the Duke's friends are uneasy and alarmed, and others are confident that this Government cannot stand. Not so Granville; confident it will. I am meanly glad that it is not a finer thing. It seems to me *cosa da ridere.* I

[1] The daughters of Sir Thomas Hardy, Nelson's friend. He had just been made a Sea Lord.

cannot say how glad I am that, as Huskisson gave up, all did.

I cannot write *longuement* or pleasantly to myself or you to-day. Of course you know, without my telling you, what Granville does, and you will not say, like little Jumilhac, 'Mais vous ne parlez pas. Ce n'est pas sûr, vous n'avez pas reçu votre congé.' Granville is anxious his letters should be received before his friends talk of the future.

Here is Mr. Sneyd, very agreeable, thunderstruck at the news.

To Lady Carlisle.

Paris : June 12, 1828.

My very dearest sister,—Pray thank Blanche and Agar for their letters. Tell the latter I will untake the apartments I had taken for him at the Hôtel Bristol, and that I cannot tell him what our plans are.

I think, upon our leaving Paris, our first move will be to Dieppe ; but whether we shall spend the winter in England or Italy cannot yet be decided. I am happy the decision does not rest with me, as between all the *pours et contres* I should go distracted. My longing wish to be with you would combat painfully what I think most desirable for Susy. We shall know by the next courier the probable date of our departure from hence. Nothing ever was like the kindness of the regrets expressed here, and I shall have some, but there are immense compensations. The worry and packing and settling are fearful, and I long to be wound round the card, whatever it may be.

To-night's post brought us the majority of 106.

I have begun the great task of paying bills, burning and settling papers, and I take a great deal of exercise and have much occupation with my girls. A week later they will set out for Dieppe.

To Lady Carlisle.

Paris : June 20, 1828.

The courier brought no letter to Granville from Lord Aberdeen, therefore the official announcement of Lord Stuart's appointment has not yet been made.

How can you ask me what I think of Francis Leveson's conduct ? Can there be two opinions ? He leaves a worse place upon principle to accept a better. ⌋ Our letters were all read beneath the conscious moon, the garden bright with lamps, sweet with orange flowers. One honourable man had received what follows. ' We '— that is Tories, Whigs, and Radicals, the writer a Whig— ' are all prostrate at the feet of the Duke of Wellington.'

Never may F. L. G. know what in that garden was thought of him. We say that, since Cardinal Wolsey, there never was such a power in England. But I have done with politics. Mr. Canning is forgotten, and honest men must look on with everything but surprise at anything that may happen. Is it true that Brougham is coming into office ? I was told last night, at Mme. de Flahault's, that my brother had attached himself to the Duke.

We cannot remain here long, but until the official announcement nothing of exact time or place can be settled.

We dine at a great hot dinner at Pozzo's, and return to this garden, it being Friday, where we shall find lamps in the trees and Baudouin's band, so that the little dears may hop if they like. We go on, as is the nature of the beasts, as if we were here for ever. God bless you.

To Lady Carlisle.

Paris: July 7, 1828.

Granville has not had any letter from Lord Aberdeen announcing Lord Stuart's appointment, but the dili-

gent young Lord has written himself to say that he
shall be here in a fortnight. We are therefore as busy
as bees. We shall go straight to Dieppe, remain there
two or three days with the girls, and then, my own
dearest sister, we shall go to London. Hart has offered
us Devonshire House. After a few days there, we shall
return to Caudecote, but our plans for the future are
quite *en l'air*.

I love the people here for their excessive kindness,
and for the universal and strong feeling of admiration
and esteem felt for Granville. I have the delight of
seeing how entirely his character is appreciated, and
his departure lamented.

My dearest, we shall be so happy, and I shall see
Mary!

Pray forgive this scrap. I am now going to write
to Mr. Bradford, as we have determined upon sending
Granville to Mr. Chapman at Eton.

To LADY CARLISLE.

Paris: July 11, 1828.

Dearest G.,—Your amusing long letter gave us
great pleasure. Is it true that the King did not like
the Court, and the stars and garters upon the dandies?

Our day of departure is Wednesday. Did I tell
you that we have settled to return for six weeks to
Dieppe on the 1st of August, after a fortnight in
London? I pine for the journey and sea air, as the
oppressive heat here is almost unbearable.

Granville went to the signing the contract at Princesse Bragration's [1] last night. The *trousseau* was *étalé*
like an illuminated bazaar. Fireworks, bands of music
and dancing! Crowds of people.

It is such a delight to think I shall find you in
London, which seems to me to be subsiding every day.

---

[1] Princess Bragration married Lord Howden.

I am now going to have two hours of receiving visits, at four to pay them, but then come home to a quiet dinner, the garden and a drive after sunset.

To Lady Carlisle.

Paris: July 14, 1828.

Here am I, writing in an empty drawing-room, all my packing done and ready to go.

Never was anything like the fatigue of Wednesday. We dined at St. Cloud with Mme. de Gontaut and Mademoiselle, who is charming. Walked on the terrace, where the King and Dauphin came. Then to Neuilly. All this after a hot day of visiting duties.

Remember that somebody said, 'Whatever you do, do,' which is just what I think wanting to the *siècle*. Granville is very sorry, but sorry like an honest, noble-minded man—no repining, no irritation. He stands by his own conduct, without one shade of bitterness or unfairness. In short, I think more highly of him than of any human being—happiness enough for any woman, Lady Carlisle.

To the Duke of Devonshire.

Devonshire House: July 20, 1828.

Comfortable is not the word; we are in luxury and delight of every sort and kind.

Whilo is no bird, so thinks Marie, who, upon my desiring that he might not come to pay me his accustomed visit yesterday morning, as I had a bad headache, said with a look of fear and awe: 'Oh! J'irai vite, car il était au moment de monter.' He has said all he has upon his little heart. He sings 'God save great George our'— farther he cannot, or rather will not, go. I suspect he is not quite satisfied with the present state of things. He laughed so heartily when he saw Mrs. Graham and Lady Charlotte Thynne come in in their great Herbaults that they were quite put out. He says to me whenever I go about the room, 'What are you afraid of?' which shows great insight into character.

I sit in the delicious drawing-room and my friends pour in. On Friday we dined with the Carlisles and ran to see Mars in 'La Suite d'un Bal Masqué;' yesterday with the Staffords and then to the 'Crociato,' where Velluti sang hideously, Sontag divinely.

Monday Lord Granville is bidden to Windsor, between one and two, to dine and sleep there. Great wishes to have us all later; we think he is waiting for you.

Morpeth is gone into Yorkshire. Lord Normanby has had a fall from his horse and has sprained his ankle, yet hobbles to the theatres. Walewski thinks Lady Ellenborough the most divinely beautiful creature he ever beheld, but sickens at her dress. God bless you, very dearest, kindest of brothers.

To THE DUKE OF DEVONSHIRE.

Devonshire House : July 24, 1828.

Granville and I have been walking up and down your new balcony. *C'est une promenade ravissante.* The garden looks spacious from it, and to-day fresh, green, and bright.

We were disgusted yesterday. Granville devoured dirt. We went to dine with Lord Harrowby. The servant took us upstairs: 'Milady is gone out driving.' It was eight. A quarter of an hour passed. Lord H. appeared. I saw in Granville's looks that he had thoughts of burning his father, but a basin of soup and the sound of Lady H.'s carriage appeased him. We dined at nine. Lady Wharncliffe came at twelve, Mr. Sneyd a little before one. The consequence of these absurd ways is the heavy headachy *accablement*, the growing older and flatter that comes with a London life.

On Friday we dine at Leopold's, on Saturday we go to Beaconsfield to bring Granville to town. Madame de Lieven comes to me every day, pleased about Russia, of course. Lord Palmerston came yesterday and told me much that interested me. Everybody thinks that Parliament must meet towards the end of October, and we have given up Italy. Ireland, still as the breeze but dreadful as the storm, hangs over the Government by a single thread.

I am going with Granville to West Hill. I have not another moment.

To the Duke of Devonshire.

London : July 25, 1828.

We shall be at Brighton this day week. Will you secure us a room at the New Albion?

Your offer is most kind. If Leeds will not move and if Parliament meets in October, as it is now confidently asserted it will, we shall be most happy to avail ourselves of it.

I saw the world at Lady Barbara's [1] yesterday evening, dropping in at midnight in old satin hangings and jewels, and caps and hats, a mixture of all fashions, and something that makes a soirée look like a fancy ball. I could not see Ellenborough, Norton, Foresters, or Brudenells.

Continuation of the programme.

Saturday.—Beaconsfield : dinner here, to which we have asked Carlisles and Morleys.

Sunday.—Chiswick.

Monday to Wednesday.—Windsor.

Thursday.—Dinner at Lord Aberdeen's.

---

[1] Daughter of the fifth Earl of Shaftesbury, married Mr. William Ponsonby, created Lord De Mauley in 1838.

I am in agitated hope of the Carlisles being asked to Windsor, and obliged to put off their journey. It would make all the difference to me.

I expect Lieven every minute; she never misses a day and is very delightful. She has a little flesh on her bones in consequence of late events and vague hopes for the future.

God bless you, very dearest D. I will write an account of Leopold and Aunt George's drum.

To the Duke of Devonshire.

London: July 1828.

The rain it raineth every day, obstinate, pelting rain. The Carlisles are not bidden to Windsor. The Lievens are not. Granville rejoices at the bad weather. He has one engrossing fear, the Virginia Water, comprising boating, fishing, damp tents, and all the joys of an English summer! Mine is being driven by a Lord of the Bedchamber.

Granville and I went this evening to the Opera. Pasta, still unrivalled Pasta, in 'Semiramide.' First came Uncle George, complaining of London and rheumatic. Then Leopold very gracious and very happy, for he is much made of by the beauties and drinks tea with Mrs. Fox. Villa Real and Brook Greville. The pleasant people are almost gone. The Worcesters and Grevilles are going to Dieppe, and all the world to Brighton. I love my liberty better every day, and after being so long *en place* delight in the prospect of junketing about and seeing the world.

Leopold in spite of all resistance dragged me out before the Countesses. Glengall cared not a fig. Not so Aldborough, who was frantic; but I in going out from dinner stood with less than ' I am a dog ' face, and kept everybody standing and waiting five minutes till the Countesses had marched *en avant deux.*

Much do I fear that I am the only woman going to-day, and must sit by H. M.

To Lady Carlisle.

Windsor: July 29, 1828.

I think, my dearest sister, you will like a little line ; it may be no more, as I have desired to be told of the first conveyance. The drive here was delicious. I sniffed up country air, and felt better and better every mile. We found the two luxurious, large pink rooms, with blazing fires, a pleasure beyond all moral ones, and I had an hour and a half before dinner. We found here the Duke of Cumberland, the Polignacs,[1] and Lord Amherst, with Strathavons, the Duke of Dorset, etc. Nothing ever was so gracious as the King has been to us both, and he talked to me with such affection of all those I best love that I was charmed. The Duke of Wellington is not here or expected. I like it so much as it is. The Polignacs are excellent people, and she is a comfortable, no-how, little, good-natured thing. There is nobody to *gêner* or awe me.

The King and Lady Conyngham both asked if you were not gone, said they knew you only waited to see us and therefore had supposed you had left London. The King speaks in the highest terms of Lord Lansdowne, praised Mr. Huskisson very much. William Lamb is also a great favourite.

We are going to the Castle and the Virginia Water.

To Lady Carlisle.

Brighton: August 8, 1828.

Dearest sister,—Here we are. On Friday we found Hart looking better than I ever saw him. Yesterday we drove in flys, walked on the pier and all over the

---

[1] Prince de Polignac was Ambassador in London. In 1824 he married the Marquise de Choiseul, a daughter of the first Lord Rancliffe.

town. After dinner we went to tea with Lady Hardy, where we found little Johnny Russell. On the pier in the morning we saw the Grevilles and Sophy embark for Dieppe, and Cambridge, Montrond, Commissioner Irby, Lord and Lady Mount Charles.[1] She looked handsome, like the genius of the gale which blew hard upon the poor Grevilles.

The Worcesters and Walewski arrived here last night. We dine to-day at the Pavilion.

Bad as the weather is, I cannot say how I enjoy being here. My brother is extremely kind to little Granville, which doubles my pleasure. He is such a delightful little companion, so independent, docile, and all full of natural tact and instinctive civility, which prevents his ever being *de trop*.

We hope to be able to cross over to Dieppe on Tuesday, but at this moment the sea is impossible. I hear the place is overflowing with French and English. Whist every evening at the Duc de Coigny's, four shillings stake.

To Lady Carlisle.

Brighton: August 7, 1828.

Now this time we are really going. The morning is fine, very hot, and the sea only swelling with the effects of the two last days. Leopold and suite are going with us. He is going on to Berlin. I shall be a very pleasant companion for him, able to talk mild Liberal politics or of Mrs. Norton's charms, as he likes best. It is very great happiness to think of being with the adorable children again. Hart is quite well, and I think he has enjoyed having us with him, as we have been with him. How happy I was to hear from you! How ten times more happy to be at Castle Howard! I think it will be soon, Lady Carlisle.

[1] A daughter of Lord Anglesea. She became Lady Conyngham in 1832.

Now for the walk to the Chain Pier. Guinea has just been to tell me that the sea is getting calmer and calmer every minute, and it looks like a large blue sheet with a silver veil over it.

To LADY CARLISLE.

London : September 16, 1828.

There is not a woman who would feel more deeply the pangs of a week at Doncaster. I hope you will have the bright, sunshiny weather we have here to-day to gild its horrors.

We all disperse to-morrow. Cock and hen to roost at Dunchurch to-morrow. Chickens to Devonshire Place, Marine Parade, with a kitchen-maid on their dicky.

I hear Mrs. Norton is to be at Chatsworth. I am sorry we are to have an original amongst us, somebody impossible to like and ungracious to dislike. I am happy to think that Cradock and Walewski are to be with us—a great relief to the sober part of the community to have such game for her to point at.

We dined at Holland House. Lord Holland is uncommonly well, and I think his crutches are more a habit than a necessity. So thinks my lady. 'Put away your nasty crutches, Lord Holland ; you look as if you were in prison.' 'Oh, dear woman, pray let me have them ; I like to have them near me.' 'Impossible. Mary, take away your papa's crutches.' She is in high spirits and, as you see, in force.

Falck, the Prince de Chimay his *attaché*, a good-looking, straggling *attaché*, son of Madame Tallien, and desperately in love with Mary Fox, Sir James Mackintosh, Doctor Holland,[1] Allen, Charles. It was very agreeable, and we stayed till half-past ten.

---

[1] Sir Henry Holland, father of Lord Knutsford.

To Lady Carlisle.

Chatsworth : September 22, 1828.

How anybody exists anyhow, anywhere, without Morpeth I do not know. From the moment he arrived all has been gaiety and animation, and really to-day, the general joy has been so exhilarating that if Susy and Blanche were here I think I should die of it. We have already had charades under his management, so perfect, so beautiful that even the *blasés* and fastidious Montrond and Punch were in ecstasies. What charms me is that your modest, unpretending Caroline comes out like a glowworm in the dark and outshines them all. Her acting, her figure, the sweetness of her temper, in short all she is, is the theme of everybody.

We are to have to-morrow evening three charades. I am in the secret. One is to be 'Shylock' acted and spoken. First, Lord Morpeth and Maria Copley—young Marlow and Miss Hardcastle—in ' She Stoops to Conquer.' Shy.

Second, Lord Clements and Maria Copley—the Count and Juliana in the ' Honeymoon.' Lock.

Third, the trial in the 'Merchant of Venice.' Mr. Sneyd, Shylock ; Caroline, Portia ; Miss Wortley, Nerissa ; Coppy, Antonio ; Messrs. Townshend, Morpeth and Lascelles, the remaining characters.

To the Duke of Devonshire.

Castle Howard : November 6, 1828.

We shall be most happy to be a day at Devonshire House before Panshanger and West Hill, where we have promised to go.

The Granthams are here. Miss Robinson is one of the most delightful girls I ever met with, a fine, open-hearted, unaffected creature, very clever and full of talents. Mary, the second, is a sweet-tempered, fat,

soft-looking thing, without, I take it, much in her.
Lady Grantham is infinitely more lovely *à l'heure qu'il
est* than either of them. Her spirits are much improved. They leave Castle Howard on Saturday and
the Wharncliffes arrive, also Sir Joseph Copley and
Coppey; Maria is too unwell to come, and they leave
her at Scarborough.

We are much calmed about Penenden Heath.[1] It
cannot have much influence as a precedent, or I think
influence the minds of anyone; the only fear is its
frightening the King.

Varna news was received with different feelings.
The Granthams, who detest the Russians, groaned. I
thought no deeper than that you and Lieven would be
glad. I am an idiot about distant politics. A battle
in Ray Wood, a triumph on the top of Meg's Field, anything near fills my mind, but it is really very odd how
little I can present to myself what happens at Varna.

TO LADY CARLISLE.

Escrick: November 11, 1828.

My dearest sister,—I felt so flat on my way here
that I was afraid I should be unable to exert myself.
I had a headache and was much stupefied, but these
people are so good, amiable, and obliging, that I felt
immediately quite at my ease.

Mrs. Thompson[2] is clever, sensible, and excellent,
and I am happy to tell you that I don't mind the fine

[1] A meeting was held there to protest against the proposed concession
to the Catholics. Two thousand people were said to be present. Lord
Winchilsea and Sir E. Knatchbull supported a petition against the
concession. It was carried by a large majority, although opposed by
Lords Camden, Darnley, and Teynham.

[2] Mrs. Beilby Thompson was a daughter of Lord Braybrook. She
married Mr. Lawley, who took the name of Thompson, and she lamented
her fate—to be born a Neville, to become a Lawley, and to die a Thompson.
She, however, became Lady Wenlock in 1839, when her husband was
raised to the peerage.

VOL. II. D

words and quotations a bit, because she is perfectly unaffected. Her manner and diction is a laborious mistake in the art of pleasing, but does not offend, for nothing is put on.

I have been walking with her, looking at the nicest village, and the infant school. They have a glorious day for shooting.

The place is ugly, the house luxurious. They live in the most comfortable manner; very nice food and a most comfortable bed-room.

God bless you, beloved sister! I miss you not every day, but every moment. I have not yet at all recovered leaving you, and am your flattest, most affectionate of sisters.

To the Duke of Devonshire.

Escrick: November 12, 1828.

Your letters are such perfection! I see everything as it happens. You always tell whatever one wishes to know, and, rare and blessed art, every line is a picture.

There is one little trial to me to-day. Mr. Thompson has made such a point of Granville shooting to-morrow that we found it impossible to refuse, and by this means I shall not receive any letter till Wednesday. I must live upon my yesterday's delicious packet, and have the delight of two bulletins on Wednesday. Mrs. Thompson is a very excellent, sensible woman, doing a great deal of good in the village, over which we have been walking all morning. She has established an infant school, where there are children of even eighteen months old. All these clean happy babies are well clothed, well fed, kept out of harm, and taught obedience. In one cottage we found a pleasant, conversible old woman, sitting by the fire, only ninety-five years old. Old and young seem to doat on Mrs. Thompson.

There are very few people here—Sir Joseph and

Miss Copley, Georgiana Vernon, and her brother. The two girls have been prancing all over the country upon two fiery white steeds.

We are all very anxious about the King. Some say dropsy to the most dreadful degree, and that the Duchess of Gloucester is terribly alarmed.

To Lady Carlisle.

Trentham: November 19, 1828.

Lord Stafford is better than I have seen him since his illness—stouter and much more alert. She is also in robust health and in perfect good-humour, and their reception of us has been most gracious.

No words can say how I enjoy the beauty of the place, the charm of country in England. They were out when we came and I rushed to the *potager*—you know my weakness—and walked up and down between spinach and dahlias in ecstasy.

This is in many ways a beautiful place, and the *tenue*, the neatness, the training-up of flowers and fruit trees, gates, enclosures, hedges, are what in no other country is dreamt of; and then there is a repose, a *laisser aller*, a freedom, and a security in a *vie de château* that no other destiny offers one. I feel when I set out to walk as if alone in the world—nothing but trees and birds; but then comes the enormous satisfaction of always finding a man dressing a hedge, or a woman in a gingham and a black bonnet on her knees picking up weeds, the natural gendarmerie of the country, and the most comfortable well-organised country. Then at home, if the people are there one loves, the whole day is passing from one enjoyment to another; if not, one escapes, follows one's own inventions.

The idea of being at Chatsworth with dearest Hart is transport mixed with awe and timidity. Norton[1] will ask me who I am and suppose I cannot love. I.

[1] The beautiful Mrs. Norton.

D 2

mean to form an alliance with Lord Cowper, whose liveliness will not overpower me.

To LADY CARLISLE.

Trentham: November 22, 1828.

Dearest G.,—Granville has the gout, but he feels so well in health to-day that I hope it will be but a slight bout. The weather is delicious, and windows open, which gives something less dismal to a person tied by the leg.

Elizabeth is in the greatest beauty, and very pleasant and amiable. He wins me by his good-nature and devotion to her. They really are admirable as a pair. But his thirst for knowledge is frightfully minute, and there is something in his voice and manner that makes his talk appear worse than it is. Lady Stafford seems excessively fond of her and tolerant of him. I never knew anything like Lady Belgrave's praise and admiration of Lady Gower—thorough, heartfelt appreciation of her, and justice and kindness about Lady Francis. When she was alone with me and serious, I thought her delightful, but her *pleasanteries* set my teeth on edge. God bless you.

To LADY CARLISLE.

Trentham: November 25, 1828.

Dearest sis,—Granville had more gout last night, and we have given up Sandon and Teddesley.

Five Sneyds and Tom Grenville replace the Belgraves. The latter only arrives to-day. Walewski is just what you say. I like him, and when I am in for it I go on contentedly and pleasantly; but when I see him set out to walk round the garden at Chatsworth I shall follow, not meet him.

So Lord Grey's brother has not St. Botolph's. It is given to a *protégé* of Lady Conyngham, who, Mr. Sneyd says, is mother of Mother Church.

To Lady Carlisle.

Sandon : November 28, 1828.

We arrived here yesterday. I had a long and most affecting conversation with dearest Lady Harrowby. Her grief, so deep, so hopeless, is the more painful to witness, as the struggle of her life is to suppress and command it. She gave me the most minute, heart-rending details. She is very fond of Georgiana and interested about the younger ones, but nothing does or ever can fill up the blank, the dreadful blank.

There is an enormous world at Ingestre [1]—old Sarum, [2] the intended, and all the sons and relations.

Sidney Smith has been at Teddesley, handicapping Dick Bagot and Mr. Littleton for a day's shooting, the latter to carry six of the Dean's discourses to make up the weight.

We shall find the Wharncliffes at Chatsworth, which charms me.

To the Duke of Devonshire.

Westhill : [3] December 8, 1828.

What a delicious letter yours is, dear, adorable brother!

Westhill is dissipated. We found here the Gowers, and the Poodle running tame about the house. This morning, and a warm, spring, ravishing morning it was, arrived on foot Agar and Agress, both fat and healthy, and he in raging spirits, bringing us a good piece of news that, strange to say, was news to us—namely, that our goods have sold at Paris at an enormous value, the pianoforte at double its original price. Lord Ashley

[1] For the marriage of Lord Ingestre to Lady Sarah Beresford, daughter of the second Marquis of Waterford.
[2] Lady Salisbury, widow of the first Marquis. She was burnt to death at Hatfield in 1835.
[3] Lord Stafford's Villa at Wimbledon.

and Mr. Luttrel came with the Ellises, and soon after Mme. de Lieven. 'Bonjour, ma chère. Ah! quelle santé. Je suis si heureuse d'avoir une amie qui a de l'embonpoint;' and this upon the very threshold of our meeting.

They say Brougham is to fire off for an *éclaircissement* of the Duke's intentions immediately after the Address.

To LADY CARLISLE.

Westhill: December 8, 1828.

One moment. Lady Stafford, Granville, and Poodle are finishing their breakfast. Coach and four at the door to go and see York House [1] and shop.

We go to Panshanger to-morrow; we shall meet three generations from Lord Clifden to Bossy,[2] and Lieven, *qui me lira beaucoup de choses*. I hope I shall be intelligent, not *étrangère aux affaires*.

All here are charmed with George's speeches; both excellent, full of feeling and judgment, and so exactly the right tone and measure.

Nothing ever was so kind as the Hollands have been. They have Freddy[3] to dinner constantly; he always sits next to Lord Holland, and they talk without ceasing all dinner-time. Susy says they say we do not appreciate him nor think him the charming child he is, and she, Susy, agreed with the opinion.

To THE DUKE OF DEVONSHIRE.

Panshanger: December 13, 1828.

Dearest brother,—All our possible friends and children are here brought together. Yet the flatness is infectious and our tails are between our legs.

---

[1] Which was bought by Lord Stafford and became Stafford House.

[2] His grandson, who succeeded him.

[3] I was nine years old and at a school in Brighton, where the Hollands were staying.

I will give your message to Prince Lieven. Their
arrival last night was an immense improvement. She
is in very good spirits, making herself available in every
way, working a bag, playing a rubber, cajoling Huskisson, who, by the way, is a fat, robust, digesting man.
Mrs. Huskisson, a pitiable case of small health and low
spirits. Sir Frederick Lamb is very ungracious and
bitter and growling. Lord Melbourne exactly the reverse, exuberant to a degree. Madame de Lieven
suddenly gave a start in the middle of a deal. Emily,
three rooms off, was vociferating ' Bethgelert : ' ' Ah ! ma
chère, le voilà, cette terrible chanson. Figurez-vous
que c'est un chien qui se meurt pendant treize couplets,
et je l'ai entendue deux fois et cela fait vingt-six.'

To give you an idea of the way here. I am at near
two returned to my room, fire out, no housemaid having been near it, not a single morsel of writing-paper in
either of our rooms, one bad pen and a drop of ink.
This is a *galanterie* of Agar's ; I keep the other half for
Susy, after little Granville's arrival.

I have no news. Montrond comes to-morrow ; Lord
Melbourne is going to shoot at Mr. Baring's.

How happy Freddy will be at the ball, to be sure !
They say she is—Madame Michaud [1]—severe, but would
make the Simplon *chasser croiser* if she had a mind.

---

[1] The dancing mistress who gave the children's ball.

1829

To Lady Carlisle.

Brighton : February 19, 1829.

A thousand thanks for your political news. I think it seems tolerably calm and secure now. How amiable of Lord Clare to be sorry, if he is ! I should be so pleased never to see her again.[1]

We have all been out all day, and sitting at Lady Wharncliffe's open window like citizens on a Sunday to see the folks pass.

I am glad you are in London, as if you were not I could not be got there by force or persuasion.

We are rather angry with you for not talking a great deal of the opera relatively to Blanche.[2] We are dying to know if she liked it, if she felt shy. I have been questioned, but could not answer.

To the Duke of Devonshire.

London: May 6, 1829.

I am just returned from the bridge over the Serpentine. Even London is delicious to-day. The park was as fresh and green as ten miles out of London.

Yesterday I went to the 'Cenerentola.' Sontag, thinner than anybody I ever saw, looking as if she had cried her eyes out, sang beautifully sometimes, sometimes false, which she never used. There is more

---

[1] Lady Clare had just left him.

[2] This refers to the courtship of Mr. William Cavendish, who became successively Lord Burlington and Duke of Devonshire, and was the father of the present Duke. He married Lady Blanche Howard in the following August.

effort, weaker in health. She has had a baby, but she is married and has been so two years. She has told her story to her friends, because of the malice of her enemies. She had sworn to conceal it, but trod upon a peach-stone, was known to *accoucher*, and therefore now is obliged to confide the truth to a few. Madame Appony has received her since with the highest honour, the French ditto. The husband she will not name because of her oath, but nobody doubts its being Count Clam.[1] The mystery necessary because old Clam has promised to shoot himself if his son marries her.

I think William looks after Blanket.[2] The widow in your box, black satin hat and white feather, looked a beauty ; and the box, what with sons and men that looked like medical ones or heads of colleges, choke full.

You never saw such a ' *disette* of the men ' at Emma's.[3] No smart ones, and none of the fine ladies, few of the beauties, no Cowpers, Brudenells, Sheridans, or Baileys. No dowager dandies or young lordlings, save Villiers,[4] who hopped about like a bird with a broken wing, sandy-coloured and blear-eyed, yet a sweet smile and amiable expression.

God bless you.

To the Duke of Devonshire.

Bruton Street : June 22, 1829.

I had not a moment yesterday ; no post to-day, but I prepare for to-morrow.

The King uncommonly silent and low the two first days, in high spirits the last. Very gracious, very well, walks much better, his sight very bad. He was quite pathetic about your absence. I must say, to him, to us, to all, it was irreparable.

Ascot was a beautiful sight on the Cup Day. The

---

[1] She was married to Count Rossi.   [2] Lady Blanche Howard.
[3] Lady Brownlow.   [4] Lord Jersey's eldest son.

King bore his loss like an angel and was very gracious to
Lord Chesterfield, Zingonee's[1] new papa.   The dinners
not very long or hot, though Leeds sat on one side of
me, drunk as a fish, quite incoherent.   'I don't know
if you will quite take my meaning, see my view, but it
has always struck me that scarlet strawberries in
private conversation are very agreeable to meet with
occasionally.'   Little Dorset very pleasant on the other
side of me.   Our girls behaved very well and were
enchanted.   All the men more or less in love with
Emily Cowper.

What events, the election and the good effect of
inhaling!

Monday morning.—I should feel more remorse had
I been really capable of anything but getting through
Ascot.   I never got up but for the race, and was
obliged to repose in the interval before dinner.   As to
your health, you do not think yourself famous enough.
Clinton sent bulletins to her lord, and I knew of the
success of the inhaler in the Stand.

I think everything is to your heart's consent.
Who would not love and be proud of William![2]

To LADY CARLISLE.

Tonbridge Wells: August 23, 1829.

My dearest sis,—I have hardly had a moment.   We
have lived in junkets; yesterday Penshurst, Bayham
Abbey the day before.

We have had most agreeable, delicious little repasts
at the Lievens.   The first day Cowpers and Lord Ashley.
I did not take Susy, as I thought it would be a *gêne* to
her to find herself with the *amanti*.   Emily was in the
most captivating beauty.   Lady Cowper very much in
love with Lord Ashley and I too, we agreed, much more
than the girl.   However, I think her pleased with him

---

[1] The horse that won the cup.   [2] The late Duke of Devonshire.

and that she will like and marry him. He is quite willing to wait and hope and try everything to gain her affections. His manner of making up to her is so exactly what we all like and admire that everybody was in astonishment at her *insouciance*. So *passioné*, so devoted, yet so manly, *si noble*, nothing of the commonplace *rôle* in it. It is hardly possible to judge of her, she has been so perseveringly spoilt, but she is natural, gay, and good-humoured. Her only chance, I think, is to marry a good sort of man whom she likes very much.

Yesterday we had Lord Aberdeen and Lord Abercorn. The day before only the Lievens. Lord Aberdeen very great friend of the Princess's. To-day the Stratford Cannings perhaps.

The Lievens are of course much in raptures at the Russian successes, all but everything. Lord Aberdeen says there is nothing to oppose them now between their present conquest and Constantinople, a distance of only one hundred and twenty miles. He tries to look up about it all, praises Jules' understanding too, but certainly the Government here is not at its brightest moment. The Duke must be amazingly annoyed at the *début* of Monsieur de Polignac.

To Lady Carlisle.

Brighton : August 27, 1829.

Dearest of sisters,—I received a letter to-day from Lady Cowper, begging us to go to Panshanger, which we shall not be able to do. She says : ' We are still in a great state of irresolution about Lord Ashley. You cannot think how much anxiety I feel, and indeed so does she from the difficulty of making up her mind.' I shall really break my heart for him if she decides against, yet I should break a dozen, if I had them, for him if she marries him without loving him. So I am glad to have no voice in the affair and to have always advised, as she always consults, leaving the girl to her own decision.

Mrs. Hamilton describes all that we read in the papers of the dismay of the French. She says Lady Stuart is coming to England immediately. Lady Aldborough, who is in this hotel, gives up going back to Paris and says the English will probably all come away, as we are execrated there.

The Russian details are most interesting. They say the Sultan is quite mad and quite resolved not to give way. His fate must be decided now. He is the image of Lord Aberdeen, with a violent, nervous twitch in his face, lately come. Poor man!

To the Duke of Devonshire and Lady Carlisle.

Bruton Street: September 1, 1829.

Dearest brother and sister,—We arrived here yesterday. London is at its height of loneliness—one end of Bruton Street mending and blocked up—so that there is not a sound or a creature in it. Yet I have seen Madame de Lieven this morning. She came up from Richmond. There was a Cabinet yesterday. I hear the Duke remains in town, has too much to do to return to Walmer.

The report is that the Russians were at the gates of Constantinople; Gordon and Guilleminot[1] gone to their quarters. Madame de Lieven talks immensely big, says they will not stay in Constantinople, but that they will enter it, and then and there show their moderation.

The post bell! I must leave off with a thousand things to say.

Susy is perfect, admirable—the deepest feeling with such simplicity, such reality. Poor Eward terribly low. It is a most severe trial to her.

[1] The English and French Ambassadors.

To Lady Carlisle.

London: September 2, 1829.

We dine at Holland House to-morrow, which just now I must add to the list of my grievances. The two Granvilles rode there yesterday. In Kensington they met Lord Ashley looking blooming and radiant. He is coming to see me to-day.

I hear Emily says she is not in love, never was, and never shall be; that she supposes she must marry some day, and hopes when she does she shall love her husband, because it is right, but the later the better. Lord A. knows this, and Lady Cowper begged him to consider how much his love and grief would be augmented by coming to Panshanger, but he persists. He does not care what risks he runs for the slightest hope.

The girl, I know, was often so rude and *revêche* that Lord A. was wretched. Then Lady Cowper, in an agony of pity, scolds and tells her she has a heart of stone, and writes a kind note to the spark. She said to me that Emily said to her one day, ' You tease me so, you talk of nothing else. Let me forget it, and then, perhaps, I shall like him better.'

To Lady Carlisle.

Chatsworth: September 1829.

Dearest sister,—I am so enraptured at being here with my girls. There is but one cloud, but it will pass, and I cannot lament it. My adorable Susy continues to be very low.[1] I find, with all her calm and enjoyment, her feelings are of the deepest kind. She has the most melancholy smile that cuts my heart in twain. My dearest brother is all kindness, but it is a sort of disappointment and damper to him, and he asks when it will be over, as one does at a dull play. Georgy,

---

[1] At parting with her governess.

par contre, is—and this is most natural—quite an altered
being. She thinks she is very sorry and felt very
properly about it; but her almost wild spirits, her
countenance, and her good looks in consequence are
perfectly marvellous, and I must say her joy and Susy's
grief give me satisfaction. They would not be as
natural or loveable if either were put on or put off.
Then to see them together is quite beautiful, and very
soon the only drawback will wear away.

I feel quite nervous till to-day's post. If the account
of her is tolerably good, we shall all feel much relieved,
though I cannot believe for a long time she will recover
anything like cheerfulness or composure. The moment
of separation was harrowing. There is no other word.

To Lady Carlisle.

Chatsworth : September 1829.

Dearest sister,—I 'saw Blanche set off yesterday in
high health, spirits, and beauty, and my brother not
only delighted to take her to Derby but to leave us, his
charming guests, for a day.

Morpeth's arrival yesterday has given a new turn to
our amusements, and the young are all practising a
charade for to-night in the State rooms. He looks uncommonly well, the family somewhat excited by his
arrival. Caroline has pined for it, as, now John is
gone, she sighs only for representations.

I have invented something very ingenious, Lady
Carlisle. I come every morning to the music-room to
write to you. It has all the appearance of being sociable and pleasant without paying the tax. If you could
hear the many well-known voices from the drawing-
room ! Lady Cowper loud yet languid, Mme. de Lieven
dry and conclusive, Lady Grantham's purling stream,
Clanwilliam's shout of scorn. Then it is so amusing to
see them come out one by one, full of their last impres-

sions. Dearest Lady Wharncliffe sits alongside of the torrent always, and Lady Newburgh is quiet too, always bursting with her last squabble. Mrs. Damer has been through, dying with laughter. The Wiltons and Charles Greville come to-day, and the Belfasts and Stanleys have announced themselves. I enjoy myself to the greatest degree ; it is so noisy that it is easy to be quiet, so gay that it is comfortable to be dull.

Emily loves sport, nothing else. Lord Clanwilliam's vanity gives way to his fear of committing himself, but he allows himself all the amusement short of that. She is attractive and lovely, but I am a little tired of seeing her colour and shy, and have a wish for more of heart and opinion. Blanche is universally admired and approved of. H. de Ros : ' What uncommonly pretty women your two nieces are, Lady Granville ! '

I think the Lievens will scarcely get to you. If they do, it will be the end of next week.

To Lady Carlisle.

Chatsworth : September 14, 1829.

Lady Gower arrived yesterday. I do not think Lord Stafford at all in an alarming state, and I think Lord Gower will be able to join her at Doncaster to-day. Granville goes with her to Doncaster. My brother and little John, Mr. Shortbut [1] as Harney Cavendish [2] calls him, set out to-morrow. Charles and Catty are gone to Ossington and Mrs. Arkwright gone home.

It seems to me so strange to be left here in possession of this kingdom alone with my two girls, for Guinea went to Eton to-day with Sir Geoffrey Wyatville straight on end. To-morrow we three go to Stoke to stay there till Friday. I delight in Mrs. Arkwright, and my girls are delighted to go to quite a new place. Susy has recovered her spirits, and I never saw her look so

---

[1] Mr. John Talbot, who was very tall.

[2] Miss Cavendish, who became the second wife of the late Lord Stratford.

well. We have most affecting but comfortable letters
from Mlle. Eward. Her health is perfectly good.

We shall all meet here at dinner on Friday. We
long for Blanche. How the happiness of that *ménage*
seems to double my brother's!

To Lady Carlisle.

Newby: September 22, 1829.

Yesterday we spent a delightful day. At one we
set out, Catley, Susy and myself, in a britschka, and
Dody and Mary in a chaise, and went to see Fountains
Abbey and all the places. I never saw anything more
beautiful. We returned in fur cloaks by moonlight to
rest in our rooms till dinner. Granville, Lord Clanwilliam, and Charles Cavendish rode, but not with us.
Catty and the girls are the picture of comfort, drawing
as if Page [1] was amongst them.

Lord Clanwilliam is very agreeable at times, at
others yawning and bored, but happier here than I
have seen him elsewhere, as he is cock of the walk.
If I was asked what he was and not knowing names
and relations, I should say an only son, idolized and
spoilt by his doating parents and devoted sisters.

Susy and Dody like it very well, but do not get on
with the young and are a little too much patted and
stroked by the old; in short, they are very happy to go
to Wortley to-morrow.

To Lady Carlisle.

Lilleshall: November 20, 1829.

My dearest sister,—We have been this morning
driving and walking to the Abbey; the day has been
delicious. Mr. Sneyd is just arrived. He looks very
pretty and manly in a fur coat and seems uncommonly
amiable. Very low and flat, which I think such an

Their drawing master.

improvement to him, as he has quite enough in him to afford to be below par, and it is so much pleasanter than when he is all becks and wanton smiles.

We have had a pleasant little dinner. Mr. Sneyd seems become a regular country gentleman, improving and planting. God bless you.

To Lady Carlisle.

Sandon: November 22, 1829.

We arrived here before five yesterday, found Lord Harrowby alone, looking as if he was surprised we were come and not glad. But this is only his charming manner, for he doats upon Granville and loves company.

Lady Harrowby came to us in a minute, kind beyond measure, in wonderful looks, and her spirits quite as good as ever. The girls are in ecstasies to have mine. Dody is charmed with Louisa;[1] Susy very well pleased with Harriet,[2] who is a most excellent, good-natured creature.

Ladies Sandon, Mary Saurin, Harriet and Louisa Ryder, devouring the two annuals you gave my girls. They had seen none and are enchanted, twittering like hedge-sparrows.

To Lady Carlisle.

Sandon: November 24, 1829.

Dearest sis,—We left the Gowers with the very greatest regret. We have all been enchanted with her, and, independently of all she is, her amiability to us all was more attaching than I can say. We never were more snug than in their unfinished, unfurnished house; but then to be sure they gave us up their own apartment, with two dressing-rooms. I had no idea how clever she was, as well as excellent.

[1] She married Mr. George Fortescue.
[2] She married Lord Charles Hervey.

VOL. II.   E

Hart goes to Brighton to-morrow to see if his house is fit to live in.

To LADY CARLISLE.

Sandon : November 25, 1829.

The girls are very happy. Their evenings are spent giving letters and other innocent pastimes, which Sandon animates and leads with all that unselfish perfection of character which makes him enter with pleasure into anything which gives it. The Dowagers, Lord Harrowby, Mr. Sneyd, and I, play steady rubbers at shilling whist.

I have picked up a little news for you at breakfast. Mr. Fortescue writes from Dropmore that Miss Fanny has been rehearsing ' Belvidera,' and that the scene-shifters and lamplighters all wept, and the other actors and actresses could not go on with their parts.

Georgiana Wortley tells Lady Harrowby that Lord Ashley talks of giving up his office and going to America, and that Emily advises him not to be so discomposed, and not to go. What an odd footing ! Georgiana adds that she supposes it will end after all in her marrying him.

The Talbots are going to Hatfield to meet Lady Cowley,[1] who is arrived from Vienna. They come here on Monday for one night, on their way with Arthur the clergyman, very inferior to little John, I believe. I hope we shall none of us fall in love with him.

We have a quantity of leisure here, and go on in a spirited manner with Dante. I am now reading a book that interests and enchants me, Sumner's ' Records of the Creation.' Ask Morpeth about it. God bless you.

[1] Sister of the first Marquis of Salisbury, and wife of the Ambassador at Paris.

To Lady Carlisle.

Sandon: November 28, 1829.

Dearest of sisters,—We expect all our world to-morrow, when I hope to be more entertaining. We were half way through dinner yesterday, when the door-bell rang, and in rushed Mr. Montagu, with an orange comforter round his neck, loud, fearless, garrulous. He talks as he did, but I am less used to it, and though often amusing, it is as often *de trop*. He falls into a little knot of women not to his taste—at least it is to be hoped so—as Beckett, Powlett, and even Lady Lonsdale [1] are his heroines. ' A younger woman than any of you, rides to cover, plays at start-up, and none of us can catch her.' Playful seventy !

Lady Frances Sandon set out early this morning to travel by slow journeys into Devonshire. Sandon is to join her there. My girls adore him, and it is every-thing to them to have him stay. He puts everything *en train*. They conglomerated yesterday evening again, with shouts of merriment. Mr. Sneyd is very amiable, his spirits raised, and all his little airs and graces gone.

Mr. Wilmot writes to Lady Harrowby from Paris. He says the Liberals are perfectly secure, that the Government cannot stand, and that instead of gaining they lose by having got rid of La Bourdonnaie,[2] as they look upon it as a proof of timidity, have redoubled their confidence, and will not hear of any compromise.

To Lady Carlisle.

Sandon: November 29, 1829.

It is said and believed that the Duke of Wellington has bought all the Tories excepting five. This proof of

---

[1] Their mother.

[2] An active politician during the Restoration. He joined the Polignac Ministry upon its formation, but three months later, on the Prince de Polignac becoming President of the Council, he resigned. He said: ' Quand je joue ma tête, j'aime à tenir les cartes.'

where he seeks for strength will drive Lord Grey in strong opposition.

Mrs. Siddons is very much pleased with Miss Fanny.

Cradock has left Brighton. Lady Jersey adores him. Lady Lyndhurst thinks him too fat. Lady Conyngham is recovering very slowly.

Lady Dacre is in raptures with Miss Fanny, and has written two plays for Lady Frances.[1] The first was supposed to be too sentimental, so she has translated a French thing for her, 'Le Premier Amour.' Lord Palmerston is going to Paris.

Madame de Flahault says Monsieur de la Bourdonnaie's retirement proceeded entirely from his refusal to recall the Jesuits. Great treason talked in the Liberal *salons*, amongst those even nearest the Court.

Monsieur de Talleyrand still in an unsatisfactory state and will go to Rochecotte, which his friends think very imprudent.

Yesterday was charming. The Gowers came, to our immense delight, and Lord Goderich, whom I think charming, as a private character. We played at whist and *de petits jeux*.

To Lady Carlisle.

Sandon : December 2, 1829.

My dearest sister,—I write to write, for I have nothing to tell you. Lord Talbot and his son are gone to Teddesley. Lady Cecil is just returned to Ingestre. My girls are very much enchanted with her. They think her captivating beyond measure. I just stop short of that. I think her excellent, amiable, unselfish, unpretending, gay. I hope you think that enough, but I should be surprised if I saw anybody very much in love with her.

---

[1] Lady F. Leveson had private theatricals in which Miss Fanny Kemble appeared.

To-day being our first morning without company, Lady Harrowby is going to put on her jacket and go labouring ; I am going to trudge in my raw *baptiste* with Dody, the rest are going to ride. Mr. Lister comes here to-morrow. I saw him the other morning. He is uncommonly pleasing in his look and manner— such a pretty smile and unpretending quiet way, but his health appears very bad. I never saw such uncon- querable languor, so evidently constitutional.

Poor Lord Harrowby ! he is now snapping all their noses off, one after another—never Susy's—with little sharp scissors. There is something in her face and Granville's that quite prevents his ever snubbing them.

To Lady Carlisle.

Sandon : December 8, 1820.

Dearest sister,—They are all talking of Lord Howe's appointment, some saying it is a proof that the Duke is making up to the ultra-Tories ; others know that the King and Howe have always been great friends.

Granville is getting impatient to be in town, as our relations, the Kutzlebens, are come. It is insisted upon that I should crack this joke by Mr. Sneyd and Lady Harrowby. They say Lord Carlisle will know who they are, descendants of a Miss Wrottesley, and there is an advertisement in the paper that they are arrived in Gracechurch Street, Bishopsgate. God bless you, dearest.

To Lady Carlisle.

Bruton Street: December 7, 1829.

Dearest sister,—We were parted with at Sandon with kindness and regret beyond measure—Lady Har- rowby with her warmth *d'autrefois*,[1] and Lord H. was

---

[1] What she was before Lady Elrington's death.

quite sentimental with Susy. We had a delicious evening at Stony Stratford and arrived here at four. Granville went to White's, where he met Esterhazy, who
told him that Polignac and the Liberals talk equally big,
but that somebody who met the former thought his
confidence assumed.

The Emperor of Russia is alarmingly ill—a fever.
Madame de Lieven said to D. : 'Nesselrode me rassure,
mais ne me tranquillise pas.' Duke of Wellington very
equal in his attentions to both sides as the meeting
approaches. My brother very civilly disposed towards
him, as I have no doubt Lord Winchilsea is. Is he
the cleverest of us all? Lord Stuart disgusted with
Paris. Lady so much affronted with the French that
she all but cuts them. Lady Jersey and my brother
acting friendship. It seems now her *marche* to be con-
ciliating.

Aldborough has given up Paris and is going to buy
a house at Brighton. She said to Lady Holland, 'Is
the Archbishop of York straightlaced?' Holly answered, 'No, not at all, at all, but he is,' pointing to
Allen, sitting in a corner.

To Lady Carlisle.

Bruton Street: December 9, 1829.

I write to-night because I am afraid of not having
much time to-morrow. We found assembled at Madame
de Lieven's D., the Lambs, Punch, Mr. Luttrel, the Duc
de Laval, Alfred de Vandreuil, and Montrond. The
Lievens are low and uneasy about the Emperor. Laval
extremely distressed at the death of his mother. He
will be very popular, as he is civility and tenderness
itself—at the foot of every woman and the button-hole of
every man. Susy sat between Laval and Montrond.
Dody had Punch and was charmed with him. He wins
my heart by his admiration of Susy. 'Monstrous hand-

some girl she is, charming girl,' every second word.
He puts forth all his powers of amusing when he talks
to her, and she thinks him uncommonly agreeable, but
her head is not one that turns to anything but Blanche's
and Nussey's [1] attentions, and Dody admires him twice
as much as she does.

We hear from little Guinea that Miss Kemble was
received with rapture last night. Shouts and throwings
up of handkerchiefs, and somebody at the Travellers'
said it was infinitely superior to her Juliet. So to-
morrow we shall see.

[1] Miss Wortley.

1830

To Lady Carlisle.

London : January 1830.

I have seen Lord Carlisle, full of Abercromby Chief
Baron of Scotland.[1] Well done, beau Wellington ! I
have seen Mrs. Huskisson, thunderstruck about Wortley,
delighted about Brougham. So am I doubly since this
last hit of the Beau's, which will make Hart awfully
grateful. Lord Essex carries Lord Carlisle to the
House. Granville is just gone to hear the little Duke.
There is a rumour that the vacant place is to be offered
to Mr. Stanley, Sandon, or Lord Howick. I feel sure
that neither of the first would accept. Granville went
to Madame de Lieven's ; only six women had braved
such a night. The Duke was there, looking old and
careworn, very well in health.

Lady Harrowby is arrived. I wonder if her energies will carry her to the House.

To Lady Carlisle.

Bruton Street : February 1830.

Well, dearest, another impossible day. I saw but
violent rain and unfathomable dirt, muddy dirt, but
quiet.

I saw yesterday morning Lord Wharncliffe. He

---

[1] This office should have been bestowed on the Lord Advocate of
Scotland, but that course was violated in order to conciliate the Duke of
Devonshire. Mr. Abercromby was his man of business, and had long sat
in Parliament for one of his boroughs.

sat with me an hour, tells me the Duke of Wellington is in high health and spirits.

Great indignation at Mr. Herries's appointment.

How can I have written so long without saying anything of poor Mr. Tierney's death! It seems to have been sudden, although he had been previously ill. Granville saw the Hollands yesterday and dines with them to-day. He says they are very much grieved, and say nothing had been so unexpected. Mrs. Tierney had left him the morning of the day and had called proposing to take a walk.

The Session is expected by everybody to be stormy: violent and agitating discussions. I suppose the Duke will sit cracking these nuts and leave the different parties to fight it out with each other.

To Lady Carlisle.

London: February 8, 1830.

I have been shut up with the girls, and yesterday was my first dissipation. I dined at the Lievens. Greece [1] on one side, so low, so flat, so thin, that the log was a better King than that. Nobody knows what is to be, but he whispered it all in German to the Princess, who did not tell us anything about it. I had Morpeth by me on the other side, and he paid me as much attention as a man can who has Emily Cowper on the other, beautiful and buoyant. The Wharncliffes were amongst us with their tails between their legs. Huskissons, F. Lamb, Lord Palmerston, everybody, says the Government cannot go on as it is. We shall see. The report of Lord Ellenborough going out is general. The effect of the two last debates in the House of Commons would necessitate a change under any other Premier, but I feel convinced he will weather it if Peel is not alarmed and does not refuse

---

[1] Prince Leopold.

to wade through the dirt of the Session. F. Lamb is
bitter beyond measure ; angry with Lord Holland for
being lukewarm ; says we have dawdled till their
moment of danger has passed ; suspects Brougham ; has
got a story of his pushing back the Whigs who were
following him, saying, 'For God's sake, don't come
after me, you will leave the Government in a minority.'

Dearest sister, of all things that did not affect those
dear and near to me, Lord Graves' death [1] has shocked
me the most. It leaves a sort of horror in the mind at
all he must have undergone ; what she must now, and
those poor children. I had heard nothing since I told
you that Lady Mount Charles said the whole history
was a lie. I knew he was living with her again and
had asked Lord George Seymour, whom he met in the
street, to call upon her.

To Lady Carlisle.

London : February 1830.

There is every sort of speculation afloat about
politics, and I feel a conviction that the Duke will not
throw himself upon any party, but fish in all. Madame
de Lieven has asked him to dinner on Sunday to meet
us, Lady Cowper and Lady Harrowby, and is extremely
amused at the prospect.

I saw yesterday Lady Canning, very much softened,
perhaps partly by the sorry figure her enemies cut just
now. I hear the Duke floundered out his vindication
of Lord Ellenborough. I admired George Lamb's
speech very much, but am told it was foolish and imprudent and gave the Government an opportunity of
saying many things they wish, and played their game
in short.

I am convinced of poor Lady Graves' innocence,
and believe that he had been goaded to suspect and

[1] He committed suicide.

tax her with what is certain he never discovered, that he was extremely furious and violent, and that his misery has been the having by his accusations ruined her character. Think what those must feel who were in the habit of exciting his mind against her and sending him all the paragraphs and accusations!

To Lady Carlisle.

London: February 1830.

My beloved sister,—I have nothing new. Johnny Russell has just been here. Lord Ashley behaved most beautifully last night. How that girl can help liking him, seeing his devotion for her, with something so noble, so manly in his whole manner and conduct! He danced all night with the girls, did not follow her at all, and his spirits appeared good without being forced, though I, who know, could have cried over him.

Lady Graves has not had a moment of consciousness since she heard; in fainting fits, and delirious at times.

To Lady Carlisle.

London: February 11, 1830.

Dearest sister,—Pretty speeches of Husky and Grant, and very proper butter spread upon Abercromby by the former.

I have been walking to Lady Harrowby, who is in bed with a severe cold and can scarcely breathe or speak, but in despair at giving up going to the House of Commons to-night. The Wharncliffes came and tea'd with us last night. There is a slight *gêne* because we never mention politics, but they are such nice people and there are luckily so many other subjects in the world.

I see Peel is very touchy about Husky's pleasantries.

Lady Graves continues in the same state. When

she speaks, it is to ask why he does not come to fetch her to some place where they were to have gone together.   The Duke of Cumberland has been sent to by the police to tell him that they cannot answer for his life if he goes about.   I must pity him.   There is a fatality about him, and I hear the nervous horror of his manner is dreadful.   It is now made a crime that he called at Hampton Court to inquire how Lady Graves was.

To Lady Carlisle.

London : February 1830.

Dearest of sisters,—Morpeth is much pleased with Miss Fanny, though he sees the faults I see and is not foolishly enthusiastic.   How glad I am that Brougham accepts and is coming in for Knaresborough !   Somebody said, J. Wortley between Lords Ashley and Ellenborough will be the tame elephant between the wild ones.   Mr. Luttrel was asked whom he had met at the Hollands.   ' The quick and the dead,' Lord Clanwilliam and Mr. Rogers.   Mr. Montagu was full of joy at the people at Melton, after Lord Clanwilliam had been over, unshaved and very grand, holding all of them as cheap as dirt, asking, ' Who's that heavy swell?' The name is a good one.

I am poorly and don't feel jovial.

To Lady Carlisle.

London : February 18, 1830.

Dearest of sisters,—I have seen my brother in such spirits, so happy with the little *ménage* at Devonshire House, disgusted with John Wortley—indeed, I never saw so general an opinion as the one of his having so lowered himself ; delighted about Abercromby, satisfied with himself about Brougham.   The minority last night must have been a curious sight—O'Connell and Sadler walking out side by side.

Agar has just been. He seems to think Lord Ashley and Emily will certainly be ; do is another question. They say Frederick Lamb is strong for it now. God bless you.

To the Duke of Devonshire.

Saltram : August 22, 1830.

Many thanks for your letter, dearest brother. We have here the mildest, prettiest weather; nobody but Theresa and Mr. Lister, engaged and seeming perfectly happy.

To-day Lord Graves [1] and his French wife, some Frenchmen and sparks quartered at Plymouth, expected. I had forgot the Bulteels, the happiest couple I ever saw, devoted to each other, fond of all the same things, their children and place, drawing like artists, singing like nightingales.

Eward has reached Paris in safety. She says the French look extremely happy, with a sort of arrogance and *bravade* about them. Charles the Tenth is to have Lulworth Castle for the present, *en attendant.*

Lady Morley is dying for Chatsworth in the winter, but cannot tell what her plans are. We, dear brother, are *comblés* ; we have no sort of engagement but the Carlisles for October. A winter has always been a *beau rêve* of ours.

But, private and confidential, think of Guilleret,[2] who says we shall perhaps go to Paris to see the new state of things.

To the Duke of Devonshire.

Bruton Street : November 4, 1830.

Dearest brother,—Everybody is full of the Beau's speech. Some think it a proof that he is determined to resign, others that he will propose an enlarged plan of reform in the course of the next six weeks.

[1] Son of the man who committed suicide.
[2] Lord Granville.

Morpeth spoke well last night; so exactly the moderate, sound view to be taken of things just now. To-day I have been to see the Staffords, violent reformists. Lady Stafford observed, 'Mr. Brougham made a very good speech.' 'Francis is a foolish, provoking boy. What was the use of being such a fool? And when he knows his father has declared himself for reform.' I have also seen Lady Clanricarde in the most brilliant beauty, to be sure.

Lady Aberdeen's rout was immensely full and hot. Granville was there, and Ministers, Dips, and a few extras. I heard of Madame de Lieven's and Lord Grey's faces expanded with delight.

Billy has forty people to dinner to-day, Lord Gower among them.

To the Duke of Devonshire.

London: November 5, 1830.

I begin at an early hour, as I may not have much time. You read Lord Winchilsea wishing to see Lord Grey in. I begin to pity the poor Beau.

Granville and Dody [1] dined at Holland House. Holly having caught a young bird, they were *tête-à-tête* after dinner, pumped her hard upon all the distressing subjects she could think of—religion, the Wortley marriage,[2] etc.—but Doddles turned round and round in her hands like a ball of soap. The Duke of Bedford dined there; she is in Scotland.

Theresa is to be married to-morrow morning, and we are to breakfast at Lady Clarendon's at two o'clock.

Saturday.—I had no time yesterday, and regret it less, as G. wrote. Loch votes for Reform. Lord Stafford is all energy, ratting with speed yet dignity, as his principles do not allow, etc. I saw Lady Canning, very much pleased indeed.

[1] His daughter Georgiana.
[2] Mr. Charles Wortley to Lady Emmeline Manners.

Granville went to Lady Lansdowne's last night. Lord Grey *rayonnant*. He and the host most affectionate together. The bets were that the Duke would have been out yesterday, others that he will be a Reformer before Saturday.

Susy has been at the marriage at St. George's. Theresa, very pretty in a white pelisse and white hat and feathers, dreadfully nervous, shook like a leaf. I hope it has given Susy a horror of matrimony. Mr. Lister looked very happy.

I shall wait now for the chance of news. Mrs. F. Frankland Lewis has been, but communicated nothing. Bathiany has been, and the report is that Ministers are out, but I cannot vouch for it. Lady Cawdor told Morpeth that Edwin Lascelles told her that Mr. Algernon Greville [1] told it him.

To THE DUKE OF DEVONSHIRE.

London : November 8, 1830.

Granville dined at the Lord Chancellor's yesterday. The Chancellor came in after they were all seated from a Cabinet that had lasted five hours, returned to be at it again till two, and the result you see in the papers. It may have been necessary to put off,[2] but what indignation it will create! It is really appalling, and I fear for the Duke. It would be a national disgrace if any personal harm awaited him, and it is impossible not to fear it from the exasperation of the people. The Government must have received information of the most alarming nature to justify this measure. I am terrified for the first time. Cold paws, my heart in a curb rein, and my ears erect and listening—out or in, who, when, all, seems secondary to me to-day.

I hear Lady Jersey is terribly low. Did I tell you

---

[1] Duke of Wellington's private secretary.
[2] The King's visit to the City.

that Lord Talbot had sent to the Duke, *à la* Stafford, to
declare himself for Reform?   Lord Wharncliffe came to
see me yesterday, holding up his hands and eyes at
the Duke's last speech and declaration,[1] saying unto
everybody that he must go out, and extolling Lord
Grey's most sound and temperate speech.   God bless
you.   Nobody knows what determined Ministers, and
of course all judgments upon it are premature.   Some
say they had notice of a house taken from whence
the Duke was to have been shot, others that the trades-
men wished it, and that there was a plot to detain
the King as a hostage.   I am uneasy about the House
of Lords, where Granville has just gone, as they say
there will be a piece of work.   Abercromby says the
report was that twenty thousand men were coming up
to-morrow from Liverpool, Manchester, etc.

Lady Cowper has just been, making me brave.
She says Lady Wilton is in despair at there being no
Guildhall, thinks it was all prepared for battle; which I
therefore conclude she would have liked.   I feel rather
less frightened.

To the Duke of Devonshire.

London : November 9, 1830.

You will see by the debate that the insufficiency of
the reason for putting off was almost unanimously
felt.   Nevertheless, I am sure it was right ; but it has
given the final blow, if one had been wanted.   Lord
Haddington said to Granville after the Duke had
ended : 'If I had not thought he must resign before, I
should be convinced of it now ; ' and even his own people
hold the language that the sooner he goes the better.
Everything is dropping from beneath his feet.   I hear
he looked extremely low and annoyed.   I am dying for
him to go for his own sake, for, as to his place, who can

---

[1] Against all Reform.

wish to be unfortunate enough to get it, and I think of Lord Grey with profound compassion. *Ainsi ne va pas le monde*, and there are many *rayonnant* faces about.

Wilmot Horton is at breakfast here, having turned up like small fish in a storm. He must think himself lucky in having kept aloof, when *agacé* by the present Government. He may not be lucky with the next, but at least stands fair like another.

I am happier about danger, as I am laughed at, and nothing has happened yet, but Mr. Wilmot met just now a policeman. 'Was there any row last night?' 'No, your honour, but there will be.' The Queen to the last was dying to go. Lady Cowper called on Lady Jersey yesterday. She says she showed her feelings in excessive crossness. I go on Friday to dine at Ludolf's[1] to meet Berri, on Saturday at Lord Stafford's to meet Talleyrand. The other Berry dines and sleeps at Stafford House on Saturday.

Susy went with Lady Morley to hear Lord Burghersh's opera. They thought it wretched. Two pretty things—one out of the 'Gazza,' and the other out of 'Masaniello.' Lady Wharncliffe is charmed with Miss Fanny in Mrs. Haller.

Poor Lord Mayor! The City have turned him out, and sent into the country for Mr. Copeland to be the new one. It is *très dur*, but I suppose right, as to have had an unpopular one in the City just at this moment would have been the deuce to pay.

I am just come from *la Princesse*. The carriage was at the door to take her to Richmond. She walked out of an inner room, Le Gris[2] following. He looked fair, sweet, like a spring morning. She is in a great state. 'Mais, est-ce vrai? mais que faut-il penser?' She was at Billy's last night. He was all fondness and civility to the Beau, and drank his health four or five

[1] Neapolitan Ambassador.　　　[2] Lord Grey.

times. He, the Beau, holds the most *hautain*, *prononcé*, confident language. He says Government count upon a majority of a hundred on Tuesday next, scoffs at the idea of danger to himself. 'On l'essayera, mais on ne le fera pas. Ce n'est pas si facile de tuer un homme.' On the other hand, she says that he does look, not only ill, but low, *abattu*, downfallen.

Lord Grey told her she would be pelted, and she was in a great taking. 'Mais, donnez-mois donc un nom. Que faut-il dire? qui doit-on nommer? qui est populaire? Vous, Milord—mais que sais-je? Je ne sais pas qu'on vous aime. Qui me dira la vérité?

I have just seen Lord Haddington. He thinks they cannot be sanguine. All the Government people talk the most desponding language, but the Duke puts on a face and is determined to fight it out to the last. He looks upon Billy's civility as conclusive ; says he never heard of its being otherwise from a King to a Premier at the last gasp.

Lord Haddington says he understands all the Royalties were at Billy's last night, talking the most open, unguarded defiance and dislike of the Duke.

To the Duke of Devonshire.

London : November 11, 1830.

Dearest brother,—There is no news. The girls went with their papa to Lady Aberdeen last night. The Duke talking a great deal, Lady Jersey ditto. The brides in great beauty. Lady Lilford, red gown and white hat and feather, the prettiest. Lady Gower and the Duchess of Buccleugh dine at Court to-day. G. and I, both in the last stage of decrepitude, rush there at eleven, yet I think she rather likes the thought, having a more junketous soul than me. Hardys just asked, driving about distracted for feathers and flounces. Blanche very much affronted. Morleys not asked, she who lodged and fed them. My girls enchanted. Eight hundred friends.

The report is that the Duke offers his resignation incessantly. Billy will not hear of it. The mob continue peaceable, in spite of all the provocation. Some say the rise of the Funds is because Ministers are out, others because there is a conviction of their going. Lord Strathaven votes for Reform. William Banks with Ministers. Lord Grey and Dolly sat together the whole of yesterday evening. Lady Jersey, Talleyrand, Lord Clanwilliam, and a Minister or two got together into a little room and made a great noise.

When the mob cried 'Liberty or Death!' to the soldiers, one of them said, 'I am very sorry I cannot give you liberty, but I can give you death, if you like it, this very moment.'

To the Duke of Devonshire.

London : November 13, 1830.

I know not when I shall get to Brighton; you must know how much I wish it.

I am low about politics, yet I know nothing; but there seems to me a reaction, and people are so shabby that I think the King's fondness and allegiance to the Beau will tell. I begin to think there is no chance of beating them on Tuesday.

Well, last night was the completest failure.[1] Elbowed by the navy, numberless queer figures, and at eleven, in the midst of a dull rout, with scarcely any dancing-men, an impromptu was got up, and two reluctant, serious quadrilles performed to one or two squeaking instruments taken out of the band and playing out of tune.

Lady Chesterfield beautiful, I am told. I did not see her.

[1] A party at the Palace.

Lady Seymour beautiful, I thought, but people say she has lost her good looks by being grown one of the fattest women you ever saw.

Lady Ashley, body and mind too much out of curl. Lady Clanwilliam, a fine girl. Her husband out of his wits for joy and all devotion to her; so was Lord Seymour to his corpulent lady.

Talleyrand crawled past me last night like a lizard along a wall. Dino dined there, so did the Lord Mayor and Mayoress; good-natured of Billy.

God bless you. The Queen enquired most graciously after you—in detail.

To the Duke of Devonshire.

London: November 14, 1830.

Dinner [1] was solemn. The Chancellor looked black, the Beau bored, Lieven in a taking; she does not know what to make of it.

I have just been told that the Government means, if possible, to meet Brougham's motion with a sort of concession, the members for the great towns perhaps. Nothing ever equalled the shabbiness of the Duke, and there is only one thing all agree upon—that he will stick on as long as it is possible. I can form no guess of what will happen; there is no calculating with such a man as the Duke. Berri, though our object, looked amazingly out of water amongst us all, with Lieven in velvet and diamonds and the Beau basking by her. Dolly [2] was in a very stormy state; looked uncommonly handsome. God bless you. I could not squeeze out another word, if to be hung.

[1] At the Ludolfs'.   [2] Lady Lyndhurst.

To the Duke of Devonshire.

London: November 15, 1830.

My dearest brother,—I am so sorry you are still unwell. I cannot get rid of my hoarseness and general *malaise.*

Why, Orange is uglier and thinner and animaler, and nobody seems to think about him. He is in high spirits, driving in a cab and dining with Worcester, and I dare say will fall in love with Fox or Beckett and be a very happy particular.

The interest is immensely strong. Dating from to-day the Opposition are very sanguine. The Beau has disgusted so many of his friends, and the officers, by keeping them up three days and nights in readiness for action. They now call it, whatever may have been the truth, a nonsensical panic. Lady Wharncliffe was here yesterday. She said he had cut his own throat, that, even if he has a majority on Tuesday, it will only be dragging on the same weak, miserable Government. I saw Punch, frantic against him if he turns now to any modification of Reform. Old Charles Greville says : ' I wish to God they would go out ; they make themselves more and more ridiculous every day.'

Interrupted by the Swedish woman. She wonders at Mrs. Berri, how she can go on and gobble up all the Ludolf property. She tells me Mme. Esterhazy is very angry. She called and they said Mme. la Marquise *est chez elle.* She walked up the narrow stairs and there found our Berri, standing up in the middle of the room, Ludolf and Bouillé arranged like d——d honours behind her. She bowed, asked after the Emperor's health, never offered her a chair, and bowed her out again before her carriage had had time to turn round.

Dolly says the Beau means to swallow Reform, but I cannot believe it, and most of his friends deny it. It would leave him too contemptible, and he has not now popularity enough to shield him.

I dined at Stafford House last night. Lady Stafford has a sort of *engouement* for Dino.[1] She can talk of nothing else, and her manner to her is affectionate homage. She can say nothing but 'Is she not beautiful? Is she not interesting?'

To the Duke of Devonshire.

London: November 21, 1830.

I am better, but so languid and flat, in spite and in the midst of all the excitement, and that's why I did not write, knowing that sister G. did.

Everybody seems to be charmed.[2] I told her some little changes, which I saw her put into her letter to you.

Lady Grantham has just been here. She came from Silence, who is in a real taking and says she has been the only consistent person, reviled Grantham, who turned upon her. Brougham called on her yesterday. She would not speak to him, only grunted. Granville is gone to see him take his seat. Miss Berry came here yesterday, had dined with him at Lady Charlotte Lindsay's; never saw such a sweet *couleur de rose* lamb.

I have not seen Mme. de Lieven. Some people think she had travelled so far and fast on the late road, that she must have a little time, like a ship after a storm, to settle into her way again.

I am very sorry for the Lyndhursts, all the more for everything that makes others glad.

All the minor rats are running in upon the Government, which must be troublesome. God bless you.

[1] Daughter of the late last Duc de Courlande. She left her husband, the Duc de Dino, in order to preside over the house of his uncle, the Prince de Talleyrand, with whom she remained until his death.
[2] At the Duke of Wellington's resignation.

To the Duke of Devonshire.

London : December 20, 1830.[1]

My dearest brother,—You are most kind and adorable, but are you sure this time there are not objections you may feel when the moment comes, some grand affair at which you would like them [2] to hang on Blanket, or a wish to show them to the future Duchess of D., the morning after your proposal? A Revolution and a wish to sell them. Think this over and say ' Send them back '—without scruple, if my logic strikes you.

There was a debate last night, good for Government, I am told. The Beau let slip the words, ' The late misfortunes in France.' Lord Grey spoke extremely well; much talking in the other house, Paris and Vienna not to be cut down. I have had letters from Madame de Flahault, and some *parlez-vous*, most flattering. Nothing yesterday from Lord Stuart, but Mrs. Hamilton writes, evidently, I think, begged, to deprecate our coming soon, yet go we shall.

I must answer all of them to-day, so a longer letter to-morrow.

[1] Lord Granville was re-appointed Ambassador at Paris on the formation of the Grey Government.

[2] The Duke had lent his sister some diamonds.

1831

To Lady Carlisle.

Dover: January 1, 1831.

We have had a most prosperous beginning, dearest beloved sister—a day like October, brighter and clearer than any we have had since Castle Howard, making everything look distinct and beautiful.   There is not a breath of wind and the sea is as calm as a pond.   We are to go over to-morrow in the ' Duke of Wellington,' not a Government packet, but a good large one.   We are promised a three hours' passage.   G., Stewart, Guinea, and Dody are all in the agonies of looking forward to to-morrow, and sick already from fright.

We met on the road somebody we took for Mons. Van de Weyer,[1] and a number of *calèches* coming to London.

Good night, my dearest sister.   I never let myself look at this as a long separation.   I really could not.

Sunday morning, half-past nine.—It is a delicious day, as mild as spring, with very little wind—just enough, I am told, to steady the vessel.

The girls are quite well, very sorry; but change and bustle and their own adorable sweet buoyant natures would carry them through everything.

To Lady Carlisle.

Calais: 10 o'clock.

We had a passage of three hours, the sea very rough, till we got near the French coast.   Granville and I

---

[1] The Belgian statesman, who was prominent in the movement for separation from Holland.   He was a long time Belgian Minister in London.

perfectly well on the deck all the time. Susy well in
the chariot, Dody in bed very ill, Stuart, George, and
Guinea the same on deck.

The weather was fine, very cold as we got here.
We walked about the town, smelt the peat, saw the
National Guard with his gun, the merry noisy people
all over the place, in this cold weather on round-
abouts and *jeu de bagues*, the women in caps as usual.
Came back to dinner at five o'clock. Our rooms—not
the large ones, which they think too cold and are shut
up—are very comfortable.

Going abroad, anyhow, anywhere is such a lark;
not more, not less, but a lark. Neither comforts nor
grievances are as substantial as in England. I am to-
night in the humour that I like being on the road so
much more than being arrived in Paris.

We shall not get there before Thursday.

We have the two latest French papers here. Nothing
can, I think, be more promising than the state of Paris.
Good night.

To *Lady Carlisle.*

Paris: January 10, 1831.

Your letter was, as always, a happiness. Let me
now try to settle my thoughts, and give you a
sketch of my four days. I have done immensely in
them, yet I tremble when I think how much remains;
but this is our May and June in London, with all the
labour of dress and visiting, for Paris, *malgré* the
retraites, the *absences*, the *bouderie, les résistances*, is Paris
still, swarming with English, and the French rising from
their ashes every day. Balls beginning, dinners constantly, every Frenchwoman at home three days in the
week, ten of them, I am told, on Saturday. We have
thoughts of a ball in about a fortnight, before Guinea
leaves us.

Yesterday I went at two to the Palais Royal, desired *de me faire bien belle*. I find to my despair that the great wish is that one should dress a great deal and very fine to encourage trade.

I found the Queen, the Duke of Orleans, two Princesses, three dames and one man, most amiable, most kind, most gracious. They talked of everything—the difficulties of the times and *surtout* France. I think their great wish is to pursue the late firm though very moderate course the King has taken to restore the tone of society by degrees, to promote a return to amusement, hats and flowers. *Les boudeuses*, you must know, amongst whom predominate Alfred, Jumilhac, Girardin, do not go out and dress like beggars.

The Duke of Mortemart's appointment to Petersburgh has electrified this last set. He is high in everything—rank, character, high-mindedness, connections—and such a man, chosen and accepting, is an immense step for the present people.

We have had the *attachés* to dinner. They are all civil and good-humoured. Ashburnham rheumatic, languid, and upon my woord I doon't kno-o-ow *genre*, which is not useful or efficient, but he seems sensible and gentlemanlike. Magennis well-meaning, good-tempered, would be a puppy if he knew how, rather prosy. Waller good-natured, vulgar little man. Lord Harry Vane,[1] good-natured, inoffensive. Cradock, a very fine thing, a Russian prince of high degree.

To LADY CARLISLE.

Paris : January 1831.

Granville is extremely busy. I delight to see how he is considered and valued here; my only regret is, *entre nous*, that he has such a man as poor Mr. Hamilton,

---

[1] Third son of the first Duke of Cleveland. He succeeded to the dukedom in 1864.

who, as he grows older and less sanguine about his own affairs, is left with the outward man entirely unstuffed, not one idea or *qualité* of understanding, that can make him of the slightest use or relief in any one branch of Diplomacy.

We like Paris better every day. Though it is the *Carnaval*, there is not an oppressive quality of gaiety, and we often sit at home, my girls at a round table with John Ashley, Guinea, and G. Stewart—occasional *attachés*—every now and then a Monsieur or Mademoiselle presented to them. They are daily improving in looks and dress, and their countenances and manner—I must say perfection—make them so popular and so much liked that I see they will be amused and happy.

To the Duke of Devonshire.

Paris: January 1831.

I must begin a letter fresh from the mint. We are just come from the Palais Royal—a dinner given to the English Embassy. Our reception was beyond measure gracious. The King and I talked without ceasing. He gave me a detailed account of all the terrible days. The Queen was *très souffrante*, and is more low than her relations. Madame Adélaïde very sprack and delightful, sitting by the King and Odillon Barrot, the most violent of the Radical party. I was very fine, in a grey satin gown, my diamonds, which make my fortune, and a Herbault all feathered and bowed—very fat, but squeezed into a *tournure*. My sister Dalmatia[1] by my side, still fatter and tighter. The girls looked uncommonly well. Susy, between an old Maréchal and a National Guard, chattered away and *emerveillé'd* them with her French, and was for the first time in high spirits. Dody, very nice and *piquante*, made her play upon a pair of *attachés*.

[1] Wife of Maréchal Soult.

To the Duke of Devonshire.

Paris : January 14, 1831.

I have been writing a volume to G., my very dearest brother. I am expecting Mme. Appony every moment. This is only detached sentences.

Pozzo has just received his letters of credence. Princesse Bragration is too ill to move off her couch, so how can she go to Russia?

The *housses* are on; the room, the green beauty, looks just like its old self, with the sun broiling upon it.

They talk of balls at the Palais Royal, but one of the Princesses is ill.

Baronne Delmar[1] the great thing; concerts charming. Mme. de Flahault the other great thing, *soirées*, and the few French who show.

The Poodle is worrying the Pug,[2] but good-humouredly, and it is a great relief to have him here to do the dirty work. He says it is not to be told the good you have done him. He is really worthy of it, and likes to bark and wag his tail about it.

Quiet is the word for this great town, dearest; one must *savourer* it, for it cannot last long. If you could know how like a dream it seems to me, to be so perfectly settled here, as I now feel!

Bourke is very happy, very valiant, very fond of Soult;[3] likes his energy and promptitude. To be dawdling in these times is making *bouillie pour les chats*, says she.

God bless you.

[1] A great beauty, sister of Sir William Rumbold, and married to a rich German Jew.

[2] A nickname of Mr. Frederick Howard.

[3] Marshal Soult formed part of the Lafitte and Perier Administration. He was President of the Council from 1832 to 1834.

To the Duke of Devonshire and Lady Carlisle.

Paris: January 17, 1831.

Bourke has promised one party, and Lent falls early ; how much my girls will like it ! They agreed, even last night, for the first time, that it was like a house in the country. The billiard room, in which they spooned, and two or three people, added to ourselves, sitting over the fire.

To-day we are all writing. The *attachés* and the Poodle dine here. It is well I got up early, as that too kind woman, Mme. Appony, has sent to ask if I will see her, out of all rule and etiquette. Mme. Castelcicala would see me d——d first. Mme. de Flahault is coming by appointment at three, Bourke at half-past four. I hear Lord Stuart is in force and good-humour ; she unwell and very low, being, I am told, in despair at staying on here, but he insisted upon it.

I think the case a little more complicated than I did. I mean as to society. Appony, I see, though she loves and honours the Queen, lives on tears and sighs, and all one set of my old friends weep with her—Noailles, Girardin, Jumilhac, &c.

Mme. de Flahault sees few but the violent Orleanists, the Ministers, and some of Flahault's greatest friends from all parties.

Poor Lady Ellenborough[1] is just going to be confined ; Schwarzenberg going about flirting with Mme. d'Oudenarde.

To Lady Carlisle.

Paris: January 21, 1831.

Dearest of sisters,—I hear that Talleyrand found all the Ministers junketing when he went up for the conferences. The Duke of Orleans has been ill, but is

---

[1] She was divorced in 1830. Prince Schwarzenberg was involved in the suit.

better.   He looks a little delicate, but is by way of
being quite well and dances all night at the balls.

Mme. de Polignac is still here, wonderfully calm.
Lady Stuart has seen her, and so had Mme. de Davidoff.
She says she can see one person at a time—any hurry
overcomes her.   I am going to make the attempt.

What have I done since I saw you?   Apponys'
ball.   We were not amused.   There is no conversation.
The girls are led out by unknown parleys, who caper
by their sides and then give them back to my care.   It
has given them a disgust of balls, but what they do
like is the *genre de vie habituel*—the dinners here, and
being at home of an evening, and Mme. de Flahault's.

The Stuarts and Mintos dined here on Wednesday,
and yesterday I took Betty to the Opera with me.   She
is good, sensible, has behaved perfectly well in a difficult
situation, but she talks too much, too loud, is too absent,
too busy—huffy, with notions of all kinds about civilities
and ceremonies.   This makes the pleasure less of endeavouring to make the self-imposed awkwardness of
situation as little irksome to her as possible.   To paint
her in one word.   Do not tell.   Mrs. Hamilton hinted
to me that what would console her most would be being
considered as a cut above the general society here,
first in all times and places.   So I see it is.   She even
likes a nod and a smile occasionally, in the midst of
the things, and, in short, would like to enact with me
ex-Queen and *régnante*.   So, when she comes, we play
at Ladies, and all is as smooth as possible.   Lord Stuart
and I are, *tout autre*, as happy and as little dignified as
need be.

My only grief and care is economy.   I flatter myself
there is an immense difference, but it is the eternal
subject of lighting that vexes me.   Granville does not
care a straw about the thing looking less well than
formerly.   It is all in reasoning perfectly true, but I

find to my shame that I have not a mind that can raise itself above dark rooms and an ill-lit ball.

To the Duke of Devonshire.

Paris: January 24, 1831.

Perhaps the Queen may like you to read to her the following sketch of Paris this moment with regard to society and the Court. Most of those absent from Paris, who have quite retired into the country, are personal and devoted friends to the ex-royal family, such as d'Escars, Chasteleux, Damas, Narbonne. Here there are two different parties, into which, though there are many shades, society divides itself. Those who go to the Palais Royal, who support the present state of things *chaudement*, who were all ready to rush to Court in the first stormy days. These are called *Les Dames du Mouvement*— Mme. de Vaudemont, des Boigne, de Montmorency, de Valençay, and de Laborde. On the other hand are *les Dames de la Résistance*. Amongst these last almost all the Faubourg St. Germain—Mme. de Girardin, violent; Mme. de Maillé and others almost ruined; Mme. de Jumilhac; the Noailles; Mme. Théodore de Bauffremont, daughter of the Duchesse de Montmorency. These last are expected. 'Elles portent le deuil; cela ne durera pas; c'est un très petit deuil.'

All wish for peace. All the sound-headed and right-minded pine for order, all love and respect the present Royal family, all condemn Charles X. and Polignac.

There is a third class, *les Dames de l'Attente*. They are said only to be watching the weather.

I send this small talk in case it may be of use to you, but you must be discreet and consider my gossip as private. The Queen here is adorable and adored.

We have done little: sitting at home—Opera—nasty damp weather. Two hours trying to get to the Grand

National Ball; obliged to come back; cause of liberty.
Messieurs les Gardes Municipaux said they would not
let their *Roi* or their *Père* pass. God bless you. Our
ball is on the second.

To Lady Carlisle.

Paris: January 27, 1831.

The Ball at the Palais Royal was splendid and
beautiful: four immense rooms, dancing in each. The
supper *magnifique.* We sat all night, the Queen and I,
with our girls on either hand. Mine danced with French
and Italian unknowns, but enjoyed themselves very
much. We supped in State also; I between Susy and
Madame Adelaide, Ad. and I eating *poularde au gros sel*
and asparagus and very jolly.

I forgot to say that Redem and Daniskiold are
footing it in these parts, both disgusted and pining
after England; but though the first is a bore and the
second vulgar and familiar, it is something for the girls
to see a well-known face, which can talk to them of
their English friends and Almack's.

Guinea is very low at the thoughts of going to-
morrow with the courier to London. We decided
upon sending him once more to Eton, as his enjoyment
here was much too great to allow it to go on. Poor boy!

The courier has just brought me your letter—most
dear sister—smelling, as usual, of sea air. The Pavilion
must seem to you 'home' by this time. I approve
extremely of the King.

My girls are such loves. They will be very popular
here, I see, but nothing will shake their fidelity to
England. As yet they are not even much pleased, only
sweet-tempered and contented.

Do you see me, Lady Carlisle, in my dressing-room
—hartshorn and oil on the chimney, cloves in a saucer,
a piece of flannel airing at the fire, Michaud—do you

remember him ?—and Richard arranging *paravents* in the bedroom to keep out the blustering wind ? I think things seem tolerably quiet here. Belgium is the eternal subject, the stubborn knot. ‘Après tout,’ says Vaudemont, ‘c'est le hasard seul qui pourra décider la question.’

I must not write any more, for I have got all sorts of business relative to my ball, which is to be this day week. It was very different *autrefois*, when I had only to say like the children—more, more,—as to light, flowers, etc. Now, most laudable it is, we are all a re-trenching and vexatious public can wish, and Kulbach and I are expected to *on dansera* half price exactly of what it was. This makes me foolishly nervous and anxious, especially as I must say the Stuarts, who saved in everyday life, gave splendid balls. I have, however, obtained dearest Granville's consent to light much more, and have dancing in two rooms, the long and the middle one. Think of Betty's spirit, who had three double lamps in the conservatory, seven or eight hundred francs' worth of flowers, and yet called stingy because she put up some pretty white moreen instead of hideous red silk! *Ainsi va le monde*, and who would fear its criticisms, but those who have taken calomel and starved! God bless you, my dearest.

To Lady Carlisle and the Duke of Devonshire.

Paris: February 8, 1831.

Your letter last night amused and interested us beyond measure. We devoured the accounts of dearest Blanche's presentation, of your green and gold tail, of the ball, etc. Of politics the little you say is reassuring, as I had heard the same exaggerated fears for the Ministry as you hear of our troubles. What odd reports I spy in ‘Galignani’ about Sir Robert Peel!

I wish he was with us or against us, only because I hate him in a merciful protecting attitude.

Dear Duke, who is la Vicomtesse d'Hénin, *née* Dickson or Dixon, who says if you were here, how I should love her? As it is, I have sent my card, because Lady Codrington loves her. I took the Mitfords to Madame de Flahault's last night, and an irritated, discontented flower sat she, knowing nobody, the company all screaming at the top of their voices, and Mercer, dear, honest Mercer, putting her best leg out to her, but that a stiff, unbending one.

We hear our Charles and Emmeline think of coming to live at Paris, and we are also told that nobody else does, and that Mrs. Cavendish and Fanny are derided and scoffed at for having such a mad project. I will not press it, because I will not be responsible, but it will be a great disappointment to the girls if they do not. I see here how very English they are in what they prefer *dans tout genre*. They love Keith. God bless you, dearest, dear brother and sister.

To Lady Carlisle.

Paris: February 1831.

Dearest of sisters,—When I read the newspapers and see the accounts of Paris, I tell myself I have been here in the midst of *cette fièvre*. But so perfect is the tranquillity now, and so daily did I walk round the Tuileries each of the stormy days, that it is difficult to fancy it all. Yet these accounts I believe are all accurate. The truth is that, where there is such a bulwark of defence in the National Guards, actually lining and paving the streets at a moment's warning, I cannot believe in danger whilst they remain true and unwearied; and as each of them rests upon the preservation of his individual property, I do not doubt they will.

There have been most animated debates. For a moment the present Ministry was said to be out. I believe now that even Montalivet remains. The dissolution of the Chamber is to be almost immediate. It is popular, and expected by most people to be returned much as it is. In all the late elections the Moderates have been chosen.

I went to the Palais Royal on Saturday. I thought them all terribly low and *accablés*. The zealous champion Lady Keith, who went with me, said, ' I never saw them in this state, but don't tell.'

We had been at a forty dinner at Pozzo's—Diplomacy and English—and I ended my evening in two very different *salons*—Broglie and Ranzau—but both equally dull. Mme. de Broglie, like the Queen, quite beat down by the nature of the late disturbances, and nothing can be more alarming than religious feeling being made a cover or a *but* for such proceedings.

Our great dinner is on Thursday. Does it not seem odd to you that Montalivet, Dupin, Lafayette, and Odillon Barrot are all *convives* at it? *Je crains pour les digestions.*

I have seen Mme. Delphine Potocka. She is *gracieuse, pittoresque, polonaise—en un mot*, regular features, very fair, large eyes. She is just like a martyr on a wooden screen. She seems agreeable and certainly very pleasing. The take off of her beauty is a want of *fraîcheur* in her skin and teeth. Sapeiya was with her, a large, gentle, merry, natural, handsome daughter of Madame Zamoyska. Mme. Delamarre came too. She looks just as she did, but is grown civil and sociable, and is a nice little woman.

I have had a long letter from the Duchess of Beaufort, which I must answer. She is just as I knew she would be, almost more than resigned. She says she[1]

---

[1] Her daughter Lady Isabella Kingscote, who died on February 4.

turned to me from him and said, her countenance
evincing the pleasure she felt, 'Do you hear what he
says, that he would not keep me if he could from the
happiness into which I am about to enter?' I cannot
talk about this, as it gives me pain to feel what I do
about it.   This, however, is certain, that people who
feel thus are beyond the reach of human infirmity and
misery.

God bless you, dearest dear sister.   My best love to
D., Lord C., and Morpeth.

Pray tell me all that is political.

To the Duke of Devonshire.

February 16, 1831.

I find it is thought bold of Dody and me to have
walked round the Tuileries to-day.   Nothing could be
more lovely and delicious.   Air like milk, blue sky and
bright sun.   The Chambre des Députés and the Tuileries
guarded.   Live toys of National Guards, some on horse-
back, parading on the quays and over the bridges.
Little knots of people whispering, everybody excited.

I never felt so safe anywhere, though I believe there
are many who would avail themselves of the folly of
the Ultras if they could.   Some of the Faubourg St.
Germain people got up a crowning of the Duc de
Bordeaux's bust at the church of St. Germain l'Aux-
errois.   This caused irritation, an attack upon the
archevêque's house, an attempt to throw the priest who
officiated into the Seine.   The National Guard restored
order and are now everywhere on the alert.

I had Salvandy in the evening.   'Aujourd'hui c'est
le mouvement populaire, demain le mouvement politique.'   His talk alarming and gloomy.

Noailles stept in ; she, the Just, had been at church.
Ma foi, had seen nothing.   'Oui, j'ai vu une dame de
ma connaissance, et il y avait un jeune homme, et puis—

il n'y avait rien, et j'y étais moi-même—vous voyez, donc—mais comment—voilà pourquoi—ah.'

In stept Decazes, grave, solemn, exaggerating the horrors, describing the poor priest over the parapet.

Juste was amazingly put out, in horror at *les outrages*, ashamed of having been on the spot, though before the confusion anxious to vindicate everybody— would deny the Revolution if she could.

I have had a rhapsody from Lady Westmorland at Lausanne, which she is to follow shortly *en personne*—a request that I will be kind to an Englishwoman here, a widow in deep affliction, having a child dangerously ill, adding, 'She is not pretty, indeed I never thought her so.' She then writes a small essay on Lady Stuart and myself, ' an odd case.' She wishes to be impartial. The letter ends with a slight memoir of Sir Sidney Smith, his deserts, his grievances, his brilliant exploits, his expected honours, ungrateful public, injury, and inadequate recompense.

The whole is interspersed with eulogiums on Granville's beauty, nature and prevalence of rheumatic fever, view of English country gentlemen, the haystack, and the turbulent, fashionable habits, calamitous paradoxes, and texts from Scripture. She is on her way to her natural protector, and will pass two months in England.

What is all this? I am all impatience for tomorrow. What is this *pas en avant* and *chasse en arrière* of Cousin Jack's?[1] Write, I beseech you.

To Lady Carlisle.

Paris : February 17, 1831.

My dearest dear sis,—Paris is restored to tranquillity, but there is going to be to-day a most important debate, one that many think may turn out the

[1] Lord Althorp.

present Ministers. I think all parties are against them, either from original feeling, or most of the Deputies, at their not having met the last disturbances with more vigour. *Nous verrons.* How glad I am to see that things are so smooth and improved in England, and that Jack is rather lauded than otherwise! I was frightened to death when I read the debates upon the transfer tax, though George's healing speech soothed me.

I am just returned from the Panorama of Navarin. Sir E. Codrington, the girls, and I were rolling along the Boulevards at ten o'clock this morning—such a bright burnished morning, clear as crystal. The view of the battle is beautiful; you see it from an exact representation of the 'Sirène,' De Rigny's frigate. Nothing can be more striking, and Sir Edward's descriptions were extremely interesting. We were there an hour and a half.

I feel so all you say of the comparative pains and pleasures of our two capitals. I should enjoy nothing more than Paris, if you were all coming.

We went to a little soirée at Flahault's last night. Prodigious excitement about politics. This is the measure of all we are doing now. Nothing big and smart, but constant means of seeing a few people, and talking of all that is interesting before our eyes. *Relâche* for balls till the *Mi-Carême*, when Montalivet, if still in, will give a great one, and the Flahaults perhaps a small one.

My girls are very popular. As Granville is too busy to ride, I must leave you to walk with them in the Tuileries, where at two all the fashionable parade; but we shall keep out of the line—*la terrasse sur le quai*, which is like walking in Bayswater.

I sat with Mme. Appony yesterday. She has been ill, and looks deplorably, and is miserable at all *la profanation* and *le scandale* of the last days.

D. wrote me a delicious letter. I see him at the

pictures with Blanche, and you with her at the very gay drum. I don't see Lady Wharncliffe at Belvoir, or only as a poor little fishing smack in the midst of all those ships of the line.

To Lady Carlisle.

Paris: February 19, 1831.

Dearest of dear sisters,—I am sorry you had any worry about us; we are safer than any people, I believe, and all seems to me in a political way going on smoothly. But how are we at home? You and Hart do not alarm me much, but others do. I put on the boldest face to Molé and others, who come and tell me of letters they receive. Doubts of the stability of the present Government in England. I do not despond, though some of my friends write to me from thence : ' Your friends get on very ill; the House of Commons and people begin to talk of them as very unsteady in their places. Lord Palmerston was a complete failure last night. Peel excellent.' And then that odious story, which you and Hart allude to, of that Joseph Surface Peel allowing us to remain in. Write dearest of Gs., and give me courage and facts. Miss Mercer is in a spasmodic anxiety about it all, for she too receives desponding letters, and her fears are all doubled, as she says, ' If your Government falls, ours follows.'

Sister, the reason I did not write was that I attended the Chambers all day. Odillon Barrot speaks incomparably well; he has a fine determined countenance, a fine voice and *subjuguant* manner set in a vulgar frame. Benjamin Delessert looks like an excellent English farmer, a Frank Lawley grown immensely large; La Fayette has *par excellence* the manner, tone, and voice *de la bonne compagnie*, leans on the *bord* and speaks to the Deputies as we should say, ' Were you at the Opera last night, Mr. Such-a-one ? ' Sebastiani spoke uncommonly

LETTERS OF HARRIET COUNTESS GRANVILLE 1831

well; his voice as clear as a bell, and the solemnity of his manner is not amiss in his ministerial attitude. The compliment to England was most warmly and strongly articulated. The *Loi Electorale* was debated with all the childish, noisy, petulant vehemence still reigning in their debates. They run, they ring, they squabble, they scold; and if such a thing you like to behold, you must come, Lady C., and, like Betty and me, sit up in a charming tribune, where one is in perfect comfort, like in a box at the Opera.

Our great drum and soirée for the Queen is over. We had all sorts of shades and colours. Odillon Barrot and Casimir Perier, Castelcicala and Lafayette, and in the evening the old Duchesse d'Escars on one hand and the Duke of Orleans on the other. But she did scamper when she spied him!

My individual and immediate prospects are bright. No dinners coming, nothing but small things, and Lady Georgiana Mitford come. *Elle me fait l'effet* of the first swallow, a woman of the right sort from England. Come upon a lark too. I think her pretty and pleasing and *élégante*, a nosegay and kerchief in her hand, a boa twice round her neck. I make much of her, that she may bring other birds.

To LADY CARLISLE.

Paris: February 21, 1831.

My dearest sister,—Your letter last night delighted, and above all, touched me. You are a kind angel and make me most happy. I sometimes feel a tight pang come across me, head and heart, when I feel that I am away, but I have much to console, to please me, and next year, even if nothing hastens it, we must meet.

I am glad that things look so well in England, and that the two last debates were more satisfactory than the first.

I have just been sending out notes for a fatal dinner on the 24th, the Queen's birthday. Myself and forty-nine sparks of high degree. Granville will not let the girls dine. In the evening I shall have a stuffy drum, but that they like.

I cannot let my thoughts dwell on Betty. She comes in and out whenever she likes, and is like Helena Robinson or any other here. I shall be sorry when she goes; to lose a very pleased, happy person, miss her in my society, she being a most efficient talking, animated member of society. Always glad to come early, stay late, talk without ceasing. *Bon jours* and how-d'ye-does all the visitors much more audibly and busily than I do myself. She is esteemed and popular, and whatever was amiss in the doing here was, and is known to have been, singly and wholly his work. I do not feel as if she was here, never think of her but when I see her. Nobody feels the least *gêné* at finding her always sitting near me, and all her toads toad on because they see that I toad her too. Mexborough [1] is ravished, and sits with her mouth wide open, like Paul the dancer, only very still, not comprehending what she sees beyond that 'nothing meets her eyes but sights of bliss.'

Alava [2] bores me to death, but I am very good to him, from a sort of feel as if he was the best of men, and an old uncle or relation. Why, I wonder—a profligate old Spaniard, I believe.

Your account of the Duke's and the ladies' moderation is very satisfactory. I think things here look tranquillizing. I have no fear of war or any mischief but what comes from those horrid Belgians, and they, I think, must soon end in troubling nobody but themselves.

[1] Lady Mexborough, Lady Stuart's sister.
[2] A Spanish general devoted to the Duke of Wellington.

Cradock is gone, and going to you. He has made
himself a great loss to both Granville and myself, so
attentive, so anxious to please us. Never was there
such a pleasant, delicious repast as ours, *chez lui*; but
it is in business that Granville, and in society to my
monde that I find him really not to be replaced.

MISS LEVESON GOWER TO LADY CARLISLE.

Paris: February 25, 1831.

My dear aunt,—Mama is gone to the Chamber of
Deputies and has people to dinner, which makes her
fear she may not perhaps have time to write to-day.
She is a happy woman, having got over her long
Diplomatic dinner. It was reckoned very handsome.
We had a *grande réception* in the evening. I did not
like it much, chiefly from feeling such envy in thinking
of you all at the ball at Devonshire House. In many
ways our life is pleasant here, but I cannot say my
wish of going back to England is the least diminished.
Independently of mama's wish to see you all again, she
certainly does enjoy her existence here extremely. The
way of living, the early hours, and the climate do all
suit her better; and also the occupation and little excitement of her position she does not dislike, and it
must be a pleasure to her to feel how well she does it
all and how popular she is.

I rather despair of Blanche's coming; what you say
of her seems to make it unlikely—a great disappointment to me. You have no notion how much affection
I feel for her, and what a privation it is to be away
from her. I am afraid the disturbances will frighten
people from coming. Everything is quiet again and
seems to promise to continue so. Lafayette was here
all night and seemed in good spirits. He talked away
with Pozzo for some time very eagerly. There were
numbers of pretty women last night, both French and

English. A good many quizzes among the latter, as the house was open, in Adelaide's honour, to everybody. Some people observed, 'Quel beau birthday!' in looking at the brilliancy of the house and mama's toilette, which was dazzling.

It is dreadful to send so stupid a letter instead of mama's usual one, but I thought it was better than nothing.

TO LADY CARLISLE.

Paris: February 28, 1831.

Dearest of sisters,—Your life is too vivacious, and you are more dissipated than we are. My own throat is gone. Sister, how does yours do? I have gained by it four days at home, but to-night we start again. A second ball at the Palais Royal, another on Wednesday, and our own on Friday. 'Settimana, che piombami sul core.'

Lady Mexborough is arrived with a pretty, tiny daughter, whom my girls think a love. I pity the Queen the day before her ball.

News from Belgium is still what one thinks, talks, hopes, and fears most about. I think everything in England—Ireland included—looks so much better that it is quite reviving. Here, I also think, if that one source of endless perplexity and wrong was set at rest, all would do well also.

My girls go on reconciled, satisfied, merry, sometimes amused; but oh! what a difference!

I like Betty much better as we go on. Her faults of manner, or at least the impression they make, wear off, and she is become happy, easy. She is constantly here, and sometimes very droll, always shrewd and clever. People have left off looking surprised at seeing her here in the evening, when they drop in with their best speeches, which is a great comfort to her and to me. He comes rarely, prowls about among *les douairières*, as he tells me.

To Lady Carlisle.

Paris : March 11, 1831.

You can have no idea of the state of excitement here. The Ministry is changing, but they do not think more of that than of our affairs. We were one day convinced that a majority of sixty-seven had beaten us, a story got up for stock-jobbing purposes. I cannot help feeling very sanguine now. My own small wit had told me how injudicious Lord Howick's speech was. Robert Grant is a darling.

You will see that the mob have been attacking Pozzo. His court and street were crowded with soldiers the whole of yesterday, and he was advised not to go out. His nerves are at all times terribly shattered, and he must be in a dreadful state. Pray tell Mrs. Cavendish that she must not mind reports. There never was a safer place than this for the English. The little *émeutes* are, as somebody said the other day, 'commandés comme un pâté,' and never was protection so immediate and efficient. If there is the slightest alarm, you have National Guards everywhere on the alert, crossing all the streets and standing at all the corners, and, in short, for the time in full command of the town.

Andrew Barnard is anti-Reform, which startled me at first in that courtier, but they tell me it is because he is the bosom friend of Croker. Sir Andrew says that, whatever is thought of the measure, there is but one opinion of the man, that Lord Grey's popularity and the respect felt for him are general.

To Lady Carlisle.

Paris: March 14, 1831.

Dearest sister,—The change of Ministry here makes a great sensation. The Dips are all pleased that Sebastiani remains, as he is decidedly pacific. Casimir Perier [1] is a man of great talent and energy, and will have his own way, which in the situation of things here is essential. The idea of strength anywhere gives hope and confidence.

All is as quiet as possible. It is so much the interest of many to exaggerate and alarm, that I do not wonder at alarm being felt; but you know I am not brave, yet I never have had a moment's fear. Even Pozzo, though pelted and obliged to barricade, was safe. A man was heard saying, ' Vois-tu, un ambassadeur—sais-tu ce que c'est qu'un ambassadeur ? C'est comme un parlementaire, on n'y touche pas '—a pleasing view of the subject.

Paganini is the *idée dominante* just now. They say there is a new religion called Paganinism, and talk nonsense, when *exaltés*.

To Lady Carlisle.

Paris: March 19, 1831.

Dearest sister,—Fanny spent the evening here yesterday, looking very nice and very happy. This morning my girls take Mrs. Cav. and her to the Louvre, and they dine here.

Lord Normanby and I are just setting out to hear a young Murat, a very handsome Buonaparte-looking man, propose at the Chambers the taking off of the penal punishment attached to the family of Buonaparte's return into France. We hope *qu'il y aura du bruit*.

[1] Lafitte resigned and was succeeded by Casimir Perier.

To Lady Carlisle.

Paris: March 21, 1831.

Dearest and best beloved sister,—I am very sorry indeed for poor Lady Cawdor's accident. How strangely accidents happen, like *émeutes*, never when they are expected or with apparently sufficient cause! Yesterday, the threatened day, the 20th, when we had been foretold a crowning of Napoleon the Second's statue and the breaking out of a civil war, was more than quiet. Susy and I walked all about the streets alone, and were only struck by the total absence of carriages, why, I know not. But we found the town looking like a large village with a fair in it from the swarms of people walking.

Mrs. Cavendish was never so expected and hailed in her life. I look forward to having them with the greatest pleasure. Fanny will be such a delight to the girls, and Mrs. Cavendish will sit among the flowers.

We shall not go out at all during Passion Week, as Granville is to be confirmed. I do not think the Cavendishes will mind being quite quiet just at first, as we shall tire ourselves and them in the morning with sight-seeing, drives, and walks. In Easter week *je les ferai danser.* They are also, I believe, seriously enough disposed to prefer not having great dissipation just at this season.

To the Duke of Devonshire.

Paris: March 24, 1831.

Now hear! your letter arrived by the post and we gave up the Bill. Yesterday Waller came at five and said Rothschild had received a despatch by telegraph. The Government beat by a majority of sixty-seven. The Funds fell enormously. Bonfils the Jew ruined by it. I go to Appony's drum, in an attitude of decent composure and ignorance of probable consequences. Granville goes to Mr. Louis Philip, who asks him what can make the Funds fall so. ' The news from England, perhaps, sir.' 'Why, Lord Granville, there is no news from England to-day. Rothschild has just been here, and has not had a word of news to-day.'

Well, your Grace, this comes on to Appony's, all the world in a hubbub, the Dip. faces lengthening again. This morning we get up ignorant, helpless, uninformed. No courier till Thursday.

To Lady Carlisle.

Paris: March 25, 1831.

I know you will forgive me, my dear sis, for only writing a line to-day. My ball is to-night, and I think you will pity me when I tell you that I and my girls have, for the last three days, done nothing but receive and write notes, and I with so bad a cold and sore throat that I have for the last two been doing nothing but gargle, and the night before last was obliged to blister my throat. But your sprack sister, being well dosed and entirely starved, is in perfect good trim for the hop, and I do not mind appearing in a *negligé* of velvet and flannel.

To Lady Carlisle.

Paris: March 28, 1831.

My very dearest sister,—Lord Normanby is loaded with all sorts of messages to you both. He has made himself extremely amiable here, and I regret him very much.

Dearest brother, your letter and speech have given me the greatest delight in you. George, the silent George, burst out with ' What a noble speech!' and eloquent too, and quite worthy of you. I am so glad that William succeeded so well.

Now for a sketch of Glinfashy. She is happy and *couleur de rose*. They dined here yesterday, and this morning we went after church to Passy in the carriage, to the hole in the wall which you, your Grace, taught me, and walked down to the Champs de Mars, she linking and looping with Mr. Mitford, and there, having hired chairs for twopence apiece, we stood in the midst of forty-five thousand infantry and cavalry, and twice the number of populace, as quietly and securely as I sit to write in my own room. The King was received with enthusiasm. He stood bowing to the shouting multitude, and all their language around us was good-humour, applause, and delight. 'Oh, si Charles Dix voyait ceci!' with some wishes expressed, 'à présent nous aimerons voir les Anglais à Calais.'

I am just come from Casimir Perier's reception. The *salon* was crowded and many Ultras in it, as they consider his being Minister as a triumph over the extreme *gauche* party, of which Lafayette and Odillon Barrot are the chiefs—'L'odieux Baron,' as *les dames de la résistance* call him.

Guinea is a dear. He brought us a great deal of London gossip. He said he found Fordwich at Lady Hardy's. We asked him, 'Does he seem to admire them?' He said, 'They seem to admire him very much.'

Mme. de Flahault is becoming happier about English politics in consequence of a cheerful letter from Lady Grey. She is not so much so about the stability of the Government here, and frets over Casimir Perier's health, and the chance of war. Yet she admits that things wear a much better aspect, but she is a great croaker and alarmist.

I was at the Palais Royal last night, and thought they all looked in better spirits than I had before seen them.

I must seal my letter, for Mrs. Opie[1] is coming to

[1] The widow of the painter. She wrote many popular works, chiefly novels. Late in life she became a Quakeress, and was much esteemed for her benevolence.

play with me at two, and at three my girls and boys have a little reunion in the conservatory. Lady Minto's twelve children, from sixteen downwards, Lady Stuart's two girls, and Master Murray, Freddy's bosom friend, from Wick. Fanny, Sneyd and Tchann; all ages you see, and my dear Mme. de Chasteluse to sit with me, and Mme. Juste to say 'Ah' with Mlle. Sabine.

To the Duke of Devonshire.

Paris: April 1831.

I am a little frightened. The Bill, my dears? and is it true that the King will not dissolve, and that if beat, Earl Grey bolts, and then what, where, who? and how will the country bear it? and shall you all soon come swimming over in a long boat? *Emigrés* to set off with us to take lodgings in Pekin? I am not really afraid. Don't dine with Reform Bill, as I hear he is called. It is not worth a risk, and you had better do some pleasanter thing for your *début* a week later. How happy I am to hear such excellent accounts of you *de toute part*!

Yesterday my children all exclaimed, 'How kind and amiable Mrs. C. is grown!'

You can have no idea of the delight and feeling she has shewn at our attentions to her here. She melts like jelly before all the little kindnesses and civilities of society.

To Lady Carlisle.

Paris: April 29, 1831.

I went to Flahault's last night, and must own I enjoy having my good news[1] to tell to the sceptical and discontented. Everybody, however (Lord Stuart and the Chancellerie, red-hot Tories to a man, excepted), seem delighted and soothed at the universality of wish and

---

[1] Of the sudden dissolution of Parliament.

opinion in England. *Les bien pensants* think it ought to destroy all fear of unpleasant results. Ireland too, a little lamb !

It is quite true all you say about Mrs. ——. There is no pleasure in giving her pleasure, but there is the satisfaction of paying a debt, doing a duty, avoiding a storm. But there is 'no pleasure in her song, no summer in her year.' Then I think of all she has suffered, and scold myself instead of her.

Mr. Stuart is very ugly, very intelligent, uncommonly agreeable, and we all are fond of him.

To the Duke of Devonshire.

April 24, 1831.

My very dearest brother,—Your letter is the most interesting, the most entertaining, the most curious, the most eventful that ever was written. I have read and read again every line of it. The King is beyond all praise for the manner in which he has given his confidence—so wholly, so frankly, and so courageously; but the pretty, piquant, delicious part of the business to frivolous me is Lord Wharncliffe in his closet ! His preposterous intention, his stubborn will, his proud anticipations, mowed and squashed. Humpty Dumpty sat on a wall.

Write again, more, more. How interesting everything is, and will be ! Are you sanguine about the elections ? Are you easy about Ireland ? Our domestic Tory, Harry Vane, talks of a reaction in the country. The interest about it all here yesterday was intense amongst English and French.

On Friday, at my hop, it was known that there was a majority against us. I had an *out* feel, and the natural antipathy to being beat, independently of larger and finer feelings, but I talked big and confident of dissolution to Perier, Pasquier, etc. My spirits rose upon Lord Stuart's coming in as cross as a lapdog and as rude as a bear. I thought this promised well. Mme. de Flahault sat like a thunder-cloud, and her friends declared that when spoken to she could not or would not answer. I understand that yesterday she sat at home, taking joy upon the rumour of certain dissolution We hope that during this falling of the sky we shall catch larks. Susy says, ' Uncle Duke will certainly come.'

To Lady Carlisle.

Paris : April 29, 1831.

A thousand thanks for your most interesting letter, and for being so well, but not for going to dine with the King. I hope and trust it will not tire you.

How it delights me to hear that Granville is so appreciated! It is true he slaves, and slaves alone. The place of Secretary of Legation is filled, but not occupied. Mr. Hamilton, harmless, inoffensive man, can neither comprehend nor reply to even a question about etiquette or the news of the day. 'What sort of weather is it to-day, Mr. H. ? ' ' God bless my soul, it never occurred to me to make an observation. It seems to me, I may err, I would not pronounce rashly, but I'll step out and make a point of ascertaining it ; ' a nervous, bilious, conscientious, *pauvre sire.*

Lord and Lady W. Russell are arrived. She is really beautiful, grown into a very large woman, brighter and clearer than anything I ever saw.

The poor King of Sardinia's death, hourly expected, is dreaded by the young and dancing part of the community to a degree that is almost shocking, my young *à la tête.*

We are safe for to-night, but I doubt whether I shall be able to have a fourth.

H 2

To Lady Carlisle.

Paris: May 2, 1831.

What you call your election gossip is read like a
sentence or reprieve by your devoted relations. We
savourer every line, and when we have done, begin
again. Why, sister Carlisle, what times? I have no
doubt of the elections going well. I should not like a
Reign of Terror over the elections. In any other case
I like to think of dearest Morpeth successful and triumphant again.

Granville is a good deal better, but very languid, and
unable to walk. I hear him now laughing with Pozzo.
You know, they never laugh so much with us, Lady C.

The King of Sardinia is dead, and Court and Court
ball, all that would have been so *accablant* to me, over.

Lord Wallace is on his way to England. Yesterday
he paid Granville a long visit, and gave him accounts
of the Harrowbys. They were driving home from an
expedition in an open *calèche*. Lord Harrowby felt
himself collared from behind by a man, who held him
back with one hand, and with the other held a stiletto
to his breast. Lady H. seized that hand. They told
him he should have money, watches, etc. He departed
with them.

To Lady Carlisle.

Dieppe: July 4, 1831.

If you could know the delight of having Granville
sitting opposite to me! He goes, alas! to-morrow with
George Stewart, leaving us Guinea and the *calèche*, two
great improvements in our circumstances. Our plans
here are uncertain. We are to remain here till he
beckons to us, and I shall not be surprised if that is the
whole month of July, unless Lady Harrowby arrives at
Paris towards the middle of it, in which case we should
go there to meet her.

Good-night and God bless you, my very dearest sister.

To Lady Carlisle.

Dieppe: July 12, 1831.

I have just received your letter, my very dearest sister, and wish you joy a hundred times of your birthday, and of its being a year less than I thought, and mine also in consequence. This very day I told Guinea I was forty-six.

I have no fears for the *trois jours*, as they say the people are in a good humour, but even if they were not every precaution has been taken.

I heard from Granville to-day. He had been dining at Sebastiani's, where he met Mme. de Flahault, Lord Lynedoch, Lord William Russell, Belliard and Guizot.

My three are gone to the play to-night with Mme. St. Clair.

I expect Willy and Freddy per kettle on Saturday. I am waiting to know from Granville if we are to set off on Sunday or Monday. We go back by the uglier shorter road, cutting the Seine and sleeping at Gourney.

Friday.—Well, here's an event, *je ne me possède pas de joie.* Who do you think came in the night, is now asleep at Clarke's, fancying himself known only to me? I shall not tell the girls. They shall have all the surprise of seeing him walk into my room. My dear, adorable brother crossed in the night in a pelting rain, which still continues. I will not direct my letter till I have seen him.

Here he is, looking so well. I have not a moment. We dine with him to-night.

To Lady Carlisle.

Dieppe: July 16, 1831.

I prepare my letter for the first occasion, my dearest sister. We have had the most delicious weather since

I last wrote, and sat by the sea till ten o'clock last night.

Lady Westmorland is arrived, but has not yet appeared, and I have prepared a willing victim, poor lonely Mme. St. Clair, to be her *souffre-douleur*, and to represent me as a sad, unsociable, unprofitable listener. Two or three Frenchwomen that I know only to bow to, and the Sardinian Ambassador, who never does anything but bow, are our only other events.

We are going a long expedition to-day to Arques, tell Morpeth, to finish the steeple and draw the Castle, to come home to a late dinner at six. All this is very exciting and delightful to the Leveson family.

Sunday morning. I had a long letter from Granville yesterday. He went on Thursday evening to St. Cloud, where he found them all in pretty good spirits. He was to return there on the evening he wrote to present Lord William Russell, and that *débutant* Lord Lynedoch. The elections are favourable to the Government, and there is a decided majority of Ministerialists.

The steamboat came very empty last night, only thirty passengers on board. My brother wrote me a line by it, too busy to cross. He says: 'London news is dull and flat—Reform stale and grippe triumphant.' What a picture! Freddy writes: ' As to politics, I don't care a pin about Prince Leopold. Reform is my principal aim, and I am afraid it will not be carried in the House of Lords.' He is rather a prig, but an amazing darling.

I was dying for the comment on the debate, having been enraptured, by myself, with Mr. Macaulay, pleased with G. Vernon, and amused with Mr. Lytton Bulwer.

To Lady Carlisle.

Dieppe : July 17, 1831.

Dearest sister,—I hope G. Morpeth has been pleased here as well as at Paris. He is now in a warm

bath. So are my girls. They go into the sea to-morrow, Morpeth on it. He is to start at seven. No
words can say how I shall miss him.

I support all my privations, however, better here
than elsewhere. There is to me a charm about this
place, its perfect quiet, not a friend to be had for love
or money, the air, the waves, the hours, the hunger,
the sleep, that keeps up my spirits against my sorrows,
for it is a great one to be away from Granville and to
part with George. My girls are too dear and nice,
just as gay and contented here, as they are charmed
with such a different existence elsewhere.

We are longing for letters from England. This
moment is so interesting and curious, and to know
what Granville's plans are and how long he will be
there.

Lady Westmorland was very reasonable and amiable, very eloquent, very droll, and only seen the eve
of our departure, brought no bother and tax upon
one. I think her ten thousand times superior to Lady
Jersey in every way. We miss at Paris, my dear Lady
Carlisle, by this lark of ours a prolongation of the
society of Lady Westmorland, Cheerful,[1] *ne vous
deplaise*, Lord Burghersh, Lord and Lady Conyngham,
Lord Howard of Effingham.

Poor Lady Emmeline and poor Cornet. She is ill,
he is foolish. He talks of her being so cross and in her
tantrums. Only to Verity, who told my boys, so do
not betray. Charles said to him, ' She won't see you ;
I can't help it, I don't know what's to be done next.'
She never would come out, and would not see me
when I called, but wrote me a very grateful note next
day.

         [1] Nickname of the Duke of Rutland.

To Lady Carlisle.

Paris: July 29, 1831.

Dearest of sisters,—I hope the gaieties of London are indeed ending, and that if we are so blest as to go there for the Committee of the House of Lords, we shall find society and no *fêtes*. I wish it more and more, but as yet have not the slightest encouragement from his Excellency.

On Monday evening Lord and Lady Harrowby, Granville and I went to the Palais Royal to the work-table. The Queen looked gayer than usual.

On Tuesday we returned there, zealous, loyal creatures with the four young ladies to a concert. There we found the Dom,[1] the Empress and French music ; very hot, but amusing from the circumstances, very much so to see the Emperor and Lafayette in a confab.

Yesterday we went to Berci, and there we saw a *joute*, pretty from the gaiety and dress, but wretched as a water-work. At two we adjourned in the broiling heat to the mounds by the Champs de Mars, where we found a miserable spectacle, two wretched jockeys racing, *courses de chevaux libres*, but myriads of people all gay and enchanted. In the evening the town illuminated, every tree in the Champs Elysées lit up.

Friday morning, *balcon* of the Hôtel Bristol *chez* Monsieur Motteux. A beautiful sight, day blue and gold, the Place cleared of the populace, but every window and *balcon* full. The King on a white horse with his sons. Pedro with all his green feathers rode up to the Queen's *balcon*, like a *tourney*, Lady Carlisle.

[1] Dom Pedro and his wife, the Emperor and Empress of Brazil.

To Lady Carlisle.

Paris : July 30, 1831.

The troops are going to be reviewed. M. Motteux has taken for the occasion a large apartment and ordered us a feast. In one window Lord William Russell, Susy, F. Howard, Freddy and the little Russell boy.[1] Lady William, Motteux, and Mrs. Rawdon in the next one. Dody, Harriet Ryder, Guinea, all the others too late and are lopped off. The carriages cannot get back for them. The crowd is immense, the cheering very well, but less striking than the perfect good-humour.

I am writing in a corner, as comfortable as if I was in my own room. We have a soirée this evening, lamps and seats in the garden, the roof and garrets for those who like to see the fireworks.

They are hurrahing now. It is so beautiful, and all like lambs and doves.

There is a report of a great victory by the Poles. It may only be got up for to-day.

Lord and Lady Harrowby have with admirable dexterity just run across the Place through the soldiers' legs, and here they are.

I have been dining on cold chicken. Freddy is as drunk as a piper with champagne.

I am to tell you that Pedro starts at eleven to-night, in spite of all the efforts made to retain him.

To Lady Carlisle.

Paris : August 3, 1831.

Dearest sister,—We had a most curious repast yesterday at the Palais Royal, an immense affair with all the diplomacy. We must have been most unwelcome.

---

[1] Who succeeded his cousin as ninth Duke of Bedford in 1872.

Perier's resignation [1] occupies everybody, and nothing is as yet decided as to his successor.

The heat has been perhaps a shade less oppressive. I have, however, done nothing since *les trois jours*, the dinner yesterday the only exception. Tell Morpeth that Madame and I had an hour's political talk after it. I liked her very much, thought her wise and feeling. The Queen looked worn. We met all the ex-Ministers coming in as we went out.

From thence to Madame de Flahault's. Found all the people in despair at Perier's move—remove. She dines here to-day, and Madame Appony and Lady Conyngham are to run in in the evening.

We are threatened with a ball on Tuesday at the Palais Royal to celebrate the King's accession, but I hope in this heat there will be none.

To Lady Carlisle.

Paris: August 10, 1831.

What interesting times! I have just heard of the *échec* in Belgium, General Daine's defeat. I feel so much interest about Leopold, and he seems to meet the crisis so manfully. He must be embarrassed with the novelty and difficulty of the situation.

Lord Harrowby sets out for Beauvais to-morrow and Granville dines at Appony's, so that our solitude will appear striking.

To Lady Carlisle.

Paris: August 13, 1831.

My dearest sister,—I am charmed with Leopold's conduct, and, forgive me, with the idea that all the vulgar English will prefer Brussels to Paris. I think Pedro is too frisky with all the ladies.

---

[1] Casimir Perier withdrew his resignation and remained in power till 1832, when he died of cholera.

Lord Harrowby is or rather has been very poorly here, which he always is when his mind is worried and irritated as it now is to the greatest degree by politics, and I should gather from all I see and hear that he is goaded on by his friends in England, yet totally unable to make up his mind. Altogether, he is in a pitiable state of mind and spirits.

Lady Harrowby is well, but thinner than anybody you ever saw. The girls are not in particularly good looks, though I think Louisa better looking than she was. But they are all very amiable and happy to be here, and my girls return the compliment, and are delighted to have them.

I conclude from what I hear that Lord Spencer is in a very alarming state. I am glad to hear that the disgust inspired by the conduct of the Ultras in the House of Commons has done us good, and that many of the Lords, even the factious, are become more moderate.

To Lady Carlisle.

Paris: August 16, 1831.

My dear, dearest sister,—Nothing new. The two royal Dukes gone to join the army, which saves us from a ball at the Palais Royal on Tuesday.

All our old friends, Perier, etc., remain in office. Everybody wondering and speculating about Dutch land.

The Conynghams and Lord Orford dined here yesterday, and we had quite a brilliant soirée. Madame Appony sits by *la Marquise*, as Lieven used. Her beauty is much admired. She is wonderful, as fresh as a daisy, *bouche comme une rose*, in a light blue gauze hat with white feathers, a salmon-coloured gown made extremely high, with long sleeves ; she looked infinitely handsomer than when in a satin frock, swaddled in

jewels. Lady Maria is inoffensive and good-humoured.
Lord C. begs to be remembered to you and my brother.
He is grown larger and meeker.

Lady Harrowby goes to England on Thursday. We
shall miss them very much. The girls are extremely
fond of Harriet. They think her in every way improved
by her travels. Louisa is so also. Her countenance
is uncommonly intelligent, and she is so to a remarkable
degree.

To Lady Carlisle.

Paris: August 20, 1831.

Lady Conyngham and her cubs come to-night. She
is so much better than her brood. The foreigners are
much excited about her, Madame Conyngham, and
think her, as she is, still beautiful. I thought Paul of
Würtemberg would have screamed with curiosity and
excitement, and Madame de Vaudreuil with anxiety to
see which had *conservée* herself best ; not having met for
twenty years, the result must have been mortifying.

Lady William came last night. She has interesting
letters from him. Great praise of the conduct of the
Prince of Orange, noble and temperate when he had a
strong temptation to take advantage of his position and
power to conquer. As to Bob Adair, he is a hero and
the youngest man going.

The English Press ! What license, what a *ton* !
Do tell me what you think of the progress made, and if,
as Lord Napier says, the Lords will be at it in ten days.

To Lady Carlisle.

Paris : August 1831.

I am so glad to hear of Lord Carlisle being well
enough for Windsor, and that you are up to so much
of various sorts. We are now as if we were in some
château every evening. The conservatory rings with
the shouts of laughter of the young ones. To-night we

old ones go to the Palais Royal, to-morrow to Tivoli, but life is as quiet and enjoyable as possible.

We have got a Mr. Sneyd, but a very little one, almost imperceptible. When does the House of Lords go into Committee? Guess, suppose, but don't say, like Lord Granville, 'Impossible to conjecture.'

To LADY CARLISLE.

Paris : September 17, 1831.

How grieved I am for poor Lord Durham.[1] Is it quite hopeless?

I am much better; went to the Opera on Tuesday, and saw 'Anna Bolena.' Rubini, perfect, enchanting. Pasta, older, thicker, her voice as well as figure, but always very admirable. Yesterday had a longish soirée, more French arriving. Conynghams go to England on Monday, to some place they have near Dover. She longs to see you, and is an amiable, good-hearted woman, irrevocably dull.

The new peers occupy us. Whom will my brother bring in for the county? We wonder at Northland. He lives abroad, and we say why.

The Dips came from the Palais Royal yesterday evening. They had left the little Queen [2] at play with the Princesses, putting bits of wood in mosaic shape, *très enfant* and delighted.

Madame de Dolomieu and her daughter are nervous about l'Heredité question, which is one of immense difficulty for this Government. The discussions are to begin on Thursday or Friday next.

Madame de Flahault is in her new house, and ill. She was at home on Thursday. Granville went and thought there was a strong smell of paint, which may have disagreed with her. Our Harry Vane stuck his

---

[1] On account of the illness of his eldest son, who died on the 24th.
[2] Of Portugal.

elbow through her new glass door and smashed it, rather an ominous beginning in the Rue d'Angoulême.

To Lady Carlisle.

Paris : September 20, 1831.

It has been great repose both to body and mind having those dear Talbots here, a chaperon for everything, the walks, drives, sights in the morning, operas and plays, and last night a hop at Lord Granard's, all without my having anything but the accounts, which I delight in.

I believe there was a great deal of disturbance in Paris yesterday. The cavalry, impatient and goaded, were very violent. I heard of one man killed and many wounded. The slackness, or rather coldness, of the National Guard is a bad symptom. I can hardly think this set of men will weather it, or that any other will be found to undertake it, or succeed if they do.

John Talbot is just come in from the Courts of Law, and says that everything seems perfectly quiet in the town to-day.

Charles Canning was the recommender of Mr. Shore.[1] Mr. Chapman says he is very glad he was going to him. We saw some letters to Charles Canning, which we liked. I blush to say we neither of us know the terms. It is a singularly dull place, one of its great advantages in our eyes.

To Lady Carlisle.

Paris: September 23, 1831.

Weather hot as June. The Talbots and girls gone to Vincennes and Père-Lachaise. They are indefatigable. I went after dinner to the Palais Royal and from there to Madame de Flahault's. I found the King

---

[1] Young Granville was with him till he went to Oxford.

delighted with the majority of eighty-five. I saw Monsieur Thiers at Madame de Flahault's. He says the Chamber is not so ill-disposed as ignorant, easily *emporté*, but *bon* and inclined to be *bienveillant*. The Ministers are in spirits again.

I could hardly believe when I read the ' Times ' that my girls had dined at the Palais Royal and been to the Italian Opera on the night of the disturbances and *vitres brisées*. There is nothing like being in the midst of anything for knowing little of its danger.

My plans all in uncertainty, but I feel and Verity says that I ought to do something wholesome. Aix en Savoie ! Granville consented. Verity offered to go too, but I gave it up. I am morally quite unequal to a journey of six days without Granville, when if anything was to go amiss I should go into a nervous madness. St. Germain ? Very easy, still on the cards, but hardly enough, as I want bathing, *des eaux* and sea air.

Boulogne ? Sea air, sands, the journey with Granville, to wait for him there and come back with him. Very tempting, though it is a hideous place. What would make me think it a Paradise would be if you would join me there. One day's drive, two hours and a half crossing, excellent for your health, a quiet you never enjoy. I could give you a room in the excellent inn ; we would drive and dawdle all day long. It would be too delicious.

You will perhaps say, Why not come to Brighton, Lady Gran. ? I will tell you, dearest sis, it would alter the whole thing. What I want is perfect repose. If I went there, I must prepare dress for self and girls, go to the Pavilion, struggle against dinner and balls. If you come to Boulogne, a gown, cap and a bundle will suffice.

I have seen Verity. He will not, I think, say anything to you unless you begin. Do you think, if D.

knew the romantic motive of the wish,[1] that he would?
I have smashed all his hopes.   He is unhappy and his
manner touched me much.   You cannot, just as I cannot. I shall ask Granville to-day to let me write to Lord
Grey, but I am sure he will say no.   Doctor L'Affan
was made a Bart. merely after being with Lord
Anglesea in Ireland.   D. asked Verity once, I believe
in Russia, if he would like it.   He then, having no
reason to wish it, said he did not care a farthing
about it.

To Lady Carlisle.

Paris: September 29, 1831.

Granville will set out next week, perhaps on Monday. I intend to go with the girls to the Hôtel
d'Angleterre at St. Germain.   The air is next best to
sea, and the nearness a great object, as the long
journey would, perhaps, have been rather trying to
me. You will see that I have made *volte-face* to my
Boulogne plan with a good grace.   I put all my hopes
in the month of April, when I trust Granville will have
a satisfactory holiday.

I am shocked beyond measure at poor Charles
Lambton's death, and for his poor father.   Frederick
Howard heard from his mother.   He is very low, and
I find had no idea of how bad or near it was.

We were in despair at losing the Talbots.   I met
Prince Koslowski on the Boulevards to-day, fat and
timid.   ' Un Russe, ose-t-il se montrer?'

I saw yesterday morning, at Madame de Bourke's,
La Princesse Belgiojoso,[2] small, *distinguée*, sallow, eyes

---

[1] Dr. Verity wished to be a baronet. It was only on this condition
that the father of the young lady he was anxious to marry would give his
consent.

[2] She belonged to the illustrious Milanese family of Trivulzio. Her
husband deserted her, and she afterwards led an adventurous life. She
took an active part in the Italian revolutionary movement, writing articles
and reviews in support of it.

like saucers, little, tiny hands, *grandes et gracieuses
manières*, full of everything : ' De l'esprit comme un
démon.'

TO LADY CARLISLE.

Paris : October 3, 1831.

To-day seems to me like a dream.   Granville is just
set out at five for London, where he expects to be at
the division on Wednesday night, which seems like
flying.   He determined last night to go.   This morning, when his horses were at the door, he received a
letter from Lord Palmerston saying he need not start
till the result of the second reading was known ; but as
he was one foot in chaise, had dined at three, bid good-
bye, told the King at one at Court that he was off, he
kept to his first resolution.

I am dying to be out of Paris, my girls dying to
stay in it.   They have gained to-morrow.   We shall
go to Montmorency and dine there, walk about the
forest, and come back to see ' Anna Bolena ' in our
things.

I shall be too anxious for letters and news.   What
a moment !   I have all at once ceased to be sanguine,
and feel as if the Lords would carry their wicked
measure, beat us, and then ?   Where can we look, and
what will happen ?

Give my love to Lord Granville, tell him that we
have walked, since he went, down the Boulevards, by
the Rue de la Paix.   No adventure, but one cross old
woman, who called us *ces chiens d'Anglais*, because
Dody trod upon her toe.

TO LADY CARLISLE.

Paris : October 10, 1831.

Dearest sister,—It seemed so odd to read yesterday
evening yours and Granville's letters, having known

the tremendous majority[1] since eleven in the morning. Sebastiani received it by telegraph, nobody seems to have expected it. The girls and I sit looking at one another. We cannot go back to St. Germain ; and, indeed, bad, rainy weather would be reason enough against it. We hope every opening door will bring us some intelligence.

We have got the papers and the debate. I doat upon Lord Grey. I am sure he will do nobly. Perhaps I am foolish in having no misgivings about public tranquillity, but ' cela ne se commande pas,' I have not. Yet when I read in 'Le Temps,' 'ils ont fait leur 25 Juillet,' it gives me a shudder.

To-morrow we dine at the Tuileries. I hear they and all here think of nothing but ' le Bill.'

I have seen nobody but Madame de Bourke, who always believes whatever she wishes.

I have been much better, came back like a young rose from St. Germain.

To Lady Carlisle.

Paris : October 24, 1831.

It is great happiness to me to have Granville back again. We are still basking in a summer sun and all the leaves are on the trees and our windows open. We are going in a *calèche* to the Jardin des Plantes to show Eward the giraffe. You never saw anything like her happiness at being with us again. She looks ten years younger than she did when last I saw her.

Apponys, Werthers, Pfeffels, Schlegel,[2] such an old flaxen bore, like Mrs. Fitzherbert, and covered with rings, sentiments and souvenirs, and Humboldt dine here.

---

[1] The Lords threw out the Reform Bill by a majority of 41.

[2] The famous German critic. He was a great friend of Madame de Staël, and devoted himself to the education of her children.

The concert at the Tuileries on Friday was handsomer
and much cooler than those at the Palais Royal.   The
Duchesse de Braganza looks a good, dear, patient thing,
fine eyes, ugly mouth.   Toque evidently Devis, which
made the Appony and Werther sick.   He looks fond
of her.   Madame de Loulé, his sister, is peculiar-looking,
but handsome, black as ink, the two sides of her face
quite different.   The *tournure* of an opera-dancer.   The
Duke of Orleans is supposed to be her lover.   There
were rather more people I knew than I have seen
before at Court.

To the Duke of Devonshire.

Paris : November 1831.

If Mr. Landseer had sent me a thousand pounds I
should not have been half so much obliged to him.   It
is the only picture I ever thought really like you.   I
beg your pardon for being so enthusiastic about a cari-
cature.   What a love you are to have given it to me,
but Eward is at this moment exclaiming, ' How should
he dare make such a things ? '

Nothing ever was so happy as that dearest old soul,
walking between them, taken bodkin to the Opera, and
adoring them both.

I have nothing to tell you.   The terror of the Sun-
derland cholera knocked me down yesterday morning,
but our last accounts reassured us.   It is, however,
awful.

Paris is quiet, and there is as yet a delicious absence
of all dissipation.   We have had Pasta at the Opera.
She is gone and Malibran makes her *rentrée* to-night.
Lablache and Rubini *font nos délices.*

My girls delight in my Fridays, which makes me
enjoy them.

I wish you could have run over for a week, before
the business begins again.   There could be no happi-

ness as great as ours to see you, and Mme. de Delmar's spirit would then be laid, as she is more persevering than ever in her enquiries if you are coming.

Mme. de Flahault is in her new and pretty house and he is here. We have a terrible dearth of good English society. The French are a little *en mouvement* in consequence of Pozzo the little marrying Mlle. de Crillon the day after to-morrow. Yesterday Granville and I went to the soirée, where he and some others *ont signé le contrat.* The trousseau was all over three large drawing-rooms. Mme. Appony wept bitterly over my incapacity of appreciating its beauties. Pozzo *oncle* has given the most magnificent jewels. The bride is the prettiest girl here, and ran about like a little *marchande* amongst the goods. ' C'est le seul qu'il y a à Paris. On m'a promis de ne pas faire une autre garniture dans ce genre avant le jour de l'an. C'est du vrai cachemire. Le chalis est broché.' Little Pozzo walks about. ' J'aurais mieux aimé être garçon, mais tout ceci est bien beau et ma promise est bien belle.' Mme. Appony clasps her hands, the tears flow down her cheeks, ' Ma chère, il ne l'aime pas du tout—mais pas le moins du monde.'

Yet they are all in their way as happy as they can stick, and really the bridegroom, with six thousand a year settled upon him, a house given, the prettiest wife in Paris, of the *plus haut parage*, is not *à plaindre*.

Mme. Appony is adorable ; her unvarying sweetness and kindness gild my *existence sociale* here. Her feelings may not be deep, but they are always there for everything that is, vexed, disappointed, or in any shade of sorrow. No *humeur*, no bitterness, no *rivalité*, no *exigeance*, like those beautiful flowers, that the fastidious can only criticise as being too sweet.

To Lady Carlisle.

Paris : November 1831.

Dearest sister,—Lord Durham and his two girls dined here to-day. My girls are enchanted with Miss Fanny, the eldest. They have begged me to ask them again on Wednesday, preferring that to Meyerbeer's new opera, which, by-the-by, is, I believe, a doubtful piece of business ; at least they talk of ' une danse de nonnes en chemise.'

Lord Durham seems pleased with the letters he has received from Lord Grey. Mme. de Flahault says that Lord Wharncliffe and Lord Harrowby are become tractable. Is this possible? I suppose Parliament will certainly meet *chez vous* the beginning of next month. I have no idea of what Granville will do with us, take us or leave us.

Sir Stratford Canning, with three men, Colonel Barnett, Mr. Buchanan, and Mr. Hammond, at his heels, dines here to-day.

To Lady Carlisle.

Paris : November 1831.

I have written to Lord Brougham to ask it plump.

My Harry [1] is the least sentimental of men, likes me better than the girls and Cuvier better than me, and so on. Science is his love. He is the best of men and I love him, but such a spark, and, luckily for him, seeming to think women so many artichokes, never wasting look or word on them.

I will talk fast enough when I come, dearest. If they would send something efficient here in poor Hamilton's place, I think we certainly should, but how can Granville leave Paris with nobody but him here?

Lyons is subsiding. Weather cold and bracing, my health better again.

[1] Lord Harry Vane.

To Lady Carlisle.

Paris : December 5, 1831.

The Tuileries is enchanted at the entry into and reception of the Duke of Orleans at Lyons.

The wonder is that after all the alarm and searching so little cholera can be found, as I believe at this time of year it is always hovering over us.

I laugh when I look at Harry. It is as if Frederic Foster in our young days had been talked of for us, only Harry is solemn, not facetious. Susy sat between Lord Rivers and George Villiers on Friday at dinner, and talked most to the latter, whose agreeableness is *entraînant* to the greatest degree. Lord Rivers seems amiable and pleasing, but he pays us no court. She is in tearing spirits, the most adorable darling that ever lived, and really doated upon by all who know her. Dody is a dear girl too. It is not the same cloudless, radiant nature, but full of goodness and intelligence, and she will be a very delightful person. But I cannot talk fully or clearly about them till we meet, my dearest of sisters.

To Lady Carlisle.

Paris : December 9, 1831.

Here we are, without a courier from England, dearest of sisters. The wind has been blowing tremendously for the last three days. How the King's speech came over I do not know, but it is here. We like it.

The Nugents are only too tender for a hard world. Unutterable looks across the table, fond murmurs. ' Excellent sherry, a glass of it to Mrs. Nugent,' ' Any of this *consommé* slightly flavoured with essence of,' etc., and she sits quite passive, quite devoted.

George Villiers will be popular here beyond measure : he is in bad health, but gay and more agreeable than anybody. Very much charmed with Mme. de Caraman. Mme. Alfred came out for a wonder, very *spirituelle* and improved by having given up youth and beauty.

On Tuesday we had at the Opera Rubini, quite delightful in the 'Italiana.' Pedro in the box, which chases away meaner and better birds.

The newspapers are just come with Lord Harrowby's moderate speech.

1832

To Lady Carlisle.

Paris : January 20, 1832.

Dearest of sisters,—I know I have been meagre and unsatisfactory in my letters of late, but I shall improve. I also live in the hope of going to England when Granville does, and then I can talk of a hundred things I cannot write.

We are now in the enjoyment of a London November fog. We went yesterday evening to Madame de Flahault's, and the girls were amused, as they found Amélie de Gréfuhle, Auguste de Morny,[1] a charming spark, *né* Hortense and domesticated at Flahault's, Guinea and Frederick Howard, and formed a little establishment of their own. I sat distinguished in Meg's state bedroom, with the Duke of Orleans, Mesdames d'Istrie, Caraman and Delessert, and Count Walewski.

Lord Elphinstone [2] and William Cowper left Paris on Wednesday. They are an immense loss. The former the most amiable loyal person I ever met with. They are delightful partners, real Englishmen, and we have now only George Villiers, who, charming as he is, does

---

[1] Better known as Duc de Morny. He became the intimate adviser of Louis Napoleon, and was the chief promoter of the Coup d'État. He was for many years President of the Corps Législatif until his death in 1865.

[2] Was Governor of Madras from 1837 to 1842, returned to India as Governor of Bombay in 1853, and rendered great service during the Mutiny.

not dance or talk to any one but married ladies of distinction, and therefore is no lark for us.

Lord Yarmouth has taken to good company and appears at the drums and balls. He is the greatest pity that ever was. Such powers of being delightful and captivating, *grandes manières*, talents of all kinds, *finesse d'esprit*, all spent in small base coin. He walks amongst us like a fallen angel, higher and lower than all of us put together.

I dread a ball at Casimir Perier's on Monday. An immense temporary room, two or three thousand invited at a Minister's in these times. I hear the roof is to be covered with *pompiers*, who are to inundate us at a moment's warning, and that there are eighteen doors to go out at, and this is my comfort.

To Lady Carlisle.

Paris: February 12, 1832.

We do not appear as *émus* on the spot as we must at a distance. We were at one of the small balls at the Tuileries on Wednesday till two o'clock. It was very brilliant and pretty, and I thought they all looked better satisfied and calmer than I have seen them for some time. Only think what the Queen must at moments feel when she fears for the safety of all she so devotedly loves, and without one taste or object gratified that can bring one grain into the balance. She has more dignity and calmness of manner than anybody, and I never saw any one who brought such conviction to one's mind that ' her help is from above.'

I cannot help being much amused and pleased with Lady Harriet Baring,[1] but I am sensible it is an opinion that requires a dash of apology. She is uncontrollably

[1] Daughter of the fifth Earl of Sandwich. She became Lady Ashburton in 1848. Thomas Carlyle was devoted to her.

clever and quite natural, which is very refreshing as matter of society.

Tell Lord Morley it would gratify him to behold George Villiers executing admirable steps *en avant* between two princesses, of whom he is the favourite partner. Henry Fox[1] is said to be wholly engrossed with Mme. Guiccioli,[2] and we scarcely ever see him. He is always entertaining when he does appear, but what he likes is to be the talker of a little coterie.

To the Duke of Devonshire.

Paris: February 24, 1832.

I am dying to be off. Granville will not budge from his post till it is absolutely required of him.

We are killing the Carnival as soon as possible. Tuesday week ends it. To-night your uniforms dance and mine walk, as the *parlez* cannot endure hopping amongst the drest coats. I try to make up with flowers, candles, and food for want of better sport. *Champagne et des poulardes truffées* versus waltz and quadrille. I have asked all the English I know in Paris, only two hundred and fifty after all. The Diplomacy come full fig., all their swords and diamonds. French as they please, not at all, in uniform or not. But oh! dearest, the numbers, the Carlists, the Libéraux, the hideous, the anxious. Well, there are always the Miss Levesons. Susy in a blue wreath and diamonds in her hair, Dody ditto with your turquoise branch in hers. Lady G. in all her borrowed splendour.

To Lady Carlisle.

Paris: March 1832.

Dearest sister,—I can hardly reckon on the delight of being in London this spring, yet Granville for the

---

[1] Son of Lord Holland, whom he succeeded in 1840.
[2] Lord Byron's friend.

first time admits it as a possibility. This is such happiness that I forget the only two drawbacks, health and money. I have a little dread of being unequal to a second Carnival, and how I am to meet the expense of it I know not. But the happiness of being amongst you, the vision of Grosvenor Place, to live perhaps a whole month with D——, the rapture of the girls, and the escape from a good deal that worries and bothers me, such as shoals of inconceivable English, half of them in a perpetual rage at what some call 'taking pleasure in wantonly mortifying and insulting'—all this, although mixed as it has been with a great deal of exquisite pleasure and enjoyment derived from my adorable children, makes me look with the feelings of a bird from its chain unbound to England. And I should then return to what is delicious, Dieppe and autumn here.

You will pity me to-day, for I am poorly, yet obliged to go to Casimir Perier's to-night, and gay doings every night of this week, which I should like to spend in my bed.

You will have heard that there was an unpleasant breeze at Rothschild's ball. I did not know of it till two days ago, but the result is that the Duke of Orleans —of or before whom, for the versions are various, some impertinence was said, a nickname I believe—will not come any more to the Apponys, here or into any mixed society.

This I regret very much, as he enjoyed himself extremely, and all seemed smoother, quieter. Now this has thrown an additional bone of contention into society. Do not believe, till I tell it you, that there is any particular feeling against my soirées, or me as receiving my old Ultra friends. Up to this moment, the greatest kindness, most flattering expressions have been used towards me by the Royal Family, the Duke of Orleans, and all belonging to them. God bless you, dearest.

Harry has recovered his equanimity and presence of mind. I like him extremely, he is a most good and amiable man. He would have been saved much nervous anxiety if he could have brought himself, the day of the fatal paragraph, to propose to both my girls, as his mind would then have been set at rest for ever. However, without this security he now shakes hands again with them, and again comes and talks to me. It really was very funny to see his panic.

To Lady Carlisle.

Brighton : April 23, 1832.

Thanks, dearest sister. I am delighted to hear that Lord Carlisle is to go out. What this place would be to him later no words can say. Though the wind is east again to-day, it is delicious, blue, gold, soft, and we have been since church basking on the platform under the cliff.

We are enchanted again with Mr. Anderson, so much so that with much I have heard in other quarters my great wish is to send Freddy to him. We do not mean him to go to Eton, and if he is too young, we have heard of a Mr. Arnold here, with whom Lord Grey has a son and to whom I should like to send him *en attendant.*

I saw Lady Grantham alone for near an hour yesterday; she really was perfect. I think with pleasure that she has much greater interest and fondness for her daughters than I had any idea she had. She talks of nothing but Anne, and in the most amiable devoted manner. The Duchess of Bedford is not well. I hear of many people here, but do not see them. Kemp is too charming, it is a little kingdom of one's own. How I wish you could persuade Morpeth to come here from Wednesday till Saturday. Tell him it is really too delicious.

To LADY CARLISLE.

The weather as fine as possible, not too hot, not too anything.   Talleyrand just going to be put on board in his carriage—no, he is first going to be put into a chair by my side in this room, so I shall have to squiddle to him before.   I have settled all his affairs, what he was to give to the Guard of Honour, everything I don't understand.   All the authorities came in to see him. The whole bore, with none of the pleasure of having dearest Granville.   I believe I have made him give twice more money than he ought.   *Que voulez-vous?* You would have laughed to see me interpreting between him and the Captain.

Dearest dear brother and sister, I have no words for what I feel at having left you.

I shall write from Paris.   Talleyrand says all is perfectly quiet.   The cholera very much in the provinces, but *moins que rien* in the capital.

I must write a line to Granville by Monsieur de Talleyrand, who goes on without stopping.

To LADY CARLISLE.

Yes, Mrs. —— is delighted, and really enjoys herself and is very happy, but let me laugh a little only to you and Hart.   She cannot be light in hand or pleasant, though essentially I think better of her than I ever did before.   But the *conducteur* at the Cimetière du Père-Lachaise was worn, as we occasionally are.   We went there yesterday.   The day divine but without sun. She was enchanted, but asked him who first thought of it.   That was well.   But of the people, all the buried, every particular.   Were they poor, were they rich? Did their relations come and water the flowers, who should? every day, who could? Did clever people come and water Molière's flowers? It does not look written as it sounded said, and it was *sans relâche*. To me, Should I like to be buried there? Should I like to have my flowers watered? Did I mean to buy ground? Should I water her flowers if she was buried there? I almost began to dig the hole. But now, relations, let me tell you that with all this, I have a great regard for her, am grateful for her feelings towards me, and shall be very sorry when they go.

Our little impromptu dancing succeeded particularly well, and the delight of comparing it with the last time and seeing the girls and Fanny wild with delight and my boys. As to Freddy, he turns all heads, and his own would be if it was to last more than a week longer. His dancing *fait fureur*. All the pretty and crackest girls are charmed to dance with him, and he gives himself amazing airs. 'A woman stopped me and asked if I was engaged. I saw she had an ugly wall-flower by her side, so I hurried on, and only just said, "I really believe I am."' You should have seen him say this. I must dress.

To LADY CARLISLE.

Paris : June 25, 1832.

The novel is too like one, and an unpleasant view of human nature. We know not who, but this is what we do know, though you must promise me perfect secrecy. I am not the least alarmed, because, as Susy says, she does not think it would be easy to kidnap her. A person in C. Greville's confidence here came to him and told him he thought it his duty to tell him that he had had a Frenchman with him who came alarmed at the probable risk attending to an office he had engaged in. He was in the pay of an *Irlandais*, to assist him in his pursuit of Susy. He had received a sum of money to deliver a letter to her, and promised a much larger sum when the object in view was accomplished, that of, as his expression was, getting her to the coast, which once done, he could easily elude all pursuit and discovery. The unpleasant part of this is the walks in the Tuileries, all walks indeed except with Mrs. Hamilton or me, carriage and footmen after us, being put a stop to. We have no knowledge of who it can be. *Un très bel homme*, who represents himself as having reason for hope and encouragement from *la gouvernante*. The lawyer consulted frightened the Frenchman, told him he might be sent to *les galères*, as entering into a conspiracy, and I hope this may put a stop to the thing.

Nothing was ever so delicious as this weather. We live out of doors.

To Lady Carlisle.

Paris : June 20, 1832.

Dearest sister,—I went to St. Cloud the night before last. The drive there was delicious at eight o'clock. The King and Madame Adélaïde are in the highest spirits. The Queen looks much calmer, very much occupied with the Princesse Louise's marriage, and dying for Lord and Lady Dover to be appointed to Brussels. Talleyrand was to dine there yesterday. I believe the Ministerial arrangements are still in abeyance.

Did I tell you Talleyrand paid me a long visit on Wednesday morning? I never knew before the, as Mr. Foster says, power of his charms. First of all it is difficult and painful to believe that he is not the very best man in the world, so gentle, so kind, so simple, and so grand. One forgets the past life, the present look. I could have sat hours listening to him. He raves of the Queen here, and she is admirable. I am certain nothing will persuade him to remain here, or to give up London, and indeed what a position to quit, and what a position to gain!

To Lady Carlisle.

Paris: July 31, 1832.

You are an angel, dearest G. There is but one certain means of happiness. I have the greatest pleasure in reading religious books. I find that I understand the Bible better than I ever did before, that I know much better what I am not and what I ought to be, that the subject interests and occupies me deeply, whilst I am employed on it. But I am dissatisfied with the want of warmer, stronger feelings and power of weaning myself from the clinging, aching interests of this world. I do not mean as the question of living in it or retiring from it. If my idea of what we ought to be is a right one, the whole feeling and character would be so changed and dedicated, that it would be indifferent where, how, or when. And it is to attain this that appears to me such terrible difficulty, because the chain that must be broken is the one that binds and fastens one down. I have been reading Fenn's sermons and like most of them extremely as explaining and directing. Bradley's third volume is excellent. Adams' ' Private Thoughts ' one likes better and better. There are parts that one cannot, but these always redeemed by something so true, so feeling, so practical.

I went to St. Cloud on Saturday evening, their last day there. Princesse Louise did not appear. Princesse Marie, with her eyes swelled out of her head with crying. Leopold will be at Compiègne to-day.

To Lady Carlisle.

Paris : August 2, 1832.

Most dear sister,—I wish I could go into the rooms with you. How beautiful the hall [1] must look !

We are all quite well. The weather is perfectly delicious, very hot in the middle of the day, but delightful early and late, and we went this morning to the Bois de Boulogne at eight o'clock, and walked there in the fir woods, which smell like England.

Granville has had a summons to Compiègne to sleep there to-night. It is unlucky, as we have people to dinner. Five Ellices, tiny Mr. Sotheby,[2] Ponsonbys, and the whist boys in the evening. It is very provoking, but it will be interesting to hear what the Kings are about.

The cholera remains in its diminished state. Only twenty-eight deaths yesterday ; I believe I am the only person in Paris who still looks regularly at the *chiffre.* Yet you will be surprised to hear that people here are still so prudent, that on last Friday nobody touched ice or fancy waters, nothing but tea, sherry, and seltzer-water, and everybody is temperate and prudent. We have never at dinner iced water, salad, or cucumber. A few strawberries with wine is looked upon as a sort of excess, and no stone-fruit tasted.

Caradoc [3] goes to England by Brussels to-morrow. You will soon have him in Yorkshire. He is now standing in the court, to see Granville go, in an apricot-coloured linen jacket.

To Lady Carlisle.

Paris : August 7, 1832.

Compiègne lasted till Sunday. On the Saturday they went a long and beautiful expedition. Granville

---

[1] At Castle Howard.   [2] The translator of the *Georgics* and the *Iliad.*

[3] His father having changed his name from Cradock to Caradoc, some-one asked him at dinner for a slice of haraddock.

was charmed with the Royal Family, seen so, so intimate, so perfectly amiable and happy together. The
parting must have been severe, as they say the little
Queen is quite adored by all around her. Granville
does not think her at all pretty, but says she appears
amiable, and that Leopold said she was perfectly so.

D. has not written for ages. I hope he will when
he settles at Bolton, though the life there will not be
propitious—shooting, eating, sleeping.

To Lady Carlisle.

Paris: August 17, 1832.

We had a violent storm the day before yesterday,
which has brought us the delight of cool weather
again. I went in all the freshness and wetness of the
evening after it to St. Cloud with Granville. They had
heard of their little Queen, whose loss seems immense
to them. The poor Queen looked harassed.

I enjoy my life more than I can say. My walks
before breakfast, a new work, ' Louis XVIII.,' which
I am so much obliged to Lord Carlisle for having advised me to read. It amuses and interests me. Then
delicious drives in the evening and, *confesso il mio
rossore*, three rubbers of whist.

Talleyrand is better, but does not yet leave the
house. The Flahaults are both gone to England. I
think there will be a great row-de-dowing amongst
them all. Lady Holland disapproves of Lord Grey
going to Howick. I think it will give him such fresh
energy and spirit that any little objection ought to give
way.

We are all in despair at the thoughts of Guinea's
leaving us.

To Lady Carlisle.

Paris : September 1, 1832.

The Poodle tells me that Lord Dover is better. I like to think of you and my brother expecting Morpeth and Verity on guard.

We are going on well and quietly, with but little cholera and a great deal of prudence. A small *fonds* of society. Ponsonby, who seems to enjoy Paris extremely ; Henry Fox, who is very popular among a set of gossips, Mrs. Rawdon and Lady Helena Robinson, and likes nothing so much as talking scandal with them. I like him a degree less than usual.

Edward Villiers is here only for one day. He is the image of George, only handsomer and graver. I think him uncommonly pleasing.

We are all impatience for news from Pedro, and what a moment for Belgium! Everybody seems to think it *tout simple*, and so did I, till I reflected that this is just one of the most important and critical moments we have had to steer through. I comfort myself with Lord Thurlow's answer when he was asked how he got through all his business. 'I do some, a good deal does itself, the rest is not done at all. Yet all casts up much the same, and nothing is of much importance.' If Lord Granville, sitting there with a hillock of papers before him, could even suspect the nonsense I am writing !

Monsieur de Talleyrand is better, well enough to go out to Neuilly to-day.

To Lady Carlisle.

Paris : September 8, 1832.

Dearest of sisters,—It is most kind of you to write at all on Blanche's last day. I can only be glad that a few more daughters will come and replace her.

I wish you could see us now. The two girls opposite, drawing, and all of us looking as if there were no
sparks in the world, which I sometimes wish was the
case.

No new arrival but Tolstoy, the Russian Dip. from
London. They say he is very agreeable.

I hear Lord Yarmouth is fitting up his house and
furnishing it in London, where he means to live.
When this Lord left Paris he said he was going to look
for a wife, to Madame de Flahault and others. He
deprecated violently marrying a pretty or a young
thing, says what he wants is 'something nearer thirty,
somebody he could not have a jealous feeling about.'
Well, one is also told that, odd as it is, money is his
great object, being his idol. It crossed us all one day that
he would be likely to think of Anne Robinson. Now,
if he does, do you think it possible that, with their ideas
about religion and morality, they would for a moment
think of it? This is mere talk, for I have not heard
their names, do not know where they are, or if they
know each other. I cannot think Lady Grantham
would—a man whom I, less strict, would not even
introduce to my girls.

Guinea is all gratitude to Mrs. Gibson,[1] 'found her
airing my bed with one hand, and holding out a mutton chop in the other.' A little physic also she has
administered, and is in short a darling.

I never saw Susy looking as pretty as she does now.
My head is turned by the compliments paid me about
her. Even old Tchann is quite romantic. 'Voilà,
milédi, une darling,' he said to me last night; 'mais
sérieusement c'est qu'elle devient plus jolie, plus charmante tous les jours.'

Dearest sis, what a twaddling letter this is!

---

[1] Lady Carlisle's housekeeper, who had been nurse to all her children.

To Lady Carlisle.

Paris: October 30, 1832.

I am impatient to hear more of your winter plans, though, alas! I shall be dancing at the Tuileries when you will be basking under some cliff.

I dined on Saturday at Madame de Broglie's. She is perfect, and exerts herself and is no longer absent. He is excellent and sensible, but his manner is not *prévenant*. A few black unknowns made very clever interesting talk, and I am convinced that the Doctrinaire society is the pleasantest in France.

The Lansdownes arrive in a day or two and will be in their element.

Madame de Caraman is a very pretty woman here, but would not be thought so in London. Full of information, delightful talents, draws and paints like an artist, sings beautifully, speaks English perfectly, and Italian, Spanish, and German *de même*. Detested by her *compatriotes*, protected by Apponys, Delmars and us. Her fault is unbounded love of admiration and unwearied toil to obtain it, and she overshoots the mark. People here are so unjust to her that it inclines me to an excess of indulgence. She talked to me of S., but I put a stop to it. He lives a great deal with her, has known her for years, she paints his picture over and over again, sings romances, makes eyes at him; but there is no love on her side, though to every one there is a great deal of coquetry. He is very fond of her. 'To tell you the truth it is not because I think her such a very nice person, but because she loves and dotes upon me so.'

To Lady Carlisle.

Paris: November 5, 1832.

Dearest, dear sister,—Lady Grey has sent me a letter to convey, and ends her note, 'I hope you are

likely to come to England soon for a little visit.'
Really a *première* ought not to permit herself such
says. I sit fancying that the thing is possible that
Granville may be wanted. Not really, my dear, I fear
there is no chance.

I like Lady Lansdowne very much. She has, as
you know, an unattractive manner, but she is most
unaffected, good-humoured, excellent, and pleased and
sociale to the greatest degree.

He, who is not my *beau idéal,* is now revelling in
his leisure. Beauty, music, small talk, a painstaking
laissez aller, a most laborious frivolity. The girl seems
very amiable. To-day we all dine at the Tuileries,
girls and all, no lark, but we come home to my Monday
here, which is their favourite amusement.

Edward Villiers is my love. He is delightful,
excellent, and interesting, a Villiers without any of
the shades.

The Lansdownes are expecting their two sons.
Granville seems much pleased at Oxford, and writes
very quiet, steady letters. How he will miss the
constant society of your Charles! He doats upon him.

1833

To the Duke of Devonshire.

Paris: February 23, 1833.

Our plans are still *en l'air*. Granville better, but still walking with a stick and thrown back by the least fatigue or over-exertion. I suppose his presence will be required as soon as this Irish question makes way for Church reform.

Chiswick is such a Paradise to those two darlings,[1] that no wonder they wish to remain there. Whenever they go to you, if I am not there, let me say one little word to you, but promise me sacredly secret from them and dearest G. Do not fear his *sauvagerie*, and never encourage a London going-out life. It would endanger that happiness for which I would gladly pay the price of my own, to which I have already with delight sacrificed its brightness. To live at Devonshire House with you and in your society, *spectacles*, all that line is well; but the wearisome, heartless round of what is called going out, where people cannot be devoted to each other, and are bored into being devoted for the time to others, would expose him to the only danger I could *envisager* for him. He is so much the creature of *entraînement*, impulse of the moment, with an artless, innocent warmth of feeling for those who by kindness or by design get about him, that anything that separated him from her, from her immense and hourly influence, might unconsciously to himself lead

[1] Lord and Lady Rivers were married in Paris on February 8. They spent their honeymoon at Chiswick.

him into mischief. He is excellent and adores her, but that has nothing to do with what I mean. If I did not think your understanding as good as your heart, your *finesse* and tact as perfect as your feelings, I could not venture to say this. G. would think I meant more. They would laugh me to scorn, but I give it you with perfect confidence. You will measure my meaning in its true sense ; and, having told you this, I care not where they are, so that you are looking on. You have made their happiness and you will guard it. God bless you, most dear.

To the Duke of Devonshire.

Paris: March 1, 1833.

Thousands of thanks for all, for amusing, twigging, and, above all, for telling me you are gradually getting better.

I know Monsieur Walewski. He got me into a mess with Meg Keith, and I have never said anything to him but ' Honey, my dear,' since.

I am a bad play informer, as I never go out, never leave Granville but for an unavoidable misery, such as when Meg or Appony provoke me. But I hear.

People rave of ' Les Malheurs d'un Amant Heureux ' and ' Les Vieux Péchés,' which last even to read kills one. Mrs. Hamilton says ' I Puritani' is very good. Of ' Gustave Trois ' the papers rave. Company says the scenery and decorations are beautiful, and that people will get accustomed to the music. G. Stewart says the parody of ' Lucrèce Borgia ' is good. The play is horrible, although, as always in what he [1] writes, with fine bits and cleverness.

The pair have both written by the last courier. Never did I read of two such happy beings, and in his letter such gratitude and warmth about you. Guinea

[1] Victor Hugo.

writes of them, 'They are the most perfect specimens of happiness I ever saw.'

Meg's ball last night was brilliant. The first opening of her really beautiful house. All the Apponys there for the first time.

TO LADY CARLISLE.

Paris: March 1833.

Berri [1] is to be let loose after her confinement The Carlists have dropped her already. 'Le premier jour ils étaient pulvérisés, le second ils ont dit, Mais voyons, à présent ils disent : C'est mieux, notre cause est à présent claire, cette petite femme n'était après tout qu'un embarras.' This cannot prevent their regretting and others remembering their folly in having made her their heroine and the rallying-point of her party. The jokes rain. They hope the child will be called 'Dieu-donné le second.' Chateaubriand said, 'Je comptais parler de Marie-Thérèse, je ne m'attendais pas à me trouver en face de Marie Gisbourg.' A young Beaumont, son of the General, Monsieur de Gisbourg, son of a lawyer at Nantz, and the Jew who betrayed her, are the people talked of. They say she must name a father in the *extrait de baptême*.

Mme. Juste says, ' Ah! Ah!' Madame de Chateluze and Madame de Bauffremont deny it flat, a forgery they say ; Jamilhac laughs, but also denies.

God bless you, dearest.

[1] Soon after the Duchesse de Berri's imprisonment in the Château de Blaye a letter appeared in the *Moniteur* dated from her prison and bearing her signature, in which she wrote that the serious position in which she found herself compelled her to declare that she had contracted a second marriage. She was about to become a mother, and the public learnt that her husband was the son of a Neapolitan nobleman, Prince de Luchesi Palli.

To Lady Carlisle and the Duke of Devonshire.

Paris: June 1833.

Here we are, dearest sister and brother, for I have not time or means for a double shot.

Our journey has been prosperous, crossing quick and smooth, weather quite delicious, not too hot and yet warm enough for comfort and security.

Paris is enchantingly deserted. Almost all the French people are going or gone. The Court at Neuilly.

Madame Palli, of whom it is said that Henri Cinq was her *enfant politique*, this one her *enfant impolitique*.

I never knew before to-day the story. Ruffo, Castelcicala's son, was proposed to. He asked two millions, upon which Mme. du Cayla said she could get her a husband cheaper, and bought Palli for one million and a half.

Georgy is so happy and Susy coming. I only want to know that you are both well.

To Lady Carlisle.

Paris: June 1833.

I sit before my paper with a great doubt whether I can find anything to put upon it. No courier because of the high winds, so one does not feel wound up.

Granville is better. He has been to the Duc de Broglie this morning. I saw Madame de Broglie yesterday. She is pleased at the admiration excited by his last speech, wishes he could be more so himself. She says he only wants to be more proud and exhilarated about himself, *sa modestie* accepts all that is less flattering, and his spirits are never much raised by what is more. That if he was employed to *planter des carottes entre quatre murs*, he would be as much carried away by it as he is by his present great bidding, that this has its advantages, but also prevents his putting

out all the energy he possesses and which is now so
much wanted. It is taken advantage of by the envious
and inimical to keep him back and discourage him.

The Duc d'Orléans is gone to Belgium to see his
sister. There is a report of her coming here on the
10th, which I trust is unfounded. We should be
obliged *de nous faire vifs*, which would be the most
painful thing that could happen to us.

TO LADY CARLISLE.

June 20, 1833.

Most dear sister,—My last night's post made me so
very happy. Lady Harrowby was so charmed with
you, that, with a kindness I shall always remember, she
wrote me a letter describing the immense improvement
in you.

Leveson will be here on Wednesday. I hope Mr.
Fullerton Monday week.

Mr. Luttrel and Abercromby dined here yesterday
and Lord Harry Vane. It was very pleasant, Luttrel
more amusing than I ever knew him.

To-day we have Sir F. Robinson, Mrs. Hamilton's
father; Mr. Robinson, a potentate in Edinburgh, head
of some college; Doctor Bowring [1] ('La France Commer-
ciale connait Monsieur Bowring,' *vide* French Press),
and the Poodle.

To-morrow Flahaults, Walewski, Damers, Tchann,
Luttrel, and Abercromby.

All this *se passe* easily and rurally in my bonnet
and things, and it gives me all my mornings to myself.

Eugene Anisson tells me that all goes well for the

[1] An eminent writer and political economist, at one time editor of the
Westminster Review and for some years in Parliament. He was sent
to Paris to inquire into the state of commerce between the two countries.
In 1854 he was knighted and became Governor of Hong Kong. His high-
handed policy there, which led to the second Chinese war, was much
attacked.

present people. He travelled through the south of France and was struck everywhere with the prosperity and tranquillity. You know he lives entirely with the Carlists and never goes to Court. He says there is an immense difference amongst them. They scarcely ever talk politics or read a newspaper. In short, since the birth of Miss P., it is easy to see that they will only wait a decent time to come gracefully out, and Lord Harry tells me that their language is altered. 'Après tout il faut faire danser nos jeunes personnes.'

We hope the marriage [1] will be on the 12th or 13th. Our house will be ready for us at Aix on the 20th.

To Lady Carlisle.

Paris: July 13, 1833.

Your letter is just arrived, my dearest sister. I can think of little but your dearest Georgiana [2] at this moment, and feel how much it must engross you all.

I am so happy to hear a good account of Granville, to hope for him back and to hear that he has found politics such as to reassure and satisfy him.

I never saw anything happier than Dody, and I am in every way satisfied and pleased at her prospects. Nothing can be more *facile à vivre*, more kind and attentive to her, more perfectly sweet-tempered and well conditioned than he is. He is extremely fond of her, enchanted with Paris, and the happiness to me of having her with me, contented, gay, seeing everything *couleur de rose*.

Your neighbour's faults are, in my opinion, all in her head—nothing that prevents my being very fond of her. Granville is right about her. She is weak, governed by her mother, has much to answer for in having spoilt her children, and now often misunder-

---

[1] Of her daughter Georgiana to Mr. Fullerton.
[2] Lord Dover died on the 10th.

standing and worrying them; but she is gentle, affectionate, *aimante*, and forgiving, and she flounders more than she errs.

To Lady Carlisle.

Paris : July 26, 1833.

My own dearest sister,—How happy your news of last night made me! Congratulate William[1] and your dearest Blanket for me. I know she wished for another boy. I shall long to hear how they are going on. I suppose from Granville's letter that the Duke of Sutherland must be quite given over. Granville gives me hopes of his setting out from London on Friday and arriving here on Sunday. We should then set off for Aix on Tuesday. I have most delightful letters from Rivers and Susy. They are enchanted with Geneva, its beauty and quiet comfort, and mean to wait for us there and come for a few days to Aix. He has promised to take the two boys to see Chamouny, during which time I should have my darling Sukey all to myself. We have settled to have Eward's visit there.

The *glorieuses journées* begin to-morrow. The Queen returns from her *accouchée* for them and back again for the christening. The little Queen was only ill two hours, and had little pain.

I see in the 'Globe' just arrived an account of the Duke of Sutherland's death. Lord Stafford will be so glad to have gone there and to be with his mother now.

We all dined yesterday at Flahault's. I saw a letter of Lady Grey's, very enthusiastic about Lord Grey and the effect and success of his speech. I suppose all will go smoothly now—yet those Tories?

---

[1] On the birth of his second son, the present Duke of Devonshire.

TO LADY CARLISLE.

Aix: August 8, 1833.

I think you and D. will like to hear of our arrival here, my dearest sister. We all got up at half-past five yesterday morning, my children to get into the steamboat for Vevay, we to come here in a little more than eight hours. The day was fine and cool, the country beautiful. The view of the valley of Savoy and the Mont Blanc from one height almost the finest I ever saw. The approach to this place through the most luxuriant country. The highest and most picturesque Alps—all I love—vineyards in festoons over *treillages* and round down about every cottage. Plums, apple, and walnut trees of uncommon size and beauty for hedges. Light yellow cows with bells round their necks, women with straw hats and milk pails, goats that look as if they were blown in glass, Indian corn like a fairy forest. Tall bridges with one arch, crosses and fountains.

We found our apartments here quite good enough for us, though not smart or *recherché*.

My boys will join us here.

Granville is well. Sir T. Shelley is charmed with the whole affair here, says he feels one and twenty, showed me two fingers that had been swelled and stiffened as nimble and slight as a conjuror's. The air is delicious and the environs beautiful. Granville is now taking his first bath in the house. It smells like a million of rotten eggs. What Aix would be good for is D.'s knee and Lord Carlisle's legs. Granville is hardly a case enough, as, though stiff, there is not swelling, for which the cure is certain. God bless you, dearest brother and sister. I will report progress.

To THE DUKE OF DEVONSHIRE.

Aix en Savoie : August 27, 1833.

I cannot tell you the delight it gave me to hear from you, most dear brother. It had seemed so *triste* to me to receive last week your cover containing my two letters from Geneva, without a word. I cried a little, and so I did when I got your kind, delicious, witty own letter yesterday. ' Varia e mutabile.' No, Grace, because it was all the same feeling—two springs, but from the same source. Natural image here, where everything flows, spouts, showers, shoots upon and at the devoted victim.

I am most happy at this place having been so useful to Granville, and he is so well, and we are, in spite of our rude habitation, so snug and comfortable, that I shall leave it on Friday next with much regret. Our life suits me so perfectly—up before eight, boating, walking, driving in char-à-bancs, the Lake smooth, the boats flat-bottomed, without sails, like Robinson Crusoe's rafts, the roads good or impassable, the coachmen, peasants *en blouse*, drag the horse up and down by the mouth, such a nice safe way, all cheek by jowl together. Our breakfasts and dinners are excellent ; such butter, mutton, and greengages as never were seen before. We all play at whist, the boys and I for five sous the stake, and we go to bed after ten. We have had delicious weather, and our post three times a week brings me letters from my girls overflowing with their happiness. *Que voulez-vous?* My great care is to get that dear beloved G. well and braced. As to you, I am delighted to hear of your amendment, your enjoyment of Chatsworth, your being able to go about in so many different ways. Your life till the company comes must be ecstatic. You have no idea how much more worthy I shall be of sharing it. What with spectacles, mineral waters and courage, I am a new woman. I walked the other day

four miles by myself, exploring in little, unfrequented
wild paths without a thought of danger, fearing nought
that cow could do.

Lord Hertford is much better and saw Granville
yesterday. He sleeps and has recovered his spirits,
and is going on to Naples. Lady Strachan is in great
beauty; she has the bluest eyes, most glossy hair, red
and white skin, lips and teeth; but there is a vulgar
housemaid, common look in her features and countenance which spoils the concern. I have not seen her
girls, but they say the youngest is a hundred times
more beautiful than the eloper. The ugly one is, I
hear, the cleverest. She has unbounded influence over
Lord Hertford.

Every evening we have a little woman of Colmar
singing on our balcony, Monsieur, as she calls her (I
hope) husband, playing on the guitar. It is enchanting.
I must send you two of her songs.

To Lady Carlisle.

Paris: September 15, 1833.

Dearest sister,—I write to-day, because to-morrow
we set out at eleven for Versailles. The Fullertons,
Leveson, and I to dine and make a day of it. Mr. F.
has never seen it. Granville and George Villiers dine
at the Duc de Broglie's at Auteuil.

To-day Granville dines at St. Cloud, and I have
the Flahaults, Lord Mahon, John Ashley, Brooke
Greville, and Mr. Aston to *charmer mes ennuis*. Lord
Mahon has been at Milan and seen Susy, so I like to
see him.

I went to St. Cloud yesterday evening. They all
look so happy and radiant, having been delighted with
their journey, their reception everywhere, and the
yachtes surtout. There is a chance of Leopold and his
Queen the beginning of next month, which would be

calamitous, but as I hear the baby can't come, I live in hopes that they will resolve not to leave it.

Paris is perfectly quiet, a few people occasionally to dinner, but nothing of an evening, always save and except Madame de Flahault twice a week.

We are anxious for news from Portugal.[1] How delighted those Royal women must be at our Court's reception of them! Henry Fox wished Lady Augusta to go to Court. I asked the Queen last night to receive them, and we are all going in a body on Thursday. Meg, who loves going to a Court, thinks it quite a jollification, and will go too.

Such are our pleasures, not to forget the evening concerts, transferred to the morning from three to six. Yesterday I sat it all out with the young ones. Beautiful music, beautifully played. It is just opposite our gates. Perfect order is observed, a slight paling keeps out the people. We have one little wooden chair and entrance for *cavalier et sa dame* for one franc. We think it would succeed in the Grove. Eighty-five thousand francs the musicians have already gained.

To the Duke of Devonshire.

Paris : September 23, 1833.

Your beautiful and magnificent present has turned our heads, mine, Dody's, and Mlle. Thérèse Trouchet, the waiting-woman to the possessor. Dody tells me she was overcome at the first sight of it. It is of real use, for how is Lady Georgiana Fullerton to meet the King and Queen of the Belgians, who arrive on the 4th and will do nothing but dance and drum, without jewels to bedeck her? Is not the white satin gown,

---

[1] 'The Queen of Portugal goes to Windsor to-day. The King was at first angry at her coming to England, but when he found that Louis Philippe had treated her with incivility, he changed his mind and resolved to receive her with great honours.' See Greville's *Memoirs*, 1st series, vol iii. p. 33.

trimmed with blonde, intended for the first great occasion, with your gift to *relever* it, a dainty dress to set before a king?

That beauty, Horace Pitt,[1] sleeps at the Arabins' and plays about and dines here, and drives out with me every morning *en calèche*. He is as good and happy as the day is long, and, as he says himself, quite gentlemanlike.

To the Duke of Devonshire.

Paris: December 3, 1833.

How happy it made myself and friends to hear of you at Lyons! I wrote G. word of your arrival there and sent your account of the road to Susy, to meet her and give her good heart.

The Fullertons go to England on the 10th, and the Rivers's will be here, I hope, on the 16th.

Dolly [2] has not been visible to any eyes I know since you went. Yesterday she wrote a note to Granville to beg him to call on her, for she was ill, lone and desolate. Not so Sarah of the other hotel. The Duke of Orleans calls every morning, though he meets Noailles, the Duchesse de Guiche and Richelieu. The blowens [3] are all angry and have no comfort but saying she writes to him to come and asks for the Royal boxes. She has them, all *à commande*, which is what she cares for. She looks wonderfully well and is not the least oppressive to me, in perfect good-humour, never talking politics, abuse or friendship, no care or bore to me. She has dined here once, we have paid little civil visits to each other, we go to Court together to-morrow, and she sets out for Nice on Friday, Lord Jersey having arrived last night. 'Sad and wearily the wayworn traveller,' I always sing when I reflect on him. Mme. de Flahault is furious because Silence sent a parcel from old Keith

---

[1] Lord Rivers's brother.   [2] Lady Lyndhurst.

[3] Slang for women.

without a card, because when she called in answer to
this no card, Silence talked to Montrond, her back
turned to her. Mme. Walewska is furious because
Silence sent to her to bid her come, because she had not
time to call on anybody. Old [1] Fitz is put out because
she will dine with her at her hotel, where she has no
cook. Lady Sandwich fans every spark she can find
into a flame. Damer [2] is so flustered and hysterical with
the universal hubbub that she invited a party to Fitz
two days ago. Granville amongst the number went and
found Fitz was gone to the Opera and nobody at home.
So much for you to-day. I shall write often and short.
You see this would be sheets in Dolly's hand.

To the Duke of Devonshire.

Paris: December 12, 1833.

I am glad William Cowper is still with you.
Silence means to bide at Nice during the winter. She
continued peaceable and harmless to the last, went with
me to the Tuileries. The King admired her beauty
loud enough for her to hear, and she was, as she always
is, *avec des gens en place* extremely happy.

Here is Leveson arrived. Freddy is coming with
Scarlett this evening. You have no idea of the satisfaction a school of Oxonians gives me, as I must ere long
dance, and young men are the scarcest possible articles
here. A young Oswald, Lord Folkestone, Lord Suffield's son, and several others.

The Wortleys [3] are here, the Wharncliffes in London,
thinking of coming here, but Charles and Emmeline
won't wait, and talk of setting off immediately for
Naples with Hook's new novel, ' Love and Pride,' and
the ' Comic Annual,' directed to you.

[1] Mrs. Fitzherbert.
[2] Mrs. George Damer, *née* Seymour. She had been brought up by
Mrs. Fitzherbert.   [3] Mr. and Lady Georgiana Wortley.

Saturday morning. I have little to add. Dolly arrived, looking sulky, ill and affronted, not with any one in particular, but with public opinion and private feeling, to both of which I suppose she secretly does justice as applied to her own case. *Le Préfet de la Seine* is very attentive, and Lady Sandwich and she are inseparable, a homage to Toryism I conclude. But all this does not seem to unruffle Dolly's plumes, and if she could make a noise like a turkey cock she would. Our weather is still bright and mild, and I hope Susy will arrive before snow or real desperate weather sets in. The Carnival makes me sick, and I want her as a pull against the disgust of giving and going. I do hate society, dearest Grace, more than ever, as a friend told me last night. ' C'est terrible de s'attacher aussi fortement à *sweet ome*, milady.' I was puzzled at first and thought he said sweet wine.

Dino came to see me ; she goes to England to-morrow and Talleyrand follows in a day or two. She tells me Mme. de Lieven has a party every evening, most select, herself and half a dozen whist-players. She cannot exist without her rubber.

1834

To the Duke of Devonshire.

Paris: January 16, 1834.

You will be glad to have parted amicably with poor Lady Lyndhurst. After ten days of illness she died at five o'clock yesterday. Premature labour, Lord Lyndhurst absent, and her poor little girl in a state of misery. We immediately sent my maid with the carriage to bring her here, but Mr. Greene, the nephew, said it was impossible to persuade her to leave the house. I suppose Lord L. will come. It has caused great horror; she was at a ball here, well and brilliant, on the Friday before last, and the violence against her makes it more felt.

I will write more *longuement* the day after to-morrow.

To the Duke of Devonshire.

Paris: January 23, 1834.

Lord Lyndhurst is arrived. The burial is to be in England. He wrote notes of the most grateful thanks to Granville and myself. They would have been deeply affecting from anybody else, from him they were proper, and I have no doubt he felt much shocked by the rapidity of the last events. Lady Chesterfield and Mrs. Anson pleased me. As they had lived entirely with Lady Lyndhurst, dining together every day, and going about together everywhere, I liked them for the feeling they showed in entirely shutting up, not going to the Delmar or Appony balls. They appeared for the first time at Court last night. Mrs. Fitzherbert plays about, dined here last Friday, and at twelve was still to be seen sitting on a couch between Pozzo and Sir Sidney Smith. The Carlists are all coming out again, and the little Duke[1] and everybody are in good-humour, and approve and like to look at each other.

To-day the world is at a bazaar, where the Mlles. Labordes, Madame de Massa, Mesdames Potocka and Rothschild sell in their little booths.

Diplomacy was much in doubt.

Madame Werther: 'Il faut y aller; c'est indispensable; on nous a écrit.'

Madame Appony: 'Chère Lady Granville, que faire? La bonne Werther! Les jolies petites boutiquières! Irons-nous déposer notre petite offrande de dix francs?'

Lady Granville: 'Je n'irai pas.'

This sounds dreadful, but I think more money without the pound of flesh will bring matters even *versus* Mme. Rothschild. I really had rather be hung than go.

The French do not admire much the Ladies Ailesbury, Chesterfield, Anson. What they do are the two Miss Ellices, Miss Seymour, a daughter of Sir Michael's, very fair, with long ringlets, and Mrs. E. Jerningham. They stand round those ladies in admiration. *Bijou*, *figure d'ange*, etc., and sneer at our mature fashionable beauties. *Que voulez-vous?* Every dog. There are many pretty Frenchwomen of all colours. Monsieur de Delmar's ball was almost of fabulous beauty and brilliancy. The worst was we looked like the servants come to see the apartments before the fit inhabitants appeared. It is so high, so broad, so light, so awful. Domes above, red velvet carpets all in one piece to step

[1] Of Orleans.

upon. Madame de Delmar alone is made on the same scale, and looks handsomer and fits it all.

Here is Susy in a purple silk gown and your Russian *cadeau* on, which, being cleaned, comes out like Peru.

To Lady Carlisle.

Paris: February 1834.

I have not been inspired by you, most dear sister, these two last post days, so I write flat, but I see with delight that your journey is over in the 'Morning Herald.' We are going on quite well. Granville free from gout. Susy quite wondrous. She goes out every now and then to an opera, or for a little while to Mme. de Delmar's, but is generally in bed soon after ten.

The Carnival is raging, and all full of squabbles and petty jealousies and *tracasseries* owing to the Carlists beginning to come out, and the eternal questions of who meets whom, and why somebody stays at one place or leaves another

In the midst of it all poor Lady Lyndhurst's almost sudden death, though she had been ill some days, coming just after we had all seen her at a ball here radiant and covered with diamonds, gave one of those dark, awful impressions that such calamities bring with them, even when feelings are not immediately interested.

Lord Lyndhurst is just arrived to take back his little girl.

To Lady Carlisle.

Paris: February 27, 1834.

A thousand thanks for your letter and kindness and your advice. I enclose you a letter. Will you frank it to Mrs. Lamb?

Would it not be good for you and soothing to her if you were to go to her for a little while at Compton

Place? What are your plans? Not only London, I
hope. The sea, the sea, the deep blue sea.

I can tell you little more about Lady Lyndhurst. I
think Lord L. behaved most properly. He seemed to
feel the shock very strongly, and gratitude to those
who had been kind to her. George Anson told me
yesterday that though one knew the sort of relation
they must have been upon, yet his manner when with
her was that of kindness and even fondness.

To Lady Carlisle.

Paris: March 21, 1834.

I am happier than I can say, own dearest sister.
Susy is quite wonderfully well,[1] my little grandson is
the greatest love, like an immense wax doll, but, as
Beck says, saucy.

To Lady Carlisle.

Paris: April 1834.

Susan is going on perfectly well, but, dearest sister
—I talk to who will understand—you know when
nerves take dominion, the misfortune is, and I reproach
myself in vain for it, that one rejects relief and comfort,
and this only to you, when calmed upon one terror,
another fixes its hook into one.

Here is that darling angel, relieved from suffering,
regaining strength rapidly, happy about herself and her
baby, who is also well. Yet here am I, because she is
going out for the first time to-day, and that I do not
think the weather quite fine enough, with cold hands, a
tight head, and aching, frightened heart. Just strength
of mind left to shut myself up and keep out of the way,
not to damp the ecstasy of herself and her husband at
this first lark, this proof to them of returning health
and strength and promise of more. The anxiety of the
last two months has given me an impossibility of feeling

[1] She was confined on March 20.

happy. 'I have a new fear,' which you have often written to me is the constant move of my mind, and I have for the time broken the spring that used to bring me rapidly back to joy in proportion to anxiety. Then I make to myself all sorts of reproaches. I read in a little book I like, Mrs. Fry's last, 'Fear is not sorrow.'

This too I feel: my anxiety for what I love so much is not of a kind that interests and pleases me with myself—it is not sensibility, it is not a softened softening feeling, it is more like cramps and spasms of the mind, it paralyses my power of being useful, and is to the objects themselves something inexplicable.

It reduces me to wish them away. The only thing that calms my nerves is sitting at an open window, reading Mrs. Fry or Adams' ' Private Thoughts ; ' but my religion is like my feeling, and I do not find its influence when I leave the immediate occupation of it. I know why no single act of feeling or practice can soothe, it must be what I have not, entire submission and devotion.

' It is time to have done with future prospects, or a vain imagination that we shall be happy or more at ease, when such a point is gained or such an impediment removed, whereas nothing is more certain than that every period of life and every day will bring its own burden along with it, and that there is no possibility of happiness but in bearing it according to the will of God.'

Dearest sister, I did myself very great good by pouring myself out to you this morning. They sent for me into the garden, and there I found her, delighted and able to walk round it without fatigue, and I have since seen her upstairs feeling quite well, with a great appetite for roast mutton and green peas.

I have also had a long visit from Mme. Appony.

I like and love her. We talked much on serious subjects. She was saying that she thinks that it is wrong in us to be always looking forward, fearing evil, planning good, that it cannot be approved that we should do that with what is so entirely in God's will and out of ours.

'Know your own weakness, trust and pray,' 'Take no heed of to-morrow,' are the two sentences I just now cling to. God bless you.

To Lady Carlisle.

Paris: May 20, 1834.

Dearest beloved sister,—I need not tell you all I feel for you and yours, or how anxiously I long for the next account of your darling Blanche.[1] What a trial this must be to her! If his life was likely to have been of delicate health and suffering, she may have been spared much misery. The time will come when what is left her will become everything, but all this is not now, and I grieve for her, for poor William, for you, my dearest G., more than I can express. Thank your dear Elizabeth for her kindness in writing.

Susan feels deeply for Blanche. She is herself improving daily in strength, and I think, if she continues as well as she promises, will be in London in less than a fortnight.

Her affection for Blanche has always been one of her strongest feelings, and now more than ever does she feel for her and with her at a moment of such trial. God bless and protect you all.

I have nothing to say. You will be very sorry for poor Leopold. I hear the loss of their boy has been a dreadful blow to them. They come to Neuilly the end of this week.

[1] Lady Burlington, who had just lost her eldest boy.

To Lady Carlisle.

Paris: May 31, 1834.

Dearest sister,—I trust in Verity's care of you, and my opinion of his skill and judgment is such that I cannot understand your inclining your ear to any but him.

I have seen in Susy's case within these last few days the wonderful effect of change of air. I long to hear of you from her, and of dearest Blanche, whose trials have been so severe; also to know what you think of my adorable child.

I feel that I cannot write to-day, because our ignorance about political events is so great, having only got so far as the resignation of the four Ministers,[1] that it leaves one all unhinged and suspended.

To Lady Carlisle.

Paris: June 8, 1834.

Dearest sister,—I was happy to hear from you yesterday, and all your thinks at this interesting moment. I am glad Lord Carlisle has the Privy Seal. It takes the scrub look from the present Cabinet, and is honour to whom honour is due. I am very sorry Mr. Stanley is gone, hope Lord Mulgrave is not affronted, dread Lord Durham at the head of the discontented and dissenting office, and I am afraid of our Auckland amongst the rigging.

Mme. de Flahault says Lord Durham would kill Lord Grey if in the Cabinet, will upset him if out of it. Lord Glengall, ultra-Tory, says, ' I hear that the Duke of Wellington and Mr. Stanley have long understood each other, and that the Duke says, " If Stanley and

[1] The Duke of Richmond, Lord Ripon, Mr. Stanley, and Sir James Graham left the Government on account of Mr. Ward's resolution respecting the Irish Church.

Peel will unite, I will act with them as Secretary of the
Treasury, if they like it." '

Now, my dearest G., I cannot say how glad I am
that the exchange of situation was not offered to
Granville. He not only likes Paris best, but would
have disliked the Admiralty particularly—no knowledge of Naval affairs, no turn for scraping and
economising, and a necessity of speaking. Yet it
would have been extremely painful to him, if he had
been asked as a convenient and useful thing to Lord
Grey, to have refused. England would have been
purchased at a price that I should have been grieved
to see him pay.

I cannot say all my shades of feeling and wishes
—you in Grosvenor Place, Susy at Mistley, Georgy
coming here, and no other *pied à terre*, Granville's
decided preference of Paris and his work here to anything else.

You will talk to me of Susy and her boy, and of D.,
who has dropped me. I hope and trust he has no
return of suffering in his knee. Tell him that I cried
when I read of Spot's[1] death.

To LADY CARLISLE.

Paris : June 1834.

I long for Georgy's arrival and expect them on
Tuesday.

About your plans, my beloved sister. I can let no
selfish feeling come across my ardent wish that you
should do whatever is best for you. I wait impatiently
to hear what is decided, and what dear Lord Carlisle
and Liz do. You must know what a hope of seeing
any of you must be to me—to have you *en personne*
at Aix would be intoxicating, but if the quiet of
the sea within a short journey is best for you, I

[1] An Italian greyhound belonging to the Duke of Devonshire.

wish you by it. I should have thought varied change
of air and *mouvement* better for your you, but of this you
and Verity are the best judges.

Of politics—well—what a popular, commanding,
and, one must add, cunning eloquence is our Stanley's!
What a Chancellor of the Exchequer Spring Rice would
have been; impossible I suppose! Why was Abercromby not placed somewhere?

I cannot wonder at Lord Carlisle, but it don't look
as well without him. What does Lord Morpeth do?
and any price Lady C., for what he thinks. Various
reports reach us. Great intimacy between Lords
Brougham and Lyndhurst? Was Lord Mulgrave
offended, or only looking to Foreign employment?
Do you believe there will be change or not? Between ourselves, Mme. de Flahault received yesterday morning a letter from Lady Grey. In the evening
Flahault said to me, 'We have letters, change is still
to be expected, and we know it from those who would
least wish it.'

The Berrys are happy, and so is Lady Charlotte
Lindsay, under a tree in the Champs Elysées sketching;
they have Saturdays and we all go, and the tea-table
and the girls look just as they do in Curzon Street,[1] and
Pozzo, Granville and Butera,[2] and Mrs. Damer and many
others sit and squiddle in the first room, and we *veilléd*
there till a late hour.

To Lady Carlisle.

Paris: June 1834.

Most dear sis,—Yesterday's courier made me the
happiest of women. Your letter, eight rapturous pages
from Susy at Mistley, and a delicious letter from
D. at Brighton. This, with Georgy's safe arrival,

---

[1] Where the Miss Berrys resided.
[2] Neapolitan Minister at Paris.

perfectly well and happy, set me up. She is gayer than I have ever seen her, and they are both delighted to be here again. She is enchanted with Lizzy,[1] whom Fullerton thinks very handsome. But Dody says there never was a more amiable, agreeable girl, which is really so much more essential, as I think dress is half the battle when looks are concerned, and everybody can look well so much more easily than they can be liked and likeable. *Vide* the whole French nation. There are no corsets and plaits for selfishness and ill-humour.

Abercromby's appointment has pacified Miss Berry and the ' Times.' My great fear now is that Lord Grey will be worn and tired out by all that I foresee will be Lord Durham's power of plaguing. How can he be pacified—Grand Mogul?

Dearest sis, I must have done. Damers, Berry, Lords Bruce and Elibank dine here, and I must adorn in silk and flannel with an aching ear.

To Lady Carlisle.

Paris: June 1834.

The Poodle is arrived and has seen you all. He amused and interested me about politics, putting many dots upon many i's.

Sister, the only doubt about Lord Carlisle accepting or not was his own convenience; and I think he must be glad at this moment to make a sacrifice to Lord Grey, who seems to me to have been ill-used, or, rather, provokingly used by many of his friends. To his enemies—the Duke of Newcastle and Lord Londonderry—he must *par contre* feel grateful. Did you ever know such boobies?

Miss Berry dines here to-day. She is at times excessively disagreeable, with a *fond* of some good and friendly qualities that make one get over it. But

---

[1] One of Lady Carlisle's daughters.

one thing is increased with age—no civility or attention does—it is always complaint, comparison, and
scolding.   I was obliged to give it her before Ag and
Lady Charlotte, and the joy of those two girls showed
how they had smarted.

I went to see her on her *jour*. 'How d'ye do, Miss
Berry?' 'Ah, ah! none the better for you.' 'What
do you mean?' 'I might have died yesterday with a
wretched cold, for anything you thought of the matter.'
I appealed to the young ladies present if it would not
indeed be a miraculous degree of attachment that
would have made me guess by instinct the day before
that Miss Berry had caught cold.   I am glad the
Poodle is come, because they are just well and ill
enough together to turn the stream of wrangle into
a new channel.   Herself is become so *exigeante*, that
people are positively angels or devils as they call on
her or not.   I, who have been uncommonly polite, am
just let off with sighs and groans. 'Nothing surprises
me here; no attention seems wonderful to me, remembering what I used to receive.'   To give you an idea of
it.   I offered her a very pretty cactus, which she admired excessively. 'Ah, ah! send me a plant indeed.
I used to have as many and more than I wanted without asking, only sending to the conservatory for whatever I chose.' 'You did not marry us, Miss Berry,'[1]
another rap which has been salutary to this virgin.

Bless you dearest, dear sis.

To LADY CARLISLE.

Aix: August 9, 1834.

We are here since the day before yesterday and all
well.   Granville uncommonly so, I think.   He took a
warm bath yesterday and a slight douche this morning.
The weather yesterday was most oppressively hot.   We

[1] She was supposed to have arranged Lord and Lady Stuart's marriage.

only walked after six and could hardly crawl. But how beautiful it was! The harvest all alive, and large, sweet loads of hay, picturesque people, and the mountains, woods, and vines all looking their very best, first under a setting sun and then under a small slice of moon. In the night a violent thunderstorm, to-day it is extremely fine and quite cool.

Aix is very unlike last year. I like it better, but am afraid it will be terribly dull for my companions. There is no society—a few Ultras whom we just know by name, and a French dandy or two. The only person Granville has seen is the Duke of Manchester, who is here with a Doctor Stewart. It is nice to have an English doctor about.

Leveson has been to two soirées—weak tea, Duchesse San Carlos and her daughters, Mme. Sougeous, a Greek niece of Capo d'Istria with a beautiful daughter, young Maillé, and a spark or two. He dragged Mme. Sougeous round the room waltzing and was glad to come home, the only advantage I see in going out.

Will you tell dearest D. the little I say, as I have not a single word or thought to make a second letter by to-day's post? I hope something may turn up before the next.

To Lady Carlisle.

Marseilles: September 4, 1834.

I am so happy you are better. We are very well but very hot. Since Valence we have had much enjoyment. The steamboat *trajet* of six hours on the broad Rhone with its beautiful banks. Avignon, the most picturesque of towns, Aix[1] a very pretty one, lovely seen from the hill above it just at sunset, like the town in ' Cherry and Fairstar,' bathed in currant-juice, and now Marseilles.

[1] En Provence.

Walked yesterday by the still blue Mediterranean, its little waves like crystal, and we are just come in from boating out of the harbour—which is gay, busy, amusing—into the open sea, where the view of the town, harbour, and forts is magnificent.

Our hotel is good, but smells so like Amsterdam that we shall be glad to drive in the cool evening after dinner back to Aix—only twenty miles—and to-morrow to Avignon again.

The engineer in our Valence steamboat comes from a place close to Castle Howard, and our host of the inn at Avignon, a poet and a very gentlemanlike man, gave me the enclosed translation. Granville read us the original out loud, which is beautiful, and Monsieur Pierson has meant better than executed.

We are rather languid, dry, and parched with the very intense heat, but we take our time. 'Don't hurry,' as the link-boys say. There is a great deal of amusement, interest, and enjoyment spread over our journey, with tiny drawbacks. The pill or not the pill, that is the question—carriages shaking, wheels burning, a slanting bed; but to-day we are all wound up and going right—no insects and little dust.

Castle Howard will set you quite up, and you will come to Paris, I know you will, most dear Lady Carlisle.

To Lady Carlisle.

Carcassonne: September 9, 1834.

Dearest of sisters,—Since I wrote last we have done a great deal. Aix and Avignon again, Nismes and Montpelier, two beautiful towns. We slept last night at a miserable inn at Narbonne, but found Mons. Delessert [1] there, who sent off his servants immediately

[1] Monsieur Gabriel Delessert was successively Prefect of the Aude and the Eure-et-Loir. From 1841 to 1848 he was Prefect of Police at Paris. He was esteemed by all parties, and his wife universally popular.

to his wife, who is alone here with her two little children, to desire her to feed and lodge us *tant que nous sommes*. And here we are, more comfortable, more left to ourselves, more astonished at large airy rooms, *fauteuils*, luxuries of all kinds.

She is a most captivating little woman. Her talents and charms all, however, *cèdent le pas* to-day to her delicious way of receiving us, as if she put us into a house of our own, meaning to call on us at dinner time.

We arrived here at two. She is going to take Granville and the boys to see the old town—very curious. Advises me not to stir—what a charming little woman! And sister, I have seen the amphitheatre at Nismes, the Pont du Gard, the most beautiful and finest remains of antiquity, and what for climb up to old Carcassonne, which I saw very plainly when I drove into the town. It is like Windsor Castle and Alnwick, and the only perfect specimen of a Gothic town.

To-morrow we go to Toulouse. Having enjoyed our steamboating on the Rhone so much, we had meant to go from Agen to Bordeaux in the same way ; but Mons. Delessert says the heat has dried up the Garonne so much that we must not attempt it, and we shall go from Toulouse by land.

To Lady Carlisle.

Bordeaux: September 13, 1834.

I found a letter from you at Carcassonne, my own dearest sister. It made me so very happy. You seem and write in so much improved zest and spirits. Only your delightful accounts of Castle Howard made me pipe, gave me a *mal du pays* to be there, to help you hang up the prints, to walk with you to the dairy, see the setting sun, and rich tints, and Henderson[1] on his

[1] The agent.

grey pony, and a thousand sights I have never seen and loved as I have at Castle Howard. And then the thinking you able to be more about and to enjoy is such pleasure !

We are here in this beautiful, magnificent town, in an hotel that is as good as the Embassy at Paris, every comfort and luxury about us.

To-morrow we shall have an enjoyable day, but somewhat trying. We go by steam, thirty miles to Médoc at eight in the morning. There we dine with the Consul's sister, Mrs. Barton, and see the whole process of the vintage. We set off Monday morning for Angoulême.

The road from Agen here near a hundred miles, which we accomplished in a broiling day, was beautiful. The banks of the Garonne like those of the Seine near Rouen, but more rich, swarming with *campagnes*, vineyards, etc.

The boys are like trouts, speckled all over with gnat bites. Freddy very much swelled and worried by them. Their enjoyment is, notwithstanding, immense.

We have always air, no serious heat, good roads, almost all the inns excellent as to food and beds. The country and towns beautiful. How often I think of, and wish for, Morpeth !

I, too, have heard from Lieven—a touching, amiable letter—but the Imperial child will set her up.[1]

To LADY CARLISLE.

Bordeaux : September 1834.

Your letter, which I received yesterday, tells me of Verity's sudden departure, most dear sister. I know how sorry one is at the moment, but I cannot help

---

[1] Prince Lieven was recalled from London and appointed Governor to the Czarewitch.

thinking that you will go on better than you expect without him.

If you will but come to Paris, I engage to give you a thousand and one ways of combating fear. You can have no idea how I have trained myself to overcome it, but it is quite impossible to write satisfactorily upon it. Fear is such a coward. Face it, talk to it, say 'What are you?' and you will find what large, unreal shapes it takes and how they vanish before energy and resolution. I have felt terror. For example, I was twenty thousand times more afraid of cholera than you were, of tooth-drawing, cattle, carriages, etc., of which I have constantly, especially lately, entirely conquered my terror by strong determination.

You will say yours is more a matter of health. I can only answer to this by reminding you of Chatsworth, and urging air, society, interests, amusements, change of scene occasionally. St. Leonards with poor Mrs. Lamb, a glaring sun and a lodging never seemed to me a lark of the first magnitude—Paris, Lady Carlisle, Paris.

I must not write on. We are setting off to sleep to-night at Angoulême. Our two days here have been charming. I am delighted with the Scott family. We passed the whole of yesterday with Mr. and Mrs. Barton, one of the daughters, at her *campagne*. Started at eight in the steam-packet, had a sea breeze on shore, the banks beautiful, coasted the fortress of Blaye. We there saw the whole process of *vendangerie*—scenes like in a ballet. The men tread the grapes to music, but what a nasty process, all hands and feet! An excellent dinner. *Royats* out of the sea, *bec-figues* as out of the air—not that I tasted either, but I looked at my family whilst they did, and with horror saw Freddy tasting the different vintages, '1821, Mr. Leveson.' We were seven hours coming back per steam and moonlight, and I

did not think it too long, which is *tout dire*. We arrived
here towards one in the morning. Yesterday we dined
at Mr. Johnston's, another Scott *ménage*, a mile and a
half out of Bordeaux. Such *luxe*, comfort, verandahs,
flowers—pretty, young women, nice, old, intelligent men.

Afterwards to the Grand Theatre, beautiful in and
out. The 'Sylphide,' danced by horrors, presented no
attraction, bed did ; so we finished our day at ten o'clock.

Here I am getting up at half-past six with the feelings of eleven, not sleepy or surprised, and prepared
for a long day's journey with Mrs. Trollope's 'Belgium'
and a batch of late newspapers.

I shall not, perhaps, write again till Paris, so do not
wonder at the gap. We shall have long days and some
châteaux to see.

To Lady Carlisle.

Paris : September 22, 1834.

Dearest of sisters,—We arrived here the day before
yesterday, and I have the delight of finding your long
and most amusing letter of the 17th. Wish dearest
Lord Carlisle joy for me,[1] if it will keep till my letter
arrives. I am always too late, and don't remember my
own till you or some kind friend remind me of it.

Our journey after Bordeaux was less interesting,
but cooler ; in consequence, not so fatiguing. One
sight—a Gothic castle, built by Le Beau Comte and in-
habited by the Dunois, at Chateaudun—was almost more
striking than any.

You are a darling old woman, as Lady Morley says
to me, as Mme. de Sévigné was so angry at Mme. de
La Fayette saying it to her, and you are so well and so
sprack, and so certainly intending to pay us a visit.
Receive Lady Cawdor, spend your fine autumn where
you are, then come five in number—Earl, Countess,

---

[1] On his birthday.

lord and two ladies—and give yourself a little quiet dissipation and amusement in La Belle France.

I found here Georgy well and with a child who, I assure her, is not the one I left. He is a fine, stout, fat baby, without speck or spot, taking notice, laughing, as prosperous as it is possible to be.

My boys are going this evening—a sad loss.

God bless you, most dearest sis. Granville is very well and so am I, but the heat and long journey was a pull, and we enjoy the repose and comforts, a clean, luxurious life, as if we were shipwrecked mariners.

The King was very gay last night. We are to go to Fontainebléau for three days the week after next, and the Fullertons are to be asked, I believe. It will be a great comfort to me to have her there, and he likes it, so she tries to be pleased ; but her dislike and horror of world and company are beyond even mine. We both equally shrink from it in perspective, but I bear it better when plunged than she does. I now make it a duty and an endeavour to court it more, and not to make a grievance of what is necessity and duty as long as I am here, and that's why, good-bye, ' I fly to the hill where the Berry girls blow.'

To Lady Carlisle.

Paris : September 29, 1834.

I thought you and Susy very ignorant, when I found two couriers back that you had only got as far as Carcassonne, and I cannot recover my surprise at your not having got me out of Bordeaux yet.

I am glad to be come back. Three weeks' constant travelling in intense heat is a trial.

Then I am a fool, and never can be so entirely at ease when I do not hear quite as constantly from Susy. She is so perfect about writing, and therefore it is such certainty of constant letters when I am here.

I think travelling, but not in the dog-days, most
excellent, both for body and mind. It does one good
after, and has moments of most excessive enjoyment and
delight *whilst*.

We find many English here. The Berrys run up
and down. To-day they dine here. Tuesday they go
to Fontainebleau till Thursday. We go from Friday
till Tuesday. We all think of nothing but dress, with
different shades of interest and emotion, and different
results to our thoughts. You will judge when I tell
you that the Fullertons dined at Bellevue on Saturday,
and Mary received them in *organdi* with long pink
sash, the ends floating on the breeze. Do not tell. It
is an extraordinary but harmless weakness. She is in
very good looks, subdued, very kind, and often as you
know friendly and true, and has left off all her disagreeable ways and hootings at me.

To Lady Carlisle.

Paris: September 30, 1834.

Dearest of sisters,—We have shoals of friends from
all quarters. Lansdownes, Mintos, Charles and Lady
Mary Fox arrived yesterday. The boys Lansdowne
and Minto came to dinner without their poor tired
unworldly wives. Dear Lady Lansdowne has been here
this morning, in a very shabby old bonnet, begging not
to come smart to dinner to-day.

The visit of Miss Berry, which came betwixt, makes
me say all my say over again. She has made herself so
pleasant and popular here that her going will be very
much felt and regretted. I never saw anybody upon
whom success had so happy and softening an effect.
All her bitterness and snapping-up are gone, and she is
more good-tempered and easily pleased at this moment
than anybody in Paris.

To Lady Carlisle.

Paris: October 4, 1834.

Dearest of dear sissees,—We are just setting out for Fontainebleau, and being well—Granville and Dody both so—fine, brisk weather, Mme. Appony to join us to-morrow, I look forward to it with some pleasure and less of dread than might be expected.

Berry has been at breakfast in the forest and sailing on the pond. We shall meet those fortunate girls screaming their way back, and Naples, Russia, and Prussia, who return to-day. Appony is classed for this time with Spain, England, and Belgium.

Lady Granville and Lady G. Fullerton to Lady Carlisle.

Fontainebleau: October 7, 1834.

Dearest sis,—I have enjoyed being here excessively. Granville uncommonly well, Georgy a little weak and tired, but this enabled her to rest and recruit. Weather quite ideal. The finest summer without excessive heat, a beauty of place beyond description ; château with its thousand souvenirs, and being restored in the best taste and magnificence, and the forest more than delicious. My own dearest, I must fly.

Mama's time is so filled up by all the things she is obliged to do and to see here, dear Lady Carlisle, that I have undertaken to give you some account of our proceedings. We arrived on Friday at five o'clock, sat down to a dinner of a hundred and four people, and in the evening there was a very pretty concert. Cinti sang divinely. The next day, after a breakfast as substantial and long as a dinner, we went over all the castle, a fatiguing but very interesting thing to do. It is quite a course of French history, and will soon be completely repaired and restored by the King, who is extremely

anxious to make it as magnificent as in former days.
We then went to see a game at tennis, played by Barre
and Louis, who are reckoned the best players in Europe.
Then there came a drive of several hours in this most
beautiful forest, which Mama would have much enjoyed
had it not been for the way the omnibus-and-six in
which they drove dashed down the rocky precipices
which the forest is full of. The Queen is, fortunately
for her, a bit of a coward and said all she thought. In
the evening there was a *spectacle, la suite d'un bal
masqué,* 'Le Philtre,' by Auber and a *pas de deux* in the
interval. The theatre is pretty, and all the women
being very smart it made altogether a beautiful *coup
d'œil.*

Yesterday the day was passed in a similar manner.
In the evening the 'Barbiere' and the 'Prova d'una
opera seria,' in which Lablache, Rubini, Tamburini,
Ivanhoff, and Julie Grisi all appeared.

To-day there is only a little *promenade sur l'eau,*
and to-night a great ball. The Galerie de Henri II.,
which has been completely repaired and repainted by
the King, is to be opened on this occasion, by way of a
surprise, which we all expect. Nothing can exceed the
civility and kindness of the Royal Family to everyone,
and more especially to papa and mama. The only de-
ficiency is a want of comfort and convenience in the
private arrangements of the Palace. These *fêtes* are
said to be extremely popular with the lower orders.

The party consists of the Apponys, the Friases, the
Lehons, the Ministers and Maréchals with their wives
and daughters, and some French people besides those
immediately about the Court.

There is as little formality as a Court can possibly
have. I have miserably supplied mama's place in
writing. Ever most affectionately yours,

GEORGIANA FULLERTON.

To Lady Carlisle.

Paris: October 10, 1834.

Dearest sister,—I wrote such a scrap from Fontaine-bleau that I must begin to-day to be sure of a less shabby letter for to-morrow.

Our last day, Monday, was the *bouquet*; in the morning a delicious walk in the shady large *jardin Anglais*—a junket in the Étang de François I. in a very large sort of barge boat, with circular seats and an awning, from which we saw the *château* as if it grew out of the water. We stepped into a pavilion in the middle of that *étang* where the massacre of St. Bartholomew was finally settled, because, Lady Carlisle, what is whispered on the water cannot be heard on the land. I told the King this, and he was much edified and surprised—very glad to hear it, no ways doubting, only had never happened to hear of it. I was obliged to cry out for witnesses, Mme. de Montjoie, who had told me, etc., and I came out with credit, but such are the dangers of sight-hearing.

The ball was magnificent, and a banquet after it, which lasted till half-past two, the whole thing grandiose, magnificent and luxurious, and I liked it of all things.

To come home is pleasant too in its way. Paris is just now very agreeable. Italian opera three times a week, no dinners or drums begun, delicious mornings in this heavenly weather, in what is real country, the Bois de Boulogne. On Sunday the third we think we shall run into the Tuileries, to prove our gratitude by boring them to death.

Lady Sydney *fait fureur* here; she is thought beautiful, extremely agreeable and *distinguée*. Lady Clanricarde is not so much admired. Her nose is a little red, and she is grand and dry in her manner to them. The cleverness they do not get at, as none of it is spent in small talk. She went yesterday to Valençay

with the Damers and Henry Greville. I hear the
Seftons are going there too, and then coming for a
week to Paris.

To Lady Carlisle.

October 14, 1834.

Dearest of sisters,—I did not hear from you, but
Berry did, and she told me all you say, so it was next
best to hearing.   Happy and proud was she of knowing
about Wentworth, and that Lord Carlisle is uncommonly well.

We are fond of Berry.   Since I have reflected upon
her age, which is not often present, *vu* the gaudy
colours, noise and constant about-ishness, I think she
deserves much excuse for what is disagreeable, much
esteem and approbation for what is pleasant.   Sociable
by habit, *exigeante* by situation and intimate by force.
There is something goes against one in the process, but
the result is great delight when she obtains what she
must naturally consider her due in society, and an
enjoyment of it, that neither the young nor the happy
can come up to.   The three dined here yesterday with
Mr. Aston and Bulwer.   It was very pleasant.

We went after dinner to St. Cloud, where we found
Apponys, and Lehons.   The abuse and attempt at
ridicule in some papers, amongst the Carlists, are as
weak and *manqués* as possible.

Fontainebleau was perfect in its way; the Queen is
perfect in every way, and the King is *much* wiser than
Solomon.

God bless you, my own dearest sister.   I could
write much more, but I must to D., Susy and Leveson.

My husband has had a letter from Lady Clanricarde
at Valençay.   She says it is spacious, comfortable and
like an English *château*.   ‘ A pair of neighbours, the
Damers, the Duchesse de Valençay, with whom she is

charmed; Mme. de Montmorency, shy at first, but who begins to amuse her, likes her and gives passages of her life; a drawing-master; several persons more or less engaged in Mlle. Pauline's [1] education, and a black gentleman, whose occupation she has not yet been able to define.'

Pouring rain—winter begun.

To Lady Carlisle.

Paris: October 1834.

Only one line to-day, my own dearest sis, to show you that I am not touchy or nervous, but only mindful that I have not heard from you the two last couriers.

My time has been taken up with a sort of influenza going about here. Dody has had it too; and we have been keeping our beds all day, and meeting at dinner in our night-caps—pleasant, if it were not for the aching and sneezing and shivering. And all this must put its best face on for Charles Kembles, Mary Berry, Mrs. Morier, and Lord and Lady Holmesdale, who dine here.

The weather is changing, still warm, but no sun, and occasional rain.

Valençay lasts till the 25th. Fancy Mr. Motteux's corner of eye and mouth when he dined here on Monday—'Any commands for Valençay, Lady Granville?' Talleyrand's friend. What a *finale* for him!

Mme. de Flahault returns the end of this month. I took her eldest girl [2] to the Opera last week. She is grown very pretty—seems extremely *spirituelle*—like Lady Bagot in face.

---

[1] Daughter of the Duchesse de Dino, married subsequently to Monsieur Henri de Castellane. She was said to have converted Talleyrand on his deathbed.

[2] The present Dowager Lady Lansdowne, the mother of the Viceroy of India.

To LADY CARLISLE.

Paris: October 27, 1834.

You are a darling woman, Lady Carlisle, but you do not talk enough of coming to Paris. Miss Berry cannot tear herself away. Charlotte is a little tired of it and goes on the fifth; but the girls, driven out of their house, take rooms in an hotel for ten days longer.

There is, as Bob Curzon said of his house in the country at Christmas, a great pressure just now, but it works easily, as they are people who know each other and very pleasant ones.

My favourites are Lady Lansdowne, two Foxes, and Lady Sydney; and then, pretty and agreeable people and no gigs or bores.

Lady Clanricarde is still at Valençay. Montrond came back saying, ' Ils s'ennuient à mourir! c'est pour soutenir la gageure.' H. Greville says he is happy, but can neither speak nor eat. They dine at half-past five, and the evenings are rumoured to be laborious, *difficiles à digérer*, after exquisite dinners.

Lady C. says Talleyrand is charming. She drives with him, and is fit to appreciate his cleverness and give him as good as he brings. Motteux is reported to eat of sixteen *entrées* every day. Mrs. Damer has got some of her French flirts there.

To LADY CARLISLE.

Paris: October 31, 1834.

Most dear sister,—Oh, that you could come here and let me pour into your ear all the knowledge I have acquired from Appony and Berry !

I am growing dressy, as Miss Keating would say, and am learning how to unite smartness and economy.

Yesterday the Mintos went to England, Lord Lyndhurst gone too, and the Lansdownes. He, that boy

the Marquis, in high spirits, young, frolicsome, full of
beauty, music. More striking, as she, most amiable,
enduring, and endeavouring, is not gay, especially
politically. Hush, but she portends most dismally,
and she does her bidding here with *dévouement*, but
no pleasure. I am very fond of her. Lady Minto and
I agreed last night that she is *the* best woman in the
world. Henry and Lady Augusta Baring are here. She
very English and waxen, and not half as much admired
as Lady Sydney with her pale face and large gazelle eyes.
Lady Mary Fox and Charles are a delicious pair. He
is in high spirits, which I mention as he was said to
be low last year. Vernon Smith[1] is agreeable.

To Lady Carlisle.

Paris: November 7, 1834.

Lady Carlisle,—My beauties are all coming thick
upon me to dinner and drum. Butera views with delight Madame Fairfax—*une si grande sentimentalité*—
and she really looked very handsome in black velvet
with her long fair tresses and large white teeth, and
fortunate am I that her night was one on which her
first cousin Nangle was invited, and happy they were
playing together.

Lady C., there is no making a Government. All
try, nobody can. The statesmen are so coy.

Lord C. knows how true this is, as I hope you have
constant correspondence in that line.

I will tell you how Norton[2] behaves in my next.
The French are sorry Blackwood[3] goes to the Opera in a
skull-cap.

---

[1] Nephew of Sydney Smith. Was President of the Board of Control,
and created Lord Lyveden in 1859.

[2] Mrs. Norton.

[3] Her sister Mrs. Blackwood, afterwards Lady Dufferin.

TO LADY CARLISLE.

Pari : November 13, 1834.

My dearest sis,—I have only a moment to tell you that we received yesterday the account of poor Lord Spencer's death. We have of course put off dinners, soirées, etc., and I only feel that I wish such a blessing as repose could be obtained without such melancholy reasons for it.

The Ministry here is all *en l'air*. Every day brings new schemes, and all *échouent*. The Bassano Government[1] ended last night and nobody yet knows what is to come next.

Talleyrand has not been ill. Shocked at Princesse Tyshiawitz's death, determined, it is said, not to return to England. Says he has lived eighty years and never met with so clever a blowen as Clanricarde. She praises him as in wit and courtesy bound.

TO LADY CARLISLE.

Paris : November 1834.

I have time but for a line, my very dearest sister.

How wonderful! how sudden![2] My reason and my wishes for him make me very sorry.

But the thought of being in London in less than three weeks, in Bruton Street, expecting you, rushing to see the people at Mistley !

Write to D. for me. Tell him I have received his letter, that I shall answer it by next post.

I cannot write, and that is the long and short of it, my own dearest, best loved sister. I can scarcely think, so like a bomb has this news come upon us ! and all

---

[1] The Duc de Bassano succeeded Marshal Gérard as President of the Council, but his Ministry only lasted three days. The King then turned to the Duc de Trevise, who accepted the office of President.

[2] Lord Melbourne's Ministry was dissolved and Sir Robert Peel was sent for.

opinions vary. The soundest think it will float, others say it will sink before three months are past. The Tories have been so evidently courting popularity, and paving the way, that I think there is no doubt of their leaping rapturously into the ship, and then the Duke of Wellington will hoist the most liberal sails, eat back all his words, every possible measure, Church and State, do as he has done before.

Of my own feelings I do not speak. First comes Granville. He likes being here, so I wish it; but then comes the overwhelming thought of you and Susy, my Carnival spent between Mistley and Grosvenor Place.

Sir Robert Peel has desired his letters to be kept here, not sent after him. It looks expecting.

You may imagine our impatience for further news.

I hear neither of the Clanricardes seems pleased, or Tory-fied at the news. Vane and Ashburnham unhappy, saying it is impossible and mad; but Granville thinks it will stand.

To Lady Carlisle.

Paris: November 1834.

My own dearest sis,—I have but one moment. Peel not yet heard of. Brougham arrived in tearing spirits. I have not yet seen him. He comes this evening to our last Friday. I have been so bothered with notes and people that I have not one minute.

People are kinder than anything ever was. Nobody can foresee or conjecture the result.

Granville must be gratified at the feeling about him here. He is really adored. The Court is most amiable, and I love the Queen dearly.

Next Monday I shall be able to tell you more of our movements, but I look upon to-day as our *clôture*, and shall spend a very pleasant time in the very agreeable society here and at the smaller theatres.

If one could but burke Brougham, who is in a state I hear of the greatest excitement, and will say and do everything he ought not during his *séjour* here.

To Lady Carlisle.

Paris: December 5, 1834.

My dearest sister,—I am sorry to have missed writing by the last courier, but I was hurried, and now I will be garrulous.

Brougham has caused an immense sensation here. He is in roaring spirits, not the least ashamed of his last extraordinary step, his law request.[1] Talking without ceasing, gold, copper, but as all is stamped the same people allow for the nature of the coin and fix its price, which prevents it either doing the good or harm that might be expected. He goes to the Chambers, and to all the institutions, to all the theatres, to all the dinners, to all the soirées. He sits with Lady Clanricarde, the Princesse de Belgiojoso, Mrs. Norton, two hours at a time in the morning, and I am told has, since his arrival, written as much as he has talked. He is a sublime quack, Lady C.

Mr. Hudson[2] passed the day before yesterday, and Sir R. Peel will probably, he says, be in London on the tenth, next Wednesday.

English people are hastening home, members to look about them. We have ended all our givings here, and go to little farewell dinners every day. You have no idea how pleasant society here is now—next, really, to having none. Oh, what a shame!

Brougham, Sir F. Lamb, Mme. de Flahault are all

[1] To be made Chief Baron.

[2] Secretary to Queen Adelaide. He was sent to fetch Sir Robert from Rome and made the journey so rapidly that he got the name of hurried Hudson. He became Sir James Hudson and Minister at Turin, where he was instrumental in promoting Count Cavour's policy.

good-humoured and gay, and liking to be all in a fury together.

What busy and exciting scenes we are returning to, most dear sister! Lord Melbourne has raised himself in all opinions, and stands higher than he ever has done, methinks. Bulwer's letter, some of it bad taste, but very clever. God bless you.

To Lady Carlisle.

Paris : December 1834.

No appointments yet made, so Granville has received no answer.

I am rejoiced at Lord Stanley's refusal. I prefer their going the whole game themselves, and think it such an object to have a strong party of Whigs of different shades, that, in case of the Tories breaking up, there may be much to look to besides the Radicals.

I am glad dear Jack's[1] bullock has won the great prize. I hear it puts him in ecstasies.

I am afraid it must now be quite the end of the month, or the beginning of the next, before we arrive. If we have our letter on Thursday, we shall have got to the 18th, and packing and travelling will take us a fortnight.

Brougham is still here. The letter in the 'Courier' must have stuck into him. I saw him at dinner at Mme. Rumford's that day. He was half-way through the repast grave, perfectly silent, but then the victuals and drink! Somebody mentioning the press, and Mons. Arago with a new plaything, put him in high spirits again, and he talked and laughed and was charming.

Lady Clanricarde is quite a little *puissance* here, and much admired and sought after. We dine at Talleyrand's to-morrow. I have not yet seen them.

---

[1] Her cousin, Lord Althorp.

To Lady Carlisle.

Paris: December 12, 1834.

Most dear sister,—I can only write ' How are ye ? ' as Brougham says.

I know not yet our date. On Monday I expect to be able to tell you, but you see we are at the twelfth, so to arrive in London before a fortnight is scarcely possible.

As to politics. This is what I see with my little eye. This Government will do very well. The Dowager Countess's nimbleness in ratting will be imitated by many mice. Then I think the Stanleyites will not come in, but hold by. Then I think the Greyites have all been lukewarm since he left the Ministry, and all this will boil in the great mess of fear of the Radicals, and that's the way the Duke will ' get over the stile to-night.'

Enter into argument in return, Lady Carlisle, or wink and nod.

The Fullertons are going to spend the winter at Nice. They dreaded the cold of Southampton and London in the winter, and finding the new plan both very delightful and economical, they consulted Verity. You may imagine his answer, and he has *monté* their imaginations, and they think they are going to sit fanning themselves on the top of an orange-tree.

To Lady Carlisle.

Paris: December 1834.

Most dear sister,—I long for your next letters. We expect Aston [1] to-day, so I hope in a day or two to fix our plans. He will tell us who is to come here. Lord Cowley seems to be thought the most likely.

I liked Peel's talk. I always do, but I think he

---

[1] Appointed Chargé d'Affaires at Paris.

has no idea himself how hard the task will be. All are astonished at the new appointments, and look upon his Government as more perilled by the names of Roden, Perceval, etc., than all the rest.

I think these will not stand, nor would Lord Melbourne again just now, only something new. Lord Grey or Spencer, and, I suppose, neither will—Stanley cannot—Durham must not. It's a pickle, Lady C.

Talleyrand is very ill, irritable and desponding. He insists upon going to Rochecotte immediately, much to Mme. de Dino's annoyance.

D. has written to me a delicious letter. He seems and says he is very sorry.

Lady Clanricarde I think much improved in politics. An education carried on by Mme. de Flahault, Talleyrand, Brougham, and the Duc de Laval is sure to come out a fair specimen of impartiality and reason. I think at present she likes Whigs better than Tories, though there could be Tories she would like better than Whigs. We all agree that she is, unlike the general herd, a Whig when she talks to a Tory, a T. when to a W.

To the Duke of Devonshire.

Paris: December 29, 1834.

Aston arrived and brought no message to Granville, but I conclude we shall hear from the appointed to-morrow. I shall let you know when we do. Our Georgiana[1] is, I suppose, the probable one.

I am astonished at the new names. I had been quite mollified and, like the country, ' as quiet as a mouse ; ' but I begin to think all that has passed can do nothing but harm.

We are shorn of almost all our English beams, have only left us Lady Clanricarde, a sort of Queen in the

---

[1] Lady Cowley.

Hôtel Bristol. Lady Sydney her first lady-in-waiting, Laval and Talleyrand her white- and gold-sticks.

Poor Talleyrand has grown very feeble and they say irritable, and has had very unpleasant attacks these last two days. We had some people at dinner, and I sent to inquire. Gros Jean returned and in loud distinct accents, 'Le Prince a transpiré jusqu'à quatre heures, la Duchesse a mal à l'estomac.'

Sir Adair [1] took leave of us last night. He is black by nature and opinion.

Monday.—Yesterday's courier brought nothing; but there is nothing vexatious in the delay, it is probably occasioned by Lady Cowley's illness.

I dine with Butera to-night, and, if I can, sing at Cannizzaro on Wednesday. What I refuse myself is the Duke of Orleans' ball to-night. Dody goes, and now's the time when it is better to wear a necklace than have a chariot or a trunk.

[1] Sir Robert Adair, the friend of Fox and well-known diplomatist. He was the son of a famous surgeon, and when he was sent to Vienna, he was objected to as not being of a sufficiently good family. The answer was, 'Mais c'est le fils du plus grand saigneur de l'Europe.'

1835

To Lady Carlisle.

Paris: January 1835.

Most dear sister,—We think of setting out the end of next week, to be in London about the 15th.

You may guess how much of little business I have to do—visits, appointments, notes, bills.

We are all very well, and very eager. Upon arriving I shall go to Mistley.

Dearest sis, I delight in the thoughts of London. It will be to me a pleasant city. No assemblies, balls, or operas, but dinners and *réunions* at my friends. Those who receive early, not smart—admit of cross-stitch and sketching lists of elections. Walks, drives with Lady C. of a morning, *folâtrer* round the squares, drive as far as the Colvilles. Dissipation is the sting of life, and for the first time it will be no duty for me.

Once I shall go with you to Berry, and that's all.

Granville says Mr. Lascelles has no chance. I grieve at the trouble—more if there is expense—but I feel sanguine as to the success of all good men and true.

Lady Haddington [1] will have full scope and verge for her passion for dress, and I see her, like a fairy in a play, one entire spangle.

I wonder how the De Greys [2] will like their ship. I think she is the woman for the jolly tars, if that is

---

[1] Lord Haddington was appointed Lord-Lieutenant of Ireland.
[2] He was appointed First Lord of the Admiralty.

requisite, and that he is just in his element, and will be
so wise about the mechanical part and the rigging of
the concern. I hope the First Lord has really to do
with all the practical part for his sake.

TO THE DUKE OF DEVONSHIRE.
Devonshire House : February 6, 1835.

It is a great comfort to us to know that you are not
in a hurry to get rid of us, but Mr. Orchard and Kulbach are one present and the other expected, and if
you do not find me here, you will on the sunny side of
Berkeley Square.

Lord Mulgrave has been with me an hour, and
interested and amused me. He is, I see, sanguine as to
politics in general. I fear nobody is as to the Speaker-
ship. He says on that question they are men conscious
of a disadvantage, fighting with courage an inevitable
battle. Burdett will vote for Sutton [1] and Ferguson, my
cousin of Raith, because he is related to Mrs. P.[2] as
was. This, however, does not discourage the party.
They expect the Stanleys to be decidedly with them,
and are in good heart.

Chatsworth news is delicious. If Mrs. Arkwright for-
gives me, if Abercromby has a decent show of hands, if
Brougham is well managed and pacified—great A, little
A, and bouncing B—I shall be a contented woman.

TO THE DUKE OF DEVONSHIRE.
London : February 12, 1835.

I have been constantly with G., who is now decidedly better.

Mrs. Arkwright is the best and kindest of women.
I am so glad she is coming. We shall not meet often in

[1] The Liberals started Abercromby against Manners Sutton.
[2] Mr. Manners Sutton married a Mrs. Power, a sister of Lady
Blessington.

the world, where I foresee she will be always galivant-
ing with Lady Wharncliffe and Punch, but she will
like to take a walk, look into the shop-windows, and
every now and then to a sight.

Bets were rather improved in Abercromby's favour,
but I do not, nor do any but the over-sanguine, expect
him to succeed. It seems to me that people are getting
much more violent, and I am again afraid of Radical
force being too much brought into play. Lord Melbourne is not going to Goodwood, as he intended. Mr.
Warburton makes a leg to Brougham. It will be
anxious, exciting, but I feel sure that nothing immediate
will take place against the present Government. When
the King read the paragraph about his spouse,[1] he was
heard to mutter 'd——d stuff.' Nobody seems to
believe it.

Lady de Grey and Berry sit at home every evening.
Pozzo is arrived, very low, and cannot conceal his *juste
courroux*; for, do you know, Nicholas sent here to find
out if the enclosed despatch, which was the appointment, was approved of, desiring it might be sent on to
Pozzo if it was. Then no Madame Graham, and the fog
and the cards to be returned, and visits paid before the
lapse of four days. You will not wonder that in his
confidential moments he neither minces nor measures
in his talk.

Leveson is at Oxford, had been to Middleton, found
Silence sick, sanguine, her politics all heaped on one
intense delight, joy at the grand conception of Addy's
situation. I daresay she sees herself governess to the
future.

Lord Clanricarde has been scandalising the world at
Paris by riding a race in the Bois de Boulogne in a
yellow and white striped jacket, and cap to match.

---

[1] There were rumours of a future heir.

To the Duke of Devonshire.

London: April 12, 1835.

One line out of breath, most dear D.[1]

I hear Johnny is likely to be Foreign Affairs. Unless something unforeseen and imperious occurs, I suppose Gilleret will be the man, so universal and flattering an opinion is there of his fitness. I shall be very sorry for Lord Palmerston. He must have something, and what will he accept?

Now, my dearest brother, look at this picture and on that. On one hand, you and Paxton, sitting under a red rhododendron at Chatsworth, under the shade of palms and pines in your magnificent conservatory, with Arkwright and Harrowby in the evening, but no thought of your country's weal and woe.

Now, walking up and down a terrace in the Phœnix Park, arm in arm with Morpeth, your secretary, saving that hapless country, adored and worshipped.

Think of the gratification to them, of the power to you of doing good. Damp but glorious.

I hear they want you to go to Ireland. I cannot, intimate as I am with your intelligence, guess what you are thinking at this moment.

Che sarà sarà, for all of us.

To the Duke of Devonshire.

London: April 13, 1835.

I have had two great pleasures this morning, a beautiful nosegay and Mrs. Arkwright for an hour. She was quite delightful, and so I saw she thought me. I give you my word of honour, I do not think I spoke twenty words the whole time she was here. I listened intensely and was well repaid, for I do not think I ever

[1] Sir Robert resigned on April 8. Lord Melbourne was commissioned to form a Government.

heard her so agreeeble. She told me many droll things. Among others of a poor tenant who wrote to petition Mr. Arkwright for something, and began, 'May it please your opulence.' We think it would be amusing to docket one's friends and call each of them your something.

Johnny was to come from Woburn this morning to Lord Melbourne. Of course you know that Lord Melbourne is to declare himself Premier in the House to-day. I hear Lord Grey has been as kind and cordial as possible, giving sanction and promising support, advice.

Mr. Sneyd is busy organising Conservative measures in Staffordshire. The Tories can never say a word more against political meetings, societies, etc.

Miss Berry has been agreeable, but I had the satisfaction of telling her that she was not a Whig at heart and that I always saw the Tory foot.

Lord Palmerston. He talked most openly, told me there was a report that Johnny was to be at the Foreign Office. He looked much *ému* when he said it and added, 'this I cannot believe.' Then he muttered, 'I suppose I shall be shortly there myself,' and then loud, 'in which case I hope you will instantly prepare and pack up for Paris.'

Lady Lilford, looking lovely.

Horace Pitt : 'Well, all up with us, I suppose. No more chance for the Tories. Any chance of Paris—I shall come.'

To the Duke of Devonshire.

London : April 15, 1835.

I know of nothing new to-day, but am told everything is going on well. Foreign Office still doubtful. Brougham came to Grosvenor Place last night, very amiable, but I thought very low. It is a moment that makes it distressing for the curious and concerned to hear only of holidays.

Morpeth went yesterday to Roehampton to Lady Dover, the Hollands to Holland House. Lord Carlisle (private) is not upon rose leaves, at least they are amazingly doubled. It frets him to see in the ' Globe' and to hear everywhere of speculations and plans about Morpeth, and not to have received one word of communication either in the way of suggestion or consultation.

To-morrow we go, and all those I know are going also. Morpeth joins us at Mistley on Saturday.

I am now going to Mrs. Arkwright to hear her sing.

To the Duke of Devonshire.

London: April 16, 1835.

Lord Mulgrave came last night to Grosvenor Place. We are not yet got to appointments. Billy is still corresponding and conversing. I suppose something more will be known to-night. My own private think is that he will execute another voluntary. 'Well, my Lord, good morning. I find with all our endeavours we are come to no arrangement'—and then he will throw himself on his late advisers.

To Lady Carlisle.

Paris: May 29, 1835.

One line, my most dear sister, to tell you that we arrived after a most prosperous journey at four to-day.[1]

I found my little grandson quite well.

We have had the attachés to dinner. Poor Henry Greville straining every nerve to be useful; laborious and plodding, and making himself extremely agreeable during our repast.

It looks so like what always was; visits have begun,

[1] Lord Granville returned to Paris at the end of April.

and in the course of five hours one invitation to a ball and another to a dinner. Leveson will enjoy the hop, and I shall like the dinner at Butera's better than usual because he has asked my friends and no formal company.

Madame de Flahault is very *agissante*. Mortal strife between her and Madame de Delmar. Tell D. that Madame Ferrari,[1] Madame Vallambrosa, Caraman's sister, and Mme. Meyendorf are going to London immediately. I believe he knows them all. God bless you.

To the Duke of Devonshire.

Paris: June 1, 1835.

Paris is awfully hot and gay. We dined at Butera's yesterday. Lady Stanhope is here, but sick and flustered because there is no governess to govern Lady Wilhelmina and no *duenna* to guard Miss Gardner and Harbord.

To-night I go to the Tuileries. On Friday dine at the Broglie's to meet Talleyrand and Madame de Dino.

---

[1] Better known as the Duchesse de Galliera. She was the daughter of Count Brignolé, a Genoese who represented Sardinia for some years in Paris. She was the last of her name and a first cousin to the late Lord Granville's first wife. She was clever and original, fond of the society of politicians and literary people, and received at the Hôtel Monaco the *élite* of French Society. Both she and her husband had enormous fortunes, his much increased by railway enterprises. Their only son is inclined to communistic ideas, and would only accept a small portion of the wealth of his parents. His father gave 800,000*l.* towards the enlargement of the harbour of Genoa. When someone shortly before his death complimented him on his generosity, he said: ' Vous voyez, si je pouvais emporter cet argent dans l'autre monde, certainement je ne le donnerais pas ; mais comme cela ne se peut pas, et que Philippe [1] n'en veut pas, je n'ai rien d'autre à faire.' His wife conjointly with her son gave to the town of Genoa their palace and one of the finest private collections of pictures in Italy. She built and endowed two hospitals in the environs of Paris and another one near Genoa. She gave in her lifetime an estate in Italy to a member of the Orleans family, she left her hotel at Paris to the Austrian Government for an Embassy, and a large legacy to the Empress Frederick, for whom she entertained great admiration.

[1] His only child.

Whenever anybody who hates me dines anywhere, I am always fetched for them, poor souls. The evenings I decline, as in London. I do not see in these summer days why I should not.

I am going to write to Aix for your rooms.

Henry Greville is making himself most popular, with me at least, and nothing can be more amiable and efficient. I hear he does all the work possible. If he could but become a Whig and hold his tongue, he would be a model.

To Lady Carlisle.

Paris : June 4, 1835.

My most dear sister,—Your two delightful long letters fully repaid me for the disappointment of the first courier without one. How well I understand all you tell me on various subjects, and all you tell me of you and yours is so interesting. The Fifteenth takes away my breath, but I wish I was as sure of everybody and everything as I am of Morpeth [1] doing whatever he does well. As to enjoyment, that is another question. He will find compensation in usefulness and success, and he will like his pretty house and garden, as I do mine.

Granville is gone a round of Ministerial visits. Leveson is gone to dine at the Café de Paris and a minor theatre with Lady Stanhope, and I am with the window open, the orange flower smelling too strong, the nightingales singing too loud, and this in the middle of a city is very delicious. There is a beautiful passage in Mrs. Norton's book about that, the gifts so impartially granted to all and what ought to be our gratitude. How excellent, how beautiful I think some of her writing; but somehow or other she does not fit into her own frame, she is not in keeping with her own opinions and feelings, and it is impossible to bind her up with her own stories.

[1] He had become Irish Secretary.

Paris is full and gay. I am at this moment remorseful at not stepping up the Elysian Fields to Meg. We dine at Court, full dress, on Saturday. I went the other evening and was most graciously received, though Dino sat to see us with her gaslight-eyes, but we all did as if she was not there.

The Duke of Orleans has been to see me and was very amiable. He is grown very handsome.

To Lady Carlisle.

Paris: June 11, 1835.

It was Lady Wharncliffe who wrote to me of the harmony in Yorkshire. Lady Jersey says we shall never do any good whilst we are so sentimental on the hustings, which makes me laugh heartily. The public, she says, don't understand such refinements, and I believe she is right.

Dearest sister, how interesting politics have become! How Morpeth puts energy into our feelings! I am extremely sanguine, and so is Miss Fitzgerald, about the good that is going to be done in Ireland. I feel so proud of and confident in him, that he will be ballast to that light, squally vessel Lord Mulgrave. I am glad, however, to hear that Lord M. is so popular, and that she is very much liked.

To Lady Carlisle.

Paris: June 1835.

Most dear sis,—We have ordered a room to be got ready for Charles.[1] It will be a great pleasure to have one of yours and Leveson is charmed.

I have had a long visit from Lord Fitzwilliam, who is in high glee and good-humour, but he won't dine.

[1] A son of Lady Carlisle. He was private secretary to Lord Melbourne and for many years member for Cumberland. He was the father of the present Lord Carlisle.

He is intent upon museums and *procès*, Père la Chaise, and the partition of land, but he thinks he will come and dance this evening. Luckily, it is almost a cold day, so that we shall not expire.

I am distressed at your asking me to be political, as I really don't know how. I know nothing of French politics. Madame de Montjoye hopes and trusts no mischief will happen in Spain, and says they are all going on admirably here. De Broglie is in high spirits and doats upon Granville.

God bless you, our dearest sis.

To THE DUKE OF DEVONSHIRE.

Paris: June 17, 1835.

I cannot attempt to repay you for your letters. I cannot fill, like you do, whole pages of everything most interesting. I shall not attempt to perish like the frog in the fable, but I shall write constantly scraps of gratitude, and whatever I see, hear, or do. What is to become of me when you leave off writing? which you will do some day—nobody knows why—all at once, *à propos de bottes*. This is written in the spirit of the Viddy.[1] What will she say of George? I long to hear how she takes it.[2] I think it a very nice, fitting union.

A thousand thanks for poor Mr. Brummel. There never was such an act of charity. I am in good heart about the subscription.

Tell my dearest, darling Lady Carlisle that I have no time to write to her to-day. Lord Fitzwilliam has been a great love. He chews the cud of conversation; takes no notice at the time, but two days after: 'You said so and so,' not, as one expects, to confute, but merely to state it over again as digested and approved.

---

[1] Mrs. Cavendish.

[2] Her son George's engagement to Lady Louisa Lascelles.

It is, at the moment, discouraging, like Miss Fanny,[1] when the audience would not applaud till the end.

To-day Broglie, Guizot, the St. Aulaires, Fréville, Madame de Praslin[2] without her husband, Monsieur Decazes without his wife, Caramans, Henry Greville, Aston, and William Ponsonby dine here. Caradoc and Howden drink tea with us; and I have asked that poor lemon, that old rag, that most faded and death-like bride, Bragration, to join the domestic circle. She sent me a message that she dreaded the numbers and heat of Friday. Mrs. Lambton drops in whenever she likes— pretty, gay, natural, sociable, brusque, most attractive little woman.

To THE DUKE OF DEVONSHIRE.

Paris: June 20, 1835.

Lord Fitzwilliam, tell G., and five offspring came. He will not dine, but could not resist dancing. Nice, unaffected girls—dear people. Meg took them under her especial care, hurried them off to a couch in the ball-room, got partners for the girls, offered her own two pretty little things up to the boys. But the youngest, Wentworth, preferred sitting all night in the drawing-room, studying the comic annual, and, that done, beginning 'Belford Regis.' Meg pinioned the Earl down by her side. I felt relieved of any anxiety about the race.

To LADY CARLISLE.

Paris: June 29, 1835.

We think the majority[3] admirable, and what repose to Morpeth to have done with it! Tell that adorable

---

[1] Kemble.

[2] This was the Madame de Praslin who was murdered by her husband in 1847.

[3] There was a majority of thirty-seven in favour of the Government Bill respecting the Irish Church.

man that I love him and care about Irish politics because of him, and wish him in the midst of trees and flowers in his beautiful park. But I have done being able to read the debates, *ru* that I cannot understand so practical and calculating a question. Granville tells me that Sheil made a very good speech.

When will Parliament be over and you free to roam? I resign myself to staying in this large cool house during this *assommant* weather, but I do hope that in about a fortnight we shall go and wash in the deep blue sea.

How much I could wish you could know how nervous I and everybody feel sometimes, and about nothing at all, or rather everything. There is but one real *calmant*, and that it is difficult to cling to in this perturbed world. The great difficulty is to rely wholly, to cast ourselves. We will be planning, hoping, and fearing. The truth is told us in the Bible. ' In returning ye shall be saved and rest; in quietness and in confidence shall be your strength: and ye would not.'

Mrs. Fry says : ' Think not to do anything or be anything, but throw yourself helpless into the arms of redeeming mercy. If we did this in temptation, in pain, in terror, we should have rest.' Mrs. Fry also says : ' We consume our lives with anxiety and waste our days in care, our hearts are continually departing from the Lord. Then comes what must come. Instead of calm in the midst of danger and confidence in the midst of uncertainty and holy composure amid surrounding or impending ills, there comes anxiety in the midst of blessings, fearfulness and carefulness dry up every source of pleasure and wither every fresh bud of joy.'

To the Duke of Devonshire.

Paris : July 29, 1835.

Yesterday was a horrible day.   In the morning an attempt to assassinate the King, his sons and whole *entourage*.   De Broglie had a button and his *nœud de cravate* shot off, Flahault his horse's ear.   The Duc de Trevise killed, and several other generals, distinguished officers.   Five men are taken.

In the evening we went to the Tuileries.   Nothing ever so perfect and adorable as the Queen.   The enthusiasm shown for the King beyond anything. There are crowds at the Palace, and many who had not been before.

To Lady Carlisle.

Paris : July 31, 1835.

Most dear sister,—I have only a minute to tell you how much your last letter delighted me.   The reason I cannot write much is that I have so much to do.   My brother has written from Havre that he is coming perhaps to-morrow, and about some business which has given me *de quoi* to bustle about.

I have had to write to Meg at Enghien, and to Lady Mary Stanley to tell her to come to tea this evening, having rudely on account of my business shut the door in her face this morning.   *Cela ne lui cassera pas le nez.*[1]   Nothing came out yesterday, excepting that the assassin is not Gerard, but Fieschi, a Corsican from Bastia, that he has been before tried for robberies and been engaged in all sorts of mischief.   He is of Herculean strength, sometimes slightly touched but generally reckless, beyond anything docile to his physicians.

The great event seems to me the Archbishop having been yesterday to the Tuileries for the first time, and having proposed to perform the services of Tuesday and Wednesday at Les Invalides and Notre-Dame.

[1] She had a very small nose.

TO THE DUKE OF DEVONSHIRE.

Paris: August 1, 1835.

What you feel for the family is generally felt here. Nobody dares show or express anything but horror and awe. The impression does not fade, and at Paris this is wonderful. We feel more tied here. The Court remains, Mme. de Broglie gives up her Swiss journey, the Deputies are all back again.

Nothing will make the man confess. Decazes and others told me last night they go to him, try every mode of getting at something. He says he repents, that he was *fanatisé par les journaux.* ' J'ai fait cela comme un enfant qui fait sauter un pétard.' He has once said that he will tell everything half an hour before his execution. He was a soldier under Murat ; it is an eagle, not a *fleur de lis*, that is tattooed on his breast. Crowds flock to the Tuileries. I begin to think it may have a good effect.

TO THE DUKE OF DEVONSHIRE.

Paris : September 7, 1835.

It is difficult to talk about politics, and I don't wonder that Sir Frederick Lamb would not bleat. The Bill is all afloat again. Sir Robert Peel's speech at Tamworth is bitter and wincing. Some write that Lord Lyndhurst is perfectly ready to form a Government and confident of success. The poor Beau [1] is much hurried, being considered to go along with favours and cakes when a Tory marries. He was to breakfast with Lord Stuart and to dine with Lord Verulam on Saturday, and then has to see-saw between Peel and the Ultras.

We sleep at Mantes to-morrow, on Wednesday see Rosny [2] and sleep at Rouen.

[1] The Duke of Wellington.
[2] A fine château where Sully was born, and which the Duchess of Berri had bought.

Balzac is a fat, red man, whose locks flow. He sits in the pit at the Opera, looks about him, and said Lady Jersey in a box aloft was the *vrai type de l'aristocratie Anglaise*. 'Le Père Goriot' I have not read but will, and will ask with a fan before my face if he is historical or fabulous, ancient or modern, and let you know.

I long to have G. here. Your details of them all, the way you tell me all I wish to know and nothing I don't, the pound of flesh, no *parler après avoir dit*, the best style of writing with no manner of doing it, makes your correspondence one of the greatest pleasures in the world.

To the Duke of Devonshire.

Dieppe: September 19, 1835.

Le Havre was as you said. I delight in it, worth fifty Dieppes. The parrots all talking at once, the pier, the scarcity of Bulls, all colours, all nations, all curiosities.

George is just seized with lumbago, Fullerton very well. The baby most glorious and victorious, for he rules them all with a rod of iron.

Oh, how Nemours' visit pleases me! He will be so pleased, and so will that dear woman the Queen. He will tell of Chatsworth, seen in the sun's broad rays.

We go to Paris to-morrow. The Carlisles have not announced their day.

To the Duke of Devonshire.

Paris: September 28, 1835.

We arrived here the day before yesterday. I have tried twice to see Lieven; have had a most melancholy and affectionate note from her. She lives *chez elle*, drives all morning with a beautiful niece who lives with her, receives from eight till ten, *avide* for news.

'Causez' is her cry, and she writes to me, 'distrayez mon esprit!'

G. is arrived, better than I could have hoped for after a tiring journey. Madame de Lieven is better also, and I shall find a comfort in being of use to her, although I am very stout about not letting her be more *exigeante* than suits me.

There is going to be a most beautiful Mass performed on Friday, all the French and Italian singers are to sing at St. Roch. Poor Bellini! I feel how much shocked you are, and they say he might have been saved.

To the Duke of Devonshire.

Paris: October 28, 1835.

The Sutherlands are to land to-day at Hôtel Loban. Talleyrand and Madame de Dino are come, and he is to spend every evening at Madame de Lieven's. The Duc d'Orléans is going to-day to Algiers. Leopold and Louise are here, she dried up into her mother in miniature. We and Lord Carlisle dine at the Tuileries to-morrow. Canterbury and the lovely Purvis [1] walk in to-night. If all the other Bulls run out, I shall bear it.

Now that your guests are dispersed and that you get stronger than ever, are you not inclined to come to Paris? The Hôtel de Duras, exactly opposite, is one of the best hotels I know—immense airy rooms, *entre cour et jardin*. Lieven is looking for sun and an easy ascent. She is now putting up with a high perch in the Rue Castiglione, where the sun never did and never can come. As Talleyrand is now her great object, as she says, 'Je vais remplacer toutes ces vieilles femmes qui sont muettes,' she is naturally anxious to be *à plein pied* to make constant intercourse with him easy.

---

[1] Lady Canterbury's daughter, Miss Purvis.

The ambassador Pahlen is a very handsome, fine-looking man, something *brave et loyal*, talks quick—not, I should think, clever. Picks his teeth with his knife, scorns sugar-tongs, a grand specimen of a Russian soldier. Nicholas is as happy as the day is long.

1836

To Lady Carlisle.

Paris: February 1836.

My own dearest sister, your dear people are just arrived from Versailles. It is everything to me, her being here.

Mme. de Lieven is coming this evening. I dined yesterday at Prince Talleyrand's. Mme. de Dino and I are as smooth as glass. She comes this evening to play with Lieven. Mr. Ellice is the little pet of both these ladies. The most *répandu* of men. He is thick with all the new Ministers, and we can scarcely catch him for a dinner, so devoured is he. God bless you, my own dearest sis.

To the Duke of Devonshire.

Paris: March 17, 1836.

Your letter, my most dear brother, refreshed me like one of your visits. I miss you everywhere, but these visits are what nobody and nothing can replace.

Your life at Calais must be delicious, and I read with envy; liberty, sea air, the excitement of uncertainty, and the certainty of repose. But I pity you a little, and should others more, for nobody but me like their larks to be without wings or legs.

You are universally regretted here. I have not seen Sugar [1] since, and Orloff has never been near me, morning, evening, or Friday since she dined. But Mouchy [2]

---

[1] Countess Schouvaloff. Lady Morley called her Sugarloaf, and Prince Gortschakoff, Got-such-a-cough.   [2] Duchesse de Mouchy.

came, all over violets and nosegays, so that she looked
like a stick in the midst of an immense one. She and
Dody linked and looped about in sham friendship.
More nauseous than an emetic is Flysy to the said
Dody. The family see it, but try and keep up her
spirits about it, and Antonin[1] says : 'Peut-être cela ne
va pas bien au commencement, mais vous aimerez ma
belle-sœur.'

To-day there is a treat that beats all that ever were
projected in excess of suffering, Pahlen's meal. Thirty
convives. Thiers and I run into it together. They say
his dinners are good, his plate beautiful, but the length is
great—till nine last time, sitting down at half-past six.

Georges d'Harcourt[2] with a friend went for the
first time to your stalls. He was perfectly delighted
with the 'Huguenots,' all his prejudices were up, and
he came back enchanted. But what do you think,
dear Grace, of what is beyond all whats? Why, on
Sunday last, Thom had an amateur singing reunion,
and Mrs. Jauncey warbled. Well, nobody but Grisi
ever had such a pipe, and a perfection as to taste
and skill that leaves all the other singing-birds in
Society at an immeasurable distance. People returned
in ecstasies.

Friday.—Forty-eight we were at Pahlen's.

Sugar sends you the most tender messages. After
I went to Lieven and Meg, and now I go to the bird-
fancier, Porte St.-Martin.

To the Duke of Devonshire.

Paris: March 25, 1886.

I have received your two delicious letters, the second
from Calais, the first from London, and the Duchess
read me your ecstatic account of the Fancy Ball.

---

[1] Duc de Mouchy's brother.
[2] Was afterwards Ambassador in London.

I have been shut up for weeks, as Granville has had the gout, and now there are Easter holidays.

Guizot has made a most magnificent speech. The sensation it made in the Chambers was unparalleled—his high tone and commanding manner.

Only think of the Duke of Sutherland having bought the 'Prodigal Son' and the 'Abraham,' two of Soult's finest pictures.

How your account of the Royal boys amused me. Is the second to marry his cousin?

Lieven is uncommonly well. Will not hear of Mr. Ellice marrying Lady Pembroke. 'Je mettrai tout mon savoir-faire à l'empêcher.'

I brought Madame de Noailles and Princesse de Lieven together on Monday. The French Power made a mistake, she took the line of *folâtre* gaiety, incessant talking and improper tales. Lieven was—I have no word—sickened. 'Ma chère, quel genre! quel bavardage! quelle incroyable personne! Une femme qui vient me raconter au milieu de cinq ou six hommes qu'elle a rencontré le matin une femme à cheval, ses jupons d'un côté, sa personne de l'autre.' And all Lieven's petticoats stiffened round her at the recollected recital.

To Lady Carlisle.

Paris: March 1836.

My own dearest sister,—We were quite delighted with your beautiful verses. What power of description to the very life you have! How much power of painting and feeling your subject! Poetry in short, rare quality amongst poets.

To Lady Carlisle.

Paris: March 1836.

I am sorry to say Granville has again been confined for near a week with return of gout. We were obliged to put off a great diplomatic dinner and the evening after it to-night, and now we have a fortnight's holiday.

Guizot has been making a magnificent speech, one that caused great sensation in the Chambers. It renders Thiers' perplexing situation still more so.

I believe Lord William Bentinck and perhaps W. Ponsonby start for England to-night to be in time for Monday's division. Mme. de Lieven is pining for the Bear, and frantic with the report of his marriage with Lady Pembroke.

All the lions and lambs in society are going to lie down together. Mons. de Talleyrand and Mme. de Dino are going to dine at Flahault's house some day next weak.

I didn't enjoy the concert at Court, leaving Granville ill at home. Heat beyond Calcutta, the worst possible choice of music.

To Lady Carlisle.

Paris: April 22, 1836.

My own dearest sis,—We are all excited about Norton—that is, all but me; the Fullertons extremely curious. I hear the great thing said against him is that he swallows the lovers or not according to their rank and position. Lord Melbourne yes, Captain Trelawny no.

On Friday last we had a very numerous soirée. I asked scarcely any English, as I knew the foreigners would come and digest the ball. Tell the Duchess that I am really overwhelmed with inquiries and messages, and real regrets and speeches, such as Caramania's, made for exportation. But she really is lamented here more than I can say. The Mondays are attended by her adorers, male and female. To-day come Lady

Acton and Mme. de Praslin and Mme. de Coigny to take leave.

Mme. de Souza is dead. I have just been at Mme. de Flahault's door.

God bless you.

To Lady Carlisle.

Paris: April 26, 1836.

My most dear sister,—I love to think of you at Roehampton, seeing all the green buds and hearing the birds sing, as I do in my garden at this moment. We are in hourly expectation of Edward.[1] I wish he may come for dinner to-day. It is the Ministerial one, put off on account of Granville's gout before Easter. There are mitigations ; we were to have been about fifty, and we are only thirty, as half the *convives* dine at a great repast at Pahlen's. We have Talleyrand, the Ministers, Appony and Alava, Rothschild, Sir Adair and Caradoc, those two wild Lotharios.

Paris will soon be perfect repose. The *jours* are diminishing, the Bulls going, the Queen gone, and the only dinner we were engaged to was put off by Lady William Bentinck letting us know on the day itself, having heard rumours of our approach, that 'she did not expect us, indeed she did not.' This with my particular compliments to the Duke of Sutherland. How I and the world miss them is not to be written. Poor little Schönbourg cried about it, and Maurice[2] looks like a pistachio nut, and has retreated entirely into his eyes.

I must now have done, for my half-past six dinner is after me. Perhaps between Thiers and Talleyrand. Mme. de Lieven we see seldom, or Marie. They live with the Flahaults and Ellice. I conclude the latter will come

[1] Lord Carlisle's son, created Lord Lanerton in 1874.
[2] Count Maurice Esterhazy became eventually Ambassador at Rome.

this evening. Mme. de Dino is always with Mme. de
Lieven. It is supposed that she, Dino, has been
making a violent and successful attack on the heart of
the Duc de Noailles, and that his family are doubly
frantic at the infidelity and the chance of her persuading him to attach himself to the present Court. A
detachment of Carlists have left Paris to form a Court
in Switzerland for Henri V. ! ! It is so like them, so very
absurd, and so sure to miscarry. The men are Messrs.
du Cossé, Fitzjames, A. de Jumilhac, and Monbreton.

To Lady Carlisle.

Paris : April 29, 1836.

Ten thousand thanks, my own dearest G. Your
letters are delicious. We see your dear daughters.
Did I ever tell you how delighted we were with your
account of them at Court, dearest Liz as well as the
best of them? How I agree about Blanche, who must
look uncommonly picturesque, and like the Lady of a
Tournament, in the present ancient style of dress.

I have a letter from D. Everybody raves of his
ball, and I am so pleased that he should see his
endeavours to please answer. I agree with you so
entirely in all you say about him, and the cleverness
and charm which make frivolity, and sometimes a
degree of want of proper consideration of, more than
of feeling, for others, more attractive than the sense and
savoir of others, who look down, and with reason, upon
dress and dissipation.

Granville fell from his horse on Monday, but most
happily was not hurt, though he felt a little shaken by
it. But how one does think, upon such occasions, of
all that one is spared, of the mercies one ceases to
dwell upon. The terrors one magnifies and amplifies
that are not permitted to be realised ! It seems to me

that life ought to be spent on our knees, and how is it? Carelessly, ungratefully.

Our present plan is to set out for England the beginning of July, to stay there six weeks, then return and tour about the Rhine, douching and bathing at the different places—not a course of it, but a wholesome pastime.

Tell Miss Berry she will find much of the sort of society she most likes, everybody at home always and out-of-doors pleasures abounding. I cannot promise that Miss Ferguson will like it as much as she will. Mme. Durazzo is now taking a house here. She is a very great and universal favourite—she is here, there, and everywhere; abhors, I am told, Miss Berry. She has never mentioned her name to me. I am afraid her loud and ceaseless notes will not dispose people more favourably towards, what had always a sort of hitch in it, the approval of the three virgins.

Mesdames Lieven and Schönbourg are all rapture at Sir Frederick's expected arrival to-day; but nothing will keep the former from Valençay after the fifteenth.

To LADY CARLISLE.

Paris: May 6, 1836.

Most dear sis,—Sir F. Lamb arrived two days ago, but a twinge of gout prevented his appearing till yesterday, when he came looking very well—much younger than he has done for some years, I think. Great was the clamour for him in Lieven's house till he did appear, and I suppose she will keep him till she goes to Valençay.

Can you see us? I fear you will not quite approve. The green room. Granville and F. Lamb in two *fauteuils* opposite the fire. Lady Elgin and Dody in a theological controversy on the green couch. Lady Mary Stanley and William Lambton together. There I ought to be.   Caradoc and young Montalembert in the middle of the room, Mrs. Lambton with all the attachés about her.

The Seine is overflowing, the weather like January. We are all in hopes that Mme. Appony will put off her breakfast.

To Lady Carlisle.

Paris : May 13, 1836.

Most dear sister,—F. Lamb looks in spirits again. He never leaves Princess Schönbourg—such an old beau I never saw.

Yesterday we had a great Russian dinner at Pahlen's. I think, next to Devonshire House, his banquets the most beautiful I know, though far inferior in real solid splendour, but the new *or moulu plateau*, the servants, the light, the room, the salt-cellars made of two dolphins !

Round it sat : Lavals, Schouvaloffs, like a white heart cherry and a bud just dropped ; Ambassador Pahlen, supported by me and Mrs. Werther ; Duke of Hamilton 'twixt Mme. de Lieven and Kisseleff ; then Marie Menzingen, Paul Lieven, Meyendorfs, Mme. Schöppung, F. Lamb, and Schönbourg at play.

In the evening we made Mme. de Flahault happy. All rushed, and there I saw for the first time Nicholas and his love. She looks desperately smitten, which really is a sight to see.   He pulls a long face, looks like his brother's ancestor, and Vallombrosa waits upon them with a sort of expression of ' bad enough but might be worse ' in his countenance.

Yesterday Durazzo, Dody and I in the garden never took our eyes off the eclipse till it had done all its operations.

So Miss Berry is really to be here on the 23rd.   It will be a great *embarras* in a society where Durazzo walks over the course.

We have a breakfast for the King's birthday on
the 29th.   At three meet, at six eat, dance till twelve,
eat a morsel more and then to bed.   It will be really
the last gaiety.

To the Duke of Devonshire.

Paris : June 7, 1836.

My own dear brother,—The breakfast went off very
well, people seemed pleased ; but yesterday was the
curious day.   Our dinner : Mr. and Mrs. William
Locke, Lady Wallscourt, Mary and Agnes, Fergusson,
Knutzen, Ladislas Zamoyski, and Mr. Angerstein.   As
soon as Mrs. William Locke saw our Berry she went into
a sort of hysterical fit.   I took her into the garden.   She
cried bitterly, said that when she arrived at the door
she said to Mr. Locke, ' Good God, what's to become of
me ?   There's Mary Berry.'   She had not seen or heard
of her for years, had resented bitterly her not writing
at the time of her son's death.   Well, I led her back
and dinner soon set her up again.   Antonin de Noailles
sat by her, did not know who she was, but with that
peculiar fatality which attends Lord Rokeby, George
Harcourt and some others, seeking to enliven his neighbour with something of narrative, began relating to
her the melancholy fate of a *jeune Anglais*, Mons. Locke,
drowned in the Lake of Como.   This time the stound
away was remarkably slight, so much so that Pius remarked, ' J'ai tout lieu d'espérer que Madame ne m'a
pas entendu.'
We came out, all was smoothed down, and we sat
after dinner or rather sailed upon a placid lake.   At
half-past nine in walks Durazzo.   In ten minutes Dody
was led out into the conservatory.   ' Oh ! I must open
my heart or I shall die.   Lady Georgiana, connaissez-
vous cette dame ?   C'est la plus grande calamité de ma
vie d'être venu ici ce soir.   Elle a dit des horreurs de

moi.' Durazzo was led back. I soon saw Berry, her, Brignolé, the whole kit, Agnes and all, talking, bowing, smiling. Berry is all civility and came boasting, 'Did you see us?' I do not think Genoa will be friends, but Berry is dying to be well with them, and pursued and was more gracious than I ever saw her. These girls are wonderful.

It was the gayest soirée, owing to Mary's excessive zest and rapturous *accueil* of one after another.

We are struck with the four giraffes, but have ourselves got an ourang-outang who receives and sits at table eating his dinner. Bourke has sent to ask what day he would like us to call.

How much I do admire Lady Wilhelmina,[1] I thought her the prettiest girl I had ever seen. Who flirts with Miss de Rothesay?

To the Duke of Devonshire.

Paris : June 11, 1836.

My dear sister, Miss Berry is very well and amiably disposed. I do not know if it annoys her, but the whole Genoa tribe has disappeared from the face of society ; neither Brignolé, Durazzo nor Ferrari ever show themselves. She just remarked it to me, and I said so it seemed, nothing more.

Give Lord Carlisle my best love. In less than a month I hope to be with you all.

Paris is very delightful now, the garden lovely.

Madame Vallombrosa brought her boy to see ours yesterday, the same age. We beat him in intellect, but he is magnificent and beautiful, taller than little Fullerton, and though he cannot speak yet runs and leaps like a child of four years old. He is not his mother's child or his aunt's nephew for nothing. He flew to embrace little F., seized one hand, and with the

---

[1] Stanhope.

other extracted from him his new drum. No words can describe the scene that ensued, only like what must have been that when Césarine [1] called to tell her sister [2] that an Italian Duke was no Duke.

Our most darling baby did not cry, but he clenched his fist and cried out, 'Allez, dirty boy!' and then came the tug of war.

To Lady Carlisle.

Paris: 1836.

The Fullertons have almost settled not to go to England, but to pass the time we are away in Switzerland and return to us for the winter. The *homéopathie* only did good whilst he observed the rules of diet, air, and exercise, and I am now convinced that there is nothing in pill or powder. Its marvellous reputation is because novelty and hope give the patient zest to follow rules which would give us all health if we could bring ourselves to follow them habitually.

Let me now congratulate you and dearest Lord Carlisle on Morpeth's speech. Granville was delighted with it, and all our letters praise it.

Miss Berry has made Miss Ferguson very smart, *très bien mise*, herself ditto. They go about everywhere with the support, not figurative, of Knutzen the Dane, a Mr. Crawford, and one or two *pendant* men. She joined us at Musard's on Saturday, and we went from thence to Mme. Appony. Not a Genoese appeared there, or at my Friday. I really believe Durazzo means to encounter her no more, for to stir out of one's house is to see Berry.

I have letters from Mme. de Lieven.[3] Pauline [4] has a fever, and she tells me *on est inquiet.* Nobody there as yet. To-morrow the Poix and Montrond are to arrive.

---

[1] Madame de Caramar.   [2] The Duchesse de Vallombrosa.
[3] At Valençay.   [4] De Talleyrand.

Paris : June 23, 1836.

I am so glad you are going on pretty well, but long for July. We set out about Monday week.

We are in breathless expectation for the verdict.[1] Nothing even by telegraph this morning. So afraid of what he may have bleated about our Gracious. Who could bear to have their letters ripped up for evidence ?

We are told that Narvaez[2] is much admired. If ever le Comte Duchâtel and Monsieur Duvergier de Hauranne[3] come across you, please remember the French.

Paris is now all made of odds and ends. Lady Kinnaird and Lady Belfast creep out and bore about you. Duke of Hamilton in green slippers because of gout, and a cord round his throat like a *huissier de la Chambre*, nobody knows why.

Three things impend. A dinner at Neuilly, the Belgian Court being arrived; then to help to marry Mdlle. Sophie de Castellane and Monsieur de Contades at a distant church at eleven ; and on Monday morning a whole day at Madame de Boignes, drive, walk and dinner—a complete treat.

The Flahaults are still here. They are trying to persuade Madame de Lieven to go to England instead of to Baden. Madame de Lieven all on one leg about it. 'Mais voyez donc, on me demande pourquoi je vais à Bade ; je n'ai rien à dire, mais c'est un vrai serpent du Paradis que votre femme ;' to Flahault, 'je ne sais plus où j'en suis !' She sees more of Kulbach than anyone else, as

---

[1] The Norton trial.   [2] A beautiful Spanish lady.

[3] A conspicuous politician during the reign of Louis Philippe, whose Government for some years he warmly supported. Eventually, when no concession was made to the demand for reform he went into violent opposition, and was a promoter of the banquet the suppression of which led to the Revolution of 1848.

there is a carriage and a *maître d'hôtel* to be secured before she can stir.

The Turkish Ambassador has just sent me two beautiful *écharpes* for turbans—one painted, the other embroidered in silk and gold—a scented purse, a necklace, a bottle of otto of roses, and a parcel of gilt and brown pastilles. The same to *la fille de l'Ambassadrice.* We think this a pretty custom.

We are still in suspense, harmless letters and awkward facts, but no verdict come yet. God bless you. I have not another moment.

To LADY CARLISLE.

Paris : July 2, 1836.

My dearest sister,—You must pay for a letter today, for I cannot let such a time pass without writing and I let yesterday's courier slip. It is hotter than I have felt it for years, and this and the thought of seeing you all so soon makes me terribly lazy.

The Poodle is arrived, and we set out *sans faute* on Saturday, this day week.

Pozzo is come, and Mme. de Lieven stays till Monday. I believe they dine here to-day, if not tomorrow.

Berry and Durazzo had a formal reconciliation here last night, made up, and shook hands like the boxers.

Georgy is still confined to couch or chair in consequence of the sprain she gave her leg last week, but she is much better and was downstairs yesterday evening with Menzingen, who is in great beauty, but I think is much disappointed at there being now no chance of England. She is in high sprits, more at her ease with Lieven than ever, dying to remain on with her. So much for the stories current about severity on one side and terror on the other.

Mme. Vallombrosa is gone to Boulogne. N. Pahlen

P 2

told Mme. de Schönbourg, *naïvement,* that he always had a great curiosity to see the *établissements de bains* in France.

We dined at Neuilly on Sunday. I never saw anything so melancholy. They were all terribly cast down, and in that scene of perfect repose, everything looking so still, smelling so sweet. The people themselves so united, so good, and amiable, to think of the assassin's unceasing aim is so dreadful. Leopold looks much as ever. La Reine Louise much improved and an admirable little person.

Dearest sister, what happiness it is to go to England! And you know I delight in all, the journey and crossing.

To the Duke of Devonshire.

Devonshire House : August 14, 1836.

Your letter, my dear brother, found me here yesterday. No flower arrived, cruel Paxton.

I had a note yesterday from Mme. Schouvaloff. They are odd people. *Souffrante,* unable to move or she would have called. I wrote I would, if possible, go to her. Luckily I was prevented. Granville and Leveson had an interview with her. Where do you think? Driving round the ring.

I found G. very well, the Lords squabbling, our hurrying to Paris no longer considered necessary. We are this moment setting off for Mistley; Granville and Leveson go to Lilleshall. On Monday the 22nd we all meet here again, to start for Paris possibly, but certainly for Wiesbaden on Wednesday. We dined Saturday with the Hollands. At the turnpike we met Landseer, still lame from his accident. He has painted the most perfect little picture of Lord Melbourne. Rogers was looking very ill. It is a compliment to

him to say so, one had thought he could have gone
no farther.

Lady Dover came to us yesterday evening at
Grosvenor Place, looking lovely and in very fair spirits.
Afterwards Punch, large and grey, very agreeable.

The Peers were all going yesterday, put it off for a
week, and assembled at the Duke of Wellington's. We
all say, What for? But no answer yet.

The Speaker and his Lady dined at Holland House.
He a great dear *au bout du compte*. She, in green satin,
with sleeves ornamented with bows, and a wreathed
cap, looked at my blue silk bags and ribboned cap and
said : 'We are in error, I see, we over-do a little ; we
ought to adopt on these occasions *demie-parure*.' We
complimented her much on the Speaker's looks, but she
shook her head, 'You should look at his person,'
slightly designating her own upper leg.

To Lady Carlisle.

Frankfort: Sept. 13, 1836.

We arrived here yesterday, and have a charming
apartment, with a large fire, and I look out of window
upon a broad, beautiful street, and see umbrellas of every
colour. I arrived here with the remains of a bad cold,
and Granville with some pain in his face. This makes
me unable to give you an account of the Fair, as we
have left all the pleasure and bustle to Freddy, and in
consequence are much better this morning. We go to
Darmstadt this afternoon and to Heidelberg to-morrow,
and by that time hope to have a less wintry day than
this.

Here is Freddy. He says the Fair is very animated
and gay—not very pretty, excepting the booths on the
Quays. We are going to start, all muffled up, having
warmed ourselves well at the fire, and by treating it
like the month of November are very comfortable ; but

it is in June that I hope we shall all meet at Wiesbaden next year. You will now direct again to Paris.

The Duke of Rutland writes Sir F. Trench word that there will be no change of men, but that Lord Lyndhurst's speech is making an immense effect in the country—Lord Granville sneers at this. *Che vi par*, my dear Lady?

To Lady Carlisle.

Paris: September 1836.

We arrived on Tuesday, my own dearest sister, and found a clean, enjoyable house, and your dear little letter.

Georgy arrived an hour ago, most extremely pulled and weakened by her illness. If she is well enough they will set out for England to-morrow week.

Miss Berry has been very rheumatic and *souffrante*, but bears up with excellent courage and spirits. Lady Charlotte Lindsay is come. Mme. de Lieven paid them a long visit to-day, which surprised me as much as it pleased them.

We all, the girls and ourselves, dine at Neuilly to-morrow, where we found them last night, looking better and more cheerful than when we left them.

Mme. Appony is here, very happy at Appony's having received the Order of the Toison d'Or, something like our blue riband.

The 'Luxor' is to be put upon its legs to-morrow week. The Royal Family and all Paris are going to look at it. I mean to imagine.

Mons. Molé looks very thin and bilious. Monsieur Guizot in high spirits. Lord Clanricarde and Caradoc are at Compiègne with the Duke of Orleans.

To Lady Carlisle.

Paris : October 1836.

I have but a moment, my own dearest sis, because these are the last days of Georgy and Freddy (they set out on Tuesday), because the house requires a great deal of attention, and because Mme. de Lieven is on her couch for two or three days, and because neither Mme. de Dino nor Mme. de Flahault nor Lady Cowper are yet arrived. Put this all together. In another week I shall write volumes.

But my subject to-day is my despair at your not having received a long letter I wrote to you from Frankfort. How strange you must have thought it! To tell you how Granville and I both felt Lord Carlisle's kindness.[1] But till I hear you have not received my letter at all, I still think you may, and I will not repeat all its contents. Only that Granville had begged he might know if there was likely to be a contest that would entail great expense, as *that* he should be quite unable to meet. But let me know, indeed I shall next post, and I will again say all my say.

I am delighted that the Fullertons are going to you, because it delights them and I know will be a pleasure to you and yours.

English are flocking to and fro, and we have had large dinners almost every day.

The Royalties return from Compiègne to-night, and the Queen is to see the 'Luxor' put up to-morrow. There is no Fontainebleau this year, and nothing in prospect but a great Russian dinner at Pahlen's on Wednesday.

We have a Friday this evening in the green room, and I hope a very small one. We shall be able, *vu* the house, to rest on our oars for a long time. We have

---

[1] In offering to return Lord Leveson for Morpeth.

much that must be done, but all of dinner sort upstairs
—Pendarves, Wynnes, and such like. Sir Robert Peel
and his family are expected to-day.

To LADY CARLISLE.

Paris: November 7, 1836.

My dearest sister,—Where, oh where, are our
letters? It seems to me that we do nothing but write,
and you do anything but hear.

Your message delighted Georgy, and they will go
to you the end of November.

We have had one Friday. Do you see Georgy
sitting with Menzingen and Lady Mary Herbert,[1]
reckoned alike, and having taken kindly to each other?
Great talk of which is the handsomest. All the sparks
saying Marie, Georgy and I Mary.

I like Lady Pembroke and Lady Peel. Sir Robert
is playful and prudent, seems perfectly happy doing
lion and lark, and only prims when Lieven calls him to
the Bar.

John and Mrs. Talbot arrived on Tuesday. They
are great dears and help us much with the Tory camp.

Give my love to Leveson. D. writes again to me,
delighted with him. We all dined at Neuilly the day
before yesterday. Sir Robert can scarcely speak any
French. The King talked English to him, but what was
distressing, the Queen, under a natural *embrouillement*
that being deaf to the language was the same as being
deaf to the sound, bawled out every word to him as if
he was stone deaf, loud and distinct. 'J'es—père que
vous—vous plai—sez—à—Pa-ris.' An odd effect, and
made Sir Robert fidget on his perch next to her at
dinner.

---

[1] She married Lord Bruce and became Lady Ailesbury.

To the Duke of Devonshire.

Paris : November 11, 1836.

My own dearest brother,—Think of my leaving your two most delicious letters unacknowledged. I have lived with you and have never told you the pleasure it gave me.

I see Rodolphe [1] with you, but I have heard from him too. He wrote me a letter of his rapturous gratitude and unbounded admiration, and all Austria thanks me and loves me the better. The Zichys are here, but oh ! where is Ossuna ?—not, I fear, in your pocket.

Now what are the things to dip into to-day ? Lady Harriet Baring is most uncommonly agreeable, and with me gentle, amiable, and by no means censoricus. I think the dislike of her is mitigating, and it is only, I am more and more sure, that the world is upon its guard, gun cocked, to be in the proper attitude for receiving the shot it always imagines her about to fire ; and then it is such a shot when it comes, so direct and so piercing. She goes back in a few days, which I regret exceedingly.

'Esmeralda' comes out to-night, opera instead of ballet, Mlle. Falcon singing instead of Mlle. Taglioni dancing it. Words Victor Hugo arranged himself, music by Madame Bertin, niece of Bertin de Vaux, the great man of the 'Journal des Débats.' Mlle. Schivoni, the new Jane Seymour, beautiful, a fine voice and promise of excellence ; Grisi reconciled to her husband, and singing and acting divinely.

Read Picciola. It is to me the prettiest thing I know, though it *prêtés* to the scorn of the worldly and unfeeling. Read it without prejudice, letting yourself go to your impressions about it.

---

[1] Appony, nephew of the Austrian Ambassador.

To the Duke of Devonshire.

Paris: November 20, 1836.

Well, I went to the ' Esmeralda ; ' the finest *mise en scène*, dresses and processions beauteous and gorgeous. But oh! the music! The tune the old cow died of throughout, grunts and groans of instruments and voices without a *soupçon* of harmony.

Poney[1] sat, her eyes, sometimes filled with tears, fixed on my face instead of the piece. 'Oh! ma chère, l'horreur, mais fi donc ! ' The priest in love all the time, the constant church music and the regular solemn Mass must have been misery to her, and so shameful, I think.

Now, my dearest brother, did ever anybody give you a commission ? Andrews[2] annually sends us the annuals, but don't choose well. Will you or direct somebody of taste to select there or elsewhere the best, to spread upon our table ? Shall you say like Granville, when I ask him to do anything, 'Oh yes, that's the way, Jack of all Trades ? ' to which he adds ' non-compliance.' God bless you.

To the Duke of Devonshire.

Paris: December 29, 1836.

My dearest brother,—I can only find this morsel of paper to thank you a thousand times for your letter.

Of gaiety there is none in its usual sense ; it is like society in November in London. People run about to each other's little soirées, not a notion of dancing. Mme. Ferrari has a concert this evening to which we had all promised to go, but influenza prevents me, Dody and my boys, as it is no joke taking one's new-born cold into a deep snow over the frozen *débordements* of the Seine.

[1] Madame Appony.   [2] The bookseller.

Madame de Lieven's little *salon* is becoming a great resource for the destitute.

On Friday last I had my first soirée. On that evening sat in a row, gorgeously attired, Zavadowska, Simloff, Wittgenstein, and Kisseleff. They make a much greater display as to dress and diamonds than any other nation, and the above mentioned are all more or less handsome. Lieven kotows to Simloff because she is the Empress's bosom friend and correspondent. She has just been here and bids me say a thousand things to you from her.

How glad I am that you are going to feed the d'Harcourts. I am so fond of the little pair here. It inclines me to work at having the d'Henins [1] to dinner one of these days, though, dearest of Graces, an *entrée* more difficult to obtain from his Excellency I cannot figure to myself. I never yet have got him to consent to have Ranfurly. If you could drop over and wished it in person instead of through Dody, it might be effected, as he would see a reason, which he will not see now, as we are already more civil to them than to most ; but I will try.

Great excitement about the opening of the Chambers. Thiers is *très monté*, a great gathering about him, pushing him on to extreme opposition.

The *Carnaval* of five weeks will be very flat. For years there has not been seen here such snow and slipperiness and such a hard winter.

Talleyrand is very well. Mme. de Dino in great beauty. She and Meg meet and dine each other, but it is like the meetings in cock- and bull-fights. The

---

[1] General, Madame, and Mlle. d'Henin. The mother a Derbyshire lady, an old friend of the Duke's. The daughter very handsome, much admired by the Duc de Nemours and Lord Prudhoe and others, but she never married. After the death of her parents, she settled in England and became a great friend of Bishop Blomfield, who converted her to Protestantism. She was a general favourite.

night before last Dino ran into Lieven's *salon*, saw Meg and shrieked, 'Oui, ma chère, c'était un cri épouvantable.' She did not apologise or say for why. Explanations have been asked. Dino says it was a 'cri de surprise,' Meg says it was a 'cri d'horreur, et voilà où nous en sommes.'

I am more delighted than I can say at your going to hear and liking to hear Mr. Beamish.[1] So is the Duchess,[2] who has written me a letter about her delight.

Fullerton is looking much better, but still very languid. She is very well and delighted to be here again with her boy, and we more than delighted to have her. Leveson is more resigned than Freddy to the idea of a very dull *Carnaval*.

A dinner at old Bourke's is quite a thing talked of in these days. I thought I should have died of a scene she had with Tchann. He called the day before yesterday, was led through numberless rooms till he found himself *au pied du lit de la belle*, her head buried under the clothes, nothing visible but a sort of black *toque* and top knot, one professor, two marchesas and a *bel fanciullo* grouped round *le dit pied*. 'Approchez, mon cher, approchez.' He did. 'Mais, venez donc plus près.' He found himself with his head buried under the *oreiller*. 'Mon cher, vous êtes né coiffé—ah, pardi, vous êtes né coiffé.' He was in suspense and painfully placed, but she played with his curiosity before she said, 'Vous dinerez ici, et vous aurez la Duchesse de Sutherland et des bécasses qui sont venues hier de la Bretagne.'

My cold saves me Ferrari's to-night, *ouverture des Chambres* to-morrow morning, Mme. Molé's reception to-morrow evening and perhaps a dinner at Monsieur Le Hon's[3] on Wednesday and Appony's drum after it.

---

[1] A popular Evangelical preacher.   [2] Duchess of Beaufort.
[3] The Belgian Minister.

1837

To Lady Carlisle.

Paris: January 1837.

My most dear sis,—There is compensation in all things. The street is mended, the carpets and hangings arriving, the smell of paint going off, and we must begin again drumming and affronting.

Mme. de Lieven in great beauty and high spirits. She has always an *entourage*; she can keep off bores, because she has the courage to *écraser* them. The sublimities sometimes clash, but that for her taste is a small evil. It would kill me to have Berryer and Molé *tête à trois,* looking daggers at each other, *mais elle sait nager* and gets out of every difficulty. The pleasantest women here, in my opinion, go constantly to her. Mme. Appony, Schönbourg, Durazzo, and Marie, who makes tea like a Goddess.

This scene *se répète* here, only with more assistance, merrier perhaps but less genteel. Here fools rush in, there angels fear to tread. You will observe that there is a great deal of conceit in my humility.

Lady Harriet Baring is wind and wave bound at Calais, and yesterday if Walewski did not hear from her he was to take an apartment for her at Paris. I believe I am the only person in Paris who would be glad to see her again. I cannot understand her extreme unpopularity. Pray be discreet, as I wish her to get rid of the idea of its extent, which only exasperates her and sharpens her wit, and makes the matter twenty times worse—where she thinks she pleases she is as amiable as she is agreeable. She ought to be managed like Beatrice, whom she closely resembles.

Granville has fallen in love with Mrs. Young, *née* Dalton, which makes us very civil to them, and she and Mrs. Burrowes, *née* Sitwell, are lovely, and had been great friends as girls, and not met for years till in our Opera box the other evening. You see I am very Irish.

To the Duke of Devonshire.

Paris : January 20, 1837.

I have been really very unwell with this influenza, and it has left me so pulled that I can scarcely exert myself to do anything. Luckily nothing is required. F. Ponsonby's death has closed our doors for the rest of the month.

Georgy presents the Duchess of Roxburgh, Mrs. Cavendish and Fanny at the Tuileries to-morrow. A ball then or Wednesday of four thousand people, two small balls later.

Lord Lyndhurst left Paris yesterday, Mr. Ellice goes Wednesday. Lord Pembroke opens his house next week—first a concert, then a ball. No sparks but the very youngest here. I hope Fanny will not delude any of them. I am afraid they are not of an age to, what is called, do, which is a serious word.

Charles Greville is arrived. Mme. Sebastiani blinked at him and kept sidling up. 'Ah! oh dear me! Je crois, oui, je reconnais le mari de Lady Charlotte Greville.'[1] I hope he did not hear, but I did and writhed. Will you send this to G., when read ?

---

[1] His mother.

To Lady Carlisle.

Paris : February 1837.

My dearest sister,—You will have as soon or before this Charles Greville, who to our immense regret sets out at six to-day for England.

I believe the melancholy death of Sir Richard Acton added to the general indisposition a gloom that made everybody appear and feel worse. What I really think is that something or other and constant melancholy events have for once given everybody a distaste for dissipation.

The sensation at the non-mention [1] is great. Mme. de Lieven tells me Talleyrand was loud and vehement about it at dinner yesterday, where she went to wish him joy of his 83rd birthday, with an ancient goblet, rich and rare—inkstand rather— to present to him.

Molé is in bed with the *grippe*. The *Carnaval* ends on *Mardi Gras* with a ball at Lord Pembroke's. God bless you.

To the Duke of Devonshire.

Paris: February 11, 1837.

Thanks for your letter and the delicious account of the marriage.[2] How do those, not fire, Brands look ?— sleek and contented, I hope. If she has one quarter of the simplicity, ingenuousness, unartificial modesty that Lady Dacre says she has, it will, I trust, turn out very well.

To Lady Carlisle for the Duke of Devonshire.

Paris: February 17, 1837.

My very dear, dear sis,—Here we are, the Suther-lands, fattening and reviving *à vue d'œil* in the south rooms upstairs, the children having room to stretch and

---

[1] Of France in the King's Speech.

[2] Of Mr. Brand, the future Speaker, who was created Lord Hampden in 1884, to the daughter of General Ellice.

spread themselves at the Hôtel Meurice. This evening
the dear Pair come down into the green drawing-room,
where they will have a *partie fine* of their friends. The
ball tempts her dreadfully, but I have arranged this
plan above in hopes of keeping her out of it, but my
real hopes rest upon her being obliged to muffle up to
the chin.

What happiness it would be to all if the Burlingtons
would but come immediately to Paris, if only for a lark
of a fortnight!

How delighted we are about dearest Leveson and
all we hear and his speech![1] The Chancellerie is *émer-
veillée*, and I think he will be chaired in the court when
he returns. Will he return?

To Lady Carlisle.

Paris: February 1837.

I believe it is partly Leveson's eagerness that has so
inoculated me, but I feel out of breath about politics.
I dread the next majority, as I hear none but ill omens
about it, and *entre nous*, dearest sis, I think matters
look as ill for us as possible.

Lord Bruce is evidently much in love with Lady
Mary. She betrays nothing. Lady Pembroke looks
anxious. They dine here to-day, one and all. Daniskiold[2] is a sort of a chaperon, and never leaves either
Lady Pembroke or Lord Bruce. The green room is
matrimonious.

I see poor Lady Canning's death in the papers.
Her existence had less of bright in it than that of almost
any person I know. I hope her children were with her.

Letters from Rome say that Miss Stuart is going to
marry Mr. Tomline, 25,000*l.* a year, handsome, agreeable, young, but that Lady Betty opposes. It is the

---

[1] Lord Leveson spoke for the first time in the House of Commons.
[2] A Dane who married a sister of Lord Bruce.

girl's doing, but *la madre* wants rank, especially Lord Douro.

We are all very busy about our Charity Ball, sketching and talking costume.

Schönbourgs and Maurice Esterhazy go to London in the spring, as also Delphine Potocka. They call Sostègne de la Rochefoucauld 'Le futur passé.'

My best love to Leveson. Tell him Baba put aside a great lump of *compote* at his dinner yesterday, 'for Uncle Leveson, he coming'—nobody had mentioned him, so it is touching.

To Lady Carlisle.

Paris: March 3, 1837.

My own dearest sister,—How happy I am to think of Edward's relief![1] The ship heaved off all our hearts. I have been upstairs, rejoicing over this with your dear daughter.

Dearest of Dukes. Your letter delights me. I favoured the Duchess with select passages only.

Do I know the Miss Bennetts? A mushroom, not to say a toadstool, and a jessamine.

The Schouvaloffs have never appeared—still very poorly, I believe. Mme. Zavadowska came to both balls, to the last really like the Queen of Golconda—a whole diamond and sapphire crown, a white tissue floating about her like clouds, looped up and streamed upon with jewels.

Give my love and my thanks to Miss Berry for a most interesting and amusing letter.

We had a dinner yesterday, most successful and useful. Mr. Munro of Novar, Monsieur de Chabot and General Cass[2] and his wife. The Sutherlands so civil and gracious, the *convives* so charmed; and to-night, as

---

[1] Lady Carlisle's son. His ship had stranded. The court-martial acquitted him of all blame.

[2] The American Minister in Paris.

Georgy will not appear, think what it is to me to have her Grace in a white crape pelisse, buttoned with diamonds.

To the Duke of Devonshire.

Paris: March 24, 1837.

One word, dearest Grace. How can I thank you enough, half enough, for your kindness to Eward? She is penetrated to her soul, the happiest, the most grateful, and the most enviable of women.

Lady Pembroke has a house in the Champs Elysées. Do not tell, but Georgy did see in the middle of the populace, linking and looping and gazing at the Longchampites, first, Lord Pembroke and Lady Mary, second, Lord Bruce and Lady Emma—more conclusive than romantic, I think.

We are all busy as bees about the Charity Costume Ball. I hope it will be a beautiful sight and, what's better, profitable.

Paris rings with Lord Pembroke's magnificence, who has sent us a donation of a hundred pounds. We have Mesdames Flahault, Menou, Caraman, Molé, Sebastiani, Coigny for our French patronesses. The Duchess of Sutherland will be Night. Oh, what a glorious night! Her diamonds the firmament, and poppies as the Zodiac and a veil with crescents. Dody, a patroness, sits over her list and looks wistfully at it. She has but one name, but that is a thumper. James the Revd. Ellice has sent her 300 francs for three tickets, but not another customer. Meg has scraped up countless numbers, and I have a respectable catalogue of friends.

To Lady Carlisle.

Everybody seems to think the Duke of Orleans' marriage settled. They say the bride is tall, thin and plain, *adorable de caractère*, and perfectly well brought up. Bad teeth, red hair, amiable countenance.

I will write more and better next time.

To the Duke of Devonshire.

Most dear Grace,—I am very poorly, only out of bed to have bed made, unable to speak, hear, or speculate.

The Molé Ministère remains in ; is called *le Petit Ministère*.

The future Duchesse d'Orléans must be prettier than Mrs. Berri was. Maréchale Lobau is to be *La Grande Maîtresse*.

I wonder what is going to happen *chez vous*. Peel, I think.

Caradoc goes to town to-morrow to wait on Victory for a month.

Grandmamma Mecklenburg brings Miss all the way to Fontainebleau for the marriage. Therefore there is no marriage by *procuration*.

God bless you. Oh, if you knew how poorly I feel! Grippe has put all his fangs into me—tooth, ear, nose, throat and head.

To Lady Carlisle.

My dearest, dear sister,—We are all very curious about our political fate. Report and surmises are so various. Paris is becoming pleasanter, all that is disagreeable in society is over, spring approaching.

Now, my dearest, business. I throw myself on your mercy. Will you obtain a few names and pounds for a subscription I have set on foot here? It is the most interesting family I ever met with—a widow with eight young children. They lived here when the father was alive, supposed to be immensely rich. Houses at Paris and Auteuil, the prettiest furniture, equipages, etc., everybody going to their house. The husband died, and left them to starve. I never saw anything so interesting as the widow's courage and resignation. She brought us her beautiful children. The singing of one of the girls twelve years old is delicious. I cannot resist a wish to serve these poor, unhappy people, but I have quite exhausted my own means and the good feelings of my relations and *entourage* here. I have tried till I am ashamed, so that my only hope is in a few names from England, that may induce others of themselves to contribute to it here.

I would like to do what Lady Julia Howard wishes more than most things, but will you tell her that I have an invariable rule, French by the French, and though this lady is English she is now Madame d'Auchamp, and therefore Lady Julia should recommend her asking some one of my French friends, a lady, to ask to present her. This is my only way of drawing a line in French society.

To Lady Carlisle.

Paris: April 1837.

Dearest of sisters,—A thousand thanks for the kindness and for the money. You have no idea how interesting a family it is that you have all been so good to.

We are very curious and impatient for political news. The Archbishop alarmed me. The last debate must, I think, have done good, and Sir Robert Peel was evidently much ruffled, which I think he deserved.

I am delighted to think that dearest Leveson is so much interested and so keen about political business, and also to hear from all of his popularity. He is become also such an excellent correspondent, and Granville delights in hearing from him so constantly.

To Lady Carlisle.

Paris: May 5, 1837.

We have had one fine hour to-day after torrents of rain and I spent it walking round and round the garden with Madame de Lieven. Madame Appony came also to bid me good-bye. I dread the coming *fêtes*, and Madame Appony's absence is a great additional annoyance. Madame de Brignolé is a dear comfortable woman and will in some manner compensate.

I know not what the Schönbourgs do, but they both talk of England. So does Madame de Lieven; but I do not think myself that the latter will go, she has in many ways such a nervous dread of it.

The effects of the amnesty and the expectation of Mlle. Mecklenburg are the reigning subjects. Lady Lincoln is much the same. I saw the poor Duke [1] yesterday, looking miserable.

Madame de Lieven was much affected at seeing Lord Lyndhurst to-day; she says his grief is so deep. He sets out for London to-morrow.

We are in hourly expectation of the result of the Westminster election.

How long is the Court mourning for the Queen's mother [2] to last?

[1] Her father, the Duke of Hamilton.
[2] The Duchess of Meiningen.

To Lady Carlisle.

Paris : May 1837.

Dearest sister,—Granville has continued very poorly. I much doubt if his gout will leave him so entirely as to enable us to accept an invitation we are to receive ' de faire une petite visite à Fontainebleau.' I went to the Tuileries yesterday evening and found them all in great spirits. The King really in ecstasies at all the late measures, his increased popularity and augmented liberty. The Queen happy, but wholly occupied about the marriage. She says it makes her terribly nervous. She praised the Princess, and all she heard of her was in her favour. She has tried on one of her gowns, and though the dear Queen is like an asparagus she is shorter and broader than her *belle fille*.

Lady Stuart and her girl called on me the day before yesterday. I think the latter beautiful and exceedingly improved.

The success of Evans [1] is some pull up against our election disasters. Sister, what do you think of things in general?

Tell me if my dearest Gink [2] has any flirtation visible to the naked eye ?

To Lady Carlisle.

Paris : May 1837.

My dearest sister,—I have little to tell you. The King went to the Jardin des Plantes yesterday, with only two servants behind his carriage. He was much cheered and hurraed, and is in a state of ecstasy at having recovered so much liberty.

---

[1] Sir de Lacy Evans was returned for Westminster.
[2] One of the names Lord Leveson was known by in the family.

The Duc de Broglie, who was to have gone to-morrow to meet the Princess, has a *fluxion* and swelled face, and may be prevented, which will be unlucky.

The picture has come, and the Duke of Orleans has locked it up. I hear ' c'est atroce.' Mons. Bresson sends word that it is a very unfavourable likeness, but that she, Miss Meck, insisted upon sending it. Wise, I think.

The Duc de Coigny is to be her first gentleman *écuyer*—not *Mesnard*, I hope.

I must leave you, as I have had much to write to-day, and my life does not give me much news to relate.

To Lady Carlisle.

Paris: May 1837.

My own dearest sis,—The presentations to the Duchess of Orleans are to take place on the fifth and sixth of June. We intend going on the fourth, if the diplomacy is received apart; if not, on the fifth. We take apartments at Versailles, one week before the *fête pour* Monday week. We shall go there as soon as Granville is well enough to move for the benefit of the change of air, his first ride and the comfort of being on the tenth, the day of the great doings, within a stone's throw of the *spectacle* at night, the *musée* in the morning. The Fullertons have taken the apartment above us.

The Duc de Broglie and all his suite write enchanted with Princesse Hélène. They say she has perfect self-possession, the best manner, never the least put out, knowing what to do and say on all occasions. But I shall soon have satisfactory intelligence, as Dody[1] is to write volumes from Fontainebleau.

---

[1] Lady Georgiana Fullerton.

5 !!! I was glad to hear that the Bear rather likes it [1] than otherwise.

Lady Stuart came to see me to-day with her daughter, looking less well than usual and rather stormy. Betty, too, in a fuss. Lord Stuart won't come. They both wish to stay to see the opening at Versailles. Betty is puzzled, opens her mouth, looks like a very hot red and white spaniel.

Then came Meg, very happy and merry, enchanted at the coming week at Fontainebleau, at the past month in London. Princesse Hélène has black eye-lashes and a fine complexion. The Duc de Broglie says she is *très polie, charmante, et distinguée*. All the young men with him were captivated. Mons. Bresson says she is the gentlest and most determined person he ever met with, that never out of France was such a manner and *tenue* seen. Her teeth are little black stumps, the foot very big.

To the Duke of Devonshire and Lady Carlisle.

Paris: June 4, 1837.

My dearest brother and sister,—I have just sent off Georgy, Mlle. Eward, Baba and Hayes,[2] Fullerton, Boringdon, Lady and Miss Stuart to Meg's house and garden, which are all open to the fashionable public to-day. Granville was offered a window in retirement upstairs, but though he is much better he thought it more prudent to decline.

The King would not allow the Duchesse to come alone, and the *entrée* into Paris will be a great affair. He is to ride in before the *calèche*, which *entre nous* is much sneered at and ridiculed by his foes and regretted by his friends. 'Il se fait postillon.'

---

[1] Majority for Government in the House of Commons.
[2] The little Fullerton boy and his nurse.

(Secret.) The Megs are returned from Fontainebleau, the old pair in a most hostile humour. They join in the chorus of praise, but without either zest or satisfaction. Is it that Meg and her girl were put into one small room, their gowns hanging round them, laundry like, having none of the comforts and conveniences of life? Is it that all the *convives* at the château were at a very proper distance, no preference shown, no distinction made to any?

Emilie is in great beauty. Boringdon and Leveson will have her and Miss Stuart to themselves, I believe, as we hear most of the other lordlings fail. Lady Stuart has just been with me, sitting up on her hind legs in great distress. The *fêtes*, the young lords, the Cannings coming, the London season going.

Monday.—I am just come very tired from Court. Charmed with the Duchesse; not pretty perhaps, but everything else and equivalent. Such a manner, *tournure*, dignity, grace, no sort of pretension, modesty, *parfaite obligeance*. He looks the happiest of men, and Mme. de Montjoie says they are the greatest specimens of true love that ever was seen.

To the Duke of Devonshire.

Paris: June 12, 1837.

Dearest D.,—We wait with anxious expectation for news from England, so much seems precarious.

I was at the Reservoir Inn at Versailles at three— Count Pahlen, Nicolas, Medem, the Brignolés, the Schönbourgs, Aston, Heneage, Emilie de Flahault, Fullertons, myself and Leveson dined at five. At six we went to the château. At near three in the morning we drank tea, then put on our bonnets and shawls again, and I and Mrs. Foster[1] came

---

[1] Her maid.

back to Paris, *ventre à terre*, and arrived at half past four.

Versailles was as beautiful as possible within and without. I hear the banquet, 1,500 at dinner, served with ease and rapidity, was something miraculous. The Salle de Spectacle is beyond description or imagination. Though entirely red and gold, as light as day. The full dress, Duprez's voice, Miss Ellsler's legs, Mlle. Mars' conversation—'Spare me the details,' you will say, ' as I take in the newspapers.'

What I admire most is Versailles, the thing itself, human beings streaming over all its glories and amongst the *jets d'eau*, clumps of roses, and under, thanks to the late season, the lilacs, laburnums, horse-chestnuts, and all the busy delight and bustle—a hum of millions of people looking their smartest.

Nothing ever was in my opinion so perfect as the Duchesse d'Orléans' manner, so calm, so quiet and still, yet always more attentive, more gracious and more perfectly up to it all than any of those around her, a sort of *tenue* that would make any defects of manner in others (were there such) remarkably obvious.

Things not in the papers. Mmes. Valençay, Castellane, Vallombrosa, Caraman would not so much have minded not being asked at all, had not our Menou been one of the invited. They did not see her superior claims—officially, physically or morally. The *Diplomates* were much pleased with their box. Mme. de Flahault says we were degraded. We mean to inquire how. A reconciliation between her and Dino.

The foreigners of distinction very indignant at a great *gaucherie*. Stuarts, Lady Rendlesham, Staffords, Marie Menzingen, Mmes. Durazzo and Ferrari, having been all asked to the dinner, the day before received formal printed un-invitations, desired to consider their former invites as *nuls et non avenus*.

Nobody knows why the Flahaults are stormy. He has not the Grand Croix of the Légion d'Honneur ; and Emilie spent her evening alone at the Reservoir, being asked neither to dinner with her mother nor *fête*. But there are many precedents of like grievances. However, it makes her mother take up all our different causes of humiliation with even unwonted energy, but she leaves me alone, having long felt in scorn—' Wretch, whom no sense of wrong can rouse to vengeance.'

All my belongings are still at Versailles. I expect them late to-day.

On Wednesday the *fête populaire* here. On Thursday a dinner given to the Royal Family at the Hôtel de Ville. The Duc de Broglie told us yesterday evening that immediately after the repast there will be a Diorama. ' Rambuteau,[1] avec sa galanterie accoutumée, fera passer devant les yeux de la Duchesse le Palais de Ludwigslust, où elle a été élevée. Après cela le Roi, à ce qu'on dit, fera deux fois le tour de Mme. Rambuteau[2] après le bal.' Repeat not this levity of our dear little *doctrinaire*. He is in tearing spirits.

To the Duke of Devonshire.

Paris : June 23, 1837.

I hope Granville will be well enough to pay a visit to England, and he much wishes it himself ; but he cannot yet walk, and it must be some time before he can risk making any exertion or undergoing any fatigue. We therefore remain here for the present, *avide* of news, devouring newspapers, gasping for letters, and marking days by the intelligence received ; for it is history, fate, romance, all in one.[3] Everything new, nothing to be calculated upon. Such a little love of a Queen ! Lord Melbourne must take care to throw a

---

[1] Préfet de la Seine.   [2] She was very stout.
[3] The Queen's accession.

something paternal into his manner. We pine to hear of the First Lady. All point at that other Queen, Harriet the First.[1]

I alone say she never can or will make such a sacrifice. Granville, Georgy, Aston, all say, it is her duty to make it.

Mme. de Lieven gasps for breath and cries over the young speech, which she and we admire *à l'excès*.

All the *fêtes* here are at an end, the Louvre concert put off, on account of our King's death, till the end of July.

God bless you. If you have any pity, write.

To Lady Carlisle.

Paris: June 30, 1837.

Most dear sister,—I congratulate the Government and the little Queen on your Duchess's appointment. It gives such immense pleasure to them as a party and brilliancy to a Court. I hope she has secured to herself as much liberty and as long holidays as the case admits of.

We grieve to hear of a contest at Morpeth, but I do hope it will be but a slight breeze and do no harm.

I need not say how glad I am of Harriet Pitt's appointment.[2] It is delicious.

Mme. de Lieven entreated me to tell the Duchess that she had not a moment to write, but that she sets out to-morrow, Saturday morning, and hopes to arrive in London Monday evening or Tuesday. She will be much missed here, as she is really more liked than I think it is easy for a foreign woman to be. Nothing can be more agreeable and amiable than she has been to us.

---

[1] Duchess of Sutherland.
[2] Lord Rivers's sister, appointed a Maid of Honour.

To Lady Carlisle.

Paris : July 1837.

My dearest, dear G.,—You may judge of the deep interest of letters from England. We are delighted to hear from all of your Duchess's liking the little Queen so much, and of Lord Melbourne's intimacy and favour. But elections are the great *point de mire* now, and as usual everybody seems equally sanguine.

Tell me a few things. What is the real state of Sir Robert Peel's health? What a loss I, *malgré* my thinking him *peu de chose* as a consistent politician and a bit of a humbug, think he would be, as he has integrity, energy, and is in his family so valued and beloved.

Does the Duchess think the Queen cares about politics, and is she a Whig or a Tory in her innermost heart?

Can you forgive me for this letter? I have not a single thing beyond gratitude and curiosity to make a letter out of.

Paris was never known to be so empty, and is becoming dry and dusty. Our drive in the Bois de Boulogne is delicious and daily. If Granville was well he would not endure Paris in its present state, but as it is we can command comfort and quiet. Amusement must be looked to a month later.

To the Duke of Devonshire.

St. Germain : July 14, 1837.

Dearest of brothers,—I was just going to write to you without the stimulus of your delightful letter to tell you that we go on as well as we have begun. We think of being in England for a fortnight the very beginning of August. Dieppe and Brighton on our way.

We came here yesterday evening. The weather is divine, the air pure and bracing as at Kemp Town.

Granville has taken his first walk without being the worse for it and I am happier than I can say or sing.

How I hope I shall find you on the pier. Is the passage out of steamer on to pier very unpleasant? I think I can recollect having it in horror, but if Mme. St. Clair has achieved it, carrying her fears and legs featly over it, I will give my alarm to the winds.

We are intent upon election news. Mme. de Lieven writes me the most perfect letters.

To LADY CARLISLE.

Paris: July 21, 1837.

My dearest sister,—I can never say enough of the pleasure your letters give me.

Mention, my dearest, Lord Gwydyr and Lady Willoughby. You will be surprised, but I am desired to ask about them and their politics and how they stand at the new Court.

There is nobody I pity like Lady Lansdowne, few that I admire more. Mme. de Lieven dotes upon Lord Melbourne. She praises him to the greatest degree, and tells me of his excessive favour with the most eager pleasure. She is also amazingly struck with the little Queen, and says of your daughter, 'La Duchesse de S. est admirable dans son rôle, si belle, si tranquille, si noble.'

To LADY CARLISLE.

Paris: August 4, 1837.

We have been in a state of great excitement. The elections seem to be going on favourably. I can bear London and Planta, and in another direction Roebuck and C. Villiers.[1]

Politics in general have a much stronger interest now. They are vivified and brought home to one's feelings. I feel so much interested about that little

[1] The Right Hon. Charles Villiers, then looked upon as an advanced Radical.

wonderful Queen, and admire all I hear of hers and
Lord Melbourne's relative positions.   What a strong,
anxious tie it is that binds him to her service, so unlike
anything else of the sort one ever heard or read of!

Mme. de Lieven writes always in admiration of
sovereign and subject, and the most grateful expressions
about *les adorables Sutherlands*, but she seems low and
really very unwell.   Mme. de Schönbourg has written to
me a most interesting and clever letter.   She says of
your daughter, 'Si je pouvais l'admirer et l'aimer plus
ici qu'à Paris, je crois que je le ferais.   Je trouve qu'elle
remplit si parfaitement la belle place et position que
le ciel lui a donnée ; son activité, toujours calme et réflec-
tive, me remplit d'admiration.'

To the Duke of Devonshire.

Paris: August 5, 1837.

How shall I ever thank you, my dearest brother ?
You have painted the Queen to me in general colours,
but nobody had sketched Pitt,[1] Tavy,[1] and Mama [1] to
the life like you.

What tact the little woman seems to possess !
What determination !   And how much security there is,
I think, in her friendships, *engouements* and *entourage*,
making her go on blowing in the right quarter.   When
I hear of Lord Melbourne looking very ill and worn,
and see how neck-and-neck the election runs, I feel as
if our great dependence was in her grace and favour,
and I hope, as you say, we shall do uncommonly well
with that.

Monsieur de Bray—perhaps you remember his papa
and mama, who used to live in the house Colonel
Thorn has now—is a very gentlemanlike young man,
known to the Princess Schönbourg, etc.   Great would be
my renown if he gets his nose into Chatsworth, and great

----

[1] Miss Pitt, Lady Tavistock, and the Duchess of Kent.

will be the wonders he will tell of it to his love, Madame de la Châtaignerie, when he returns.

If you fret at not having got the copy of Pauline, you may order four large sketches or eight small ones to put in your album. Animals in water-colours, with pencil backgrounds. The large ones ten francs, the small ones five francs. They are done by a man whose great amusements were field sports and drawing. He is now in great distress, and selling these sketches for bread. Dogs of all sorts, deer, pheasants, feeding sheep, the best and prettiest of all. I took them into Granville's room without a hope. He bought instantly four, and Aston six, so lovely did they consider them.

He is now making me a sketch of women washing in the Seine. Do not let the remembrance of the ' Vicar of Wakefield ' make you scorn the sheep. I do assure you, two hillocks with two sheep on them is one of the prettiest things I ever saw.

My artist is young—about thirty, I should think—very dark, and Spanish looking. Suffield Gunton by name —an odd, if not intentional combination. Extremely proud, as hard as a stone, till moved by a dry cold statement of his distress I said something kind, and then he cried. I know nothing of him. He wrote with his sketches, and nobody had mentioned him to me.

Caradoc is arrived, looking wretchedly and old but very domestic as he drives in the Champs Elysées with the Princesse Bagration and his daughter, a fine well-grown girl of sixteen, mother unknown—an odd family party to brave the public eye.

I must not forget that Lieven writes delighted with her delicious *journée* at Chiswick. She is *pénétrée* with your kindness. It has not reached me from her if there has been disappointment in other quarters.

And now good-bye, or you will say ' I hardly can bear it,' as Georgy's boy does when he is thwarted.

He is the greatest love. Georgy's mild, firm rule has *écartéd* all the usual signals of wrath, roars 'I won't,' etc.; but he is naturally very violent and particularly abusive, and when *outré* begins as above, and always, like the Irish, far wide of his mark. The other day at dessert: 'Grandpapa, give me some strawberries.' Georgy in a great hurry: 'Oh, no, not to-day. He must not have anything but biscuit.' Very red, after a minute's pause: 'I hardly can bear it.' 'Bear what, my darling?' 'I can hardly bear big people.' 'Oh, that's nonsense.' Much redder: 'I hardly can bear nasty, dirty, tiresome, big people, who won't give me strawberries when I want them.' And all this without a tear or *geste*, speaking as plain as we do.

To Lady Carlisle.

Paris: August 7, 1887.

The Poodle tells me Rivers looks like a fat yeoman. I hope you like him as much as ever.

We remain quietly here; not even St. Germain at present. The weather is not too hot, and the Bois de Boulogne and our garden delightful.

I am so glad you have been to Court. How universal the admiration is! A question or two as you approve.

Is it true that the Queen likes nothing but London, and dislikes the thought of Windsor or Brighton?

Who are Sir Wetherall and Sir Stovin, the two new grooms?

Who is Miss Davies?

Is it old Miss Lister or a younger one?

Does Lord Melbourne look very ill indeed?

Elections do not elate, but I hope with Scotland and Ireland they may do. But it is very strange that it has not been more triumphant.

To Lady Carlisle.

St. Germain : August 13, 1887.

We only came here this evening, my dearest sister, to drink tea and go to bed, and we shall drive back early to-morrow. This suits us better, and it is a complete change and air bath. I almost hope we are near complete recovery.

We admired George's speech at Leeds beyond everything. Aston was in raptures over it. Huddersfield ! I have not words to express my rage. Oh, how I do wish the elections were over ! We know not what to think ; some croak and some are alarmingly sanguine. I cannot believe in late events not having a very decided and overpowering effect.

Paris.

Aston tells me that he met Molé and Montalivet at dinner at Flahault's yesterday. Montalivet says Berryer is seriously implicated, but everybody else doubts it, as he was prudent and avowed his Carlism as a profession.

And now God bless you, my own dearest, kindest sis. We shall meet at the meeting, elect who will, elect who may, and that will be happiness.

Tell me all you hear of my darling Susan. I have delightful letters from her. I hear she is in despair at the Queen's accession, being a desperate Tory.

To Lady Carlisle.

St. Germain : August 18, 1837.

My own most dear sister,—You gave us the greatest pleasure in sending Morpeth's letter. How perfectly beautiful his speech about the Queen is ! Thank Heaven the elections are over !

The way everybody talks of Morpeth—all in the sense of 'greater thou shalt be'—and *envisager* for him a situation in time, which I never, after the first gratified hot feel of pride, can much wish for any one I love as much love as I love him. But it is an elating feeling to hear people talk of him.

Is it true—*entre nous* most secretly, and I did not hear it from Mme. de Lieven—that Lord Grey's great cause of soreness and plaintiveness is a jealousy of him as standing in consideration and prospective so much above Lord Howick?

Mme. de Lieven is more interesting and amusing and agreeable than I can say. All she pours forth of all those I am fond of or curious about makes Paris alive in this dead, empty season. First, really first, affection, admiration and gratitude to the Sutherlands, with a delightful account of their attitude in their new position. Then, of you, such a delicious picture; and of politics, lastly, such a charming view. She don't value the election losses one farthing; and thinks, what I have felt all the time, the impossibility to others and the certainty to us. People will come over, and the only thing that might have made the Whig break-up—Lord Melbourne's weariness and discouragement—no longer possible. His situation is of such unexampled interest as well as his duty, that he will never give up, but be more riveted to it. Difficulties the Tories will increase to him, but that is all, and little against the stimulus of added zest and devoted attachment.

We are enchanted to hear that Leveson is coming.

To Lady Carlisle.

Dieppe: August 24, 1837.

Most dear sister,—Three days here have already braced and agreed with Granville so well that I feel I shall soon have charming bulletins to send you. We drive two hours in the morning in the intervals of stormy weather, and the air is renovating and delicious.

R 2

We dine at a quarter before five, drive an hour afterwards; in bed soon after eleven, sleep like tops; breakfast at nine.

This goes to you by Leveson, who trots to Boulogne,
the sea being outrageous. with Betsey Meyendorf, the
Zavadowskis, the *maman* of this last, *le petit, le gouverneur*,
a French spark and various other trimmings.

He could not wait, so I must send this by the
steamer, if steamer there be, that will encounter such
a black mass of sky as I see out of my window. He
will be at Morpeth on the 5th. You will probably hear
from him as soon as I do.

We are now left to the Doctor and Freddy, and
sometimes Claremont,[1] who is here for a week, to
Freddy's great enchantment.

The Canterburys are here, Mme. de St. Clair, the
Armstrongs, and a few foreigners. It is easy just to
fit one's hours in, so as to avoid them all in a lump.
When Granville is able to walk with ease, we shall
begin squiddling at the Promenade des Bains.

To LADY CARLISLE.

Dieppe: August 1837.

Adorable sis,—D. gives the most charming accounts
of you, tells me Lord Carlisle was very well also and
Castle Howard delightful, that he never enjoyed anything more. You are most kind always about my
dearest Gink.[2] I never knew him so delightful, amiable,
and gay as during his short visit to us. He will be
very sorry to miss seeing Bruce.[3] I thought we had
got his papa safe in the Faubourg St. Germain. Mme. de
Flahault tells me Lady Elgin was a strange character
in Scotland—never out of a riding habit (horses being
her passion), and wearing a beard. Shaved and in chip

[1] General Claremont, for many years Military Attaché at Paris.
[2] As Lord Leveson was sometimes called by his family.
[3] Frederick Bruce, son of Lord Elgin.

bonnets, she still looks marvellous. But I think her excellent, interesting from her zest, energy, and simplicity, and more agreeable in a *tête-à-tête* than almost anybody.

My letters from Paris are full of Madame de Dino. She has had a paralytic stroke. Mme. de Lieven says, 'Elle se remet.' But it is a terrible trial to her in all ways.

The Duchess of Orleans is with child, and the Duke has given up going to Constantine—two good things for the family. •

TO LADY CARLISLE.

Dieppe: September 10, 1837.

My dearest sister,—We leave this place to-morrow, Granville in much improved health, but still lame. Though the weather is still very fine, it is becoming cold, and I am not sorry, or afraid of Paris for him.

You will have seen that there have been most ill-natured and shameful attacks upon Mme. de Lieven in the French newspapers. She is much annoyed, and I shall be glad to see her again and to give her a little advice. Nothing is done by showing annoyance, and entering into discussions means newspaper aggressions. She must be quiet, and that is what she is not disposed to be.

Princesse Bagration went this morning. She tells me that Caradoc is now at Cherbourg, having been at Havre, that he travels alone and on foot without a servant, his clothes in a knapsack over his shoulder. She wonders, and frets, and says such an odd plan for a *malade*! But I understand his doing anything or everything for effect. When he fails to astonish and dazzle in one line, to try it in another. I would give anything to see him arrive at an inn and hear him talk.

To Lady Carlisle.

Paris: September 18, 1837.

My dearest sister,—I am delighted to hear that you are going to Chatsworth. Tell D. I never can be grateful enough to him for his ' mutton-broth letter,' which I received on Susy's birthday.

I have little to tell you. Mme. de Lieven is in better spirits; she did the honours yesterday at a grand dinner at Pahlen's. He, the Ambassador, adores Mme. de Shönbourg, who was in great beauty and spirits. Mme. de Vallombrosa ditto. Nicholas loves, they say, but there was no sign of it, and he does not stick, gaze, and sigh as he used to do.

Mme. de Schönbourg is extremely fond of a swarm of admirers. As such she encourages Lord Rokeby and Mr. Sneyd—open, innocent, and very safe flirtations.

To the Duke of Devonshire.

Paris: October 2, 1837.

My dearest brother,—I was beginning to be in despair when I received your beautiful sketch of Chatsworth. I see them all—all as plain as you did. In Paris, Betsey Meyendorf used to be in the Rue Montmartre at six to draw the anatomy of the horse. I think she must look more feminine on the ladder. I like her, and I have had such a warm, grateful note about you. She is very intelligent, I think, and so sociable and cordial. My opinion is rather in a mess. Mix it and take it, dearest Grace, and let me implore you not to let the next pause be so long.

Granville is going on perfectly well, but he wants a great deal of strengthening still. We are able to lead the most quiet and regular life here. The weather is delicious. Society made up of Mesdames Lieven, Schönbourg, Brignolé, Durazzo, Pozzo, Pahlens,

Tchann, Sneyd, Luttrel, not to mention *attachés*, and
Georgy in my pocket, very pleasant. The Opera begins
on Tuesday; we are promised 'Beatrice di Tenda.'
Granville has begun a course of sea-water *douches*,
which agree perfectly. The eyes of Richard and
Robert Verity are upon us. All this will show you
why I am not longing to go to you and Susy *pour le
moment*. I think Paris better for him.

Mme. de Lieven looks very thin and yellow; will
remain here because it is true and certain that her
health would suffer if she was to travel. Everybody
believes it at last, and Chermside has written it, when
it will force 'Vraiment'[1] out of her incredulous half.
Perhaps you wish to know the truth about poor
Madame de Dino. The Duc de Noailles received the
account from her, and told it to everybody. In three
or four days she wrote to Madame de Lieven, to Henry
Greville, to all she knew here without mentioning it,
and to everybody who made or wrote enquiries the
thing was positively denied. What is certain is that
she must now be very well, as she has just been acting
the principal character in a *spectacle* given to Monsieur
de Talleyrand on his birthday. It is certain almost that
she must have had some sort of seizure, as it would be
a strange thing for Monsieur de Noailles to have invented it in honour of her, whose devoted admirer he is.

To the Duke of Devonshire.

Paris: November 6, 1837.

Dearest D.,—We accept with gratitude, and your
troisième does not alarm Granville. Monday next (this
day week) we talk of setting out. What happiness it
would be to see you all again, Lord and Lady Carlisle,
Leveson, and Morpeth!

Sir Robert Peel arrived yesterday. Called to-day

---

[1] A nickname of Prince Lieven from his frequently using the word.

when we were out. We have asked them to an early dinner to-morrow and to go with us to Madame Persiani's *début*. Lady Augusta Fox and Henry dined here yesterday. She is very amusing.

There is much that is melancholy. Lady Lincoln has again had severe attacks. Her family miserable. Poor Mr. Graham has had a fit, not apoplexy, but something very near it. To-day we heard of Monsieur de Caraman. He has died of cholera at Constantine. He was a good man, and I feel much shocked at it.

If I was not coming in a minute, I would beg pardon for this letter.

To the Duke of Devonshire.

London : November 20, 1837.

Granville has this morning a return of gout. He is well in health, but deeply disappointed. He cannot go to the House or out of this one to-day. I dine alone at Court !

My dearest boy is very well. I think he will do well.

I cannot but feel it a mercy that Granville has not the fatigue and exertion of to-day to encounter. Now he has perfect repose, and I hope none but pleasurable emotions.

I have brought you Binet's[1] egg, but when it was suspended in its glass bell I thought it so pretty that my plans changed and I have brought it to you as a love gift.

My benefit will be great, for it will be seen on your table and perhaps obtain me orders, and you shall repay me by protecting my bazaar, and, if you ever want a blotting-paper book, a comforter or such like,

---

[1] An ostrich egg painted in imitation of one painted by Teniers in the possession of the Duke.

employing me, but this egg I am bent upon giving you.

To the Duke of Devonshire.

London: November 21, 1837.

Dearest brother,—Safely delivered and perfectly happy. Everybody tells me that dearest Leveson did well.[1] Granville is very much delighted and almost well.

I found G. at dinner at Court, in hat and feather and diamonds, gayest of the gay and in her element. You know she loves in Courts to shine. My darling Susy as thin as a whipping-post, and Rivers as fat as a partridge; both the greatest dears I have seen for a long time.

I find Queen Victoria perfect in manner, dignity, and grace, with great youthfulness and joyousness. I find a dinner at Court very curious to see, but my bad nature prevailed, and I got so impatient towards eleven that I hardly could bear it.

It is so much more like a Court than any I have seen, and I am spoilt by bobbing in for ten minutes to the Queen's back and cross-stitch at the Tuileries.

William[2] says, a little tipsy and in his impulsive manner: 'I've seen Mr. Ridgeway, and he can't say anything because he knows nothing, but the letters isn't in no ways stopped; all as usual, so I suppose,' and then he looked wistfully at me like a dog.

We sat poor Mary Gloucester and I on either side. The Duchess Suth, G., Lady Durham in a row. Three chairs were called for and placed for Duke Suth, Lords Mulgrave and Durham. We looked like the old game from chapel to church, from church to chapel. She talked almost entirely to the men, but very graciously

[1] He moved the Address.
[2] A footman of the Duke's from the West of Scotland.

and kindly to us. She [1] at whist looks careworn, but all seems smooth.

Why, here's a new view of things. Little Johnny, say some, has been imprudent, over-confident of strength, too Conservative in short. I think so right, and if we do move upon it, upon what noble springs! I think it as politic as right, but I heard of someone going up to one of us and uttering ' You're gone.'

Dearest brother, in reliance upon the Hebrides I don't stop my letter, but hope and trust it will cross you on the road.

To the Duke of Devonshire.

London: November 22, 1837.

I have seen that incomparable man, Mr. Ridgeway. He tells me you will not be here to-day, he thinks, because he is going to send you your letters. So I write. We are most comfortable here ; we want but you.

Johnny's speech has had different effects, and so has one he uttered yesterday, somewhat softening the matter. Duke Sutherland and I liked the first, and object to any backing out of it. My husband thought the first imprudent, and sees no reason for having pledged himself to so much ; it has necessitated the second, and that's just the pity. I think a grand Whig fault is always, like poor Mrs. Bunting, to jump over the saddle, instead of into it, and then, dear Grace, they are obliged to go a little into the dirt to get up afresh.

Rivers and Susy dined at Court yesterday, and she is going to take her baby to the Queen. They were much pleased with the Queen and her civility to them, and Rivers delighted with Lord Melbourne.

Leveson met Lord Ashburton at Lady Harriet Baring's. She immediately said, 'Allow me to introduce to you the future member for North Staffordshire.'

[1] The Duchess of Kent.

Lord Ashburton looked much put out, so it answered to her.

Brother, I think Lord Durham vulgar and familiar. I wish I could see your face. Pray burn this letter.

To Lady Carlisle.

Paris: December 1837.

My dearest sister,—We expect Freddy on Sunday, and are leading *en attendant* a quiet life, though yesterday I dined out for a wonder, at Lord Ailesbury's, where she, Lady Kinnoul, Lady Glengall, Lady Aldborough, Madame de Caraman, and the Princesse Charles de Beauveau, *née* Komar, appeared gorgeous in velvets and satins of various bright hues. The little soirée afterwards was pleasant till the ecstatic moment of release.

Lady Fanny Bruce [1] has just left us in tears, because the carriage came sooner than was expected. She has been taking her dancing lesson with Susy Osborne. She is the most clever, funny little thing, the image of Bruce.

Oswald is slow, heavy, and sleepy, but there is something kind and worthy about him, that makes one feel as one does when the dogs grow old. I hope he will brighten up.

To Lady Carlisle.

Paris: December 25, 1837.

My own dearest sister,—After I have wished you a merry Christmas I must tell you that Granville continues well. The weather is like spring, as mild and warm. We have resumed our early drives.

Give my love and thanks to your Duchess. Tell

---

[1] A daughter of Lord Elgin. She married in 1855 Mr. Baillie of Dochfour.

252 LETTERS OF HARRIET COUNTESS GRANVILLE 1837

her I will take care that her box is delivered, also that
the feud seems much composed between the Princesses,[1]
and is not now visible to the naked eye, though spectacles see *gêne* and coldness that did not exist in former
times. Also that I gave her message to Guizot.

We are all charmed with Lady Abercorn, she is so
unaffected, gay, and graceful. Marie and Dody like
Lady Georgiana, and say that she is amusing and original.
The Duke[2] is better, calls our Harcourt 'Dearest Lizzy'
before company, which causes surprise.

George Harcourt says: 'Are you acquainted with
Baron Hügel?' 'Yes.'

'He is a most delightful person, Elizabeth knows
him well.' 'Oh.'

'We have been seeing him daily since you left
us.' 'Oh.'

TO LADY CARLISLE.

Paris: December 29, 1837.

My dearest, dear sister,—We are expecting the
Sutherlands to-day or to-morrow. I shall give you a
true account of everything we do and that she does,
knowing how interesting is all that concerns them.

I think Mme. de Shönbourg a good deal sobered,
and Paris on the whole is quite a different arena from
what it was last year. No gaiety going on of any sort
or kind. Mme. de Delmar, confined to her sick room,
will not open her house. The French are still less
coming than usual for various reasons, and now the
very annoying melancholy failure at Constantine. The
ridicule thrown, *entre nous*, not without reason, upon the
very ridiculous telegraphic account of it. Alarm at
what Thiers may do, the uncertainty of what will be
when the Chambers meet, an unusual quantity of

---

[1] Lieven and Schönbourg.   [2] Of Bedford.

private mournings.   Charles the Tenth[1] only just beginning to subside, and the Duc d'Angoulême's death
expected, not to mention Naples and Austria.   All
these very various causes have given the greatest
possible flatness to soirées ; nothing like a ball has
been dreamt of.   Tufiakin had promised to give one
on the 28th, but the Carlist ladies of his acquaintance
prevented him.   And now comes the extraordinary
rise of the Seine to keep us still quieter.   This side
of the Faubourg St. Germain is almost impassable,
and Mme. Appony has put off an immense rout which
she was to have had on Monday.   She writes : ' Une
file de voiture à terre est bien désagréable, mais une
file à l'eau serait trop fort.'

[1] He died on November 6, 1886.

1833

To Lady Carlisle.

Paris: January 1, 1838.

My own dear sister,—Many happy returns to you and yours.

Our Bazaar has taken its *élan* and is prospering wonderfully. It is really extremely pretty. Every day brings new customers to purchase and to place their works, which they are delighted to do for their own charitable purposes, allowing Miss Coppinger the third of the profit of each article sold. She has for some days past never sold for less than twenty francs, and two days for forty and fifty.

Paris is going to be *insoutenable*, even for me, as the Tuileries and the Duchess of Orleans are going to put forth all their energies two or three times a week. All the pleasant people are going away. The Cawdors next week, the Abercorns this, and last not least the boys must go soon.

Leveson fond of going, as my brother observes, took a turn last night. Dinner at Betty Harcourt's; to parties at Lieven's and Flahault's, then to the Salon to see its close, and lastly to Delmar's. He is a snug darling, always ambulating, his wheels making no noise, but doing their work well.

God bless you, my dearest. Mrs. White of East Florida comes to the ball; Mrs. White, Lady Harriet d'Orsay's sister, has been to a soirée, and is coming to the ball—nice-looking, like her sister, without

the beauty. Mrs. Henry White, lovely, appeared last
Friday and is coming to the ball; Madame d'Auchamp,
Lady Julia's *protégée*, ditto.

To Lady Carlisle.

Paris: January 5, 1838.

Most dear sister,—Susy is much better than I could
have hoped, and in her most joyous spirits. She and
Georgy are in such enchantment at being together.
Baba and George Pitt are bosom friends, and have not
yet quarrelled once. Miss Pitt,[1] an immense success in
society, is thought beautiful, is most gracious, not in
the least shy, but is at present somewhat stormy in
domestic life. The baby is thought a prodigy. I do
not admire her much. There never was such delight
as having them all!

We frequent the Opera. On Wednesday all went to
the Delmar concert, and yesterday to the Locke *tableaux*.
The sisters ravished. Rivers in despair; but then, as
Susy says, 'he can go home,' and so he does.

Lady Wallscourt, handsome as Rubens's wife, with
H. Greville and Mrs. Locke's little girl.[2] Miss Raikes
beautiful, they all declare, as Mme. de la Vallière, hair
down, eyes up, at the foot of the cross. H. Greville
Louis XIV., Mrs. Locke an attendant nun. Antonin
and Mrs. George Rose flashed in the pan—that is, they
did not look quite as beautiful as they were expected.
He, as Lord Leicester, not distinguished enough; she,
as Amy Robsart, looked on the ground instead of at
Antonin, a modesty which is said to be only in that
excess in a *tableau*, where alone it was misplaced.
But the perfection came last. Mrs. Locke,[3] Lucy
of Lammermoor, having just signed her contract,
Douglas as Ravensworth pointing at it. H. Greville the

---

[1] Now Mrs. Oldfield. [2] Now Lady Walsingham.

[3] The widow of Mr. Locke, who was drowned in the Lake of Como.

other man. Miss Raikes, Lady Aston. Richelieu was *aux anges*, like the *malin bossu*. Susy, as in her maiden days, amused and delighted with him. 'Comme on est froid! On n'applaudit pas. Je n'ai entendu que Mme. de Poix. Quand elle a vu Miss Raikes, elle l'a prise pour Antonin, et elle a crié, "Ah, il est charmant; mais comme cela change : je ne l'aurais pas reconnu."'

We have no new arrivals but the Fitzharrises.[1]

To Lady Carlisle.

Paris : January 1838.

Most dear sister,—We are all occupied with the sad news of this morning. The Italian Opera burnt down last night. Severini, Robert's partner, in an access of *désespoir*, flung himself in the middle of the flames and perished. The fire began an hour after the house was empty, and there was no wind. Otherwise the loss of life and property would have been incalculable. It is supposed to have arisen from a beam catching fire from over-heated calorifers. Kulbach worked till five this morning, harnessed to a rope, handing buckets. Pray send this scrap to my brother, as he may wish to know about it.

Freddy starts this evening for Oxford, and leaves his fortunate parents at the Duchess of Orleans' first ball, of which I will send you an account by the next courier.

To Lady Carlisle.

Paris: January 12, 1838.

Most dear sister,—What a time since I have written! I have not been ill, but exceedingly unwell, which during the time and since made me feel quite incapable of anything.

All our English, I mean of one sort, will, I suppose,

---

[1] Lord Fitzharris succeeded his father as third Earl of Malmesbury in 1841. He was twice Minister for Foreign Affairs.

rush for the meeting. When Lady E. Harcourt goes,
all the men in Paris will die, 'not really, my dear.'
The Duc de Bauffremont and Maurice are quite victims,
it is said. Lady Norreys is less liked than her mother.
She affronts the women, and men are first elated, then
angry, but even Antoninus Pius says, 'C'est une honnête
femme.' Lady Clanricarde's departure will kill only
Mme. de Lieven and me. She has been perfect, charming, but avoiding the great world, not going to balls or
great affairs, but it is a loss for *intimité*, talk, and constant sociability not be described.

I went yesterday to the Duchesse d'Orléans; a tiny
music. The King and Granville sat whispering behind
a screen. The Duc d'Orléans said to me, 'A subject
for H. B.' The Duke was in such wild spirits that
some said a little O. was in prospect. Some that at his
dinner he had indulged and become a little elated.
Lady Clanricarde, 'It is only that he likes giggling all
night with Clanricarde.'

We are all *émerveillés* and enchanted with Lord
Durham's appointment [1]—so clever, so skilful to make
such a neat hit at such a distant mark, and then (*vide*
' Examiner,' the clever ' Examiner '), to be rewarded and
more than repaid by such extravagant, such unbounded
praise. Nothing can be more edifying and entertaining.
There never was such a step, I think, for the security
of the present Government.

We never hear the Queen talked of—a good sign.

Lord Grey writes to Mme. de Lieven in the very
blackest humour. Ellice that a Garter and Dukedom
will be nothing of a reward to Lord Durham.

[1] To Canada.

To Lord Leveson and Lady Carlisle.

Paris: January 1838.

Dearest Leveson,—We regret you more than words can say.

We have done little; had an immense Friday; quantities of Carlists.

Wednesday a dinner. Mr. Kemble and Adelaide, two Mrs. Lockes, Lady Wallscourt, Douglas, Bruce, De Candia,[1] Poniatowski, Belgiojoso, Greville, and Nicolas Pahlen. It was Belgiojoso's generous proposal to *improviser* a little concert for us. We then asked him to dine. Marras is to come and Miss Kemble will sing. Lady Norreys will regret having left us.

Dearest sister,—Forgive economy; I have no more stuff in me. There is a grand war—Flahault *versus* Baudrand. Nobody knows if the former will remain in the Duke of Orleans' household.

Bruce is lower than low. He enjoys nothing and looks wretchedly ill. In vain did Lady Harriet Galway aim all her charms at him.

To Lady Carlisle.

Paris: May 31, 1838.

Dearest sister,—Only one line to thank you for all your kindness and constant letters.

The loss[2] is irreparable. There were few as much loved as she was.

Give my love to dearest Leveson. Tell him his dear letter came from Mistley and cheered me, and that I read it when in very severe pain. You will be glad to hear that I am quite relieved, and hope to be quite well in a few days, but I have suffered extremely.

Friday.—My dear, dearest sister. I felt very much

---

[1] The celebrated tenor, who took the name of Mario when he went on the stage.

[2] Lady Harrowby died on May 18, 1838.

affected yesterday by a letter from Georgiana Wortley and a bracelet with dearest Lady Harrowby's hair. I think every day gives me a sadder and deeper regret. I have trouble in struggling against nervous feelings of all sorts.

To LADY CARLISLE.

Paris: June 16, 1838.

Dearest of sisters,—Thank your dearest Duchess for her kindness about Marras, who is grateful and enchanted.

Soult[1] is to have a large following. Ducs de Valençay and Vicense, Messrs. de Champlatreux, Bassano, and Morny. It will be well done. His character is to be *très avare, très avide,* and *très magnifique.* So he will fleece Louis Philippe and then flare away.

I enclose a drawing of St. Cloud for your *rente.* The trees are too green, but we think the building beautifully done.

To LADY CARLISLE.

Paris: June 19, 1838.

My dearest sister,—What can I tell you? Sir Robert and Lady Harland dined here yesterday, and I was delighted to see her again. The slow low voice and occasionally closing her eyes had its old effect of calming my nerves. We talked of Wherstead and Felixtowe, and remembrances vivid and sad came, but not in a painful or agitating manner.

We are just setting out, Dody Hayes, Baby and I, for Longchamps.[2] At two Baba and I dine there, upon mutton chops and boiled lettuce, stewed prunes and strawberries. The day is enchanting. Our husbands ride there late. Mme. de Lieven never misses, whether we are there or not. Georgy and I have two or three

---

[1] He was sent as Special Ambassador to London for the Coronation.
[2] Lady Granville had hired a cottage at Longchamps.

uninterrupted hours for the 'Life of Wilberforce,' which she reads while I stitch.

Chalmers preached the finest sermon that ever was heard yesterday. Georgy and Fullerton were there. I did not dare go. It was an immense sacrifice, but Georgy says I could not have stood it. The crowd and heat were beyond anything. But more beautiful, more right and judicious—indulgent—energy and ardour, yet nothing overstrained or that the most worldly could cavil at. He goes immediately. Mrs. Chalmers says, 'It is of no use staying. The *savants* don't understand the Doctor's language, and he don't understand theirs.' She said this to Georgy at a most curious collection of people at dear Lady Elgin's the other evening—the Chalmers, old Mme. de Vaudreuil *douairière*, Miss Marlay, Messrs. Mignet, Broglie, and Guizot.

To LADY CARLISLE.

Paris : June 26, 1838.

My dearest sister,—We shall be most happy to receive Harry.[1]

I have been spending my morning at Longchamps. The Apponys came to us there, Mme. de Lieven and Marie Menzingen, Lady Acton and her beautiful boy,[2] like Lawrence's picture of young Lambton and the infant John in some 'Holy Family.'

We walked, ate strawberries, and tried to cheer up Mme. de Lieven—a difficult task, as she dreads the coming months when all her friends will have left Paris, and yet can make no plan to take her out of it.

The Duc de Broglie has just been to bid us good-bye. Everybody is going or gone.

[1] Lady Carlisle's youngest son, appointed Attaché at Paris.
[2] The present Lord Acton.

To the Duke of Devonshire.

Paris: July 2, 1838.

You must know that it is quite impossible to make you sensible of the pleasure of hearing from you this morning. It was quite delightful, and Lieven was allowed a peep at the sketch. She bids me tell you she adores you, and that you are the only person capable of giving a proper notion and vivid description of such things.[1] For where is Lieven's heart and what is her absorbing interest? Why Precedence, my dear, who first, who last, who here, who there, and she studied the page intensely. 'Mais, ma chère, où est donc Pozzo et les Strogonoff? Mais votre frère est un homme adorable. Voilà Paul.[2] Dites-lui combien je suis touché.'

We are so pleased to hear from all how magnificent, beautiful, and heart-stirring it was. Little Miss Schwarzenberg over the way sent me a miniature of her *belle-sœur*, and very like John Ponsonby it was. My dearest dear D., what a happy thought was the gallery on the wall![3] All the French papers are full of it.

What a pleasant thought it is that my darling Susy is three doors from you at Kemp!

We go on Tuesday, the 10th. A new road, shorter, avoiding Lyons and the Jura, dipping perpendicularly down la Dent du Chat into hot little Aix bason. Oh, that you could be tempted! God bless you.

Let me just say that two little books you gave me were the greatest pleasure and comfort to me whilst I was sick. I am quite well now, only rather wishy-washy.

To Lady Carlisle.

Paris: July 9, 1838.

My dearest sister,—A thousand thanks for your letter. Your son is most amiable and a great addition.

---

[1] The Queen's Coronation. [2] Her son.

[3] Of Devonshire House.

His shyness is not perceptible, and does not seem to take from his enjoyment of society. Lord Milton's son is arrived, and I think him a charming boy. He and Harry are now amusing Granville, Fullerton, and Henry Greville with the latest news of London and the Coronation. We are told that Mr. Ellice is to be here some time. I believe he arrives this week—such a catch for Mme. de Lieven! Mme. de Schönbourg, too, is on her little legs again, quite well. Dined at Auteuil yesterday.

Monday.—We are still in suspense about our day, because Aston, Leveson, Freddy, and the *fourgon* are all somewhere, but neither here nor there, and we must see what's what before we decide.

I fear that the journey will be disagreeable to dearest Leveson, and I am brought to be glad that Mme. de Menou, a clever old favourite of his, the two beautiful Spaniards, Mesdames Narvaez and Quintana, and the Ellices are all going to wash in sulphur with us. I have no doubt of Freddy's enjoyment. We shall probably start on Saturday.

A thousand thanks for your kindness in having Charles depicted. Tremendously like they are, your Duchess and all, but not a resemblance that gladdens the posers.

On Saturday we took Harry to Madame Appony's reception at Auteuil to launch him in a French house.

To Lady Carlisle.

Paris: July 14, 1838.

Tall, big Freddy is arrived. He gives delicious accounts of you all.

What beautiful things Stafford House has done! The Liliputian christening is quite ravishing. It is a great pleasure to hear Aston. He took bird's-eye views of all, but, like me, shuns actual practical larking. Harry seems pleased and gets on very well in sociey.

To-day he has to stand the fire of Schönbourg and Caramania, who dine here. He is reckoned uncommonly
good-looking, and would be very handsome if he would
not stoop in a way that inclines me to take a whip.
Liz is a poker in comparison. I mean when I return
to take it in hand with your permission.

To the Duke of Devonshire.

Paris : July 21, 1838.

At nine this morning the Fullertons and Baba set
out. They wait one day at Chambery, so as to arrive
the day after us at Aix.

Our weather is quite delicious. We waited long
enough to have all the newest news from the Bear,[1] who
dined here yesterday, and whose arrival saves Mme. de
Lieven, who was in a state of utter discomfiture. She
now hopes with him, Aston, and Harry—Versailles
occasionally and Longchamps daily—to get through
the hot months.

I really believe a little douching and bathing is the
best possible thing, where no mischief is apparent and
to prevent any arising. I do not like the idea of
quaffing the hot sulphur myself, but Doctor Richard
insists, and with Doctor Robert to watch I mean to
begin immediately.

We are all well. Granville uncommonly so. Fullerton, as he always is, extremely revived and exhilarated by a plan and a lark; he and Freddy intending
to go to Milan, Venice, etc

To Lady Carlisle.

Aix-les-Bains : July 24, 1838.

We arrived here at nine o'clock yesterday evening,
after a vey delightful journey. The last part of our
journey from Bourg to Bellay, crossing the Dent du

[1] The Right Hon. Edward Ellice.

Chat—most beautiful—all that river and rock can do from Bellay to Yenne ; and then scenery a little in the style of the Jura, with more steep and winding ascent and descent. At the very top of the mountain a view of the little Lac de Bourget below, and the snow-mountains of the Dauphiné beyond. Here we found a charming little house, taken for us by the Ellices, perfectly clean, quiet, and cool, and excellent beds. The Fullertons are at Chambery ; we expect them to-day. They have apartments in this house. We are told that the town is full of Lyons tradespeople and few acquaintances. Freddy is just come back from the Ellice family, where he found Marion, the eldest girl, with her hair curling over her shoulders and a large, flat, wide, straw hat like a parasol. 'More beautiful than any girl he ever saw.' He was quite *ému* with his admiration. We have had a visit from our Doctor Vidal, who is now undergoing an interview with Doctor Robert, who will view him with the most profound contempt, as he is the best but most twaddling of his kind, and will not be up to any one long word or ingenious speculation offered to him.

I have not time to write to Brighton. Will you have the kindness to send this foolscap edition of our journey to Susy ; and will you, my dearest child, hand it on to D. on the neighbouring balcony ; and will you, my dearest brother, bring me the answers *en personne* ?

To Lady Carlisle.

Aix: August 9, 1838.

Dearest of sisters,—You are an excellent correspondent, but you must allow for me. We are *arrosés*, eat and drink a quantity, drive in a very rough *char-à-bancs*, and swim upon a very beautiful lake ; occasionally meet John Gréfulhe looking black and bilious, and the Ellice girls, who bring us butterflies, and butter of their own making. Occasional visits to and from Mmes. dc Menou and Navarres.

We never hear from Leveson. How I long to have him at Paris! Give him my best love and tell him that I do not write, as I can only return fire from hence. The essential facts and occupations here he will know from you, that the *douches* agree, and that we set out for Geneva on the 15th.

You never mention a possibility of your Paris visit. If you wish for quiet, you can always command it there. If you wish for *fêtes* and *spectacles*, there are to be many on the occasion of the christening of the child that is hoped for on the 15th. Mme. de Lieven tells me to-day he is to be called Comte de Paris, and that his *marraine* is to be la Ville de Paris. She adds: 'Représentée, je suppose, par Mme. de Rambuteau.'

I never knew anything like the rush to Italy, and I believe we shall have very few compatriots of those we wish for or those we dread for the *Carnaval*.

I have taken on Longchamps till the 1st of November, so that I shall have much rural enjoyment even at Paris, and hope to show it to you.

To LADY CARLISLE.

Berne: August 28, 1838.

Dearest of sisters,—Yesterday, to our great joy, D. arrived here in high health and spirits. He goes to Thun and does the Oberland with us, and leaves us at Neufchatel to hunt Blanche.

We shall be in Paris on the 12th. Lord Holland fears that no movement *accéléré* will bring them there before a later period of the month. The pleasure of seeing him is a very great one to us.

All Paris is *en émoi* at its little Count. I am so glad of a joy for the Queen and the poor *accouchée* herself, who seems to have suffered much. Excellent account of Susy and her *dauphin*.

D. went to Thun this morning, where Master Fullerton will receive him.

To Lady Rivers and Lady Carlisle.

Berne : September 4, 1838.

My dearest Susy,—I have so little time that I must write this letter to you and your aunt G. I found here a letter from that dearest Yorkshire lady, giving me the delicious account she had just received from you, and telling me of the Naworth [1] company.

My news is for you both. Our days in Oberland have been enchanting. Such country I had never dreamed of, the finest possible weather and perfectly good health. I wish you to imagine me coming down a steep rocky path, fit only for goats, in a chair carried by two men, quite at my ease, looking at a glacier or a snow mountain, or a cascade, or a châlet, listening to three little peasant girls, all youdling to perfection in parts ; dining in clean, excellent inns, looking upon all these glories, sunsets, full moon.

So enchanted is my brother that at nine o'clock yesterday morning he embarked at Thun on the steam-boat to go back to Interlaken. Himself and his doctor, with two footmen and Boney, in blouses and belts and straw hats and knapsacks on their backs, intend to walk from thence to Brienz, Meiringen, etc., to see the fall of the Giessbach, and to return after this romantic episode to Thun. We go to-day to Morat, to-morrow to Neufchatel, and then by very slow journeys reach Paris on the 12th.

Mme. de Lieven writes from Paris : ' J'ai appris des détails sur les couches. D'abord, les témoins ont vu

---

[1] Naworth Castle, Lord Carlisle's Border castle in Cumberland.

tout, comme aux couches de la Duchesse de Berri. Il n'y a pas eu moyen de douter. Imaginez, outre la famille, six témoins. Ensuite, dès que l'enfant a été né, tout le monde est allé le voir laver, habiller, et personne, personne n'est resté avec la Princesse que ses deux femmes de chambre. Elle a voulu changer de lit, et l'a fait bien bassiner. En conséquence de quoi, elle n'y était pas depuis deux minutes qu'une horrible hémorragie est survenue. On a crié, appelé, on l'a couverte de glaces, on a arrêté l'hémorragie; après cela est survenue une atonie complète, et pendant une demi-heure on l'a cru morte. On dit que le Duc d'Orléans était dans une angoisse inexprimable. Maintenant tout est bien. Le petit prince, que la Reine appelait hier Louis-Philippe, est énorme, parfaitement constitué, et ressemblant, à ce qu'elle dit, tout-à-fait à la mère.'

Here is Mr. Edgcumbe, looking very like the Hague. We have met no acquaintance on our route except Mr. Labouchere and his wife. Mme. de Jumilhac is perched upon the roof of this hotel.

Now, my dear relations, forgive me this once for my double shot.

To Lady Carlisle.

Dijon: September 9, 1838.

My most dear sister,—Here we are, reposing a whole day, waiting for Georgy, Baba, and G. Stewart, who remained a day after us at Neufchatel.

The Hollands intend being at Paris almost as soon as we are, and I delight in the thought of seeing him. I know not how she and Princesse Lieven will put up their horses together, but I hope well, and Mme. de Lieven so pines for society and politicians to talk to that I think it ensures keeping the peace, especially if the trial is not very long.

Freddy is much amused and pleased at Milan. Fullerton rather disappointed.

It is amusing to look out of the inn window and see the comers and goers.

A most extraordinary looking set-out—a chariot, the blinds down in mid-day, an earl's coronet, followed by an open carriage with two men and two women in it, the oddest-looking I ever saw. Countess of Clare?

A very dandy courier, chariot and four, two young gentlemen, extremely *à leur aise*, Walewski and Auguste de Morny.

The Beauffremonts.

A woman in a short yellow gown, black riband round her head, running rapidly past the window, calling out 'Courage, courage!' to a girl of four running by her side, again and again. 'Une femme qui gagne son pain. Elle court six fois d'une porte de la ville à l'autre. Elle parcourt la France comme ça. Il y a trois mois qu'elle a fait cette course; elle est enceinte et tout prête d'accoucher.' In spite of reason and the doctor, we gave the poor exhausted creature some money, so did others, and she danced across the street as nimbly as possible. She was extremely ugly and ungraceful. If a beauty was to run, she might get a great deal. The poor little girl was much fatigued.

Then all the Dijonites in their Sunday dresses, but no Georgy as yet.

To the Duke of Devonshire.

Dijon: September 9, 1838.

I do not know where to begin, having so many remarks to make. They must come promiscuous, as Mrs. Ridgway used to say.

From Morat to Neufchatel by steam was immense enjoyment. The Lake much less pretty, the boat empty, but the gliding along, the ease, the lights and shades on water and view of Ewardtown [1] made it very enchanting.

She mourned over you, but rejoiced over your gift, and is more happy, grateful, and gratified than is to be said. The Alps cheated us to an unheard-of degree, but *en revanche* the dinner, the view, the cleanliness, the quiet. Yet eighteen francs for four candles is uncommon, and the rest in proportion.

Granville and I came on with the Doctor the next day, your paper in my hand. The sun shining, the day beautiful. The views of the lake in ascending to Rochefort! The mountain streams! Châlets in valleys like Derbyshire!

The hill at Salines! so truly called the ill by our doctor. Was there ever such a one? We walked down it, and my knees and legs ached, and I really thought I should have cried. But Dôle made up for everything. What a perfect inn, like the old château of a friend, and a dinner, and tea-things, and beds all incomparable!

Here we have rested at a good inn, only rather dirty. To-morrow we sleep at Montbard. Dody at Avallon, and we meet the next day at Sens.

Mme. de Lieven writes from Paris, very low and unwell. The Ludolfs are coming to us, and the Buteras are going to London. Madame has written to press Madame de Flahault to return.

Fullerton is less pleased than Freddy. They have much company; visits and routs instead of pageants. The Coronation will, I hope, make up to him. As yet they see only the scaffoldings.

Lord Holland wrote on the 4th: 'We start to-morrow, an expression with us more significative of fear than ardour.'

Toothachy and tired, I have been writing this letter

---

[1] Melle. Eward resided at Neufchatel.

to you against the stream, that you may be induced to send me one of your delicious letters, even if you have to hark back from the Oberland.

The weather is all dimmed and chilled and we have fires every evening.

Susy writes me most excellent accounts of herself. She is expecting Harriet Pitt, who has been charmed with her *séjour* at Windsor.

To Lady Carlisle.

Longchamps: Sept. 14, 1838.

We arrived at Paris yesterday, my dearest sister, all in excellent health, and found letters from all parts of the world. From D. at Entlebuch, going to cross the St. Gothard, desiring his letters to be directed to Geneva, where I suppose he intends to find Blanche. From Freddy, having enjoyed much with some disappointment. Sir F. Lamb, as rude as a bear, occupies much of his letter. The *couronnement* very superior as a spectacle to ours. The Emperor less *crétin* than he is in general supposed to be. I begin to think a jewel of a sovereign, *magnifique*, grand in matters of representation, liberal and humane in acts of mercy. The amnesty is better than most things done by his *semblables*, and everybody admires, though many grudge him the admiration.

The first person I saw on arriving was your dear boy, quite well again. Granville is very desirous that I should tell you that Aston is quite delighted with him *sous tous les rapports*—intelligent, diligent, attentive, besides being most amiable.

To Lady Carlisle.

Paris: September 1838.

Now what have I got to say? Lord Holland is rather low, and she is suffering again, confined to her couch with the rubber employed again. She says it is

the fatigue of the journey. I say it is such a dinner as
I never saw anybody eat before. She came here on
Monday evening. Mme. de Schönbourg, Lady Sandwich,
Theresa were very civil to her. Molé *très empressé
même.*

Madame de Lieven and she are great friends. 'Ma
chère, j'étais chez elle. Il y avait Mme. Durazzo, Molé,
Humboldt. On annonce Pasquier. Elle a l'air tout
charmé, tout flatté. Elle me dit: "Restez, je vous supplie;
causez avec le Chancelier." Je résiste; elle m'implore
de ne pas l'abandonner. Je cède. Pas plutôt assise avec
tout cet entourage qui nous regarde, qu'elle laisse
tomber son sac. Elle me tape sur l'épaule: " Pick
it up, my dear ; pick it up "—et moi, tout étonnée en
bonne bête, me plongeant sur le tapis pour ramasser ses
chiffons.' Is not this a true and incomparable Holly-ism,
taking out of Lieven's mouth the taste of the little
flutter at the visits and *besoin* of her support, by treating
her like Antonio, and showing off, what I believe never
was seen before, Mme. de Lieven as a humble companion?

Yesterday the Schönbourgs, Listers, George Villiers
and Mr. Sneyd dined here, and sky-rockets and Catherine
wheels were a joke to us. I never knew anything like
the animation of a talk between the two *prima donnas.*
Sir George looks thin and pale, but is in excellent
spirits, as Lady H. Baring joins us to-day.

Lord Holland had a long conversation with the
King at the Tuileries, and I hear he intends a surprise to
go to meet them the day they are at Versailles. I do not
think the to-be-astonished are pleased in proportion.

To Lady Carlisle.

Paris: September 25, 1838.

Dearest of sisters,—We were much shocked yesterday at hearing of the melancholy termination of poor
Madame de Broglie's illness. The account of her death

reached Paris yesterday, and her loss to all those connected with her, to her husband and children and many
attached friends, to numbers to whom she was a constant
dispenser of every sort of charity and kindness, is not
to be calculated. She really was an angel on earth.
She had the same constitution as her brother, and had
suffered latterly a great deal. Poor Mme. d'Haussonville [1] is travelling in Italy and with child.

The Listers and George Villiers are very gay and
agreeable, and Theresa is in greater beauty, health,
and spirits than I ever saw her. Her boy [2] is perfectly
beautiful, and seems the most charming child—wonderful abilities, without a grain of pertness or prodigy-ism,
and a tenderness and gentleness of manner most attractive. But he looks extremely delicate, and I should
only fear his mother not being quite aware of how
much care is required. Perhaps I only say this
because she is not nervous or foolish, as I should be.

To the Duke of Devonshire.

Paris : October 16, 1838.

How shall I begin? First my thanks for your two
most delightful letters and for the gentian, which lies
in a little book with some small blue relatives, gathered
in the Val de Travers.

Cliffords remained here a week, and are gone on to
Nice, all seeming well and in good spirits. Mme. de
Lieven said Bella was a very fine girl, which I repeated
to them to their great satisfaction.

Mrs. Cavendish and Richard arrived in a dreadful
fuss, to go or not to go. They have been at Versailles
a week, returned yesterday, have determined upon
remaining here, and a house in the Allée d'Antin is
taken for them, Lord Lismore,[3] and the Howards.

---

[1] The Duchesse de Broglie's daughter.
[2] Now Sir Villiers Lister.
[3] Mrs. Cavendish's brother.

Five o'clock.—Oh, how difficult to write! Look at the Green Room.—Lieven and G. whispering; Lord Bristol rising in his stirrups and clearing his throat before them, but they don't seem to perceive him; Mme. de Stackelberg and I in each other's arms, congratulating, the Pope having sent the dispensation for her daughter's marriage.

The Hollands drop in to dinner or tea daily, and sprinkled with Rogers, Macaulay, Lieven, Schönbourg, Molé, Pasquier, and Decazes, we contrive to get up a little society for them. God bless you.

To Lady Carlisle.

Paris: November 1838.

Yesterday the Burghershes and Buccleuchs, who all leave Paris to-morrow, dined here with the Schönbourgs, Madame de Caraman, and Nicolas Pahlen. The little Duchess is remarkably pleasant, as merry as ever, and as round as a ball, with a charming countenance, and I feel, as Tchann says, ' Elle me plaît extrêmement, et si vous me fâchez, je dirai qu'elle est jolie.'. The Duke looked ému at C. C.'s[1] attentions, and at last I heard him pressing her to visit them at Dalkeith. I think some Scotch laird may take a fancy.

All Paris is going to-morrow to see the procession of poor Maréchal Lobau's funeral pass through the Place Vendôme and the Rue de Rivoli. He is much regretted, and was beloved and respected by all who knew him.

Granville has received by post a letter in the most animated strain against Lord Durham from Lord Brougham.

[1] Césarine de Caraman.

To the Duke of Devonshire.

Paris: November 18, 1838.

Your delightful letter came all alive from Venice.
You will soon be followed by those[1] whom it gave me
so much pleasure to have for a few happy, very happy,
days here. I cannot say what it was to me to see
dearest G. so strong and well, with more alacrity and
zest about her than anybody, for everything from a rout
to the Corniche. They wrote last from Nice, well and
delighted. They were to remain with the Sutherlands
a week or two at Florence. They will talk to you
of what we are all most anxious about, poor Mme. de
Lieven. I will not bore you with repeating what they
will tell you in detail, but what is beyond measure
desirable is that an impression in her favour should be
made upon 'Vraiment,' who has behaved shamefully.

Oh! do I know the eyes and backbone of sight-
seeing? and am I not going a round of *ateliers* to-morrow morning with Mons. de Vatry?

Paris is quite stagnant. The liveliest thing known
for a long time in it is now beginning, as the clock
strikes ten. Mlle. Rachel, a very ugly girl, reading
speeches out of Racine to Monsieur de Delmar. The
loveliest woman, Mme. de Schwarzenberg, sets out for
Vienna to-morrow. Our beauties are Lady Harriet
d'Orsay, Mrs. Henry White, a very pretty daughter of
Edward Bligh, and a Miss Dickinson, not forgetting
Misses McDonald, Purvis, Ellis.

Richard Cavendish does not make up to anybody,
but tends his mother, walks the streets, and buys books
with Fullerton at the stalls. Lord Castlereagh sits in
the orchestra at the Opera, and appears little elsewhere.
I think him very pleasing. Last night at the Odéon, old
'Don Giovanni.' Grisi, Persiani, Albertazzi, Tamburini,

---

[1] Lord and Lady Carlisle, who were returning from Italy.

Rubini, Lablache enchanted me. Lord J. Russell[1] is at Cassiobury with his children and Miss Lister, but intends resuming his duties when Parliament meets.

To Lady Carlisle.

Paris: November 30, 1838.

I left you yesterday in a hurry because Aston, Fullerton, and Marie Menzingen were waiting to go with me to see the bronze gates for the Madeleine, beautiful beyond description, the work of Monsieur Triqueti, husband of Miss Forster, *née* Bankes—that is, her mother was. You will see at Florence the original of this most perfect imitation. I then showed Marie the giraffe, *le palais des singes*, the 'Jardin des Plantes,' which this poor maid of honour had never seen. She and Mme. de Lieven, Lady Burghersh,[2] who is in manner, talk, and countenance most attractive, dined here. Also Lords Jocelyn and Castlereagh, Georges d'Harcourt and Castellane. If Lord Castlereagh would cut off his long hair, and take off his large turquoise ornaments, fastened with long diamond chains, making him look like a pane of a jeweller's shop-window, he would be better than most others in conversation. Lord Jocelyn is merry and good-humoured.

I have just received a letter from the Duchess[3] at Chambery. They have paid a long visit to Monsieur de Lamartine, and seem to have been mutually much pleased. Long beards, recitations of verses ; much that would have made me prefer the highway. But I am a spoon, though I would go a great way to hear such a poem as 'Saul and David' read by Mr. Milnes, not written by him. I write like Miss Bates. We went last night to see Rachel, and don't feel enthusiastic. I think some things very good, but she has no natural attraction, no beauty, feeling, nor *entraînement*.

[1] Had just lost his first wife. Miss Lister was her sister.
[2] Afterwards Lady Westmorland.   [3] Of Sutherland.

Thursday.—I am just come from an immense dinner at the Duke of Orleans—*magnifique*, the best *ordonné* in every way, and plenty of kings and queens.

After dinner, we sat listening to Persiani, Cinti, and Duprez. The O.'s were more gracious than words can say. They say the Duchess is jealous. I do not see any sign. I think it is that all the women hope she is. They tell that one day he was spying at Madame Le Hon, and that the Duchess at length, unable to brook it, put a little hand gently upon the arm that held the *lorgnette*, and said, ' Mon ami, ce n'est ni poli pour elle, ni aimable pour moi.'

Poor Lady John Russell's death is very melancholy. Spencer Cowper writes to Leveson that when Lord John was told only of danger he fell down as if dead. Madame de Lieven is in a most melancholy state. She received suddenly the account of her son's death from her banker. Monsieur de Lieven has known it since the sixth of July, and never noticed it in any way.

To the Duke of Devonshire.

Paris: December 13, 1838.

We are living a life of entire repose, bought at the price of anxiety and misery to numbers. Mme. de Mortemart is as ill as possible. The news of the Duchesse de Wurtemberg [1] is so bad that the King has put off Granville, who was to have presented thirty Englishmen this evening. Mme. de Delmar better, but still in a very weak state.

16th.—The Duc de Nemours is gone to Genoa. It is reported here that the Duchesse de Wurtemberg is dead, but the fact not yet broken to the Queen.

I will try to send you something beyond a sheet of bulletins, but it is difficult to shake off the atmosphere of sickness and anxiety.

[1] Louis Philippe's daughter.

Under the present circumstances there is nothing but dinner society, and a few lists will tell you what that is composed of. On Friday we had Lord Lyttelton, Fitzharding Berkeley, young Herries, Mr. Knox, Lord Northland's son, Captain Home Purvis, and this with Duff, Freddy, and the attachments, gave us the appearance of a school or college *réunion*. If Lord Lyttelton was more aware of what he is about, whom he is talking to, if he was more master of his limbs and tongue, and minded his stops, we should be able to get at the quantity of excellent stuff of all kinds which I am sure is in him. He has dined here twice, and I am anxious to see as much of him as possible.

Le Hon [1] has just heard from Molé that the Duchesse de Wurtemberg is not dead, but the account was as bad as possible. Poor Mme. Henri de Mortemart died the night before last.

To Lady Carlisle.

Paris : December 1838.

My beloved sister,—Joy to you for dearest Lord Carlisle's progressive amendment. I had rather stay in a good house with a good doctor than see all the ruins in the world.

We are all much rejoiced at Anne Könneritz having been proposed to at our ball on Friday by Monsieur de Bernstorff.[2] It is a love match and has thrown a romantic glow over the Diplomatic Corps.

Susan is extremely well, and perfectly happy, at Brighton. She has taken her children to the Queen, who gave them beautiful presents—pins and brooches. She prefers Fanny, who they say is the image of me, a hideous wag.

The accounts of the Duchesse de Wurtemberg being

---

[1] Belgian Minister at Paris.
[2] For some years Ambassador in London.

more favourable, at eight this evening I slide or skate to the Tuileries. Neither man nor horse can stand upon the *verglas*.

Lord and Lady Roden have dined with us. She is the most beautiful creature now at forty-five, and charming. Granville was quite smitten.

Tell the Duke and Duchess that it is not to be told how we feast upon pheasants and pineapples, with the greatest *reconnaissance* to them for such welcome gifts.

TO LADY CARLISLE.

Paris: December 1838.

Leveson is with us in excellent spirits, but tired of the world, *surtout* dancing in it; spends most of his evenings at home and flirts with nobody.

Lord Clarendon has settled place, money, everything on Lady Clarendon, and on her death to Lady Maryborough—ruin to the present George were it not that, as I am assured by Lord Harry Vane, who is just arrived, Lady F. Barham[1] and her large fortune are to be his; that Mrs. Villiers had arranged it all with the consent of both parties.

Comte Molé still holds on; some say he cannot long, but I am inclined to think he will. The *séances* at the Chambers are all but blows.

How happy Mme. de Lieven has been made by hearing from her son of the alteration in 'Vraiment's' language and intentions! Pray *liez* yourself—not matrimonially, my dear—with Alexandre de Lieven. I think him a most pleasing and gentlemanlike person, and I was enchanted with his behaviour to his poor mother at the time of his brother's death.

---

[1] Lord Clarendon married Lady F. Barham in June 1839.

1839

To the Duke of Devonshire.

Paris: January 11, 1839.

I have but little time, and I must write a great deal. You will all be happy to hear of the deep gratitude Mme. de Lieven feels for the kindness of your letters, the details so gratifying to her—nothing to add to her pain, and everything to soothe it.[1]

She feels it—naturally deeply—just as you knew her to be, and much more than those who do not see her in these moments, when all is laid open, would ever believe her to be capable of.

Tenderness for whatever called for it in the past, forgetfulness of every cloud, on her knees with torrents of tears, hoping that she had not often given pain, failed in kindness, indulgence.

Then her own peculiarity of nature—no thought of *les apparences*, power of turning soon and eagerly to other objects of interest or curiosity.

All this, the good and the weak side of which no person who knows her but little can measure. That nobody but myself should see it was my great object. I have brought her here; she has the garden to walk in, cheerful rooms, us about her. Marie Menzingen always with Georgy, never in her own little melancholy room.

They only return to the hotel at ten at night, and I mean this to go on till Paul Lieven arrives.

---

[1] Prince Lieven died at Rome on January 10.

She will see people by degrees. Mme. Appony and Pahlen for a minute yesterday, Duchesse de Dino to-day, and so on.

She is *avide* of details; more gratified and grateful for the respect shown him. Of course, dearest brother, your first letter was only seen by me; the second she reads over and over again, kisses it, cries over it. She will be equally pleased with the one I have just received.

She knows nothing of her affairs. She longs for her sons. I wrote myself to Paul yesterday to urge him to come. I trust when he leaves her, Alexandre will come. She insisted upon sending your letter to Paul, and writes now to have it back again that she may never part with it.

Richard [1] goes on very slowly, but there is nothing to alarm in his state. Mme. de Schönbourg is infinitely better. Leveson and Howards leave us next week.

The funeral [2] is at Dreux to-morrow, and all the Royal Family go there to-day.

To Lady Carlisle.

Paris: February 3, 1839.

For some days my time was quite taken up by Madame de Lieven. Then came Leveson's last days here. He set out this morning at the same time as Lord Powerscourt and Lord Norreys, so that the snow, which is now fast falling, will block up two Tories to one Whig; and he will be in such good company, according to his taste, that I am sure he will make himself as snug as possible.

The death of the Duchess-Countess has again closed our doors. You will have heard, probably, from some one on the spot that her last moments were tranquil and free from suffering. I fear the Duke of Sutherland will be much affected by this event.

[1] Cavendish.   [2] Of the Duchesse de Wurtemberg.

The wonderful *coup* of the *portefeuilles repris* and the Chamber dissolved[1] took away our breath at first. They say little Thiers is violent, and that the coalition is all *feu et flamme*, but I am inclined to think that the dread of disturbance will justify this hazardous game, but no one can tell. It is formidable to hear of the new classing of parties, 'le Parti Parlementaire et le Parti de la Cour.' Between the 4th and 10th of March will be the tug, when the elections are made known.

Let me talk of the delight of your letters from Rome. Your sights must be enchanting. I pine to hear that Lord Carlisle is able to enjoy it all. Give them all my best love. Shake hands with Morpeth for me.

To Lady Carlisle.

Paris : February 11, 1839.

You will by this time know all the comfort to be derived from the last calm and tranquil moments of the poor Duchess-Countess. Lady William Bentinck sent me a letter she had received from Lady Surrey, in which every detail which would be gratifying to the Duke to know was entered into. He has probably heard from her himself.

I have nothing to tell you. We have had ten days of Italian weather. We spend all our mornings in the Bois de Boulogne, dawdling about, as in spring.

All political eyes turn to March 4, as between that and the 12th the elections and Molé's fate will be decided. The King is in good spirits and courage.

The world is to dance at Thorn's to-morrow, *Mardi Gras*. A quadrille, the women sylphides, the men beasts, which are done in *cartonnage* to the life. Then comes the *Carême*, but all is quiet to us.

[1] Count Molé resigned on February 22, but resumed office on Marshal Soult failing to form a Government.

Have I told you that Abercromby and his wife were here for ten days, the happiest of pairs? She is a quiet, well-mannered little woman, not pretty, but very well-looking; he is in delight of what he has done and done with, and it is pleasant to hear of the happiness of Crust and Crumb [1] and their adoration of Lady Mary.

I was busy last night putting all your letters together, that if you are lazy about a journal you may find your delightful tour safe in red tape and docket.

To LADY CARLISLE.

Paris : February 25, 1839.

I have little time and nothing exciting to conquer my laziness. Yet, Ministers out of the Government and Guizot out of the question, and Thiers, Soult, Dupin, Odillon Barrot only waiting for Humann's [2] arrival and adhesion to be Lords Paramount, is just worth mentioning. Mr. Pear [3] is more low and utterly beat down than can be said. He assents and yields to everything relating to the new furniture. Lieven tells me that Guizot is miserable and in vain tries to bear up.[4] She, I suppose, will soon be anxious to go to England to see her son and friends, and there is nothing to make her wish to remain.

Lord Clarendon is here on his way home. He is not a romantic lover, but will, I have no doubt, be a very good husband.

Paris is dull. Madame Zavadoska is returned, handsomer than ever. She raves of England; says she never was so happy in her life.

[1] A nickname for their son, who married Lady Mary Elliot in 1838.
[2] The Minister of Finance.
[3] Louis Philippe's nickname, from the shape of his face.
[4] Monsieur Guizot had coalesced with Monsieur Thiers to turn out the Comte Molé, and thereby alienated some of his Conservative friends.

To Lady Carlisle.

Paris : February 28, 1839.

Our weather is finer than yours. Yesterday evening
I went out, for the first time this year, to a small soirée
at Mme. Alfred's to hear Mlle. Garcia sing. She has
great promise and power ; like her sister,[1] knows all
languages and is full of *entraînement*, but there is one
fatal difference—an ugliness ' that throws its dark shade
alike o'er her eyes and her nose,' and somebody said of
her with truth, ' Elle frise le monstre.' The house is perfectly beautiful and luxurious, the society aristocratic
and frightful, the mistress of the house gracious and
agreeable, Mme. Appony and Pahlen are hardly able
to bear up, because of a majority of nine against
Ministers ; the consequences will probably be known
to-day.

Mons. d'Arlincourt,[2] whom I met at Mme. Alfred's,
entreated me to interest myself for a Mlle. de Casteras,
the last of a very noble family, ruined, and all her
hopes resting on the sale of some of her possessions. A
set of furniture that belonged to Mme. de Pompadour,
a Titian, an old clock which was in the room of Louis
XVI., a *cachemire*, an old picture of the Tour de Nesle,
and various other objects of value. She has started a
lottery, the tickets ten francs each. I have promised
to procure some names from Rome. She is a very
striking person—perfect manners, interesting countenance. She is the dear friend of the Princesse Amélie
de Saxe, whoever she may be, but I throw it in, hoping
that it may touch the Duke of Sutherland ; and now I
am going to look at the Titian, which Doctor Robert
tells me is ' very pleasing to view.' I wish you would
monter Lady Shrewsbury's head about it. God bless
you.

[1] Madame Malibran.   [2] A novelist of some repute.

To Lady Carlisle.

Paris: April 5, 1839.

I must crowd everything into a small space. Here the Rooms opened yesterday. A great number of people assembled, quantities of workmen out of place, no real disturbance, though a little noise. They hissed Appony and made the Turkish Ambassador cry out, ' Vive la Charte.' The little Provisional Government[1] got a majority ; in short, all seems orderly but in abeyance. The Carlists hope in Mr. Third,[2] and say he means to reign in the name of the absent boy. Miss Jenkinson,[3] Ministress of Strange Affairs, and all our corps calling on her first yesterday. Odd world !

The Bear is supposed to be doing, saying, and meaning mischief. I do not think so. It is only that his inclination to *ponder* and his love of putting his large paw upon every object, and calling and complaining is called manœuvre and ill-will. The Brush[4] is his bitter enemy, gives it him at small dinners at Mrs. Graham's and little sittings at the White Bear's.[5] 'If he thinks, if he imagines, I'll show him up, I'll degrade him,' etc.

Mr. Hume and Mr. Leader were very well, thank you, at dinner on Monday ; Lord Lyndhurst and Lord Brougham ditto on Wednesday. Nobody can foresee. The Tories are not willing to seize the present moment. In a week all shades return to England and then we shall see. I know nothing of what Lord Clarendon intends to do.

Marie Menzingen is to return to Baden the first *bonne occasion.* Her sister, the young beautiful one, is about to make an excellent marriage, to the young Count of Freichstett, *le premier parti du Duché de Bade.*

---

[1] On April 3 the King accepted the resignation of the Molé Administration, and nominated a Provisional Government.

[2] Monsieur Thiers.   [3] Duchesse de Montebello, *née* Jenkinson.

[4] Brougham.   [5] Princess Lieven.

Marie is enchanted at this, and returns to be present at the *noce*, and, as she says, to devote herself to his three children, lovely little things under four years old, he being a widower. Mme. de Lieven means soon to go to England. I am glad that they part amicably. I love Marie and shall miss and regret her much.

What shall you do if the Tories come in? Wait for Morpeth and us in Italy, Lady Carlisle?

To the Duke of Devonshire.

Paris: May 26, 1839.

There is a strong Government, I believe. I cannot attempt to go over the ground uncertain if you are upon the other side of it, but for the present the Whigs have better prospects than they have had for some time past.

The country has a cry for the Queen. The story pregnant of mischief is forgotten. The Tories are furious, and above all with the Baronet, who appears to have deliberately cut his throat in the *tête-à-tête*, I think on purpose, seeing what a task that head would have if it remained on.

By-the-by I have made acquaintance with your little friend Miss V. de Spot since I wrote last. I never met with anybody who had so much determination and *caractère*, or who promises to her family and friends such uncompromising and unshaken support. I should say it is fortunate for a person who is seeking a situation as governess, where there is a large family to educate, that she does not appear to have a nerve or feeling; but this can only be known when we have obtained a situation for her, and I promise to recommend her to the French families of my acquaintance.

We had a ball here in honour of our young Queen yesterday, which was much approved of. It was a *tour de force* to obtain of all my acquaintance, dowagers included, to come dressed in pink and white, but it was obtained; Mme. Dosne in a blue turban, the Minister of Marine's wife in a yellow gown, an old Portuguese lady in green, and a Scotch lady and Mme. de Stackelberg, *par raison de deuil*, in light grey gowns with natural roses, being the only exceptions amongst about 1,200 friends!

The Duke of Sutherland is going on very well, I heard yesterday from Inspruck; but she writes, like you, ignorant of all changes, and therefore only intent upon delay on the road and the quietest of retreats, the world forgetting, by the world forgot, at Westhill—only occupied about the perfect recovery of his health. Happy dream! At least, I hope his health may not require its realisation, or know not how far necessity and a sense of duty may, if it does not, induce her to awake. The letter is full of sense and feeling. Princesse Doria was here last night, apparently enclosed in a diamond.

To Lady Carlisle.

Paris: May 28, 1839.

Here we are as to politics just the same. A *ministère* entirely Thiers announced to be announced to-day, yet nobody believes in anything but dawdle and protraction till the end of the session. This is a very perilous game.

In England the maidens are more talked of than the statesmen. The Queen was enchanted with her dinner at Lansdowne House, examining everything, lights, liveries, plates, knives, merry and inquisitive, uniting the difficult parts of a girl dining for the first time from home and a sovereign dining for the first time with a subject. I long for the Duchess to be with her.

The Binghams are here; she seems intelligent and amiable. Lady Powerscourt gone, divine, unbelievable beauty. It is pleasant having so many friends passing through Paris. The Hortons, to our great regret, leave us on Friday. He is as agreeable as ever, and she the best of women. Lady Ravensworth devotes herself to making the Flora case quite clear to Mme. de Lieven, 'Ith all talking that doth the mithchief; why will people talk, my dear Printhethe de Lieven?'

Granville has just told me that Hume and Sir Robert mean to join in opposition upon the Jamaica question; so Saturday perhaps? If not, I shall think we are really screwed into our saddles.

There is a report here that Madame de Caraman is to marry the Duc de Vicence. He is handsome, pleasing, five-and-twenty, excellent *parti*; but in memory of the Duc d'Enghien [1] no aristocrat here will accept him for his daughter. This and her having had a present of 300,000 francs from a brother, who lives out of the world, tempts me to believe it.

My best love to all yours.

To the Duke of Devonshire.

June 5, 1839.

Good accounts of the Duke of Sutherland at Stuttgart.

Lord William Bentinck going on. The sufferings less, but I have little hope of ultimate recovery.

Our Government sits at home, and so does Soult's [2] here.

The Grand Duke has left England in despair, desperately in love with Lady Fanny Cowper.

[1] Caulaincourt, Duc de Vicence, commanded at Strasburg at the time of the Duc d'Enghien's arrest. The Legitimists persistently accused him of being a party to it, which he through life strenuously denied, saying that the order was carried out by his subordinate, General Ordener, without his knowledge, and in his will are to be found the following words: 'A man does not lie to God in the presence of death. I swear that I took no part in the arrest of the Duc d'Enghien.'

[2] Soult was appointed President of the Council and Foreign Minister on May 12.

Gink [1] writes: 'The Duke of Wellington's speech has driven the Tories frantic, has quite made up for any harm that Brougham's very brilliant speech may have occasioned. It is said that the silence and melancholy produced by the Duke's speech upon the Tories after their vociferous cheering and laughing was very striking and amusing.

The Queen well received at Ascot, but Agneau [2] says 'they were too excited—not the calm approbation I like.'

To the Duke of Devonshire.

Paris: June 21, 1839.

I am delighted to hear from you, my dearest brother.

Poor Lord William's body is to go to England this evening. Lady William leaves Paris also. She is wonderfully calm and able to exert herself.

Lady Jersey is as pleasant *à vivre* as she used to be rugged. Never comes near me but when I propose it, and then is as good-humoured and pleasable as it is possible to be. Mr. O.[3] gives her pineapples, boxes, and visits. Mrs. O. takes her to the French play. Upon seeing these operations, many women, many minds. Madame Appony *outrée*, 'si grossier pour nous—pas le sens commun, inouï—inconvenable au dernier degré.' Mrs. G.[4] *pénétrée* with *reconnaissance* and delight that such penances are only inflicted upon the silent.

Some say that Lord Glenelg asked of himself to go. H. B. makes Lord John drive him out of town in a patent safety cab.

Miss Minna [5]—I alone thought her pretty. From manner, countenance, *tournure*, something uncommonly attractive about her. But spectators in general were

[1] Lord Leveson.　　[2] Mrs. Lamb.
[3] Duke of Orleans.　　[4] Lady Granville.
[5] The Duchess of Norfolk. She was a daughter of Lord Lyons.

much astonished. As we already possess Lady Harriet Galway, there was no use in having Lady Lyons, there being no shade of difference between the two.

To Lady Carlisle.

My dearest sister,—I know not if this will ever get to you, as we hope you will not stay long at Venice in this hot and stagnant weather. We are longing to hear something of your plans, but have been obliged almost to fix our own. We think of going to Kissingen, near Würtzburg, not extremely far from Baden. I have written to my brother, who is in a state of delight at Geneva. Not well, but he says it is the best place for his hay-fit. Three grottoes of rooms close to the Lake. I have written to him our plans and am not without hope that he will join us.

Poor Lord William's death was very sudden at last. The body was to leave Paris last night, and his family go soon. Lady Charlotte to England, I believe. I know not what poor Lady William will do, but I hear she has not suffered in health.

Lady Jersey is in great spirits and good-humour, doing and going all day. Lady Sarah I think very pretty, the prettiest of the three.

Lord Granby leaves Paris on the 28th, and Lady Chesterfield and Miss Forrester arrive here on the 1st. I like him and his brother Lord John much.

To the Duke of Devonshire.

Paris: June 24, 1839.

It is too refreshing to find you sitting by my plate these hot mornings when I crawl to breakfast. I am dying to hear what you will determine upon.

The Duke of Sutherland writes that he is much

VOL. II. U

better, tells us of the death of the poor little baby, teething, that the Duchess had borne it better than he had hoped.

I have heard nothing of the Burlingtons. Charles[1] has taken delighted though nervous possession of his post, Harry tells me.

The story that occupies everyone is whether or not the Duchess of Montrose kissed the Queen at Ascot, but all agree, not in the details, that the audiences, affidavits, lies, contradictions, and I fear subsequent bitterness and mischief have been parallel to those upon the Lady Flora question. God bless you.

To THE DUKE OF DEVONSHIRE.

Paris: June 29, 1839.

Kissingen does not look up this morning. We are told of its imperfections, and have no decided opinion upon its unknown sources. Dody and I have just been building a castle, but without knowing how it will take. A six weeks' tour in Normandy. The new Port St. Valery, Dieppe, Havre, luxuriously with horses and carriages. *Che vi pare?*

Yesterday the nine actual Ministers dined here. The five ambassadors (Pahlen is gone to Petersburg), Rambuteau and Pasquier. In the evening came Mme. Appony and girl, Brignolés and girl, Molé and Guizot, Helena Robinson and girl, Vallombrosa, Meyendorf, Prince and Princess de Ligne, Lady Sandwich, Mrs. Locke, Granby and John, Edward Upton, Beust, Bernstorff, Hatzfeldt, Rodolphe Appony, Vicence. I give you the list to show you the sum total of what you will find at Paris. Unless, indeed, you drop in at dinner on Friday, when Sir W. and Lady Beecher,[2] Sir Charles Doyle and his bride, late Steer, Mrs Evrington, dressed and rouged like an altar-

---

[1] Mr. Charles Howard was appointed Lord Melbourne's private secretary.   [2] The actress Miss O'Neill.

piece but still beautiful, Mrs. Johnstone and her still much-admired daughter, Lady Canterbury and her girls.

I think you will be pleased with our Turkish Ambassador. I think him a love. A fine head like Rossini, a lazy, amiable smile and manner; loves to sit looking at Harriet d'Orsay or Miss Horsford. Nice disjointed talk. ' Vous montez à cheval; je crois vous avoir rencontré ?' ' Non, cheval grand, moi petit, cela ne va pas.' ' Nous espérons avoir le plaisir de voir l'Ambassadrice ici bientôt.' She is seventeen, beautiful beyond measure. ' Oui, oui.' ' Elle sera admirée extrêmement à Paris.' ' À moi égal.' I beg to add I was not the questioner.

I forgot to say that Silence came in last night at eleven, hot, breathless from a dinner at Neuilly and Opera with the O.'s. She is in perfect contentment.

To Lady Carlisle.

Paris : July 1, 1839.

Dearest of sisters,—We are all well. Lady Hardy wrote me an account of Morpeth's breakfast.[1] Beautiful, four hundred people dining in perfect ease and luxury, fine evening, and that his *prévenant*, courteous manner and the character he bears and the love he inspires smoothed even such thorns as belong to such roses, as anything connected with politics in this day.

Mme. de Flahault writes that O'Connell is the most charming man with the most pleasing manner that she ever met with. We are imagined safe till next Session.

Aston goes to Madrid, Henry Bulwer comes here.

Leveson is in high spirits, in love with nobody. Very intimate again with Lady ——, who is playing her on and off game with many of the unwary, but he is, I think, aware and safe.

---

[1] Given in honour of O'Connell. The principal Tory ladies kept away.

I have just received a letter from D.   He writes on
the 28th from Geneva that if well he will be here on
the 4th.   We shall remain here about ten days after
his arrival, and having given up Germany, we shall go
with him and the Fullertons a tour about the coast of
Normandy.

To LADY CARLISLE.

Paris : July 28, 1839.

Your delicious letter is here, so extremely interesting to us in all ways.   Let me first tell you how
entirely your effort in going to Baden answered, as far
as Madame de Lieven was concerned.   She was quite
delighted, and so am I, with all you say about her.
There is yet peace, even for her, if she will but tread
in its path.   Is it not one of the most wonderful things
belonging to this state of existence that she can still
cling to and lean upon this, to her, miserable earth ?   I
know no one so bereaved, so desolate.   I write this
morning without having a guess where to go.   I have
consulted Granville, and he says he has not a guess
where I am to direct.   He and Freddy reproach me for
my folly in writing when I do not know what to put
on my letter ; but I, with my little eye, see that Harry
or somebody will tell me all at once when and how,
and I like to be ready with my document *pour la
première occasion.*

D., after cold, headache, and two or three days'
confinement in the Hôtel Sinet, is in the most tearing
spirits and enjoyment of the rare quiet and emptiness of
Paris.   He purchases at all the shops, dines at cafés
with Fullerton, walks into the concerts, and yesterday
evening went to the 'Huguenots.'

Georgy and I pass our mornings at Longchamps.
They set out to-morrow for Brighton, where they are
to pass some time with his family.   My brother stays

here about ten days longer. We shall, I hope, leave Paris about the middle of August.

Henry Bulwer is arrived and is extremely agreeable and efficient, and will, I think, be a great addition in society and a very useful one in business. But Aston is not to be replaced in our affection.

I shall see you somehow or other, most dear sister, for I trust we shall be the whole month of September in England.

To Lady Carlisle.

Devonshire House: August 31, 1839.

My dearest sister,—You saw how poorly I was at your house after the Palace. All the next day I was in my bed. Granville dined at Stafford House and was enchanted with the Duchess and Lady Clanricarde. He returned here to keep me company with a like seizure of cold and diarrhœa. Yesterday I recovered and dined with D. and Leveson with Lord Seaford. All the Hardys. Lord Melbourne very happy, wide awake, talking a great deal to Louisa Hardy.

Everybody moans and groans over the changes.[1] Mr. Wood and Lady Mary sat with me during my *cholérine*, almost in tears, in despair at going out, leaving their best friends, but inevitable, impossible to avoid. Mr. Wood is most grateful to Morpeth for a note, loves you for your sorrow; Mary became like a silver fruit knife in aspect, and said she must leave the room if we said a word more, so moved was she.

Well, people say Lord Clarendon's tiff is absurd. Lord Seaford says his speeches were not so very good, not to be compared with Morpeth's first speeches in

---

[1] Several changes took place in the Administration. Sir Charles Wood resigned the Secretaryship of the Admiralty. He afterwards filled many important posts, and was created Viscount Halifax in 1866.

promise of anything first-rate, and what has he done to warrant immediate eye to the Cabinet?

Sister, you see how this is to be burnt, and only for you and the Lords. Lord Howick says he goes because Mr. Wood is affronted. Mr. Wood won't say one word of why he does, so we turn it upside down.

Mantalini[1] says he is now just what he has all along wished, pined for, Home, but D. says he is in deplorable spirits.

Lord Seaford says that it is the best thing possible to have Johnny Colonial, but laments over Powlettain[2] Boat Song—most ungracious, unconciliating, and to the Aristocratic Americans, descended from tallow.

To the Duke of Devonshire.

Windsor: October 10, 1839.

It is delightful. I had forgotten the beauty of the place, inside and out. The weather is quite heavenly— every comfort and luxury. Lady Sandwich and Lady Clanricarde. The Princes of Coburg arrived. A key to go all day long into the garden. No driving required. And now, my dearest Dody, to you and your husband and my dearest brother a bundle of my observations.

Lady Clanricarde came to me, which kept me till within ten minutes of luncheon.

I have been taking a delicious walk on the Terrace into an embroidered garden, but how inferior! Lord Palmerston said that if my brother could but come here for six months en maître, Windsor would be the most magnificent thing on earth, and it is quite true.

The Queen looks lovely, much more delicate without looking ill. Lord Melbourne appears to be in as

---

[1] Lord Normanby.
[2] Mr. Powlett Thomson was appointed Governor-General of Canada.

great favour as ever, and I think their relative manners in a difficult position perfect.

We sat round in the evening, but had much to look at. ' My cousins ' are both of them very unaffected and with very good manners, perfectly at their ease with her without *gêne* or familiarity ; and Prince Albert the youngest is charming. Ladies Sandwich, Clanricarde and I are won. It remains to be seen who else will be.

Roast beef and potatoes with the Ministers and maids. Going in a real coach and horses to the Virginia Water. Lady Sandwich says she idolises the Queen. Lord Normanby imagines that there is nothing actually *en train* as to marriage. Lord Melbourne sat by her yesterday evening as usual, did not sleep at all or talk much. Prince Albert played at chess with Charles Murray. Lady Clanricarde said, ' The trial is too great ; if he wins he has a master mind.' He lost.

H. M. asked Lady Clanricarde ' Do you think my cousin like me ? ' She said yes, because he is, though much handsomer.

To Lady Carlisle.

Paris: October 25, 1839.

My dearest sister,—You will have been like us, first shocked, and then relieved about Lord Brougham.[1]

The slightest encouragement to F. Grey [2] will make what I believe will be for the happiness of all parties. As to the other branch of your domestic affairs, conceive my surprise when Baroness Dimsdale yesterday said to me: ' I am so delighted to hear of William Cowper's marriage.' ' To whom ? ' ' To one of Lord Carlisle's daughters.' Much as Dimsdale regards and

[1] A false report of his death appeared in the *Times*.
[2] The Rev. Francis Grey, son of the Prime Minister, who married, in 1840, Lady Elizabeth Howard.

values me, she does not seem aware of my *parentés*. I said, obliged to boast, I was quite sure my sister Lady Carlisle, would have told me. 'Oh, I beg your pardon; I only read it in the newspaper.'

Bruce lives entirely with his family, excepting walks and visits to Leveson, who is delightful, lives almost entirely with us, in very good spirits and as amiable, affectionate, and pleasant as it is possible to be.

Mme. de Lieven wants nothing and nobody but her *tapissiers* and Monsieur Paggenpohl, who helps her. She thinks of nothing but tables and chairs. The *entresol* is delicious; she looks out upon and into the Tuileries gardens—it is like living in a kaleidoscope. She don't let me in, she don't come to see me, but dines and talks and is charming. The house for the moment is quite sufficient, and she wants neither Bull, toad, nor Bear. Class us as you please.

To Lady Carlisle.

Paris : December 7, 1839.

My most dear sister,—Your letter of yesterday was most interesting. Lady Cowper's marriage, the early period fixed for the Queen's, all was news. The happiness that awaits Liz is the constant object of Georgy's and my talk. He is so excellent; his life is one which would have been so completely poisoned by a wife that did not suit him and sympathise with him, and will be such a blessed and blessing one with your perfect Liz. He will be of such use to us all. Georgy read me a sermon of his yesterday morning which quite charmed me on part of the Lord's Prayer, such warmth and feeling and eloquence.

Lady Cowper has courage to face her angry children. I cannot say how much I blame them for telling what they feel, but I wonder she can encounter their

antipathy.   What a happy mother she might have been
and what an unhappy existence will she have, I fear![1]
Her understanding never has been of the slightest use
to her.

Adieu! God bless you all.   Harry is in high force
and wiser, though smitten with two or three beauties.
A very pretty daughter of Edward Bligh's, a very clever
one[2] of Charles Gore's, and Madame Villa Garcia are
the favourites *pour le moment.*

To Lady Carlisle.

Paris: December 27, 1839.

My dearest sister,—I shall long to hear of Francis's
next visit.   Harry is uncommonly well in looks, health
and spirits, and we all get fonder of him every day.
He is much more wary, though certainly more devoted
to woman than I ever saw any man.

Madame de Lieven has had a letter from Lady
Cowper at Broadlands.   She seems perfectly happy at
the decision she has taken.   Says she was a *sotte* not to
have had the courage to do it long ago.   Newmann
and Brunnow were going down there.   Foreign Affairs
will be more come-at-able, I suspect, than they have
been for a long time.   Lord Palmerston's incivilities
will obtain a varnish.

The Clarendons went yesterday.   They have been
very amiable.   She is plain, but seems the best, most
sensible, inoffensive wife that can be, extremely fond of
him, and he looks happier and healthier than I ever
saw him.

[1] It turned out a very happy marriage and the children became devoted
to Lord Palmerston.

[2] Mrs. Charles Gore wrote some clever novels.   Her daughter was a
great favourite with the smart young men of the day.   She was not
pretty, but she was bright and clever, danced well and had a graceful
figure.   Her mother was very stout, and they were called 'plenty' and
'waste.'   Miss Gore married Lord Edward Thynne.

What are we to think of politics? Peel and Patience?

Brougham dined here yesterday, extremely gentle, subdued and in low spirits, keeping within the bounds of decency and sobriety, not coming to balls and routs, but to dinners and *vaudevilles*. Perhaps I am a gull, but from what he said to me I am inclined to think he did not kill himself.[1]

Give my love to your dear people—men, women and children.

[1] Many believed he had himself originated the report of his death, to find out what people would say of him.

1840

To Lady Carlisle.

Paris: January 1840.

Freddy leaves us on Tuesday and will give you another live sketch of us. Yesterday I suffered the first joy of the *Carnaval*, a concert at the Duke of Orleans. Excellent music, *luxe* of light, intense heat in the mild, fusty weather, the wearied, *excédé* unmusical family sitting in a row before us. But I enjoyed part: Scheffer's beautiful picture of Mignon, 'Regrettant le Ciel,' out of one eye, and the magnificent head of the widower, the Duke of Wurtemberg, out of the other, not to mention Madame de Talleyrand, that sublime wreck of different kinds of prosperity.

To Lady Carlisle.

Paris: February 1840.

Nothing can express the delight of receiving your letters, my dearest sister. Yesterday no papers arrived, though the courier did. Lord Holland wrote as if we had the papers. Granville brought your letter in to Dody and me. 'Perhaps your sister will tell'—and you did, dearest of ladies, everything, and clearly, amply, interestingly, as you always do.

I think five was too much, three enough, but is it not a shake? We long for the Friday result.

Dearest Leveson.[1] My time is taken up with answering notes of congratulation, and to-night I expect my throat to be sore with explanations and thanks.

---

[1] He was appointed Under-Secretary for Foreign Affairs.

Monsieur Guizot's appointment[1] occupies us much.
I think he will be much liked, I mean socially, at
Holland House and Lansdowne House. I do not think
Lord Melbourne will talk much to him.

My friend feels as they said of Richelieu, when he
died, 'Il laisse plus de vide qu'il n'a tenu de place.'
She is what I always think her, hard but true. She
says she has *épousé* Lord Palmerston and only wishes
good for him and his, that she has ceased to care about
politics but as suits them and herself. The loss of
Guizot's society is greater to her as habit and resource
than as positive pleasure. Molé charms and Thiers
amuses her more. Perhaps because with all her cleverness she would prefer the soil less rich and the surface
more polished.

What are we to think, what to do? People are
sending every minute for the Tuesday's papers, which
we have not. Lord Munster *entre autres* very huffy.

Mr. and Miss Raikes dine here this evening, and
Mme. de Lieven comes to early whist, the only thing—
how odd!—I have ever seen really amuse her.

Our wonderful mild winter enables us to go to the
Bois de Boulogne *en calèche* every day. Georgy has
ridden twice, very successfully, in all but Baba's opinion.
'She's not clever at it, she looks frightened, she goes
zig-zag,' and then he puts himself exactly in the shape
she sits, which Leveson knows.

To LADY CARLISLE.

Paris: February 1840.

I wish you joy, my dearest sister. Twenty-one,[2] and
Morpeth's excellent speech. Not that I have yet read
it, but Granville tells me that it is so, and the end of Sir
Robert's also. Lord John? I mean to go through the

---

[1] Of Ambassador to London.

[2] The majority against Sir T. Buller's motion of want of confidence.

debate when they are all at the Duke of Orleans' ball.
I have a cold and a rash on the tip of my nose, which
made me think it a pretty compliment to abstain from
ornamenting the gay brilliant little *fête* with my presence.
All our men go, and Dody, very smart and hoping to
get in a rubber of whist in the course of the evening.

How different a session I suppose this will be from
the last! Such constant—though, I imagine, fruitless
—attempts to turn us out.

You can have no idea of my present comfort with
a cup of tea, blazing logs, not a sound or wheel to be
heard, whilst at eight o'clock Harry, Heneage, the
Fullertons and Granville were all adorned and armed
for the ball. Now the truth is that I think if I go
to the great *bals monstres*, I shall do all I need. They
are the most fatiguing and the least crack, so show
most good-will. Georgy was in a blaze of jewelry.
You know Alexandre. When she proposed adding a
little branch of diamonds to her *coiffure*, he said : ' Avec
une pareille magnificence, notre pensée doit être la
simplicité,' and rejected her plan. Good night, dearest
of sisters.

To Lady Carlisle.

Paris : February 1840.

My own dearest sister,—Harry and I went to a
morning concert together this morning. We hope he
is not desperately in love with the twin Miss Zamoras.
They are lovely to behold, but do not come here; only
seen at Lady Duff's. There are four good families at
the Havannah, and they are one.

I hear the Duc de Broglie is very gay, Mme. de
Lieven very much amused and *animée*, and has Thiers
at her house this evening, which must make her very
happy.

To Lady Carlisle.

Paris: February 1840.

My dearest sister,—We are again in all the suspense and wonder and *imbroglio* of the King in a fury, the Ministers out, Monsieur de Broglie as usual refusing.

Mons. Guizot sets out to-morrow, and I have just been writing out for Mme. de Lieven a list of whist-players, and we advise her to have a Wednesday entirely devoted to the game, as she gets like a naughty child if the politicians come in the middle of her game.

All the world is occupied about a ball on Monday at Colonel Thorn's. *Costumé*, it is to be beautiful. Mme. Samoiloff, d'Aspas, Kisseleff, and Poldi as—I forget what, but something very beautiful. I have had such a note from Mrs. Thorn that, to my utter disgust and despair, I am afraid I must go. The Colonel has shrewdly said that all women above thirty may be excused coming in costume. Oh, *cela ira, cela ira!* I see my young friends.

To Lady Carlisle.

Paris: March 1840.

Most dear sister,—I hope you are as nearly out of your *grippe* as I am out of mine, but it leaves one much pulled, like a thing just come out of the wash.

Lord William Russell is just arrived, which will gladden Mme. de Lieven's heart.

Nobody seems certain of the *dénouement* of events here. Molé and his friends talk confidently of over-turning Thiers, but Broglie stands by the latter, and unless he, the little man, is brought to fling himself too entirely on the *gauche* I think he may stick for a session at least.

The King stands at ease upon the point of this difficulty.

The Duc de Noailles says, 'Soyez tranquille,. il les trompera tous.'

Georgy's translation of a French poem [1] is in the number for March of 'Bentley's Miscellany.' Pray read it, and the editor's little preface.

To Lady Carlisle.

Paris: 1840.

My dearest sister,—Your letter to-day was a great pleasure. Your improved account of Blanche made D. and myself very happy. He is arrived, snug in the Hôtel Sinet.

I made Mme. de Lieven happy with your daughter's most kind letter. D. tells me she is to pay him a long visit at Chatsworth.

Give my love to dearest Guinea. Tell him that Lord Clanwilliam has sent me a message which pleased me much, telling me how much he is liked and approved of in the office by all.

I have nothing more to tell you, and the first fine hot day has made me stupid and sleepy.

To Lady Carlisle.

Paris: April 1840.

My beloved sister,—It is not possible for me to express my gratitude for your letter. Without it I never could have poured out to you all the devoted feeling of affection, of sympathy, that I have longed to write to you and dearest Lord Carlisle. I feel what absence is, not to be near you all now. What, however, could I be that you are not to each other in the midst

---

[1] *L'Aveugle de Castel Guillé*, by Jacques Jasmin, the Languedoc poet.

of the blessings that remain and duties that occupy you, which you so adorably feel, and for which God will give you strength and grace![1]

I feel that we are all left to endeavour to follow her in all that may await us in this life of trial. I only hope to be like you.

Every moment, every thought is with you all and my beloved brother. I wish much to hear of dearest Harry being with you. We have all the strongest affection for him. I will tell Susy that you thought of her.

Dearest sister, if it was possible to tell you how I love, how I hope with you, for you!

That last look seems before me too.

TO THE DUKE OF DEVONSHIRE.

Paris: April 30, 1840.

I thank you more than I can say, my beloved brother. It would have given me intolerable anxiety not to have heard from you, and in that letter, in the midst of anguish, there is something that speaks peace.

I feel as if. in that angel's departure, there was a sort of mission to us all to suffer, resign ourselves and hope. I think the remembrance of that last expression will come in all these dark hours of trial and bitterness through which all must pass.

Your letter will always be by me. I have the greatest gratitude to you for writing it.

I am so glad you were able to see them all. I have had a letter from my sister and send you back her letters, letters that at once break one's heart and soothe it. I love you, my dearest brother. I never knew how much I loved you. You are never for a moment out of my thoughts. I cannot night or day forget what you said to me on the overwhelming subject, but I hope

[1] Lady Burlington died on April 28.

and trust you are well, and that when you can you
will let me hear from you.

To Lady Carlisle.

Paris: May 1840.

Most dear sister,—I long to be with you, to talk to
you, to feel with you, to learn of you.

I think it is a long time before we practically
believe how much is given, how little asked. I do not
think it is in man easily to understand the unbounded
mercy of God. Come unto me, and that at the eleventh
hour, as at the first. This the only peace on earth we
shrink from till brought to it by fear and sorrow, terror
and bereavement.

God bless you, my angel sister.

To Lady Carlisle.

Paris: 1840.

My most dear sister,—I am so grateful for the letters
I have received from my brother and Morpeth, so
soothing in the midst of grief, telling me of all you
have been strengthened to do, of all that has been
added to your adorable nature, to enable you to bear
your trial, perform your duty, and be a blessing and
example to all around you. I have an intense wish to
see you, but I do not form any plan or look forward.
It may be given to me, like other blessings.

Granville better after a sharp attack of gout, but
I know not what he thinks of doing this summer. I
trust he will soon be able to walk, which at this moment
he is not allowed to do, and that it will not be tedious
and weakening as the last attack.

How my brother does love you, my most dear sister !
What a comfort you will be to him !

Lord Carlisle has written the kindest letter to

Granville.   I wish it were possible for me to tell you what I feel for you both.

I shall not write more to-day.   I have scarcely left my room and his, and now I am going to breathe a little air.   I will only tell you what very strong affection we all have for your dearest Harry, and the pleasure it is to us to think of seeing him again.

To Lady Carlisle.

Paris: May 1840.

I received your letter yesterday, my own beloved sister.   I am glad you did not go to Compton Place, and am glad that Richard and Caroline were with him.

It is all, I hope, settled as the Sutherlands wish with regard to Mme. de Lieven.   She has had such improved accounts of her son that she is in doubt again as to the time of her departure.   I have made her feel that her being at Stafford House is now out of the question, and their very great kindness in offering her to be there or at West Hill later in the year.   I conveyed all the Duke had written to me to her, not as a message sent at this moment, but as an expression of their kindness and interest about her.

I have seen Mr. Blunt's letter, most dear sister. Harry sent it to me.   I find every day words, lines, thoughts that I have such a longing to show to you, all impressive of what he dwells so much on, what her perfection, her adorable character gives even to the pangs of memory—such certainty for her, such hope for what survives.

To Lady Carlisle.

Paris: May 1840.

I received your letter with the enclosed, which I return to you.   I felt, my most dear sister, more than I can express for the disappointment and difference to you and my dearest brother. You are perfect in that, as you have shown yourself throughout. You have, and my dear brother, only said and done all that must be soothing to you to think of. I feel it sure that a sense of duty actuates Lord Burlington,[1] and I hope gradually time will bring nearly the same results. Talk to me of her children. I feel to know that darling eldest boy, but I want to hear of the others and of the little girl that must be so precious to you all. Tell Liz there is no kindness to Harry. He has made himself dear to us all. I love him and respect him, for he has qualities that are invaluable. Such truth in judging, feeling and acting—such real feeling it is for all subjects, so just and so uncompromising.

Mme. de Lieven is waiting here, expecting her son soon, and meaning to go to England on the 8th of June.

To the Duke of Devonshire.

Dover: July 29, 1840.

We are going to embark on a calm sea, and I hope you will soon step into your steamer.

I do not think I have thanked you half enough for all your kindness to the Levesons,[2] always so very great to him and now to her, and so deeply felt by both.

I was pleased with her for asking Freddy in secret if he could find the nosegay of orange flowers that you had given her the day of the marriage and which she had, to her great regret, left on the table, having wished to keep it for ever. The mother-in-law, having a prudent mind, had found the nosegay, picked off all the flowers, put them in a *sachet*, and I am going to send them to her in a very pretty one from Paris.

---

[1] In his refusal to live with the Duke.
[2] Lord Leveson married Lady Acton on July 25.

To Lady Carlisle.

Paris : August 1840.

My dearest sister,—It was great happiness to receive your letter.

I do not see any prospect of war, and Buonaparte's [1] attempt and misfortune seem to have damaged no one but himself. It is almost the foolishest thing one ever heard of.

Granville's gout is almost gone. My brother is gone to-day to St. Germain on his way to Havre, where he is to take lodgings for the Fullertons and us. I long to breathe sea air.

We have had Granville Vernon [2] and his daughter here. He talked to an attentive house. We had nothing else to do, and he is sometimes a good essay, enlivened with something as good as a farce. The girl is extremely pretty, pleasing, and her singing divine, but she became low last night when at eleven, on the eve of a journey, she saw her papa in his fourth hour of conversation without a hope of abatement.

I have had a letter from Mme. de Lieven. I think she seems impatient to come back. Her niece Mme. Rodolphe Appony [3] is arrived. I hear she is quite lovely and both Appony and his wife are enchanted with her, and say that she is *douce, gentille, charmante.*

Will you tell the Duchess when you write that I had a letter from Madame de Schönbourg written on the 11th? She was perfectly well, and to embark the next day. Lord Rokeby had arrived from London to *remonter* the Rhine with her, and I think he will do as much good as the doctor.

---

[1] Louis Napoleon's escapade to Boulogne.

[2] Mr. and Mrs. Granville Vernon. He was the only one of the family who did not take the name of Harcourt when his father the Archbishop adopted it on his succeeding to the Harcourt property.

[3] She became Austrian Ambassadress in London.

To Lady Carlisle.

Paris: August 17, 1840.

You will excuse a short letter to-day, my beloved sister. We are all in the bustle of setting out. The Fullertons for Mantes and we for St. Germain, to meet at Rouen to-morrow, hoping to arrive at Havre on Wednesday. We shall find Richard Verity there. Granville is very well, but it will be a great comfort to me to have that valuable creature to look at us.

Mr. Macaulay dined here yesterday, and as we had nothing to do but to listen he was very welcome. He told us all about everything, and is I think prepared for anything. I expect nothing.

Mme. de Lieven rushed back from Wrest to Stafford House and the doctors, as she says she is bilious and ill. Lady Clanricarde is become entirely political and violent against the Government here. Leopold very busy at Windsor.

Marie has sent me the loveliest present, a bracelet with her hair and Leveson's and the date of their marriage.

To Lady Carlisle.

Havre: August 30, 1840.

My dearest, dear sis,—Forgive me for writing so little. You know what a life a seafaring one is, all outing, eating, bathing, and sleeping, for I live in warm sea water. It is oppressively hot and we are all rather languid. The doctor says, 'it takes away one's power of speech,' but it is delicious to go and sit on the pier from nine till ten, to rest by day and take long walks at night.

Granville was astonished when he saw the satisfaction I had given you all by my declaration of peace!!! Yet I persist, only he says I am bold in such daring

assertions when nobody can know. Dearest sister, I
am sure notwithstanding.

Richard Verity is still here, longing to get back to
his wife and harvest. But I do not suffer such an image
to present itself to his mind in any practical shape, it
is such a comfort to have him.

To Lady Carlisle.

Paris: October 7, 1840.

Most dear sister,—What has made me lazy has
been knowing that from others, chiefly Morpeth, you
know all, and that I had nothing to say, and that in
these times nobody can do more than wait, look and
listen for what has not yet happened—something decisive of the one great question, Peace or War.

Thursday, 8th.—My dearest, this will go to-night,
and I have just received your dear, anxious letter. It
is impossible not to feel so, but yet I trust, if events
continue to be such as to frighten Mehemet Ali, he
may be led to give Lord P. the immense triumph and
the world the immense blessing of peace.

The newspapers do their most and worst to aggra-
vate matters, but I trust the mutual interests concerned
will prevent any beyond paper explosion.

En attendant we are living the most quiet, pleasant
life apart from politics. Granville, though most
anxious and very busy, is very well. He rides every
day with Dody and Freddy, and we keep early hours.
The Seafords are arrived. They are inclined to remain
here, but ask if it is wise. I have almost persuaded
them to take a house for the winter—*sauf la guerre*,
an agreement, I understand, made and agreed to by all
who do.

Frederick Bruce arrived the day they did, but not
de concert, as he came to take care of his mother, his
father being afraid of the state of things.

Mme. de Lieven and Mme. de Flahault gasp for news, but events, though showering quick upon us, are nothing till a decision is taken in a friendly sense. Things that calm one place irritate in another. Yet still I think, and if I dared I would say I am sure, it will not end in war.

The Bois de Boulogne is *méconnaissable*, the trees all stripped and barked where the line of fortification is to go.

My love to all yours and to Lady Newburgh. I envy her being with you, because of you, dearest people, but also Castle Howard—dear, beautiful Castle Howard. Autumn brings it so to my mind. There is no place of which my recollections are so vivid. At any time I can cry over its walks, its beauties and its pleasures. I can smell it and see it with almost all the ecstasy of reality, for ecstasy there is in all the enjoyments of earth, air and sky. And you, my own dearest beloved sister, how dearly I do love you!

To the Duke of Devonshire.

Paris: October 15, 1840.

Have I not seemed ungrateful for your most delicious letter? But I have been so flat and low, such terror of over-fatigue to Granville and return of gout; and what could I say that you did not know? Tankervilles! Chatsworth! The different views of your political friends, and I with nothing to say but that I found the Duchesse de Dalberg here, kind, charming and reconciled;[1] that the English have all taken to fright and flight.

But I have to tell you that at six o'clock to-day the King was shot at by a desperate fanatic, *une bête féroce*, forty-three, a *frotteur*, who says, ' Je connais l'histoire, j'ai voulu délivrer la France du plus grand tyran qui ait jamais existé.'

---

[1] She had been opposed to the marriage of her daughter on account of the difference of religion.

Eleven o'clock.—We are just returned from St. Cloud. The King pale, but very perfect about his danger and escape. The Queen adorable, quite calm but heart-broken. The little Comte de Paris is dangerously ill, and the Duchesse d'Orléans is *saisie* by the accounts of the poor little Queen of Portugal.

The assassin had so overcharged his short gun that it burst in his hand. He was in tortures, but quite unsubdued, walking about the room, his voice quite strong, and boasting of his knowledge of history. Two of the worst books of the day, two pistols and a poignard were found on him.

Lady Seaford[1] is droll. 'Knows nothing, because she does not think spectacles look well on a bride.' Lord Seaford called at the Luxembourg. She got out to walk up and down on the *Place* full of *émeutes*. She asked the *laquais de place*, 'Vous ne croyez pas que je coure aucun danger d'être insultée.' 'Oh non, madame, pas à votre âge. Si c'était une des demoiselles, cela se pourrait.' She hastened to explain that a political assault was what she apprehended.

To Mrs. Hamilton Hamilton.

Paris: November 5, 1840.

We have had ten days of most mingled feelings. The loss of Lord Holland to Granville's feeling a most severe blow, to his existence a most irreparable privation. There never was a more devoted friend or agreeable companion than Lord Holland had been to him from their earliest youth.

We have had the great happiness of seeing Leveson and his wife. I never saw a couple so well suited to each other. She is charming, good, gay, pretty, and as a' wife the happiest mixture of spirit and submission.

---

[1] Lady Hardy had lately married Lord Seaford.

Then the mother has been all satisfaction and gracious
kindness, which she must have great credit for, as there
was strong feeling excited and only laid by amiable
ones.   They go to-day.   It is terrible to lose them, but
it would have been worse to be glad.

Granville is uncommonly well, and the quiet life we
lead by the side of the storms and supposed agitation
of the *siècle* is good for us all.   Good-bye.

To the Duke of Devonshire.

Paris : December 1840.

At half-past eight we met in the red room—Apponys,
Brignolés, Mesdames de Gontaut, Caraman, Poix, Sabine
out of breath with ecstasy, the Beauvaus, Guiches,
Mouchy, Richelieu, Rodolphe I., Albert Esterhazy,
Madame de Flahault and her girls, Percys, Rendleshams,
Ailesburys, Francis Gordon, Madame Razoumoffska,
Arabin, d'Orsay, Murray, and St. Clair.   Madame de
St. Clair's emotions were various.   ' How sweet it would
would be to have Mr. Leveson for a lover ! ' was her
gratifying whisper.   At another time Fullerton says he
heard something like the heaving of an elephant.   She
had seen the gun, and knew it was to be fired.

At nine we were all in the ball-room, the prettiest
little theatre you ever saw.   Henry Greville and Miss
Raikes, Grampus and Alice, *le grand genre*.   Harry
Howard, looking quite beautiful in a black wig like
Louis XIV.'s, acted the villain of the piece perfectly.
Freddy as Walter Barnard and Marion Ellice as Bella
had the greatest success.   Plunket, an excellent comic
actor as Jemmy Starling.   Miss Thelusson [1] had set
beautifully all sorts of the prettiest bits of opera music,
and played them with a band of Tolbecque.

The marriage procession, the dance of the girls ;

[1] Was a daughter of the third Lord Rendlesham, and was married to
the late Lord Walsingham in 1847.

Émilie de Flahault looked lovely, and all very pretty. There were no *longueurs* or mischances, the greatest possible success, immense applause, and when at the close Miss Raikes, called for, led on the modest, reluctant Marion, and curtseying, picked up wreath and nosegay thrown by Mouchy, no words can describe the contentment of all parties. To-morrow the play is again acted to an entirely new audience. No duplicates but the mothers of the *figurantes*. Gramonts, Mme. de Lieven, Albufera, De la Redorte, Castellane, Ségur, Fézensac, Decazes, La Ferté, St. Aulaire, Marescalchi, Durazzo, Chabots, Haussonville, Vallombrosa, Grahams, Salvos, Sebastiani, Kisseleff, F. Barings, the Actons, Gallweys, Rothschilds, Boigne, Molé, Délessert, Pigotts, Fitzwilliams, Casteja, N. Pahlen, Guizot, men *diplomates*, Zamoyski, Montalembert. They have all comfortable seats and refreshments to keep up their spirits and soften their hearts. Lord Howden looked and acted the chief pirate beautifully.

In short, dearest brother, it is thought that we have done it. Landseer never saw a private play so well got up, and when Harry kneels to Marion in the last act, he said, ' Was there ever a more beautiful picture than that ? '

1841

To the Duke of Devonshire.

Paris: February 10, 1841.

Your delicious letter came this morning. The pink poplin will be more than ever suitable. She [1] dined here last week, very agreeable and gay, but a trifle too young, as I see people now know what is coming and try to ward it off. 'Oh, I should like, I should like, but I must not; *vous voyez, je suis trop jeune femme pour cela.*' Kisseleff, whom I doat upon, is fond of her, but sees it all. She was on the defensive about political energy. 'Les Chambres! Je n'y vais pas, je ne pense pas m'occuper de ces choses sérieuses—oh! non, non. Vous comprenez, quand on me parle, qu'on veut m'expliquer les fortifications et tout cela—non, non. Fort détaché vous-même.' Dearest brother, if you had seen his face!

Don't tell ever and I will amuse you. Lady Ailesbury—a dear, natural, good-humoured woman, but on a fever to distinguish herself—projected a little ball. We all approved; she sent her list to Henry Greville all right, but in an evil hour she sent to Rodolphe Appony *neveu* to consult about the buffet. She says she told him she wished to know what to order— 'j'aimerai souper.'

'Ah! ah! au nom du ciel, je vous prie.' She did not see why, but said, 'mais il faut avoir quelque chose.'

'Un thé coiffé, tout au plus, un thé coiffé.'

She was very much puzzled. Had heard of many

[1] Madame de Meyendorf.

fashionable things, but not of that. However, to *tâter le terrain* ventured upon *cinquante poulets*. 'Ah! ah! l'horreur, on vous écorchera, dix, tout au plus.' I will tell you *l'historique* of the case to-morrow.

Saturday.—Mme. de Flahault pronounced Lady Ailesbury's to be the best little ball that had ever been given, well lit, just the right number of people, champagne, *pâté de foie gras*, proving Rodolphe to have had no finger in the pie, all ages prancing. Georgy relates with a look of rapture and emotion how she heard ' Lady Georgiana Fullerton coming down stairs '— sounds unknown on these shores.

Mme. de Lieven is, I hear, much annoyed at Alexandre having broken off his match with Mdlle. Dackenhausen. At best an imbecile, and I fear much worse.

What a moment! ' Un paquet qui vient de Londres.' Did it walk? Muller cuts a string and two *rouleaux* appear. The blue is so lovely that I joy in its being mine. Both well adapted to the wearers. As the pink is not too glaring, a sort of old Aurora will she look. And the blue so refined and chaste that an Abbess might wear it at a festival.

To the Duke of Devonshire.

Paris: March 12, 1841.

My dearest brother,—I write because I am so frightened at the idea of your punishing me by a long interval. My letter will be *triste*; we can think of little but the poor unhappy Flahaults. Adèle, their third daughter, a charming girl, is, I fear, dying. Richard Verity was called in, but when the case had become almost desperate. It is a terrible tragedy. Flahault is scarcely in his senses, refuses all comfort; and she is, as in all things, the very reverse of him, wretched and alarmed, but feeling, what is true, that his giving way so entirely is terrible for the other girls. But it is impossible not to feel deeply for him, for them all. He never goes to bed, but remains at the outside of her door all night. There was a slight amendment last night, but Verity does not seem to think she can live.

I am very good for nothing after my long *grippe*, and on a day like spring am not to go out. But I am sitting with lilacs in my alabaster basket opposite my great cage. If I was left out, a beautiful *tableau de genre*. All your presents and my original ones living in harmony together, all coming under the glass, where they have a garden. In the middle a *monticule* of sand from Havre. Branches of millet in a dark blue vase and bulbs of light blue Bohemian glass. The *veuve* is like a giraffe and domineers without oppressing.

Lord Palmerston writes to Mme. de Lieven in great spirits, and says the marriage [1] is approved of by them all—twenty-five years old, beauty, talent, has loved her for near three years (*c'est une espèce de roman*).

To Lady Carlisle.

Paris : March 1841.

Dearest sister,—Adèle de Flahault is calm and free from pain, but her case is considered hopeless; only a question of time. I am miserable about them, and Richard Verity comes from thence quite beat down by the scenes he has witnessed.

Politics I never know how to write about. The Whigs seem to me strong in their stirrups. When the Government does right it is triumphant and admirable, when wrong lucky and undaunted, so I have ceased to think anything can overturn them.

I hear from Vienna that Lord Beauvale [2] was seized

---

[1] Lord Jocelyn married Lady Fanny Cowper on April 25.

[2] Lord Beauvale's marriage to a daughter of Count Maltzahn.

with gout during the ceremony and cried out to the clergyman, 'Dépêchez-vous.' He was taken ill after the ceremony and fainted away. The next day, instead of the great *festin de noces* which had been prepared, she dined at a little round table by his bedside.

To LADY CARLISLE.[1]

La Jonchère : June 1841.

Dearest of sisters,—Has a rumour reached you, not of my falling between two stools but off one ? I suffered much pain, did myself no injury, and now am only desired to keep quiet on my couch.

This place is delicious, the beauty beyond description, an excellent house. Granville enjoys it, and it agrees with him admirably.

Yesterday Bulwer, Greville and Heneage dined and slept here. Bulwer most agreeable and in high force. To-day Charles and Mrs. Percy and Plunket dine and sleep, on Friday Greville returns with Alava. You see our *genre de vie.*

Soult menaced resignation upon the Duke of Orleans voting against him, and has been with difficulty pacified, principally by his son being sent for. The offer of Vienna is to be made to him, though it is not easy to think how Metternich will swallow and arrange about his title. My friend [2] of the Rue St. Florentin writes, ' Elle [3] déraisonne ; il est très aimable.'

---

[1] Lord Granville was seized with a paralytic stroke towards the end of March, from which he gradually, although never completely, recovered. In the interval between this illness and the removal to La Jonchère, a place in the neighbourhood of Paris which Lord Granville hired, Lady Granville only wrote short notes, and those chiefly referred to her husband's state of health.

[2] Madame de Lieven.

[3] Madame de Flahault, whose husband had been promised the Embassy at Vienna.

To Lady Carlisle.

La Jonchère : June 15, 1841.

The weather is becoming fine again, and Granville and Georgy are delighted with the beauty of their drives.

Mr. Percy was here yesterday. He tells us his friends count upon a majority of seventy in the new Parliament. He is in despair to hear that ours reckon upon one of eight.

We have been much excited about dearest Leveson. I do hope there will be no contest in South Staffordshire. Bridgnorth is also a most exciting interest, but I fear in spite of zeal and Marie, who must be a charming canvasser, that there is a formidable power against them.

I pity little Lady Sarah Villiers so much, as I think her happiness is embarked in this marriage. I am told *qu'il n'y a rien de si volage* as this youth,[1] and that he will not commit himself. I think nothing more likely than that he will marry somebody else when they get him to Vienna, and that all the silence in the world will not avail.

The Flahaults are much annoyed at another failure, and this after the long wished for embassy had been given and accepted.[2] I think they will, however, behave quietly and understand the difficulty that seems always imperative when there is a question of touching the hero of Manchester.[3] We heard yesterday that his son is to be made Duc de St. Amand. I should like to be called Duchesse de la Jonchère.

I think my brother will approve extremely of this place. He does not mind a drive, and from the Hôtel Sinet it is an hour and a half. We could lodge him, but I fear he would not like it, as the bedrooms, though very clean and nice, are extremely small. But what he would

---

[1] Prince Nicholas Esterhazy, who married Lady Sarah in February 1842.
[2] He eventually was appointed.   [3] Marshal Soult.

like is the dry, pure air and high situation. They are making hay, but there is no sting in it. I have not smelt it. It is damp brings out its sweetness, and its mischief is merged in this large atmosphere.

To Lady Carlisle.

La Jonchère : June 1841.

The day before yesterday Madame de Flahault came triumphant with the election news. Yesterday it was not so cheering. I think it seems doubtful if the majority will be sufficient to enable the Tories to carry on the Government, although sufficient to make it impossible for the Whigs to remain in.

Do you know, most dear sister, that I cannot resign myself to the idea of losing Morpeth's holiday and a chance of many of you by turns ? How I think he most especially would enjoy this place ! The day before yesterday, at a stone's throw from Paris, we drove, through chestnut woods and fields of waving corn, the peasants in their bright colours cutting wood, and making their *récolte* of raspberries perfuming the air, to *les Deux Moulins*. There, from one of those grass platforms that look as if the fairies had made them to dance in at night, we looked down upon Versailles, château and town, like a model. I pined for Morpeth. And again yesterday, when after a broiling morning we drove to the broad terrace of St. Germain, all the Sunday people walking with their children, and almost sea air blowing upon us. Again and again to have you and yours here would be too delightful.

On Saturday we came home to other pleasures. The Flahaults just arrived from Paris, agitated and aggrieved, but reasonable. She goes with her girls to Ems to-morrow ; he remains here, uncertain what awaits him. To dinner came Madame de Lieven, Guizot, Broglie, and Bulwer. She was enchanted with the place, and provoked because *les Français n'ont pas l'organe d'admirer ce qui est beau.* The fact is they both know La Jonchère intimately, and have seen the Aqueduct of Marly and the Palais de St. Germain, and that she was astonished and charmed at finding herself for once devoted to the beauties of nature, sneering at politicians. They all stayed till nine, and were very agreeable. Guizot anxious to do well for Flahault, but not prepared to go out on the question, curious about English politics. De Broglie behaved very prettily, though not naturally fond of the Princesse.

What a storm we had last night, and how in the midst of it did I feel at this height, with the tops of the trees bowing all round us, and the lightning in at the countless windows!

To LADY CARLISLE.

La Jonchère: June 1841.

My own beloved sister,—Morpeth's speech is quite beautiful, quite perfect. I cannot bear to think of his being beaten, I can of his being out. Mr. Raikes tells us that the Duke of Wellington writes him word that nobody can foresee what will be the result. But if you could imagine to yourself what a *beau rêve* it is to me, thinking of having Morpeth here, of enjoying with him, as I know he would do, this delicious place, you would understand my being, what I am become, terribly selfish.

All you tell us amuses and interests us so much. Dear Marie is a most zealous friend. Granville's interest about English politics is extreme, and nobody can know more of election movements than we do.

We have constant society, but it has never been oppressive. Miss Raikes has been staying with us two days. She is very agreeable and a great favourite. Her father brought her down and dined the first day.

Plunket came with them, and yesterday Raikes returned and Lord Alvanley, who was quite charming. *Le meilleur enfant,* which does not mean *homme,* but I cannot persuade myself that he is not much altered and that he will end by being a very good as he is a most captivating person. Such cleverness, *si fin, si simple,* without one grain of effort. What a receipt for being, as he is, quite charming! I am a little in love with him. Montrond brought him here but returned to Versailles. He is coming to dine here some day next week.

To-day we are quite alone. Robert Verity always comes back to dinner with the Paris news, and Freddy, George Stewart, or Fullerton generally go there in the course of the morning, so that notes, letters, and parcels are always arriving.

To Lady Carlisle.

La Jonchère : 1841.

I cannot quite bear the anxiety about Morpeth's election. I cannot bear his not being whatever he wishes to be, and his beautiful speeches and perfection in all ways deserve success wherever and whenever he seeks it.

I have been crying because he is lowest on the first day's poll. Recollect I am in a poor state of health, and because they say if he is not elected, he will not, as I had reckoned upon, be able to come here.

I do abhor politics, elections. This lovely place would make you all forget them. I hear Granville 'Globe' in hand : 'I never saw a worse statement.' Freddy : 'Nothing to console one.'

Here is the courier and Mary's kind letter. I had my roar out, which did me good. I feel all sorts of wrong thoughts. I never could bear to see another

Wortley again as long as I live.[1] Then I hoped the most dreadful mischief would happen in Ireland. That I repented of as soon as I thought it. Then I felt that I would not listen, did not care about Charles's[2] success or anybody's. There, now you have it all.

There is a sentence in Mary's letter, a slight distant hope held out of having you here. She says truly, what repose and enjoyment awaits that adorable Morpeth, and to become anything and everything, when those poor unfortunate Tories have struggled through their weary day.

Granville is improving, as he has done from the first, by degrees, not perceptible at the time. He now walks, leaning upon an arm, and his general health is excellent.

Yesterday we had a great amusement. 'Much Ado about Nothing,' curtailed into what might have been called, 'Benedict, the Married Man.'

The play was admirably acted by—Leonato, Georgy in an under cap of Granville's with tow whiskers, beard, side curls and a large silk dressing gown; Don Pedro, Freddy well got up in his own shirt-sleeves, my scarfs, and a long feather in a silk hat; Claudio, Heneage; Benedict, Plunket, both in short silk mantles; Hero, Georgy again, white veil and natural flowers; Ursula, Freddy again, perfectly well dressed, the image of Georgiana Wortley; Beatrice, Miss Raikes, beautifully dressed.

They had arranged a bower with a path behind it and all sorts of flowers with lamps.

The audience sat in clover. Granville in his arm chair. Doctor Verity and I in perfect ecstasies on each side. Fullerton perched high above us. Mr. and Mrs. Gêne, Mlle. Josephine, Mr. Müller, Mrs.

---

[1] Lord Morpeth was defeated in Yorkshire by Mr. Wortley.
[2] Mr. Charles Howard was returned for Cumberland.

Hayes [1] forming the mass of the audience. Pray re-read it and fancy them.

To-day we have all the odious papers and a long letter from Leveson. One from Marie, who will not be moderate in opposition.

The Fullertons and Freddy are gone to church in Paris, and to take back our *prima donna*, who to our great regret is going to Honfleur to-morrow, and to England afterwards. I hope the Tories will do something for Mr. Raikes.

To the Duke of Devonshire.

La Jonchère: August 29, 1841.

One line without stopping to take breath. We hope to set out for Nice the second week in October. The Fullertons with us. Freddy will follow. The Levesons join us there. We shall spend the early months there till February, and then we hope Rome. Naples in April. What happiness if you are coming! But all turns upon one thing, of course, how Granville is at the time.

The Carlisles are in great enjoyment here and perfectly well. To picture us, *l'heure qu'il est*, Lady Carlisle, Mary and Harry went off at twelve to church at Versailles, and then they are to see in detail *les Grandes Eaux* play.

Lord Carlisle, Granville and I are stepping into another *calèche* to see 'La Fête des Loges' at St. Germain. We come home to find Mme. de Lieven, Molé, and the Pahlens, who dine here.

Bolton Abbey has been ecstasy to Fullerton, Frederick Howard and, I believe, Louis de Noailles, and we have eaten up nineteen grouse from there already.

[1] The servants.

To the Duke of Devonshire.

La Jonchère: September 10, 1841.

What pleasure it was to receive your letter to-day, my dearest brother, and to know that you have received all our letters and know all about us, and mean to be of us, first and greatest of all pleasures! Fullerton says he has written to you a full account of everything.

Mme. de Salvo, *née* Claxton, about eight and twenty, lovely, refined, full of talent, sense and goodness. She would marry Salvo. *Que voulez-vous?* She has drawn his picture and hung it up in her room, and under it she has written, 'Mon cœur éprouve ce que ma pensée ne peut rendre.'

Till[1] goes to Nice by Granville's desire. Kulbach leaves behind him his fat lame old black terrier, and gladly accepts the *rôle* of travelling tutor to Till. You won't like him; he is ill-tempered, misanthropical, wrapped up in self, and it is only to Granville that he behaves decently.

I have the best account of Granville to give. He walks about the house and verandah, only leaning on his stick. I believe we shall go to Paris on October 11 to your rooms in the Hôtel Sinet for four or five days, then to Versailles or Fontainebleau for two or three days, whilst Kulbach gives up the two houses. He then joins us. We take Pater (cook), Charlemagne (*chasseur*), and Charles (footman), François Righi (courier). We mean to steam part of the way and to go as slowly as possible.

We have the Maison Grilla,[2] that which was the Brownlows and Pembrokes. Monsieur La Croix has taken it for us and is slaving for us at Madame Graham's instigation.

---

[1] A dog, a present of the Duke's.   [2] At Nice.

The Demidoffs[1] are at Dieppe. She asked Mme.
Albufera to bring her here, who wrote to ask me if she
should. Felix Schwarzenberg is coming here, sent by
Metternich to be *chef* during Appony's absence. Mme.
de Lieven wrings her hands and says, ' Il n'y aura que
des garçons.' Lady Cowley is very ill and Lord Fitzgerald likely to come, if Peel can prevail upon him.
Sir Robert Gordon to Vienna, Sir Charles Bagot to
Canada, are, I believe, certain. Morpeth has made
another most beautiful speech. Leveson is elected
without contest for Lichfield. Marie writes from
Herrnsheim, bored to death and longing to get back.
They are going to Brighton for a fortnight to drink
mineral waters and to see Susy. They join us in
November.

To the Duke of Devonshire.

La Jonchère : September 24, 1841.

This letter is entirely on business, dear Grace, first
to give an excellent account of Granville, and to say
that we intend to set out about the 15th.

I am assured that Leveson has done his election
matters well. Morpeth's retreat is beyond all praise.
Lady de Grey really in despair. The Beauforts talked
of for Vienna. Paris suspended still. A report that
Peel sent to offer it to Lord Beauvale. The Queen
would not let them sit at her round table, but insisted
on whist. Lord Clarendon says ' she might as well
have asked some of them to play on the German flute.'

To the Duke of Devonshire.

La Jonchère : September 30, 1841.

You dearest brother,—Letters will now tumble on
you like the river at Gastein. Thanks for your delicious
acount of that town.

---

[1] Count Demidoff married in 1840 Princesse Mathilde, the daughter of
Jerome Bonaparte.

I am made very happy to-day. Robert Verity will travel with us to Nice, and leave us only when his uncle Richard joins us there. Richard and his wife will follow our fortunes, independent of us, but always in the same town and on the same road, to and from. You do not know what a comfort this is to me.

The Duchess[1] writes from Windsor to her mama. The Queen in a muslin frock, all kindness, with her beautiful baby—a little low, but very proper in her conduct.[2]

Morpeth still means to go to America. He says autumn is the time for Niagara and the forests.

Lady Sandwich and Walewski are just come. She says Sir Robert is oppressed with claims. Lord Castlereagh says, 'My father wishes for Paris, and he must have it;' Lady Jersey, 'Either Paris or Vienna will satisfy us;' but Lord Cowley told Lord Clarendon he never was so well in his life, so it will be his.

Monsieur Demidoff, it is said, is sent for to his native country, where, Mme. Appony says, she will be admitted *en famille*, he not at all. How cross he will be! and when he is, they say he beats. She is a very fine girl, I think, with a charming countenance and frank manner.

Flahault dined here yesterday. Mme. de F. and the girls are gone to England. Flahault told me that he was walking round Dessein's garden at Calais. At a window was a woman playing with her parrot. 'I cannot tell how, but she was *si gentille, si gracieuse,*' that he called his girls, and they remained *en cachette*, quite riveted with this little scene. The window shut. They had the curiosity to inquire. Mlle. Déjazet.[3]

---

[1] Duchess of Sutherland.   [2] To her new Ministers.
[3] The most amusing actress of her day.

To Mrs. Hamilton Hamilton.

Nice: November 28, 1841.

Dearest Mrs. Hamilton,[1]—We left La Jonchère with much regret. Our journey was prosperous as far as Lyons, but there we were detained nine days, and in weather that made us all feel depressed—a fog like a London one, and the vapours arising from all the inundated ground. The river and road from it alike impassable. When we embarked at last, we felt as if escaping from prison. When we arrived at Valence, breathing light air and the sun shining, I cannot tell you what was the renovating feeling. All the rest was delight. Avignon, Fréjus, the first view of the Mediterranean, the beautiful Estrelles, two days of repose in Lord Brougham's excellent house at Cannes, and then a beautiful day's drive here.

And now, dearest Mrs. Hamilton, how difficult it is to write to one to whom all used to be said with such pleasure and sympathy, to drop out what used to be poured, to know neither where to begin or how to stop.

Of politics, on Lord Clarendon's authority in a letter just received, there is a dead lull. The Queen and her magnificent baby are perfectly well. Sir Robert has not let out a plan or intention.

Nice swarms with English, but we know scarcely any of them.

[1] Her husband was Chargé d'Affaires under Lord Granville at Paris and had been transferred to Rio. Lady Granville entertained a warm friendship for his wife.

1842

To Mrs. Hamilton Hamilton.

Nice: January 4, 1842.

The new year, dearest Mrs. Hamilton, has already made me two presents. Susy has a fourth girl, and is going on well. Freddy is arrived in high health and spirits.

The calamity of the poor Grahams has been generally felt. She was driving with her baby, when he was seized with apoplectic convulsions, and in a few hours all was over. Madame de Lieven says: 'On ne sait pas de quoi se réjouir dans la vie. L'arrivée de cet enfant a sans doute été le plus beau jour de la vie de cette femme; pendant un an un bonheur inconnu, incomparable—et puis!'

Douglas was at Paris, going little into society, looking fat and well. Madame de Talleyrand in radiant beauty, the Castellanes, Monsieur de Maistre, Governor of the place, Léon de Narishkin, and my brother dined here yesterday. Both the men are agreeable, the Russian particularly.

The 5th.—The *Carnaval* is exerting itself. There was a fancy ball at Madame de Talleyrand's the other night, and there is another given by half a dozen people the day after to-morrow. My brother has been entreating Georgy to go in costume. She has at length consented to order a cap and apron, and he means to say she is a Derbyshire peasant.

The christening [1] is the great topic of the day in England *en attendant* the meeting of Parliament. The Duchess of Northumberland, Lady Lansdowne, and the Duchess of Sutherland are to be the only women invited. The blue riband vacant by Lord Westmorland's death is not yet given. The Duke of Beaufort is much annoyed at its not being yet offered to him; the Duke of Buckingham's claim being, it is supposed, in the way. The Duke of Cleveland is so ill that it is thought they are waiting to give the two at once. Lord Clarendon writes me word: 'Lady Westmorland is at the Bedford Hotel at Brighton, and has told the waiter that she means to be a disconsolate widow, and is determined never to be happy again.'

The English are getting up a ball given in honour of the christening. George Stewart is disputatious and dictatorial upon the questions of what is fitting or not. It is one of the peculiar attractions he has in society, to be both without any shade of temper or malevolence. He provokes but does not offend, always stirring the cup but never putting any bad ingredient in it. Freddy is on the committee. Richard Verity has just made them happy by his adhesion, and a deputation is now gone to my brother. The resident nobility are 'indeed truly glad to see this loyal spirit.' It is hoped Lord Adam Loftus will be sober, and that the authorities of the town will allow the theatre to be floored.

Paris, we are told, is colder than ice; but the *Carnaval très animé*. The Duke of Orleans extremely gay—dancing and concerts. Madame de Montmorency has given a ball in her beautiful new house. The poor Cowleys in the meantime are suffering from the meanness of the English Government, inconceivable in Tories as it was in Whigs. All they direct to be done is the doing up the *rez de chaussée*.

[1] Of the Prince of Wales.

January 29th.—I will wind up my letter with news received from London yesterday. Lord John is in good heart and expects much fun for the party, and perhaps some little benefit to the country. The reports about Sir Robert's intentions are never two days the same. The De Greys are said to dislike Ireland; he the expense, she the bore, neither having the sense to hold their tongues. I hear that Esterhazy has again put off arriving, and that Lady Jersey has kept fixing the day and inviting all London, ' just as people ring the bell and order the dinner to make the guests who are late arrive.'

God bless you, dearest Mrs. Hamilton. My husband's best remembrance to you both.

To the Duke of Devonshire.

Milan: May 31, 1842.

My dearest brother,—You cannot know the pleasure hearing from you gives. I certainly know no pleasure greater than that of so many that I love being all assembled in one place, and hearing of them from each other, and your letters are epochs in my life.

Dogs.—Till is too clever, too pleasant, improves daily in comprehension, and from the cooks and *laquais de place* sitting in a row, when he gets into the carriage, to the Seaford family, the idol of everybody. Lady Seaford has begged me to ask you for a descendant of Boney.

Bulwer's escape was like Doctor Beamish's. He says: ' I was to have dined at the Poix at half-past six, did not reach Paris till half-past ten, during which time they must have fancied me one of those curious calcined creatures which Majendie wishes to preserve.'

Why, did not I at Tixal translate the ' Ideale,'[1] and read my translation to Francis Egerton, by that means persuading him to learn the tongue? If I had not lost

[1] A poem of Schiller's.

the copy, would not I send my poem to prove my words? It is a proof that then, as now, I think it the most beautiful thing I ever read in any language.

The Seafords set out for Turin at six this morning, the Fullertons at twelve, for an early dinner at Lecco, and a charming evening drive to Varenna.

Yesterday the Confalonieris, Abercromby, Trecchi, and Felix Schwarzenberg came, *p.p.c.*

I am just been to a sort of Passage Panorama, and, being generously inclined, bought fairings for the family. A book of poems for Dody, Bulwer's 'Zanoni' for George, two little volumes, Schiller's 'Gedichte,' for Freddy, and a map of Hamburg, all the poor burnt part blazing in bright red, for my husband. And here I am, very hot indeed. At five we have a roasted goose and beef steaks for dinner, and at six we hurry to the Corso. It is beautiful to see. Such pretty women in such smart equipages, and the *Vice Roi's* carriage and six, with liveries that, though a darker yellow, make me think of yours. Mme. Terzi took Lady Dalrymple out to drive, engaging her to dismiss her *remise*. At the entrance of the Corso the axletree refused to move, and there they sat till a friend picked them up. Mlle. Terzi is in great beauty. They go to Paris on Saturday.

To the Duke of Devonshire.

Stuttgard: June 16, 1842.

Think of us in this clean, broad, tranquil town, where we have a sort of a palace, Hôtel Margrath, and where we rest to-day. We send Kulbach on to have house prepared for us at Wildbad, where the Fullertons are to arrive to-morrow, the Levesons and Eward on the 20th. I am all fury and dread at the idea of Lord Shelburne's mastiff.

Why, to-morrow is the 17th, and on the same day we step into our respective baths. Granville is ex-

tremely well. Sometimes I think if? if only? you
were to follow your fancy and with three days' steaming
come and look at the *juste milieu moyen* between Buxton
and Gastein?

Marie writes : ' Lord Shelburne is coming with an
immense retinue, composed of bipeds and quadrupeds.'
Oh, the vile mastiff! and what is become of that Jack
the house built proceeding? Stephen [1] to Castellane,
Castellane to me, I to Leveson, Leveson to Shelburne
warning him off the premises.

We shall, I hope, stay a long time in the Wurtemberg
dominion. Yesterday we drove after an early and exquisite repast to the gardens and saw much sport.
The King and the Princess of Orange [2] taking a comfortable walk together. Then Neuperg the *gendre*,
married to the second daughter, a good-looking man.
Then Count Buhl in a large vehicle, Sir George Shee
in a phaeton, and Mr. Wellesley, walking and stalking
up and down.

This morning I followed a most distinguished-look-
ing blowen, such a *maintien* and walk, like Dino and
Orleans in her go. Wondered, till I saw the sentinel
salute her, then I started, looked at her face, called
' Till, venez ici, monsieur.' She turned upon me, a fat
resemblance of the *docte Hélène*,[3] nothing pretty, but the
perfection of grace and manner. Orange it was again,
out shopping, in a green veil and coloured muslin frock.

God bless you. My love to every stone and rivulet.
All the Splugen is like the robbers' stone and four
mile walk [4] on a gigantic scale, beautiful beyond measure.

---

[1] Stéphanie, Dowager Duchesse de Bade. She was a Beauharnais.
Napoleon adopted her and married her to the Grand Duke.

[2] The Princess of Orange was the daughter of the King of Wurtemberg.

[3] A Princess of Wurtemberg and aunt of the Princess of Orange.
She was married to the Grand Duke Michael, youngest son of the
Emperor Paul.   [4] At Chatsworth.

TO THE DUKE OF DEVONSHIRE.

Wildbad : July 20, 1842.

All our thoughts have been at Paris for the last days. Never was there a more horrible and unlooked-for event.[1] 'L'affliction, la consternation est grande, le regret le plus sincère. Une grande sympathie pour les pauvres parents et une grande inquiétude pour l'avenir. Les Chambres sont convoquées pour le 26. On y portera une loi pour régler la régence. Ce sera, j'imagine, le Duc de Nemours. Il y aura des obsèques solennelles à Notre-Dame, et puis le Roi conduira le corps à Dreux. Il y aura des réceptions chez le Roi pour les corps constitués, réceptions muettes. On le saluera. Le Roi est plus affaissé que la Reine. L'exaltation pieuse soutient la Reine, mais la désolation là, partout, est immense. C'est un grand moment pour ce pays-ci. Tout le monde sent cela, et tout le monde est sérieux. Quel sort ! Quel inexplicable décret de Dieu ! Un accident si simple avoir des conséquences aussi énormes ! Car regardez le gouffre que cela laisse à côté du trône. Une dynastie qui commence se trouver à la veille d'une régence !'

TO THE DUKE OF DEVONSHIRE.

Herrnsheim : August 1842.

In a small but very pretty luxurious drawing-room, Marie, dressed at three o'clock, with long curls and in a light blue gown. Why? To go across the court and small flower garden to an orangerie, where sits, in a light-coloured smock frock and black tie round his throat, Herr Peters, a young promising artist—not a charity. Why? To make a drawing of the said Marie at her spinning wheel, where she spins, like a real Deutsche Hausfrau, yards of linen thread. I am proud of the

[1] The death of the Duke of Orleans, accidentally killed by a fall from his carriage. The following account was received from the Princesse Lieven.

way with which she has, with a fairy's wand, that is with taste and skill, made herself, of an unbuilt house and small pavilion, a delicious country house, where she can receive whom she pleases. This orangerie she has converted into a drawing-room, and I had no rest till the Baron von Pfeiningen, our *intime* and constant guest, a great friend of her father's, with true chivalry and zeal drove off and fetched from Mannheim somebody capable of making me a drawing, which I beg you will graciously receive when Susy, who sets out for England on Saturday, leaves it at your door.

I am so grateful to you for your kindness to Freddy and the promised week at Chatsworth.

I have just had a letter from Paris. Guizot seems on his legs again, after a violent *tremblement de terre*,[1] and will go on for some time longer. 'Did I tell you I saw Lady Beauvale? *Elle a tout ce qu'il faut pour être belle*, and there's an end of it; *mais elle est vraiment charmante, douce, modeste. Elle adore son mari, ce qui a l'air un peu drôle, et il a l'air gracieux et bon pour elle.*'

11th.—The Rivers's and Fullertons returned at nine yesterday evening, the latter having dined with Stephen. A great German repast of black *entrées*, hams, sausages, and heavy puddings at two o'clock. The Palace beautiful and *magnifique*. The reception of them rapturous. Stephen in tearing spirits.

To the Duke of Devonshire.

Herrnsheim: August 1842.

My dearest brother,—How terrible the disturbances are! Derbyshire, I trust, is quiet.

Lowndes is here, and I have the happiness of seeing

---

[1] A trial of strength took place between the Ministry and Opposition on the question of the election of a President for the Chamber of Deputies, when Monsieur Guizot was nearly defeated.

that, however annoying and unsatisfactory the business may be that occupies Granville for hours, his health does not suffer, and he bears the intense heat, that knocks us all down, better than any of us. This is doubly delightful, because Robert Verity has left us, and a German doctor at Worms would be our only resource if he was unwell.

How hot! but how delicious! We sat out of doors till ten o'clock yesterday evening.

Leveson returned from the Worms station at that hour, without Douglas, who had announced himself as coming by that conveyance. He is at Baden.

To the Duke of Devonshire.

Herrnsheim : August 27, 1842.

We were out yesterday in the *carnavalette* in a *tourmente*. The coachman could scarcely see or sit ; the dust hid everything a yard beyond the ground. It was instantaneous and impetuous. We knew the Levesons, Shelburne and Fullerton, were gone to take a row in the *Lorelei*. The half hour was anything but pleasant. Nobody the worse. The boatman warned them just as they were stepping in, and we are all as fresh as larks in the delicious cooled atmosphere.

To the Duke of Devonshire.

Herrnsheim : August 29, 1842.

It was a great delight to hear from you again, my dearest brother, and I long to know that you have not been the worse for your exertions. I see you all at Bolton as plain as if I had been there. I should have liked to have been of the rubber.

Scene : a small drawing-room. Lord Granville in a large armchair in the window, reading the life of Sir Samuel Romilly. Lady Seaford in an adjoining one, listening attentively to Mme. de Flahault, who is relating many anecdotes and trials not yet before the public. She is much softened in manner, very much subdued in spirits, very agreeable, and a handsome woman, the asperity of the countenance gone, and the finest teeth in the world. Leveson as comfortable as if he was in bed, rolled up in a large fauteuil couch, not listening to Emily Hardy, who never ceases talking to him for one minute. Miss Hardy and Mlle. de Flahault, who is much prettier than ever, walking up and down a large sort of court before the windows. The Flahaults go to Darmstadt at one.

Herrnsheim is extremely gay; very *piquant*.

31st.—The first rainy day since we have been here. The Flahaults went yesterday, the Seafords to-day. The Badens returned yesterday from Baden, and are again settled at Mannheim for a few days.

To the Duke of Devonshire.

Augsburg: September 19, 1842.

Here we are, dearest brother, almost at the end of the first volume of our journey, and most successful has it been. The most perfect weather, excellent inns, and Granville extremely well. Heidelberg to Heilbronn and Geissengen are almost more beautiful than anything.

We rail to Munich to-morrow, settle ourselves in the Cour de Bavière, and wait there for Levesons, Fullertons, and O'Grady, who will all, I hope, be arrived so as to enable us to set off for Florence about the 1st or 2nd of October. It has been great happiness to have Dody, and nothing could equal my surprise at the change except my delight. Fullerton is far from well, and Italy has been advised by doctors and friends, by all but Georgy and myself, for we thought it so little possible that the idea had never crossed us. You may judge of the reprieve at the very moment of parting. I sometimes think—yes, upon my honour, I do—that you will come when you have done Ireland.

Granville has found you out in the *Fremdenbuch*, and all our friends and relations by turns.

I will write from Munich. Pray read two tiny volumes, ' Le Rhin, par Victor Hugo.'

To the Duke of Devonshire.

Verona : October 14, 1842.

I hope the details of our journey have reached you, my dearest brother, as I have begged my sister to keep you informed of them. She will, I trust, have told you how enchanted Freddy was with the beauty of Chatsworth.

Our summer here is delicious. Yesterday we sat in the market-place—the prettiest I ever saw—and to-day we have been out all day *en calèche*, acknowledging the amphitheatre (all I could do), enraptured with the six *portes*, and, above all, the Tombs of the Scaligers.

To-morrow we go to Mantua, the next day to Modena, and so on. Our next halt will be at Bologna. The Castellanes rushed into our rooms this morning on their way to Rome. They had been to the Villa Melzi and found the pair [1] alone. Her manner charming, doing the honours of her house *à ravir*, all queerness gone and health restored. The house luxurious, music on the lake, the little Duke charming. Who is Giovanni, a man like Lowndes, whom we found basking, not beaming, at the little town of Levis ? He enquired fondly after our healths, said he was come in eight days from London to see his father, but that he could not bear it; it was beyond him to stay; he must hurry back.

[1] The Duc and Duchesse de Melzi. She was *née* a Brignolé, and a cousin of Lady Leveson.

We imagined he said he had lived with the Sutherlands and was now at the head of the Victoria Station. But he talked indistinctly and rapidly, and the only thing obvious was that he thought Levis dull after Stafford House and the Brighton Railway.

We think the Levesons must be wishing the Crown Prince of Bavaria joy of his marriage, and we do not much expect to see them before Rome. Mme. de Dalberg is waiting impatiently for them at Bologna, where the hill upon which she and her sister Marescalchi perch has been inundated at its base, and they were as if blockaded for some days. How wildly they must have stared at one another!

To the Duke of Devonshire.

Rome: November 2, 1842.

We arrived at five o'clock yesterday after four long days. Sienna, Radicofani, and Viterbo. We are in an excellent apartment at Czerny's Hotel, all of us quite well. The weather like a very beautiful 2nd of June in the North.

The entrance into Rome charmed me. I felt at once I should like it as much as I disliked Florence. The brilliancy of the weather and animation of the scene—All Saints' Day—added their influence. This morning Granville and I have been sauntering in the Place d'Espagne, looking at distant bits of beauty, snubbing friars and beggars, admiring on the broad stairs the most picturesque of men, selling and combing the most intelligent poodles. The Fullertons, George Stewart, and Kulbach house-gazing. Our disappointment is that the Karolys took the Villa Aldobrandini the day before we arrived. There are objections to almost all the others. In short, we are going to make a grand effort, under the *chaperonnage* of Brook Greville, to see if Mr. Mills will let us La Villa Spada, on the

z 2

Mount Palatine. He did once, ten years ago, to the Puseys. If not, I almost think we shall remain here.

3rd.—Mr. Mills told Brook Greville the letting his house was impossible. We have one more to look at, which was the Princesse Pauline's, but I expect to bide here.

Drive with us on a glorious summer day down the Corso, by the ruins of the Temple of Peace, the Coliseum, Arch, etc., to Mr. Mills's garden, all full of roses, Cape jessamines and heliotropes; himself and Lady Charlotte Bury driving off from his door rather damaging the effect. There we walked and sat, and home again, going on our way to the Mount Quirinal and to the Pincio to see the sun set.

To the Duke of Devonshire.

Rome: November 15, 1842.

My dearest brother,—Till is well, but detests Rome. He despises the people, abhors the beggars. He has no preserves, no small woods or wide meadows to hunt in.

I am very much pleased here. We have space and air to my heart's content, less sun than we could wish, but excellent fire-places, and the house perfectly solid and thick-walled. A fresh, clean atmosphere like a country house in England, and a staircase that is hardly ascent, though it lands one at its top.

My fancies are: the Villa Mattei, with the sun setting over the wall covered with roses; Mr. Mills's Villa, where we are going this afternoon, has rather too much brick and *treillage*, though his view beats all.

The Mount Janiculum, with a drunken, rickety, *laquais de place*, who points out the domes more patiently than the sober do.

The grass before the San Giovanni, with the path to the convent and distant aqueducts.

The Pincio every day from twelve till two. There we sit and look at St. Angelo, standing black out of the light background, and St. Peter in his glory. Lady Susan Percy and her white Spitz, and Maurice de Noailles and his wife.

I was glad to hear a good account of Lord Melbourne to-day. Lord Glenelg had heard from Lady Holland.

To the Duke of Devonshire.

Rome: November 25, 1842.

My dearest brother,—The most distant hope of seeing you is delightful. We have taken this charming house for five months, and in the middle of May we talk of going to Naples. The real reason for being delighted at having taken it is—do I live to utter it?—the climate. Oh! if you could hear Granville! He declares that it is inferior to a winter in England, greater and much more sudden changes from muggy warmth to piercing cold, and sunless excepting for one bright week from the twelfth to the eighteenth, when it was heavenly to live and breathe. We shall see; it may improve.

Our young liked a dinner at the Dorias, a select blue party at Lady Davy's, and a mob at Torlonia; all amusing in their way. You know by sight the Roman people, the Murillos in the streets, the Bulls in the churches, the hideous aristocracy on the Corso, the Cardinals in their coaches. If you wish to peep behind my spectacles at any of the sights, Lady Carlisle possesses my ' Walk through Rome.' There are moments when I sigh for you, bits that, like jokes, we both take in with the same keen enjoyment. You have no idea of the amusement of reading De Brosses [1] over again here. His levity is atrocious, his want of principle

---

[1] *Lettres Historiques et Critiques sur l'Italie.*

revolting, and yet his fun, his perfect simplicity, his good-natured malice and joyous recklessness, make him an enchanting companion.

26th.—We picked the Levesons up on the bridge and have found them a lodging just over the way. Douglas [1] has written to Charles Gore that he is the happiest of men and Princesse Marie the most perfect of her sex. She has written to her friends that she discovers new virtues in him every day. Charteris is coming immediately to remain here.

Those trifles China and India occupy and interest Granville beyond measure. Leveson was all on fire when he heard it, and so rejoiced for Lord Pam's fame, though he has not the pleasure of being in for it. But how great and glorious it is!

To THE DUKE OF DEVONSHIRE.

Rome : December 9, 1842.

Our house is delightful, though with little sun. Granville's end of the long room has it all the morning from nine till eleven. It is a great object to us to be so central, and society is thus easy and pleasant. To have constant early visits would not be possible on a distant hill.

If you want my sights, *vide* Lady Carlisle, but accept a few pencillings by the way. The Ludovisi gardens and villa. The American oak and that particular ilex wood that makes a green canopy overhead and the old twisted supporters underneath, with old vases, seats, and sarcophagi. The retreat the sickliest spot in Rome and the most enchanting December walk. Then do you know one figure sitting in the ceiling by Guercino, not the Aurora?

Abdys and Mertcherskis and a few old generals play

---

[1] The son of the Duke of Hamilton, who was engaged to the Princesse Marie of Bade.

about the churches and ruins and give a *faux air* of Nice. Spencer Perceval is very agreeable and gay, but Mr. Calcraft tells me that he is still as odd as ever in opinion. 'Goes about and is all animation and spirits, but he is an angel of some church in Southampton, and goes over whenever Henry Drummond says he is wanted there.' Did you see Gibson's 'Triumph of Psyche?' Never did I see anything so lovely.

The Cadogans are coming to the Palazzo Chigi, immense and the aspect full south, but comfortless as to want of fireplaces and *dégagements.* In short, the complaints of others make us still more satisfied with ourselves.

But here comes Frederick Cadogan, the songster, and Lady Acton [1] with Monsieur Spada in her hand, and I must bid you good night.

10th.—Fullerton and I are going to hunt for ivy with yellow buds, to be found between Cecilia Metella's tomb and the bridge of Nomentana, supposed to have been brought from Greece by Adrian. The only representation of it is in a mosaic at the Vatican, the pendant of Pliny's doves, where there are two masks, one crowned with ivy with yellow buds. A pleasant little *chasse.* The said Mr. Fullerton is on the point of yielding to Lord Cadogan's earnest solicitations to go partners with him in the purchase of a bit of land at Tarquinia or Faleria, where they are to dig and share what they find. We think it will be awful when the moment comes of dividing the spoils—to whom the jug, to whom the arm.

I am told that Miss Lawley is engaged to Jem Wortley, and Lord Coke to Miss Whitbread.

We are going to meet the Levesons at the Baths of Titus, to walk from thence to see the Moses in San Pietro in Vincoli.

[1] The widow of Sir John Acton, the Neapolitan Prime Minister.

1843

To the Duke of Devonshire.

Rome : January 2, 1843.

You will have heard from my sister of our proceedings, my dearest brother. You will have seen that, after the too great delight of seeing Granville to all appearances perfectly well, we had a lesson, for which I am deeply grateful. He is now going on quite well, the only difference being that he feels himself rather less strong in walking, and that he consents to give up reading, outing, and all that can fatigue or excite.

You are most kind about Chiswick, but no. My great wish is our house in London, and then to go to all your Palazzi and abroad again if necessary.

Frederick Cadogan sings like an angel. The girls, admirable artists and good girls, seem perfectly happy. Potemkin and Lambruschini called to say that the Duchesse de Leuchtenberg [1] was extremely anxious to make our acquaintance. The lawless distich came into my head : ' The devil take Hyde and the Bishop beside,' but go I did, to make Granville's excuses, *robe montante sans cérémonie.* I found a little woman with long fair curls and red velvet cloak, trimmed with magnificent fur. If you wish to see her plainer, take Princesse Théodore de Bauffremont and Mme. de Courval, mix them in equal proportions, and take care not to drop any of the dignity and high breeding of the

[1] Daughter of the Emperor Nicholas. Her husband was the son of Eugène Beauharnais.

one or the brusque familiar garrulity of the other. Very civil to me, taking my hand, asking after you and dying to go to England. I think her a very amusing, charming little *autocrate*. Her life is very Russian ; she sight-sees from the dawn of day, goes to bed meanwhiles, dresses in a *robe de chambre* for dinner and goes to bed immediately after. She has three maids, who are waited upon by seven housemaids. When Marie was introduced to her, she said, ' Who are you ? ' Marie, almost choked by her quarters, did not answer, upon which she reiterated, ' But what's your name ? '

The joke about the Torlonia marriage is that they have put the old capital upon a new column, Principessa Alessandro Torlonia, *nata* Colonna.

We have a new great pleasure. Signor Moroni, Marie's singing master, plays divinely, and her lessons in the evening are little concerts and make variety without ceremony.

Hayes is charming with a passing curtsey—' Very pleasant on the Pinch this morning, Milady.'

To the Duke of Devonshire.

Rome: January 10, 1843.

I wish I could help writing to you so often, my dearest brother, but how is it possible ? It is not merely my gratitude for your letters, my avidity for more ; it is the positive delight of receiving them, accompanied with a longing to answer, ask, and talk, which it is the peculiar charm of your letters to give.

Scene : The long drawing-room, three fire-places blazing, which made Granville and myself, sitting by one of them in two arm-chairs, very comfortable in spite of the intense cold of the weather. Heyday ! What is this ? Clatter, shake. We rush to the window. A violent storm, large hail-stones, thunder-claps and vivid flashes of lightning. The door opens, and Kulbach, with

December 26 in his hand, and what a moment for it! and how we did enjoy it back in our arm-chairs! I have since read it again and again and once more to Granville. You give us such new lights and objects. We have scarcely seen any of the pictures and statues you mention.

Poor Mme. Zavadowska! She has just lost her son, her only child I believe, at Naples. I have only heard the sad event; nothing about her since she left Rome many weeks ago.

Think what a comfort it is to have our quiet and *far niente*, where *il suffit de regarder pour s'instruire*. The Tasso oak is utterly destroyed, the Colonna pine one half blown down. We are going immediately to Monte Mario. Oh, the Priorata di Malta! and the view of St. Peter from the Pamfili! Fullerton is going without loss of time to the palm trees, and Granville means to walk the first fine day in the cloisters of Santa Maria degli Angeli. We shall turn our attention that way and to the pictures and statues by degrees, *piano, pianino*. Fullerton adores St. Pietro di Montorio. We have only driven to the green before it, drinking in its glorious universal view. We have been to the Villa Albani, not within it, but the garden is delightful.

Charteris dined here yesterday for the last time. We shall miss him very much. He goes to-day to Naples.

I went to Stordogni yesterday, and saw the lovely little cast of Gibson's ' Psyche.' I have ordered one for you. Gibson has made six of the last groups, and Torlonia has one and the Grand Duke of Russia another. The novelties here are now things made from designs by Michel Angelo Gaetani,[1] and said to be equal to Benvenuto Cellini, which I much doubt. There are

---

[1] Brother of the Duca de Sermoneta.

leaf-openers, one an angel, another a devil. Castellani makes them in silver for a hundred francs each. Being penurious, I am going to present myself with one of each in bronze. The original casts are at a German sculptor's, whom it is a pleasure to employ. He had been one of the cleverest and most famous here, but from domestic calamities has fallen into great distress. And who should he be but the very Rohrich you name in your letter. His rulers, merely a bas-relief, are said to be beautiful. Fullerton tears his hair—he ought not, for it is growing scarce—over one Lady Davy had bought. Castellani has also made the bell that is in Raphael's picture of Leo X. Lord Cadogan has bought one of Rohrich in gun metal. Then there is Ariosto's inkstand, which Mr. Fullerton loves, but some say it is not a very pretty one. The great work of modern art began and talked of is Imhoff's ' Agar.' Ask Charteris about it when he has the happiness of seeing you.

To the Duke of Devonshire.

Rome: January 16, 1843.

I have an irresistible wish to write to you, dearest brother, because I cannot vent myself to anybody who quite understands me, and I think you will. Little Till is dead after two days of very great suffering. The servants are all in tears ; everybody was fond of him. You do not know what a pleasure is gone out of our days. We had made him such a pet, amusement and companion, that we shall miss him more than I can say. They are all sorry, but nobody can quite enter into my feeling about it, and my great object is to hide it. He is linked with so many thoughts and moments, and I had such a pleasure in seeing what a very great amusement he was to Granville. There never was such an engaging little creature.

And then the very thing of not being able to make anyone understand, and therefore endeavouring to suppress how very much I am grieved about it, makes it worse. Pray do not answer this; I write it only for my own comfort, and I have the conviction that you will entirely understand what is reason and what is folly. Believe me.

It is odd that writing this has enabled me to appear what I wish to be.

To the Duke of Devonshire.

Rome: January 20, 1843.

It is very odd. I felt, when I last wrote, ashamed of being so sorry, afraid of being thought to have been, which I was, crying all day, and I have been comforted by the excessive kindness and sympathy people have shown.

I am happy to tell you that Granville and Georgy are both well, and that to-day we have a day that can hardly be surpassed by any day in the year anywhere— soft, warm, nothing cold, nothing oppressive, too delicious. Monte Mario was in glorious beauty, seen by Dody, Granville, and myself for the first time. Hayes, a fling, pointed out a snow mountain. 'Is that in Italy, Milady?'

The yellow-berried ivy, clustering over a tall tomb near that of Cecilia Metella, is beautiful. Ask Paxton what is the *Chysocarpia* he mentions in his dictionary as Indian under the head of ' Edera.' This is said to be from Greece. Is it not the same?

Charteris writes to me from Naples that it is as odious as Rome is charming. Twenty degrees warmer, but very relaxing. The town Birmingham. Storms raging at sea, society raging on land in all its gossip and scandal. Lord Cantelupe the Apollo of the place; four ladies so in love that he cannot tear himself away. Mesdames Palfi and Hatzfeldt among the number.

The Levesons heard Clara Novello last night at the Opera, in the 'Puritani.' Nothing ever equalled the *furor* of applause, wreaths, nosegays. She was dragged home in a car, all surrounded by people with torches.

And this is all I can think of. Tenderest love to Freddy.

To the Duke of Devonshire.

Rome: February 1848.

Most dear brother,—Glorious summer almost is come. Granville is well. The Corso in full force, but I have taken the opportunity, was in bed all yesterday, and am now only just able to get up.

Monsignor Spada, a great friend of mine, who has got us orders and permissions without end, would expire of joy if his friend the *sous-secrétaire* could obtain what is written on the card.[1] I know not if the thing is easy. I think it rather an audacious demand, but the manner made it suppliant.

The Grand Duchess is come back. She has affronted the Neapolitans by her odd sayings. To the Duchess de Montebello, ' Is your father an Englishman? is he a gentleman?' This last shot to the '*nata* Jenkinson,' doubly primed. Charteris is waiting at Lady Anne Anson's feet. He has written to his father for his consent. They say such love was never seen. The Normanbys are in high spirits and he looks quite well, and what pleases me to see, they appear extremely fond of each other. They dine here again to-day and go to Naples to-morrow. We have the Chesterfields, Paul Esterhazy and Alfred Montgomery to meet them. The *Carnaval* rages. Georgy is the

---

[1] For admission and entertainment at Chatsworth.

most Amazonian of women ; Lady Chesterfield's balcony is, however, desperate also. Lords Chesterfield, Cantelupe, Leveson, Esterhazy, Fullerton, and F. Cadogan have ordered a car, and there are to be great doings on Thursday.

I cannot tell you how much I rejoice the winter is over. I have not talked of it, but I cannot say how trying I have thought the climate.

Mme. Potemkin's fancy ball for the Grand Duchess on Saturday is to be *très animé*. Marie goes in a Tyrolese peasant's dress, given her by her mother. Lady Chesterfield, Georgy, and the Cadogans powdered, Louis XIV. Our men sup at the Prince of Hesse's this evening.

I have a small oil picture of Till by Buckner, but it makes me miserable to look at it. It was painted after his death. Leveson had agreed to have him done as a *cadeau* to us, the very day that the poor little dog's dead body was carried to him, and do you know that the other dogs (Leveson's and Kulbach's) who saw the helper in the house carry out the body, flew at him for three days after with quite alarming fury ?

Lord Chesterfield's hounds have arrived.

·To the Duke of Devonshire.

Rome: March 3, 1843.

What can I say, how begin, how end ? I wait, best and kindest of brothers, to tell you all that your gift [1] bestows. Granville's delight is to alarm me, to tell me that it is still uncertain, that the Reverend may be taken ill and be unable to start. We drove yesterday to meet the hounds on the Ponte Motte, and we did peep into the carriages and wonder over return horses.

[1] The Duke made them a present of another dog.

4th.—We have had torrents of rain, and this morning a fall of snow. We see in the papers that between Calais and Paris there has been forty feet depth of snow. Oh! brother, brother, R. R. R. and his precious freight! Everything is prepared. Darling Till's basket new lined, and a new red collar, which he had only worn half a dozen times. His name is to be Tiber. Leveson says a famous breed ought to carry the first letter on.

I will try and divert my thoughts. Lady Powerscourt is still pretty, but altered, I am told, the resplendency gone. They dine here to-morrow. Her drawback is that she loves to sing with no voice at all, and without the slightest knowledge of music, but the pianoforte she reluctantly leaves. Mrs. Elliston is said to look wonderfully young and well. Kitty Oranmore is the best creature going, just like she was, only a most luxuriant wig of innumerable ringlets, put on with as little pretension as a bonnet, fidgets the beholder. Miss Browne appears to be a very agreeable, clever girl. They are miserable just now, because their youngest son and brother Henry, a beautiful boy, is on the eve of engaging himself to a young lady, who is very handsome, older than him, a case of desperate love on both sides. They say she is *perdue de réputation*; he says she is a wronged angel. Kitty hopes his uncle the Bishop of Tuam will carry him off by force.[1]

I wish you had just seen, as I have in my drive, the mountains round the Campagna covered with snow. the sun gleaming on them. 'But where is Mr. Rhodes?'

7th.—The *Carême* has brought quiet; our people are gone to drink tea with Latour Maubourg.

11th.—Great news. Backhouse has had a letter from Mr. R. R. on the road. He expects him to-day or

[1] They did not marry, and he died the next year.

to morrow, and desires to find him *deux lits de maître*. We think one must be for Tiber.

Everything is prepared, and a small negress to wait upon him and teach him all Till's tricks, of which she is perfectly mistress. This negress, born at Herrnsheim, by name Seppia, is a half-sister of Var's, jet black, very small and short-haired. A German would say of her that she has threads in her hands, sees the wind go down the street and hears the flies when they cough. I quote from memory, so I may be inaccurate. Her voice, manner, and shape exactly like Till's. We are extremely fond of her, but she is not possible as a constant companion, as a drawing-room favourite, or ever to be trusted when strangers are by. She is, to begin with, like a little hyena. There is something incredibly vicious and malicious in the way she turns up her nose and shows her teeth, when anybody but Granville or myself speaks to her, and she is then, alas! so incorrigibly dirty in her habits. We hope, that as Tiber's maid, she may learn sweetness and decorum.

We had the Oranmores the other evening, and I never saw people so pleased, especially as she had with her the youngest son, listening attentively to Marie, while Miss C. was warbling to a party at the Villa Strozzi, which I am told she does like a nightingale.

12th.—I write to-day under the influence of continual rain dropping on my spirits, and everything would seem dim if I had not the happiness of seeing my dearest Granville continue so well in spite of it.

I heard from Robert Verity yesterday of Lady William Bentinck 'having been struck with paralysis, her case, inflammation of the head, having been mistaken for nearly two months. We have now just a faint glimmering of hope.' I have a very affectionate regard for her, and what a loss her unbounded kindness will be to hundreds !

Charteris has written to Paul Esterhazy to desire him to contradict the report of his marriage.

We went yesterday to see the *petit St. André du Noviciat de Jésus, église qui est un chef d'œuvre de miniature et de bon goût*, except some sprawling figures of angels and saints, white, stuck about the ceiling. It is one of the *tre capi d'opera de ce pays-ci.*

Among the arrivals at Meurice's Hotel in 'Galignani's,' the Rev. R. Rhodes and H. Gossip. Dicky Gossip is the man, deny it if you can, who takes care of the small son of Boney. Unless the charms of Paris are irresistible, they must be here in a minute.

I believe Lady Cowley's unpopularity to be chiefly with those who are offended by her reforms in society, which all tell me have been very great improvements. She is a hundred times a better ambassadress than I was, perhaps a more stormy blowen.

To Lady Carlisle.

Rome : March 14, 1843.

It must have astonished Mons Sacer to see the hunt—exactly like Epping, I am told.

21st.—A long pause, during which I have received your long and most interesting letter. I think I have little to record beside the Duke of Manchester's death on Saturday. He suffered severely for two days, but I have not any exact idea of what his complaint was.

All the accounts from Trentham interest me, but principally the general opinion of the Duke's good health, next the beauties of the garden. There is no saying how true it is, ' How much more I shall like everything with my Roman eyes ! ' I feel a remembrance of many things in England vivid and enchanting, which I never had observed till I saw things here.

Your political news is devoured by Granville. Charteris has left Naples and there are many reports. He will be in London before this letter, so Freddy at least will know all about it. We are all well, inhaling spring, and Georgy up and down again, to the tops of steeples and galleries and bottoms of catacombs and excavations. We have been to see the beautiful little church of Santa Vittoria, with Bernini's statue of Santa Teresa, full of feeling and affectation. Our walks and drives are now enchanting. Flowers and trees all thinking of bursting out. And my brother has sent us such a live plaything, such an enchanting, coaxing little dog. Leveson and George started at seven this morning for Naples. On the 28th Marie goes from hence to meet them at Cività Vecchia, and Granville and I meditate going there also to see them embark.

Granville says we shall be in about a week at Florence, whither next I know not. The slow, lingering, dawdling journey, in delicious weather, a doctor with us, Tiber in the travelling basket, the Fullertons on and about, the *point de vue* home. Nothing can be more delightful to me than the prospect.

Everybody we know well gone or going—Mrs. Huskisson, Morleys, Normanbys, Lord Glenelg, Mr. Hay, Chesterfields, Powerscourts, Castellanes, Odiers. We have little beyond Cadogans, Lady Davy and Mr. Bentinck,[1] Lady Frederick's son, who dines with us to-morrow. The Italian part of the society is breaking up. Those we know best, Dorias and Chigis, are overwhelmed with the sudden death of Doria's sister, wife of the eldest Chigi, leaving seven children, only thirty, scarcely supposed to be ill.

[1] The Right Hon. George Cavendish Bentinck.

To the Duke of Devonshire.

Rome : March 24, 1843.

Here am I at my writing table, Marie packing up with vehemence, as Leveson is gone to Naples to meet her at Città Vecchia on Wednesday, where they embark for Genoa on the first instance. Georgy and Mr. G. F. Bentinck talking Church architecture over their cups—of tea; Granville uncommonly well, discussing the affairs of the Scotch Church with Calcraft, and Fullerton by the fire, and in a large basket, new lined with a handsome chintz, the little darling, engaging delicate Tiber, who is the greatest love that was ever seen.

Direct your next letter to Florence. We talk of setting out on the 10th and remaining some days there. What paper you write on is a matter of indifference to me. When thin I insinuate a sheet between your pages, which gives immediate solidity to the hand and facility to the eye.

The whole account of Nice amused us beyond measure. The balance is, I think, decidedly in favour of Nice as to pleasure and enjoyment, Rome as to attraction and moments of gasping for breath delight. It is so difficult. Place all for the latter, but their accidental circumstances all for former. Yourself (were you ever called an accidental circumstance before ?) living in the country instead of .in the middle of a town, the sea, German backgammon, Freddy, the novelty of Italian scenery, cactus hedges, olive groves, flowers, sun. Here the sort of nameless dreamy charm, the views of Rome from the different heights, the incomparable fineness of fine days, the populace, the bits and corners, *le mura e i sassi*, your letters, Tiber's arrival. Sum up and throw in first and foremost Granville's immeasurable preference for Nice.

Seppia is Var, beautifully made, swift as the wind, and her habitual attitude *debout*. Her residence is upon Granville's great coat and cloak, where she waits for the rapturous hour of going out, when she runs after the carriage all the way; Tiber only getting out with us when we walk, or by the great King,[1] when we sit and look on. I wish you could hear Granville, Dody, and him conversing at this moment, or see him when he calls us in the morning. He begins to know us all in different relations. All the most coaxing tender ways with Granville; pert to Dody; hates Kulbach because of the spoonful of castor oil the morning after his journey.

I did not comment on Lady Morley, because she is the one least to admit of discussion. She seems good and sensible and has an excellent manner with him.

To the Duke of Devonshire.

Rome: March 31, 1843.

My dear Grace,—Would that I could write like you or Dickens! How either of you would do justice to yesterday, the most dramatic day I ever passed!

At half-past eleven, as usual, we went out, and our first business was to leave two invitations for Messrs. Rhodes and Gossip to dinner on Monday.

From thence we went to Gibson's and found him at home. He said he seldom made busts, hating to do them, but that he wished to show us one he had just finished for Lord Kilmorey. Grazia, the famous model, a Roman peasant. We climbed up a narrow ladder into his workroom, and beautiful the bust is. On turning my head, I saw close to me an immense mass of terra cotta. I felt puzzled, and my thoughts went quick. In a niche near the summer parlour at Chiswick—Duke of Sussex—the Emperor Vitellius.

---

[1] The *chasseur*, whose name was Charlemagne.

Lady G.: Mr. Gibson, who is this? It is impossible, but if it was not, I should say it was Mr. ——

Mr. Gibson: Reeston Rhodes, Lady Granville. It is a very remarkable head.

Lady G.: It is a very fine bust, only I could never have believed when I saw.

Gibson: No, one would not. He is a very remarkable man; he comes with his pockets full of his own poetry, and he reads aloud to me while I work. Some of it appears good, but there is a great quantity of it.

We drove to the Villa Borghese. As we turned out of the Gate del Popolo, our coachman drove us rapidly up, *contra le mura*, to avoid the shock of the black carriage horses, harness, pole and all, who were coming plunging and dashing through the Borghese Gate.

We drove on anxious. On the top of the hill a crowd was gathered, increasing every moment. We stopped. The beautiful Mme. Crisi, as pale as death, told us she had seen a terrible accident—a carriage overturned, a woman she believed to be English thrown out and dangerously hurt.

Soon after Prince Borghese and Colonel Caldwell came to us. The lady was supposed to be dying, her spine hurt, and she quite senseless.

At this moment emerged from the crowd, something Johnsonian, pastoral, something I felt I knew, but could not immediately put a name to. My dear brother, poor Mr. Reeston Rhodes, in a large white straw hat, his hands bleeding and terribly nervous. He had met with a family of intimate friends, the Empsalls, from somewhere near Doncaster. He had asked this poor lady to drive with him, her three daughters following in her carriage. The accident happened, and she was thrown out into a ditch, and he, with his immense weight, upon her. Doctor Kipoch came; she was put into a litter, and we took him home.

To-day the poor lady is pronounced not quite out of danger. Mr. Rhodes has had leeches applied, and, although shook, is not in any way damaged.

He showed much feeling during our drive home, did not know how ill she was, yet much alarmed about her, mixed with much oddity. 'No Torlonia to-night. I am an unfortunate man. I tumbled out of the rumble the day before I reached Florence. Poor Mrs. Empsall, I am sure it is nothing serious. I have made my will a short time ago and have left your brother a diamond snuff-box, as a testimony of gratitude and admiration for his noble character. I have hurt the muscle of my thigh.'

My next letter will contain an account of Monday's dinner.

To the Duke of Devonshire.

Rome: April 15, 1843.

My dearest brother,—I sing Tiber. There never was such a darling. Beautiful I think, caressing, soft, help-less, and yet with a spice of the family temper, which prevents insipidity. Desperate volitions exerted with the utmost gentleness, a quiet little fury now and then. Oh! there never was such a love of a dog. You know that, from our peculiarity of our never letting our little Blenheims out of our sight they have immense advantages. We do not attempt education; all our care goes to health, and the success is perfect. He is plumping up, his coat glossy, his paws beginning to flounce and furbelow, his cough gone. I took him to Gott, who said as Gibson had done, 'What a beautiful little dog, exactly like one his Grace the Duke of Devonshire had here!' 'He gave it me.' 'Do I see Lady Granville?'

Brother, you will be jealous, you must expect it; he

beats them all hollow—much more like Boney [1] than Till. No accomplishments, it is true, but such quickness of comprehension, and when he walks with us, such ' let observation with extensive view.'   And then his beauty where he is in action, when he sees a lizard on the wall, or a crow in the heavens.

When you receive my bits of Tasso's oak, give the one you like least to Charles Percy, who wrote me a lament on the fall of that tree.

To 7he Duke of Devonshire.

Florence : April 25, 1843.

The severities of spring after a summer journey are so great here that we all feel them in different degrees.

27th.—Since which sentence I have been in bed with cold and sore throat, and *extinction de voix*. Still in that retreat, but almost well.

Rhodes detested Tiber, who howled and squeaked all the way, and whenever he did was violently shaken in his basket by the Colossus.   When they reached Meurice's Hotel, no Tiber.   Then came mental agitation of the severest sort.   ' I thought I should have died of it, but Monsieur Meurice, a most excellent man, kindly soothed me by sending off a messenger to Beauvais,' and back flowed the Tiber to his uneasy bed, having preferred the inn at that town, where he was found comfortably settled.   My love to Var.[2]   What a dear she must be!   And I long to introduce the different members of the family to each other.   If I were you, I should certainly buy Boney a, wife.   What is to become of us if the breed fails ?   Think what a charm even the illegitimate grandchildren possess !   I only wish one thing, that you could see Tiber with the flies.   They terrify him, but his ways with them, and his plunge under the car-

---

[1] A Blenheim. Landseer inserted his portrait in his picture of the poodle in the character of a Judge.

[2] A descendant of Boney, but not thoroughbred.

riage seat, his peeping out to see if the enemy is gone! What a gift you have bestowed!

The Hollands have a delicious house, luxuriously furnished, like an Eastern tale ; parroquets nodding and curling their pea-green heads, nightingales singing in their recesses, galleries, verandahs, all the possibilities of a hot climate, not available now. He is better, but has been very seriously ill. She poorly, and much out of spirits. They are much occupied with Lady Orford, and her daughter Lady Dorothy,[1] the prettiest, most captivating little creature I ever beheld. 'Fun in her eye, and mischief in all her thoughts.' The only day I was out, she rode up to me with General Ellice, hung over with flowers, a large straw hat with a red riband round it, and a bunch of peacock's feathers on the side of it. Her habit quite open, and little gauntlets, to be, as she said, like the Life Guards. We were all enchanted with her.

Our plans are unfixed, but Turin will be our next gîte.

To the Duke of Devonshire.

Florence: April 29, 1843.

I have no thoughts of going yet, but I think it will amuse you to note down what I shall have forgotten by the time I send this letter. After all that had passed, Georgy was curious to see Lady Douglas, and she and Granville called at the Hôtel de l'Europe. When they were announced, there came out to meet them, in an old purple pelisse, with her hair about her ears, a shabby, miserable-looking woman. She received Georgy with the most affectionate cordiality, and began talking of her journey. Presently Douglas appeared, thin and sallow, but looking gayer and happier than they had ever seen him. By degrees Lady D.'s spirits rose, and she became talkative, animated, and evidently exces-

[1] Now Lady Dorothy Nevill.

sively in love with him, and he extremely kind in his manner to her. Every symptom or suspicion of royalty is dropped ; no splash or finery of any sort. But you must prepare London for her personal appearance.

May 2nd.—Georgy has been all morning with the Douglases, and says he is very much in love, and that they are as happy as it is possible to be. He says, 'I am her slave,' and she, 'Oui, il fait tout ce que je veux.'

Tiber likes Florence very much indeed. Yesterday the Douglases came with Mora and Aspin, their two large spaniels, to call on Tiber, which with Seppia makes a cheerful little society for him.

To the Duke of Devonshire.

Florence : May 7, 1843.

Your letters are like Oberon's horn. I cannot help dancing. Josephe Potocki came last night, and with Paul Esterhazy entreats to be put under your feet. We have engaged Pacifico, the Genoese *voiturier*, by which means we shall dine in the middle of each day, and go small journeys.

Genoa, 15th.—There have been moments and views and enjoyments beyond description, but you know them all. Massa Carrara ! Spezia, where we slept, the most beautiful of all. Then we travel so luxuriously and slowly. At four every morning Pater, Kulbach, Tiber, and Seppia set off in the *fourgon*. At nine, Granville, Tiber, and I in the landau, G. Stewart and Dody *en calèche*, Fullerton and the doctor in a *coupé*, Hayes and Bumpy,[1] with *petit* Jean on the box, in a little *voiture du pays*.

G. will have unfolded the new plan of Arqui within two days of this, and one and a half from Turin, a pause of at least ten days, I hope. Here we have

[1] Young Granville Fullerton.

passed the hot morning in the Doria garden, and charming it was.

I have nothing to add but a sketch or two. A beggar was teasing Bumpy, *per carità*, pulling his blouse, not to be shaken off, when the Fullertons heard *petit* Jean say in Italian, 'Don't tease him, *il poverino*; he is going to school; leave him in peace.' The beggar stopped and presently joined in full chorus, 'Oh, *il poverino*; going to school; *il poverino*,' and walked away. Is not this a good specimen of two Italian classes?

I took a most beautiful walk with G. Stewart at Spezia, where there is the *berceau* of the small rose festoons and draperies—do you remember it?—and white round-headed acacias. We came close to the sea, and, to our utter astonishment and envy, in walked Tiber, perfectly happy, the greatest love, not liking the waves, but not deterred, patting and trying to put them down with his little satin paws.

To the Duke of Devonshire.

Arqui : May 23, 1843.

You can have no idea of the pleasure it gives us to accept your proposal of Devonshire House. Thank you a thousand times for that, as for so many acts of kindness that gild our life. But our arrival is delayed by our delight in this place. We all like it better than anything of the kind we have ever seen. Granville has taken the second mineral water this morning, and begins the mud bath for his leg and arm to-morrow. He is very well, but as yet the light air and perfect repose are the only remedies we have had time to judge of. There is no saying how much people would dislike Arqui who look for any sort of dissipation; a visit from the Directeur des Bains, a remarkably rough little carriage, and about a dozen invalids from the environs being all they could command.

I think Chiswick an incomparable place, enjoyed on a bad day. What will the enchantment of the folks be on a fine one!

We are so jealous of Var's accomplishments, and with some remorse, because, had not Tiber entirely put Seppia's nose out of joint, I do declare she could have done it all. She has immense talent. The manager of any theatre would be proud to engage her for any sum she would ask. But *que voulez-vous?* Tiber is so *gentil*, so full of natural grace and attraction, that he monopolises our affection, and will not learn anything. He delights in Arqui, leaps over the high grass like a kangaroo, and rushes into the Bormida River twenty times a day, but he will not go out of his depth, and Georgy and I are going to buy a duck to teach him to swim. He is at this moment romping on the terrace with Granville.

Georgy and I have been drinking this morning. Fullerton asked Baba where his mama was. ' Oh, in some valley with grandmama, where they will stay babbling all day.' God bless you.

Mme. de Lieven writes : ' J'ai vu ici Miss Gurney, merveilleuse beauté ; elle est superbe. La Duchesse de Talleyrand est ici, tellement belle et jeune que c'est fabuleux. Le jeune de Broglie va passer trois mois en Angleterre. La Princesse Clémentine y va aussi.'

TO THE DUKE OF DEVONSHIRE.

Arqui : June 12, 1843.

We have a delicious summer, but no heat. To-day might be the tenth of April. Poor Seppia has the raging distemper, and I live in dread of Tiber's having it. I never told you that I could never get them vaccinated at Rome, and when I said this to Evanson, he said, ' No more could Mrs. Abdy or Lady Rosa Greville get their babies.' I had yesterday a long letter from

Mme. de Lieven. Marie Appony's marriage is declared, and they go immediately after it to Madeira, Malaga, or Palermo. 'Mais enfin voilà un mariage dont on ne sait que dire. La mère a l'air malheureux, le père s'étourdit, le monde s'étonne. Marie est transportée d'amour et de joie. Madame Rodolphe Appony se croit grosse; toute la famille passe l'été à Paris. La Princesse Clémentine est ravie de son mari ; cela a fait une noce très gaie pour tout l'intérieur. La Duchesse de Nemours se rend très accorte et aimable. Mme. de Caraman, helas! reste Mme. de Caraman, ni plus ni moins—just the same. Marie Menzingen au comble de la joie est nommée Dame d'Honneur de la Duchesse de Nassau. Very well off. Cela l'enchante !'

We read about Ireland with great interest, Evanson representing that country. George Stewart gets into a state of excitement awful to behold. Georgy reads us Mr. Sheil's speech, as Mlle. Rachel would say it.

How I shall like to find Freddy at Devonshire House ! Is there any law ? Perhaps, as nobody will answer my question as to his sentimentality, somebody will about his legality.

To the Duke of Devonshire.

Rivoli : June 20, 1843.

We have spent three days luxuriously at Turin in the best hotel I ever was in—large rooms, a long balcony looking upon that perpetual *spectacle* the Place, endless processions with a Jesuitical *luxe* and *tenue*; puppet shows, *saltimbanques, improvvisatori,* royal equipages. Our beds and food were exquisite and our carriage like a long, low pony chaise. To-day fine weather, the snowy Alps, blue sky and fresh green too beautiful, not the least hot, yet with all windows down.

Poor Seppia died at Arqui of the worst sort of distemper.

St. Ambrosio.—Bumpy on a balcony, the Turin *voiturier* baiting whilst he dines. The invisible parents are gone to walk, I suppose. Dody in that stone-coloured Joseph, buttoned with mother of pearl, of which Hayes said, 'I'll tell you what, my lady, if you don't leave the gown off, the gown will leave you off.'

We are all rather spoilt and think this inn very deplorable after l'Univers, but we owe you the Arch, to which I first went alone, and then we *en masse* after dinner. It is beautiful, as perfect an antiquity as any in the Eternal City, and the bits of snow mountains and wooded ones between make it unique in its kind. The wind has got up amazingly and we expect to be blown across the Mont Cenis to-morrow.

Landau : 21st.

Oh, how beautiful! Glorious morning, wind gone down, but quantities of fresh air, blue and gold! You see it all. *En avant* Charlemagne and Tiber, next Evanson and Pierre with butterfly nets. No new flowers yet, only the common ones, but bigger and brighter than any I ever saw. L'Hospice curious and bleak ; the fineness of the day gives it beauty, the lake looks so blue and glittering. Tell the Levesons I mourned over Medor [1] at the fifth Ricovero. Fullerton careful over his large gentians and small beasts. Nothing new but Dody in goggles. Granville looks beautiful. Here come the trout and beef-steaks. Sans-le-Bourg, an excellent inn, and all of us as prosperous as possible.

To the Duke of Devonshire.

Lausanne : July 1, 1843.

Your letter of the 12th made me happy at Geneva. I trust I shall find you quite recovered from influenza and hay. Your 'new light' amused me beyond mea-

---

[1] Their favourite poodle, who had been run over at this spot.

sure. One does forget that one is not fifteen in moments of excitement, and after being become older, larger, more infirm and apathetic at Rome than I have words to describe, the sulphur baths and drink at Arqui have so renovated me that I am obliged to recollect I am not a mountain nymph, and to be hauled back to this hotel last night, *par example*, by Eward's strong unaltered arm. And where would not the view from the Terrace lead one ? Geneva was less pleasant than our usual halts—rainy, cold weather, like March in England. Then in your delightful rooms at the Couronne the view was rendered *nul* by a thick mist and the height made us feel somewhat imprisoned. I heard that Mrs. Craven was at the Hôtel des Etrangers.

Oh, what rooms at the Hôtel Gibbon ![1] After a delicious night's rest we woke upon the whole opposite view with its curtain drawn up. Open windows, summer, but no heat.

Continue to let me know how you are. Change of air for ten days. You get this on the 6th, put on your things, as women say, step over to Baden, where on the 12th we hope to be, take a peep at Herrnsheim and steam back all together to our native land. I cannot see one objection or obstacle, and what happiness and delight to us ! Think and leap. I have told Granville. He is all on my side and did look so pleased. Why, brother, it is little more than railing up and down to Mundy and Co.[2]

To the Duke of Devonshire.

Berne : July 5, 1843.

This is only a *signe de vie*. Your inimitable sketch of your duties at Derby alarms me, but I cannot give up my hope.

---

[1] At Lausanne.   [2] Derbyshire neighbours.

Since we parted we have had two nights of a fairy tale in the new Trois Couronnes on the lake at Vevay, too enchanting. A *magnifique* château with every luxury and comfort, a large terrace balcony, with seats, tables, and orange trees, overlooks the *parterre*, and then with parapets upon steps down to the lake.

Clifford can talk, for his name is in the book. Divine weather made the halt too enjoyable.

Granville is so well that my only fear is you will none of you be able to think how essential the utmost precaution and regularity of life are to him.

Granville, Fullerton, and George Stewart are going off in the next room like fireworks, so excited are they by a new plan. Instead of returning here we are going to take a new road to Basle, from Thun to Lucerne, which the Fullertons have never seen. The road said to be beautiful and the inns good. From Lucerne to Basle by Soleure.

Will you let my sister know my gratitude for her little letter found here? But still happier was I to hear from Lord Seaford. 'I am happy to tell you that I think Carlisle has been regularly improving ever since his return to town.'

We are very sorry that Lord Grey is so ill.

To the Duke of Devonshire.

Devonshire House : August 1843.

Granville is extremely well. The Fullertons crossed in an unexampled gale, but are all the better for it.

Let me quickly note down remarkable things. I have seen Mrs. Edward[1] and Mrs. Charles.[2] The former so *distinguée* and amiable-looking that it does as well as beauty, and Edward so happy and simplified.

---

[1] Mr. Edward Howard had just married Miss Ponsonby.

[2] Mr. Charles Howard, Miss Alice Parke, daughter of Baron Parke, created in 1856 Lord Wensleydale.

Tiber is quite recovered, only rather languid and self-occupied.

Duncannon called to-day, I think, more to see the staircase than me. He could not penetrate, but was so edified. He says it will be admirable, that the effect of the entrance-hall was what he doubted, but that it really answers perfectly. I did not understand this exactly, but perhaps you do. What was the doubt?

I have seen Lord Blantyre,[1] and approve—handsome, and a stern, calm undazzled glance around and down his new position.

We see less of Susy than we could wish, as dearest Rivers waits at Windsor in a peculiar manner—that is, he is always in town.[2]

Sunday.—Too late for the post yesterday, and now I must write. Oh! Chiswick! dearest brother, Chiswick! What shall I say? Chatsworth, be jealous. Charles Greville, who overtook us at Hammersmith and ambled on, was in ecstasies. He had not been at one of your breakfasts; it was an utter surprise. He said he never saw anything so pretty. Then your room! The carpets! The improvements in the garden, the walk through the open room to the Horticultural, the flowers, the perfect enamel of the parterre, the pink passion-flower! Landseer's picture, Lord Alfred Paget![3] Charles Greville fell from astonishment to astonishment. He had not seen Landseer or anything. 'God bless my soul! Have you seen anything abroad to compare with Chiswick?'

---

[1] Engaged to Lady Evelyn Leveson Gower.
[2] He was a Lord-in-Waiting.
[3] His portrait, painted by Sir Francis Grant.

TO THE DUKE OF DEVONSHIRE.

London : September 5, 1843.

Dearest brother,—You are a benediction to us all. Here we are again in gratitude and clover. London contains only Morpeth. Even Lady Holland is at Richmond.

The Carlisles wish Freddy to go to them; we long to see him; so when you have done with him send him on.

Charles [1] is composed, I hear; lives with the Parkes, and is going to Ampthill with them.

Can you imagine the scene at Eu ? [2]   Louis Philippe; how he will bow !—roll over perhaps.

TO THE DUKE OF DEVONSHIRE.

Aldenham : September 27, 1843.

Your dear welcome letter came this morning all redolent with Chatsworth.

Could a *pair* be a housekeeper ?   Would there be any chance in applying for the place ?

This place is very enjoyable. A large, old-fashioned, square stone house, made by Marie's *baguette* into an uncommonly pretty one.   The court, roofed in by Sir Richard and furnished by her, makes a charming drawing-room, and there is besides a library, a very good dining-room and a billiard-room.   The pleasure ground very pretty, the country round uncommonly so.

Willie,[3] to which we drove yesterday, is beautiful. The house frightful on the outside, enchanting within, where we found Miss Selina [4] and Lord John Manners; she picturesque and with charming manners, he very

---

[1] Mr. Charles Howard died on August 26.
[2] The Queen's visit to Eu.
[3] Lord Forester's country house.
[4] Miss Selina Forester, now Lady Bradford.

smart. They looked like a page out of Finden's 'Sketches of the Aristocracy'—too many curls and gold chains, but very pretty to see.

Luttrel and Sneyd are here. The Poodle, Spencer Cowper, and F. Cadogan went yesterday.

To THE DUKE OF DEVONSHIRE.

Aldenham : October 26, 1843.

We intend to be at Devonshire House on Wednesday, and at Brighton on Saturday. Imagine my happiness at the Rivers's having decided upon spending the winter in Kemp Town.

How I do long to see you! I have such quantities to say, unwritable things.

The Poodle surpassed himself. He is *incroyable*; asked Marie before everybody : ' How could she be so foolish as to marry such a child ?' One day : ' He had hoped for a leg of mutton ;' another : ' Your housemaids are all so Gothic ; they should not do so and so.' She bore it all with calm, but oh ! her indignation, and I must say natural. She is very amiable, occasionally captivating, *une sirène*.

To THE DUKE OF DEVONSHIRE.

Kemp : November 29, 1843.

It is delightful of you to have written, and such a letter ! No, never. The pleasure of reading it to myself, and then seeing Granville read it.

Yesterday, summer here ; to-day, south-west wind, not sunny, glass at fair ; your letter in my hand, all imagination and repose.

This morning brought me a letter from Lord Lansdowne, begging me to take rooms at the Bristol for him and Lady Lansdowne, Brodie having ordered him here again immediately to be shampooed. I must go and wash my hands, as they are coming to dinner. They will find only ourselves, the Fullertons, and an excellent dinner, as Mlle. Pater-aide[1] turns out to be a most able *artiste*.

How can I be so intrusive and interruptive? Only because I can wait with the dogs in your lighted room.

I know you cannot write again. I shall read over the 28th every day. I see almost all, but fret at not knowing the new top of the dancing fountain.

I wonder which of her diadems Mrs. Thornhill will put on, Ceres or Dante? she has both. Give my love to my progeny.

To the Duke of Devonshire.

Kemp Town : December 1843.

Your letters are sun and make my climate.

Brighton is doing its pranks—pouring rain and gales of wind, and yet we, ensconced in your charming house, are as comfortable as it is possible to be, and before I answer your letter I must detail its advantages. The gaiety compared with other places from the wide expanse of light and broad spaces; no sopped leaves and wet paths—a *trottoir* and two lamp-posts. In the bluster no smoking chimneys.

Yesterday at two Lord George Seymour paid us a visit, and a charming man he is. At three we went out and sat with Heneage,[2] that miracle of patience lying on his back. A moment's cessation on our return, and Granville, Tiber, and I had a pleasant walk within the shelter of the houses. At half-past six sat down to *perdreaux à l'Espagnole, émincé au gratin*, and a leg of mutton. Dowager Rivers, the pair of shoes,[3] and

---

[1] Daughter of the cook.

[2] Was an attaché at Paris. Then became a Roman Catholic and entered the priesthood. For many years an invalid.

[3] Lady Rivers went by the name of Shoes in the family.

Captain Pitt, who had unexpectedly come down. Beautiful he was to look at and droll to hear, and we had a most merry *prima sera*, the family departing at half-past nine, when we sat down to backgammon.

Now where can hopeless weather boast such antidotes as this ?

Oh, my dirty paper ! The outside sheet of a bundle out of a damp box. Alas ! alas !

1844

To Lady Carlisle.

Brighton: January 10, 1844.

Harry's letter amused us extremely. Tell me more about Miss Martineau's book.[1] I am afraid of it. The old tales, which I have been re-reading, have such an effect upon me that I can scarcely read them. She writes in a way that harrows up every feeling. It is, I think, quite a strange power, perhaps because no writer is so simple and so strong upon sorrows that come to all. Tell me some more of the new book. I must finish my letter to-morrow, as I shall be too late for the post.

Never was anything so terrible, as all Verity used to say ;[2] no chance of anything like recovery, or of any sort of restoration to what he was before the attack. In short, all that has since, by the blessing of God, been proved so utterly groundless.

To Lady Carlisle.

Brighton: January 12, 1844.

I thought Granville had a little cold yesterday, but he is much better to-day and we have been enjoying the June morning. We met in a pony-chaise and four the second Duchess[3] and the first Countess,[4] perhaps the two foolishest blowens in Europe ; but so kind and good-natured is the former that I beg you not to repeat

---

[1] *Letters on Mesmerism.*
[2] When Lord Granville was struck down by paralysis.
[3] Duchess of Somerset, the second wife of the eleventh Duke.
[4] Lady Shrewsbury, wife of the sixteenth Earl.

anything I say of her. At the instigation of her friend,
she persuaded the reluctant Duke to flare up for the
Duc de Bordeaux. Now, whatever may be his future
destiny, quiet is his game, and I hear he is wise enough
to have appeared much annoyed at the clumsy folly of
making him draw King out of a cake, called a Bourbon,
to the music of various Jacobite songs, 'Charley is my
darling,' etc. I saw the Duchess yesterday. 'Only
think, dear Lady Granville, what an odd chance!
Nothing prepared. I saw him put it quick into his
pocket.' Dearest sister, do not tell. This said woman
quêtes for my lottery, asks young Fullerton and his
sisters to dinner, and I really never knew so kind-
hearted a woman.

My lottery is prospering. We are much amused
with a doll's *trousseau*. Mme. Pater and Josephine [1]
have made her out of odds and ends the loveliest
modes. A black velvet bonnet, with pheasant's
feathers, made Lady Ailesbury studious for five minutes
yesterday. Never was there such a doll, from stays
and garters to cloaks and surtouts, and she has a
carpet bag which beggars description. And all this
for no pence, excepting the bag and a large knitted
manteau, garters and a comforter, which are worked
by poor people here. A fan and a boa will be presented to her gratis.

What a good speech of Guizot!

To LADY CARLISLE.

Brighton : January 22, 1844.

I am in your debt, my dearest sister. Many thanks
for what you tell me of Miss Martineau. Did you read
' What's to be Done ? ' or some such name, and Melville's
sermons, preached at Cambridge ?

Mr. Sneyd is gone and we regret him. He has been

---

[1] The cook's wife and the lady's maid.

as agreeable and amiable as possible. He dined with us every day but one, when he left us with Riverses and the Fullertons to dine at Lord Ailesbury's, leaving the Duchess of Beaufort to dine *tête à trois* with us, which she prefers.

By-the-by, it amuses me to hear of Mr. Luttrel, exasperated at some praise of Lady Ailesbury's figure, exclaiming, ' Just enough to keep the muslin together.'

On Saturday Lord Jermyn, Lord Polwarth, and Sir William Middleton dined with us. Lady Katherine Jermyn was not well enough ; she has been here in the morning, walked on the esplanade with us. I like what I have seen of her extremely. Sir William is a friend of Rivers. Lord Polwarth is extremely agreeable.

Mr. Sneyd gave us hopes of the Sutherlands coming to Brighton. Do you think there is a chance ?

Bumpy goes to school Thursday.

To the Duke of Devonshire.

Brighton: January 27, 1844.

Brougham has been sitting with us on the esplanade for an hour. A little low for Cannes. ' Upon my soul, this is not credible,' and it is to-day almost the finest day we have had. He was comparatively tranquil and exceedingly droll. He says the Lansdownes are much pleased with Emilie.[1] She is to live this season at Lansdowne House. Frantic about Anderson.[2] ' He has gone and given them a treacle discourse.'

God bless you, my dearest brother. We are going to luxuriate along the cliff.

To Lady Carlisle.

Brighton : January 28, 1844.

We are going on prosperously as to health and weather. Did I tell you of Lord Brougham's coming

---

[1] Mdlle. de Flahault, who had just married Lord Shelburne.

[2] The Rev. James Anderson.

on Friday morning, hallooing and bawling to us on the esplanade? He was very droll, stayed an hour, and is gone back to London.

A more agreeable arrival yesterday was Freddy from Folkestone. His journey to Paris has answered perfectly. He was received most graciously, found everybody and everything exactly as they were, the same young ladies waltzing and unmarried. He was much pleased with Lady Cowley, whom he thinks very agreeable, and was much amused at the balls at the Embassy. He was delighted to be with Harry. We had a very amusing dinner yesterday—Lady Ailesbury, so intent upon every word that fell from Frederick's lips, the George Seymours, and Lord Polwarth.

We are all much occupied with Frederick Bruce's appointment to China. Eighteen hundred a year. He thinks it his duty to go—he has not a farthing—but I hear he is dreadfully low about it. There is much talk of whether he will propose Hong Kong to Emily Hardy, and if she will accept if he does. I trust the Sutherlands are coming.

To the Duke of Devonshire.

Brighton : January 29, 1844.

Quite beat down with summer, I sit down, no fire and the windows open, to say a word or two.

On Saturday we had a pleasant little repast. In the evening, whist and music. The Moriers came. Horatia[1] has a beautiful voice, and Lady Belfast brought Lord Chichester, a great exception to her rule. He sang to us like an angel and is a charming unaffected boy, accompanied beautifully by cousin Verner.

Dearest Grace, will you indulge a whim of mine and do me an immense favour? My prizes are all settled

---

[1] Miss Horatia Morier married in 1845 Lord Algernon Seymour, the present Duke of Somerset.

and I have more than enough, but I want an extra-ordinary one from you. Do you think Mr. Paxton[1] could contrive that I should receive on the 6th a covered basket, docketed, with fruit and flowers from the Chatsworth Conservatory? Oh, what a catch for a Brightonian, fond of names and who never sees a flower! I will hope that in the natural course of draw-ing that prize might fall on a resident, and if not, ex-change being no robbery, I could manage one with some winner of a drawing or a paper knife. Brother! Mr. Paxton! I do not breathe my request to any one, only if you can't or won't, take no heed of it.

To Lady Carlisle.

Brighton: February 1844.

A thousand thanks for your kindness in telling us what gave us so much pleasure about Leveson's speech.

They are in Bruton Street, and Marie has made, I am told, their rooms below quite beautiful.[2] London has got no society or reunions. I hear Lady Holland is in a very teasing humour, and tries Lady Palmerston with constant abuse of the 'Morning Chronicle,' chiefly for its foreign politics. I should like Miss Martineau, if somebody would translate it. I have only read a

[1] The Duke of Devonshire made acquaintance with Sir Joseph Paxton in the Horticultural Society's garden at Chiswick, where he was an under-gardener. The Duke was so much struck with his intelligence that he appointed him head-gardener at Chatsworth, where he built the great conservatory; and in imitation of it he designed the Exhibition Building of 1851. He became the Duke's confidential adviser, received the honour of knighthood, and during the last years of his life sat in the House of Commons as member for Coventry. He was a man of remarkable energy. The following was his own description of his first arrival at Chatsworth. He arrived there at half-past five in the morning. He explored the whole place before any one was up. He set the men to work by six o'clock. He made acquaintance with his future wife, the housekeeper's niece, fell in love with her and she with him, and all this in one day.

[2] Lord and Lady Granville occupied the first floor, Lord and Lady Leveson the ground floor.

chapter, which I cannot understand. Good night, beloved sister.

I went this morning in a fly by myself to the forbidden fruit, the Huntingdon chapel (dissent, but the service seemed to me just the same as ours), to hear Mr. Sortain. Wonderful eloquence, energy, ardour, conquering every sort of natural disadvantage. In person like Thiers and Lord Boscawen, with a wire of a voice and bad articulation. But how new, how clever! What beautiful language and a conviction that rivets one!

To LADY CARLISLE.

London: March 8, 1844.

London, oh! London. But yesterday having found beds that made sleeping impossible was not a fair trial. I was quite unwell all day and he very languid and tired, and this added to by spring in coal smoke drest, always trying at first.

Georgy is in ecstasies with London. How unlike her mama! 'Ellen Middleton'[1] is no longer a secret and will be out in three weeks. Moxon publishes, she to have half the profits. Opinions given without her name being known have been more than gratifying, and Mrs. Sartoris read till four in the morning with intense interest that never flagged for a moment. Charles Greville is in raptures, and has been invaluable and indefatigable.[2]

I saw yesterday dearest Lady Morley and Corise. Henry Greville dined with us; the Poodle came in the evening. They laughed at my reception. 'How do you do? I am so happy to see you for a quarter of an hour,' and they were all off at eleven.

Marie has made the *rez de chaussée* like a delicious country house—chintzes, birds, flowers, and comfort. I think she will do wonders with the *premier*.

[1] Lady G. Fullerton's first novel.
[2] He helped to correct the proofs.

I cannot tell you the longing I have to be at
Brighton again. We go to-morrow, but alas! alas!
Granville threatens returning here in a fortnight. The
rule of three. If two days, what will be weeks.
Georgy says, better when all and everybody are not
crammed into so short a space.

The delight of seeing your letter, most beloved
sister. I have met, I think, all your questions. Give
our most affectionate love to dearest Lord Carlisle. I
sometimes, only sometimes, think, Oh, that I was there
with them! Castle Howard must be a paradise in this
season, and you and Morpeth and Lord Carlisle's adorable smile. When shall I see you all? But the gulph
of London must be passed first. Marie is in excellent
spirits; she hates going out now. Dody delights in it.
She was at Lady Lansdowne's. Lady Shelburne seems
very happy. I will write constantly.

To LADY CARLISLE.

Brighton: April 4, 1844.

I send you the enclosed letter from Georgy.

'Dearest mama,—I send you a few more proof
sheets. Some part of them you have already got; there
has been a change of type which has caused it. Tell
dearest Sukey that, if she has not done so yet, she may
certainly read them, if she likes it better in that way.

'I am rather angry with Charles Greville for having
shown the proof sheets to Lord Clarendon, and I regret
for my own sake that he praises it so extravagantly. I
think it is like when a new beauty appears. Instead of
prepossessing people in its favour, it will make them
find fault with it. He told Theresa Lister that it was
the most remarkable work that had appeared for years
and George Byng the cleverest novel he knew. This is
such gross exaggeration that I am sure it will do more
harm than good.'

To Lady Carlisle.

Brighton: April 16, 1844.

Whilst I am waiting for luncheon, before the half-past three train, I write a word. Susy and her little girls are by this time in Bruton Street, where Rivers and Freddy are to join us at dinner. I am glad to go to Georgy, now that she and her boy are poorly, and it is delightful to have Susy *domiciliée*, and I hope my brother will like to have us, and this is a pull against London and Court. You have no idea of what it has been this morning, sitting on a bench looking on the sea, with a high bank behind us of wallflowers, the real sweet flowers of the earth.

I have had a note from Lady Charlotte Greville with your good account of Lord Carlisle, and her lamentations that Henry Greville, universally congratulated, is not appointed.[1] He receives also daily joy about his marriage to Lady Essex. I hope when he is placed he will propose. I am very fond of him.

To Lady Carlisle.

London: April 1844.

Most dear sister,—My grateful thanks to Mary. The book-openers are beautiful. I have poured out my thanks to Francis Grey. I cannot say what I felt. The reception of the beautiful works did not *look* like pleasure, and half an hour afterwards I gave the same sort of welcome to 'Ellen Middleton,' in three volumes, so that my morning was one of delicious but deep emotion. Would that I could hear you upon this last subject! My brother is delighted. Brougham writes me a note as follows: 'Hurrah!' Not a word else. Georgy is like a mouse.

Granville is well, but there is not the same hue as at Brighton. Our life is pleasant and almost as quiet,

---

[1] To some diplomatic post.

but I have not the security. To-day he is going at
her request to Lady Jersey, and St. Aulaire says, ' Oh,
nous le soignerons bien,' etc.

The day before yesterday evening Clarendons,
Wharncliffes, Lords Harrowby, Sandon, Charles Gore,
Jem Howard. Very pleasant but hotter, later in short,
etc. Do not say anything of this in your answer.

To exemplify my meaning, we have been this
morning paying visits, he sitting with Lord Clarendon
and Lord St. Germans, and he has just announced that
he shall walk to Lady Jersey's and back, and all this
preparatory to going down this evening to a little
soirée at Marie's. This may not do harm, but keeps
me in a fever.

To LADY CARLISLE.

London: April 22, 1844.

I missed the post on Saturday and your dear letter
is just arrived.

I see I have not said enough about the Drawing
Room. The Queen bowed and smiled and hoped I
was well, but less gracious than Prince Albert, who
seemed inclined to embrace me. Leopold careworn,
absent; Kent civil. Very few people. Miss Barring-
ton extremely handsome. Lady Wharncliffe entirely
enclosed in a gold framework, just like a barley-sugar
treillage one sometimes sees over cream and strawberries in an *entremets*, a great love, in ecstasies over
the darling cream-coloured horses. Lady Jersey a very
good-natured old woman. The Duke of Wellington in
radiant health and spirits. *Ouf!* dearest sissie, it bores
me almost as much as being there to fight it over
again.

Granville is better, and I am very happy, as I find,
though he has not told me, that he will not dine or go
out. We drive and walk at twelve every morning and

drive again from half-past three till six. We are now going to the garden of Eden.[1] The Francis Egertons came to us the night before last. She was in excellent spirits, and as active and useful as a steam-engine. Lady Morley is a dear. 'Dody, you are going to Court, presented of course upon the coming event.' ' Ellen ' comes out on Saturday.

I went yesterday morning to St. Paul's.[2] I never liked anything so much as Mr. Bennett's sermon ; never disliked anything so much as the performance of the service, a sort of parody of what I do not like at Rome. The clergyman who read the service hummed it over in a monotonous rapid mutter, the new way I am told. The music constant, troublesome, lively, inefficient, so that the Litany was like charity school children divided by London cries. But then came Mr. Bennett, admirable, simple. The soundest doctrine, warmest piety, and most practical result. So here were all the *pours et contres* of Tractarianism. Excellence in fact, with why those things *à côté* ? We went to the Temple Church at three. Too long, nearly two hours, beautiful music and a very bad preacher.

To LADY CARLISLE.

London : May 4, 1844.

I have only a moment to thank you a thousand times and Mary for your dear letters to Dody and me. The third volume ! It has really affected and agitated society in a most remarkable manner. At St. Aulaire's[3] ball she was quite overwhelmed with kindness and praise. How I long to talk it with you, and it seems to me that summer is coming ! Though I am happy here and cannot wish time to go quick, I cannot but pine to be with you again.

[1] Lord Auckland's house at Kensington Gore.
[2] Knightsbridge.   [3] The French Ambassador.

TO THE DUKE OF DEVONSHIRE.

London : May 26, 1844.

Wintry weather ; too cold for the open carriage or Chiswick.

Last night Poodle and Charles Gore at dinner ; Lady Rivers, Lords Ebrington and Ponsonby, Lady Holland and Mr. Stanley[1] (Ben) in the evening.

The Levesons are to dine with the Shelburnes at Richmond. To-morrow we go to Hatchford[2] for two nights, and I dare say, as we are hardy, we shall enjoy driving on St. George's Hill.

The Stafford House concerns going on much the same, the Duke still poorly at Brighton.

Monday.—Mr. Sneyd came last night. He pleased me with thinking Lord Lorne's conceit worn off; says he is extremely clever and decidedly in love in the right quarter. Had not he dined there on Saturday with him *en famille*?

We are setting out for Hatchford. ' Winter armed with terrors yet unknown.' Never was anything so east and sharp.

TO THE DUKE OF DEVONSHIRE.

Hatchford : May 28, 1844.

How d'ye do, dearest brother? I do at Hatchford exceedingly well. A comfortable house in a most beautiful country, airy rooms, wholesome victuals.

Lady Cowper is very agreeable and droll. Lady Charlotte Greville very poorly with rheumatism. Henry will come down and tell us of the *clôture* of the Essex theatricals.[3]

---

[1] On the death of his father in 1850, he became Lord Stanley of Alderley. He was for some time Whip of the Liberal party and later President of the Board of Trade and Postmaster-General. He was noted for his amusing conversation and brilliant repartee.

[2] Lord Ellesmere's place in Surrey.

[3] At the Dowager Lady Essex's.

Lady Cadogan heard some one say ' Ellen Middleton '
was too sad. ' Oh dear, no, just what it should be
to succeed.' No, it is too melancholy, indeed it is.
People like the book because it is beautiful, but would
all the more for a little more light and shade. ' You
don't understand anything about it. That's just what
people hate, light and shade. Bulwer tried it and it
didn't do, nobody could bear it.' Georgy says she
was alluding to his ' Night and Morning.'

TO THE DUKE OF DEVONSHIRE.

London: June 1, 1844.

Dearest brother,—What a surprise upon the world
is the Emperor Nicholas—expected to-day to play with
Saxony, to bet at Ascot, and puzzle the ladies, who head
the Polish Ball! They met and settled to have it.
Lord Aberdeen says they shan't.

Yesterday evening came the Duke of Sutherland
radiant, the Duchess with a crown of black roses and
diamonds, going to the Academy Ball with Caroline[1]
lovely, Julia Howard, the Dean of Lichfield's daughter,
very handsome, Georgy Lascelles very pretty, or rather
pleasing, Elizabeth in a cap and shawl beaming with
happiness, and Lord Lorne, with whom we are all charmed.
I see no conceit or self-importance ; devoted to her and
them, ingenuous and earnest in manner, and a brow and
eyes that make one feel one's understanding growing
clearer as one looks at them. The company that came
stared at the family party. Punch, Sneyd, Dowager
Lady Cawdor wept for joy over us; Mrs. Cavendish
blinked in utter bewilderment. Fanny and Frederick
Howard and Lord Lansdowne quite enchanted at
falling upon such a troop of nymphs in garlands.

---

[1] Her daughter, who afterwards married Lord Kildare and became
Duchess of Leinster.

Then the Poodle : ' Some say Nicholas is come. I don't believe it.   Brunnow[1] slept all night at Greenwich in an agony of mind.   There is but one state apartment ready at the Palace, and the Emperor and King must sleep in one bed.'

There was a farce at the Polish Committee.   In came Ailesbury, chairwoman : ' Must be put off.'

Clanricarde : ' No such thing.'

Palmerston : ' Much better put it off.'

Sutherland : ' Don't see why.'   Lord Dudley Stuart[2] talked incessantly.   Palmerston gave way.   And now it rests with the Government out of petticoats.

TO THE DUKE OF DEVONSHIRE.

London : August 1, 1844.

The later period, most dear brother, end of September and beginning of October.   What bliss it will be !

The dinner[3] at Stafford House was beautiful, I hear, and perfectly well done.   The Duchess beautiful ; Lord Lorne very pretty in a kilt.   The flaws odd company, instead of some nearer and dearer.   Little Lord Frederick[4] waiting all dinner-time behind the Queen's chair.   At ten minutes before ten a little enforced dancing.   The going away was, it is said, quite beautiful.

We spent our whole day at Hampton Court.   Nymphenberg.   All over roses.   Groups of unknown *élégants* and *élégantes*, and military music.

TO THE DUKE OF DEVONSHIRE.

Brighton : October 30, 1844.

Never was anything like it !   We arrived at five and walked along the cliff, W. Baker having made all

[1] Russian Ambassador.

[2] A son of the first Marquis of Bute.   He married a daughter of Prince Lucien Buonaparte.   He warmly espoused the cause of the Poles, and bored people about them.

[3] In honour of Lord and Lady Lorne's wedding.

[4] Duke of Sutherland's second son, died in the Crimean War.

look as square as his own new wig. Mary showing me the house. 'My lady, look how beautiful they pull up,' and so they do, the new blinds. The new Bluebeard-looking building at the bottom of the room is very ornamental with its jars above, and many are the new kicks in every corner. Oh, it is such a haven, such repose, such freshness, and certainly the gayest-looking house that ever was! Poor souls at the Hall! [1]

We have already seen Lord George Seymour in a *calèche*.

Did you hear that Lord Bessborough has had a very bad fall from his horse? No bone broken, but a severe contusion.

There is Granville, as if he had been settled here a year, cracking his sides over an old book of plays he has found.

To the Duke of Devonshire.

Brighton: November 16, 1844.

I think, as you are alone at Hardwick, a little writing will not be *de trop*. Your dear little letter is arrived—a double pleasure to know you safe and snug at the Hall. How happy dear G. will be! And then you will come here when Brighton has shed its fashionable vulgar.

We had a very pleasant dinner yesterday. Georgy not silent as at Holly's. Lady Cowper most extremely droll, Mrs. Ashburnham very agreeable, Mr. Ashburnham intolerable, Lord Cowper charming, Lord George Seymour wonderful. How your house is admired!

To-day Corise stepped in, come to pay a visit to the remaining Miss Mitchell. I called upon Silence and found her looking beautiful with her two nice girls carpet-stitching diligently like Marie.

The landslip has frightened people. Holly quite.

[1] Hardwick.

Lady Harriet Drummond came down in terror. Anne Loftus sat near ten minutes in a tunnel, not knowing what had come or was to come next.

17th.—We found Holly at the 'Albion,' Sheepwash [1] *en action*, Sir Henry Webster sitting opposite to her, young Loch reading and the doctor. 'Very kind of you. You see how lonely I am. A horrid little room. I could ask my friends to come and eat a roast chicken, but I have no other to go into.' She dines here on Thursday. We have asked the Cowpers, James Morier,[2] and Mr. Gladstone to meet her, already furnished with Shoes and Dodds.

To THE DUKE OF DEVONSHIRE.

Brighton : November 21, 1844.

Your letter was delightful to us. Captain Bruce was caught on the way to the station by Charles Seymour and Mr. de Bathe, and these persuaded him to give up his journey and marriage.

I am writing very weary. You know what a July morning is when it falls on a November day. We walked and sat two hours, and then I turned home, leaving Granville and Doddles basking, to be in time. Lady Charlotte Greville accepts luncheon, and came with her lovely niece, and so did the Miss Fullertons, and we had an hour's social enjoyment.

Holly comes up the hill. 'Georgy, my dear, I am dreadfully nervous, are there many police in the way?'

Yesterday, General Upton, Susy and Dody, Lady Anne Loftus, and Mr. and Mrs. Ashburnham went to the amateurs. First, the 'Follies of a Night,' very amusingly and well acted. Mr. de Bathe extremely handsome, and a little foolish. Mr. Martyn very good; sings extremely well. Sister Mordaunt, good, fine eyes, flashy and

---

[1] Lady Holland's maid, who acted as rubber.
[2] Author of *Hajji Baba*.

somewhat vulgar. Miss Angel, a small part, but her beauty something surpassing. Captain Bruce, good actor, but Mr. de Bathe and C. Seymour could not get over the different passages alluding to Gretna Green, domestic happiness with an opera dancer, and rolled over, which disturbed the gravity of the action.

To the Duke of Devonshire.

Brighton: November 29, 1844.

I lament for G. and myself not to see you together. When will that happy day be ? But it is delicious to think of you between the 5th and the 12th.

I can hardly help going to a billiard table in the town to see the great performer [1] at that game, of whose play Horace Pitt, who dined here yesterday fresh from the strokes, raves. Or if you come to that, to attend to the placard, great in its simplicity, 'The Mysterious Lady.' For many of the things others do may be prompted, or some hidden aider or nodder or winker may explain. But how she could tell Lord Henry Loftus, Lord something Kerr, and three other young sparks, what fish they were thinking they should like to have for dinner, which she did without hesitation or mistake—my informant Lord Henry himself—passes my comprehension. Shoes is on fire. She is going to think of whale, and, if baffled by Miss Mystery, then she will think of *alose*, a French fish not known in England, and if Miss says, ' A fish I am not acquainted with,' she has promised to *baisser pavillon* bare-footed before her.

A great lull at Brighton. Dody writes from the fog, going to dinner with Holly. Rivers wanted to speak to Sukey, so up she railed at eleven this morning under Horace's wing ; meets him at Mrs. Bruce's,[2] and comes back early to-morrow.

[1] Kentfield. [2] Their sister.

Sir Edward Bulwer is young, blooming, and no longer deaf. The water-cure—Lord de Grey is almost persuaded to try it. Not at Gastein, not under Doctor Wilson at Malvern, but under the physician at Sudbrooke, close to Richmond, who is perfectly safe, and never undertakes a doubtful case. Sir Edward is convinced he would cure Lord de Grey in a fortnight.

All this was told me by the quite altered water-cured man. I expect to hear of him re-united to the wine-cured Lady B.

At this same repast Lord and Lady Ely figured, and, what with H. Drummond, ' Hajji Baba,' and Sir Edward, the Marquis was quite puzzled, much edified. ' God bless me,' every word any of them uttered.

1845

To Lady Carlisle.

Panshanger : January 2, 1845.

I am happy to tell you that Lord Melbourne was quite another man yesterday, appeared better in health, and more natural in spirits. Granville was struck with the *agrément* of his conversation and immense stores of knowledge. They are just gone, and so is Lord Aberdeen.

Lady Cowper is in bed with a severe cold and sore throat ; Lord de Grey rather *souffrant*, and Mr. Sneyd has a cold ; so that a quieter party will be a comfort.

To the Duke of Devonshire.

Wrest Park : January 1845.

You know Wrest, so I need not describe. Beauty, luxury, and comfort. The fog has kept us indoors almost entirely, some walking in a handsome Nymphen-berg-looking garden excepted, which must be very enjoyable in summer and in keeping with the house. The dining-room and library are beautiful, the drawing-room not finished. The tapestry *manqué* in design, execution, and colouring. The weather is unwhole-some. Granville bilious, Lady Cowper in bed with a sore throat, Lord de Grey very ailing, but cheerful and patient, and seeming to enjoy himself. Mr. Sneyd has a cold ; the Poodle well for all, opening their eyes wide to the narrowness of their vestibules and corridors. The Beauvales and Lord Melbourne and Lord Aberdeen went to-day, and we expect the Parkes and Charles Howard to dinner.

We live a great deal in our rooms. In the evening we work and talk. There was a rubber one night, but not for me, and yesterday none. We go to bed at eleven.

Since his last letter the Devonshire people call Bishop Philpotts ' Exeter Change.'

God bless you and my dearest son, if he is with you.

TO LADY CARLISLE.

Brighton : March 16, 1845.

My beloved sister,—We are charmed at the Baron taking Freddy as his marshal, and oh, that he would take me ! They are going to try Mr. Tawell.

Everybody asks why Gladstone is out, and I refer you to yesterday's ' Times.' Granville says no one can give a satisfactory answer. I said ten thousand reasons appear to me to explain it. What difficulty he would have had with regard to Church questions and probably colonial ones ! Granville advises me to have done, and abide by the late Lord Lansdowne's advice, ' When you are in the dark, stand still.' ' Then you will never get into the light.' 'I beg your pardon, the fog will disperse.'

Poor Miss Fox,[1] perhaps the most valued and beloved of all women ! I never heard a word or thought or feeling about her that was not enthusiastic.

I cannot tell you anything of French politics beyond what you know, for I have not heard for some time from Madame de Lieven. Guizot seems to rely on a dissolution of the Chambers, but French Ministers have very often been disappointed in the results.

March 20, 1845.—Freddy says he 'never had any doubt of Mr. Tawell's guilt. That it was interesting to

---

[1] Lord Holland's sister.

watch him during the proceedings, and to hear the wonderful but useless efforts of Kelly to save him. The prisoner has the most thorough air of a Quaker, a small face with small eyes, his hair thrown back off his forehead, looking particularly respectable, a bad countenance, very fidgety the first day, quieter as the trial went on, very pale, constantly compressing very white lips. Not a muscle of his face moved during the sentence.'

Mrs. Tawell [1] had sent for places for herself and five friends. God bless you, dearest.

TO LADY CARLISLE.

London: March 28, 1845.

My own dear sister,—We drove twice round the Ring in a brougham to-day. It was very reviving—a strong gale of southerly wind, the Serpentine like a rough sea.

I send you Madame de Lieven. I have not another minute.

Paris: le 24 Mars, 1845.

'Dearest Lady,—Votre lettre de Brighton est restée longtemps sans réponse, parce que j'espérais mes yeux et vous écrire moi-même. Ils ne sont pas revenus, mais ils se mettent en chemin à l'aide de Verity. Je crève d'orgueil de cette guérison prochaine, car quatre médecins avant lui y avaient perdu leur latin.

'Parlez-moi de la jaunisse de Lord Granville. Elle ne m'inquiète pas, mais elle m'ennuie. L'hiver a été abominable ici. Cela veut dire un véritable hiver et qui ne commence à disparaître depuis deux jours.

'Les *politics* ont suivi les allures du temps, avec cette différence, que les mauvaises chances n'ont pas disparu encore. La majorité est si faible que le moindre accident peut faire chavirer, et cela serait arrivé déjà, si

[1] She was convinced of his innocence and acquittal.

les remplaçants n'étaient pas si impossibles. Mais vraiment Molé est au fonds de l'eau, et Thiers très difficile. Lui-même affirme et répète qu'il ne veut pas et qu'il ne sera Ministre qu'à la Régence. Monsieur Guizot conserve toute sa bonne humeur et sa fermeté ordinaire. He does not care much about staying or going. I wish he was out to refresh himself a little. Le Roi crie bien fort et bien haut qu'il ne peut avoir d'autre Ministre que Monsieur Guizot, et qu'on peut aussi bien marcher avec une voix de majorité qu'avec soixante.

'Avez-vous vu "l'Histoire du Consulat," par Thiers? Ici on ne parle que de cela.

'La semaine passée a été toute consacrée à la dévotion. On dit que le nombre de communicants a été énorme. A Notre-Dame trois mille hommes à la fois dans la matinée de Pâques. L'Abbé Ravignan l'objet de l'adoration de tous.

'Madame de Contades est toujours sur béquilles, mais aussi jolie et charmante que jamais. Je ne vois plus Madame de Castellane. De toutes mes connaissances, c'est la seule qui ne m'ait pas soignée pendant ma longue reclusion. Molé non plus n'approche pas. Du reste, ma chambre n'est jamais vide. Thiers y vient. Monsieur Guizot l'a trouvé chez moi l'autre jour. Ils ne s'étaient pas rencontrés depuis quatre ans et demi. Il y a eu un moment de stupéfaction. J'ai éclaté de rire, ils ont pris le parti de rire avec moi, et ils sont restés une heure et demie à causer ensemble le plus agréablement du monde, abordant tous les sujets, situation ministérielle, situation parlementaire, le présent, l'avenir, décidant qu'il n'y a plus pour la France que Thiers ou Guizot, Guizot ou Thiers. Tout cela se disant avec une indépendance et une liberté d'esprit parfaites. C'était évidemment *a treat* pour chacun d'eux, et moi j'ai été parfaitement amusée.' Nothing more to say, my dearest Lady.'

To Lady Carlisle.

London: April 4, 1845.

Most beloved sister,—We go on favourably, but very slow. Verity threatens departure. Granville has seen the Duchess of Beaufort and Lord Clarendon. The latter was on his way to the House of Lords to make a motion. The Duc de Broglie came yesterday. He quite adores Granville, and it put him in roaring spirits, and he chattered and joked as I never before heard him and stayed near an hour. Granville was not the worse for the visit, but I was, as the fear of fatigue was on me all the time. I called by Granville's desire on Lady Holland; she was much pleased and inoffensive.

I hope soon to write you more interesting letters, but my days are gasping just now—one eye on the thermometer, another on the door, so afraid of visits.

To the Duke of Devonshire.

London: May 10, 1845.

First, flowers. An orange orchid in full bloom sits in the middle window, the wonder of all beholders. You are much too amiable. Then the delicious 7th, all but in not announcing your return. The glories of your reception,[1] so *fêté*, is the small talk of London. Decazes' dinner would have been published as an essay by Charles Lamb. I have a mind to sell it at the Repository.

Though we are just returned from sitting in an alcove in Kensington Gardens in a half hour of radiant sunshine, the weather here, too, is atrocious. Wind east and north, west for moments to delude one, and then back, 'armed with terrors.' But Granville is going on delightfully well.

[1] At Paris.

Lady Lorne's happiness is delightful to see, she is grown so natural and gay.

The Levesons are gone to Aldenham for the holidays. The London news you hear from all and I don't know it.

Mrs. Arkwright adores old Smoky, I hear; lives in it as at Paris or Rome, sees sights and *savants*, has a few *chez elle* in the evening, or goes and larks at Mrs. Sartoris's, where she has Mendelssohn and good music.

To the Duke of Devonshire.

London : May 15, 1845.

I know the Viscountess's perfect repast—a model, I think. The only flaw when I dined with her were the minstrels at the door, all in some full national costume, which looked too Shrewsburyish.[1]

Jesse! May Tiber marry her some of these days. Mrs. Spaniels are so like the Princesse de Sagan.

You see I am flat. I have seen Miss McTavish, and am captivated by her. I think her lovely, charming, gentle, feminine, neither twang nor slang.

The fancy ball is the talk of the moment. The Ministers have made a respectful appeal. H. M. has written to them *à la ronde* to say she cannot let them off, nor the *Corps Diplomatique*. Van de Weyer says there is an epidemic beginning amongst them.

To the Duke of Devonshire.

London: May 20, 1845.

I have an excellent account to give you of Granville. He is going on as well as possible, in spite of the dreadful cold weather. I love the dear people who have felt solicitude. The paragraph in the 'Standard' was quite incorrect, but still the attack of the stomach was sharp

---

[1] At Alton Towers a harper played at the door to welcome a new arrival.

enough to make him very weak and languid for a few days.

Marie says the ball at Court was dreadfully hot and crowded. Step's daughter,[1] extremely put out, stuck close to Lady Canning, resisted messages from the Queen to go and sit, dance reels, etc.—in short, rebellion to the dull honours offered her.

The costume ball rages in all senses. Beauvale, Sandwich, Norreys not asked, whilst Lady Gertrude Sloane Stanley puts out her nose and, with her whole brood, is invited.

We are going to the Regent's Park and have been to Covent Garden, which is too fragrant and delicious.

To the Duke of Devonshire.

London : May 26, 1845.

Only one line to thank you for two delightful letters and for fruit such as never was tasted—peaches and grapes. I hope McTavish, who dined here yesterday, takes it for a wedding present. Her singing is beautiful, like Mrs. Jordan's. Her manner perfect. At Mr. Bennett's beautiful church it will be a very pretty sight on Thursday.[2]

This morning it[3] was not pretty, but deeply interesting to see those bereaved Drummonds give away the comfort and delight of their existence. But they wished it, *ainsi va le monde*, though his face was a deep tragedy. Lord Lovaine looked very happy and the Beverleys are delighted with the marriage. She, Lady Lovaine, is an incomparable person. But again I say it was not pretty to see whole herds of Percys and Drummonds, Ladies Haddington, Wharncliffe, and myself the ornamental extras.

[1] Lady Douglas.

[2] When she was married to Mr. Henry Howard.

[3] The wedding of Miss Drummond, married to Lord Lovaine, who succeeded his father as Duke of Northumberland in 1867.

Dress rages. Freddy has got a charming suit[1] lent him by Lord Glengall, as the unfortunate household have been ordered to bedeck themselves in new suits and this is one Lord Glengall had worn last year. It is remarkably pretty, white with scarlet facings—V. and A. as yet secrets.

To LADY CARLISLE.

London : May 29, 1845.

I had a happy day yesterday, taking Eward to Chiswick. On the 28th of May some few years ago I took her there with Susy on her lap to make their first acquaintance. Always, as usual, owing to your kindness. I never saw anything so happy as that dear old thing, living it all over again, and I heard with pleasure records of old time, that never ceased from one door to the other.

To THE DUKE OF DEVONSHIRE.

London : May 30, 1845.

Dearest brother,—Scene : Freddy in an armchair, very poorly, cold, swelled throat and headache. I in another, very ill, got out of bed in a dressing-gown. In the back court, Levesons, Sabine,[2] and half a dozen little dogs, some shaggy, some smooth. Leveson is to give her one. Miss Pea is very grumpy. Shoes thought not at all civil, did not like any of them. Somehow or other London has not answered to her, yet dinners, invitations, civilities are showered upon her. We do not know what lacks—lovers and husbands perhaps.

To-morrow it was hoped a repast at Villa d'Este,[3] Levesons, Freddy, Miss Raikes to meet at six and to go and see Miss Cushman,[4] had at last pleased her, but this morning she was grumpy again and conjecture more

---

[1] Copied from a portrait of the Pretender Charles Edward.

[2] Mlle. de Noailles, daughter of the Duc de Poix.

[3] Mr. Fullerton's house in South Street, previously occupied by Mlle. d'Este.   [4] An American actress.

active than ever. Nobody admires her or thinks her good-looking, which may go for something, and she does look and dress like Mlle. Sterky. Some wonder if she is disappointed that Henry Greville does not offer his hand and Number Two Hobart Place.

The Queen is going again to Osborne House. Shoes dines at Court to-day.

To THE DUKE OF DEVONSHIRE.

London: December 1, 1845.

Good bulletin. We drove this morning to Addison Lodge and saw Charles Fox at the door. He was much touched by Granville's visit. He joins Lady Mary at Paris to-morrow.

Lady Portman says Prince Albert and the Queen are very busy and happy at Osborne House, planting, improving, *vie de campagnard.*

I was happy to see the Duke of Wellington ride up to Lady Jersey's door and go in to-day. A little promotion and good sense, both in his line, may dry the torrents and bring all right.

To THE DUKE OF DEVONSHIRE.

London: December 1845.

Excellent bulletin, most dear brother.

We had an hour and a quarter's drive in Hyde Park. He said he never enjoyed anything more. He is stronger and all things are improved, but I know I must not feel sanguine. Yet I accept with gratitude and adoration all that is sent to soothe and cheer.

Soon after Lord Granville became seriously worse and he died on the 8th of January, 1846.

INDEX

—◦—

Coventry, Lady, i. 370
Cowley, Lady, ii. 50, 180, 326, 353
Cowley, Lord, ii. 179, 330
Cowper, Lady (afterwards married Lord Palmerston), i. 77, 255, 302, ii. 10, 42, 46, 64, 296
Cowper, Lord, ii. 36
Cowper, Lady Emily, ii. 42 *sqq.*, 50, 59
Cowper, Lady Fanny (married Lord Jocelyn), ii. 287, 317
Cradock, Major (later, Lord Howden), i. 348, 352, 362, 395, 435, ii. 31, 52, 74, 90, (name changed to Caradoc) 129, 192, 203, 240, 245
Cramer (musician), i. 255
Cranston, Mr., i. 253
Craon, Mme. de, i. 397
Craven, Mr. Berkeley, i. 258
Craven, Mrs., ii. 366
Crawford, Mr., ii. 209
Crillon, Mlle. de (married Pozzo di Borgo), ii. 116
Croker, Mr., ii. 92
Crombie, the Abbé, i. 285
' Crust and Crumb,' ii. 282
Cumberland, Duke of, i. 358 *sq.*, 361, ii. 29, 60
Cumberland, Duchess of, i. 75, 93
Cunningham, Mr., i. 357
Curzon, Major, i. 388
Curzon, Mrs. (*née* Bishop), i. 31
Cushman, Miss (actress), ii. 397
Cuvier, M. (naturalist), i. 326, 352, 357, ii. 117

Dacre, Lady, ii. 52, 228
Daine, General, ii. 106
Dalberg, Duc de, i. 326, 380, ii. 18
Dalberg, Duchesse de, i. 326, 397, 401, ii. 311, 339
Dalrymple, Lady, ii. 332
Damas, M. de, i. 317, 333, 369, 401
Damas, Mme. de, i. 322, 328, ii. 79
Damer, Mrs., ii. 47, 147, 157, 173
' Dames de l'Attente, Les,' ii. 79
' Dames de Mouvement, Les,' ii. 79
' Dames de la Résistance, Les,' ii. 79
Daniskiold, M. ii. 80, 224
Dartmouth, Lord, i. 31
Davenport, Harriet, i. 433
Davidoff, Mme., i. 333, 378
Davies, Mrs., ii. 241

Davy, Lady, ii. 341
Davy, Sir Humphry, i. 352
De Bathe, Mr., ii. 387
De Brosses: his ' Lettres Historiques et Critiques sur l'Italie,' ii. 341
De Candia, M. (Mario, the tenor), ii. 258
Decazes, M., i. 95 *sqq.*, 101, 107, ii. 192
Dedel, M., i. 263, 271
Dedel, Mme., i. 285
De Grey, Lord, ii. 389
De Grey, Lady, ii. 182, 184, 326
Déjazet, Mlle. (actress), ii. 327
Delamarre, Mme., ii. 83
Delessert, M. ii. 87, 161
Delessert, Mme., ii. 120, 162
Delmar, Baron, i. 411, ii. 3, 133
Delmar, Baronne (*née* Miss Rumbold), i. 411, ii. 76, 150, 188, 252
Deluge, a destructive (St. Petersburg), i. 317
Demont, Mlle. (Queen Caroline's maid), i. 158, 170, 172 *sq.*, 174, 184
Demerara, i. 299
Demidoff, Count (married Princesse Mathilde Buonaparte), ii. 326 *sq.*
Denison, Mr. (afterwards Speaker), i. 255, 393, 400, 425
Denman, Mr., i. 157, 165
Dentistry, French, i. 364
Derby, (twelfth) Earl of, i. 27
Derby, Countess of (Miss Farren), i. 27, 171
De Ros, Mr. (married Lady Georgiana Lennox), i. 159, 180, 231, 292, ii. 47
De Rothesay, Miss, ii. 208
De Ruyter (artist), i. 274
Devonshire, (Elizabeth) Duchess of, i. 3, 11, 127, 135 ; death (1824), 269
Devonshire, (sixth) Duke of, i. 55, (journey to Russia) 92, 145, 175, 185, 192, 201, 211, 267, 298, 381, 383, (special ambassador at coronation of Emperor Nicholas) 400, 415, 422, 437, ii. 5, 14, 54, 71, 81, 86, 97, 101, 115, 145, 156, 185, 204, 246, 261, 266, 279, 304, 315, 394
Dick, Mr. Quintin, i. 167
Dieppe, ii. 103
Dijon, ii. 268
Dimsdale, Baroness, ii. 295

THE END

PRINTED BY
SPOTTISWOODE AND CO., NEW-STREET SQUARE
LONDON

A

Classified Catalogue

OF WORKS

IN

GENERAL LITERATURE

PUBLISHED BY

LONGMANS, GREEN, & CO.

39 PATERNOSTER ROW, LONDON, E.C

NEW YORK: 15 EAST 16TH STREET.

1894.

MESSRS. LONGMANS, GREEN, & CO.

*Issue the undermentioned Lists of their Publications, which may be had post free
on application :—*

1. MONTHLY LIST OF NEW WORKS AND NEW EDITIONS.
2. QUARTERLY LIST OF ANNOUNCEMENTS AND NEW WORKS.
3. NOTES ON BOOKS; BEING AN ANALYSIS OF THE WORKS PUBLISHED DURING EACH QUARTER.
4. CATALOGUE OF SCIENTIFIC WORKS.
5. CATALOGUE OF MEDICAL AND SURGICAL WORKS.
6. CATALOGUE OF SCHOOL BOOKS AND EDUCATIONAL WORKS.
7. CATALOGUE OF BOOKS FOR ELEMENTARY SCHOOLS AND PUPIL TEACHERS.
8. CATALOGUE OF THEOLOGICAL WORKS BY DIVINES AND MEMBERS OF THE CHURCH OF ENGLAND.
9. CATALOGUE OF WORKS IN GENERAL LITERATURE.

INDEX OF AUTHORS.

MESSRS. LONGMANS & CO.'S STANDARD AND GENERAL WORKS.

CONTENTS.

History, Politics, Polity, and Political Memoirs.

Abbott.—A HISTORY OF GREECE. By EVELYN ABBOTT, M.A., LL.D.
Part I.—From the Earliest Times to the Ionian Revolt. Crown 8vo., 10s. 6d.
Part II.—500-445 B.C. Crown 8vo., 10s. 6d

Acland and Ransome.—A HANDBOOK IN OUTLINE OF THE POLITICAL HISTORY OF ENGLAND TO 1890. Chronologically Arranged. By the Right Hon. A. H. DYKE ACLAND, M.P., and CYRIL RANSOME, M.A. Crown 8vo., 6s.

ANNUAL REGISTER, (THE). A Review of Public Events at Home and Abroad, for the year 1892. 8vo., 18s.

Volumes of the ANNUAL REGISTER for the years 1863-1891 can still be had. 18s. each.

Armstrong.—ELIZABETH FARNESE; The Termagant of Spain. By EDWARD ARMSTRONG, M.A., Fellow of Queen's College, Oxford. 8vo., 16s.

Arnold.—Works by T. ARNOLD, D.D., formerly Head Master of Rugby School.

INTRODUCTORY LECTURES ON MODERN HISTORY. 8vo., 7s. 6d.

MISCELLANEOUS WORKS. 8vo., 7s. 6d.

Bagwell.—IRELAND UNDER THE TUDORS. By RICHARD BAGWELL, LL.D. (3 vols.) Vols. I. and II. From the first invasion of the Northmen to the year 1578. 8vo., 32s. Vol. III. 1578-1603. 8vo. 18s.

Ball.—HISTORICAL REVIEW OF THE LEGISLATIVE SYSTEMS OPERATIVE IN IRELAND, from the Invasion of Henry the Second to the Union (1172-1800). By the Rt. Hon. J. T. BALL. 8vo., 6s.

Besant.—THE HISTORY OF LONDON. With 74 Illustrations. Crown 8vo., 1s. 9d. Or bound as a School Prize Book, 2s. 6d. *Although this book is primarily intended for a School Reading Book it is also suitable for general use.*

Buckle.—HISTORY OF CIVILISATION IN ENGLAND AND FRANCE, SPAIN AND SCOTLAND. By HENRY THOMAS BUCKLE. 3 vols. Crown 8vo., 24s.

Chesney.—INDIAN POLITY: a View of the System of Administration in India. By Lieut.-General Sir GEORGE CHESNEY. New Edition, Revised and Enlarged. [*In the Press.*

Crump.—A SHORT ENQUIRY INTO THE FORMATION OF POLITICAL OPINION, from the reign of the Great Families to the advent of Democracy. By ARTHUR CRUMP. 8vo., 7s. 6d.

De Tocqueville.—DEMOCRACY IN AMERICA. By ALEXIS DE TOCQUEVILLE. 2 vols. Crown 8vo., 16s.

Fitzpatrick.—SECRET SERVICE UNDER PITT. By W. J. FITZPATRICK, F.S.A., Author of 'Correspondence of Daniel O'Connell'. 8vo., 7s. 6d.

Freeman.—THE HISTORICAL GEOGRAPHY OF EUROPE. By EDWARD A. FREEMAN. D.C.L., LL.D. With 65 Maps. 2 vols. 8vo., 31s. 6d.

History, Politics, Polity, and Political Memoirs—*continued.*

Froude.—Works by JAMES A. FROUDE, Regius Professor of Modern History in the University of Oxford.

THE HISTORY OF ENGLAND, from the Fall of Wolsey to the Defeat of the Spanish Armada.
Popular Edition. 12 vols. Crown 8vo., 3s. 6d. each.
Silver Library Edition. 12 vols. Crown 8vo. 3s. 6d. each.

THE DIVORCE OF CATHERINE OF ARAGON: the Story as told by the Imperial Ambassadors resident at the Court of Henry VIII. *In usum Laicorum.* Crown 8vo., 6s.

THE SPANISH STORY OF THE ARMADA, and other Essays, Historical and Descriptive. Crown 8vo., 6s.

THE ENGLISH IN IRELAND IN THE EIGHTEENTH CENTURY. 3 vols. Crown 8vo., 18s.

SHORT STUDIES ON GREAT SUBJECTS. 4 vols. Crown 8vo., 3s. 6d. each.

CÆSAR: a Sketch. Crown 8vo., 3s. 6d.

Gardiner.—Works by SAMUEL RAWSON GARDINER, M.A., Hon. LL.D., Edinburgh, Fellow of Merton College, Oxford.

HISTORY OF ENGLAND, from the Accession of James I. to the Outbreak of the Civil War, 1603-1642. 10 vols. Crown 8vo., 6s. each.

A HISTORY OF THE GREAT CIVIL WAR, 1642-1649. 4 vols. Crown 8vo., 6s. each

THE STUDENT'S HISTORY OF ENGLAND. With 378 Illustrations. Crown 8vo., 12s.

Also in Three Volumes.

Vol. I. B.C. 55—A.D. 1509. With 173 Illustrations. Crown 8vo. 4s.
Vol. II. 1509-1689. With 96 Illustrations. Crown 8vo. 4s.
Vol. III. 1689-1885. With 109 Illustrations. Crown 8vo. 4s.

Granville.—THE LETTERS OF HARRIET COUNTESS GRANVILLE, 1810-1845. Edited by her Son, the Hon. F. LEVESON GOWER. 2 vols., 8vo.

Greville.—A JOURNAL OF THE REIGNS OF KING GEORGE IV., KING WILLIAM IV., AND QUEEN VICTORIA. By CHARLES C. F. GREVILLE, formerly Clerk of the Council. 8 vols. Crown 8vo., 6s. each.

Hart —PRACTICAL ESSAYS IN AMERICAN GOVERNMENT. By ALBERT BUSHNELL HART, Ph.D. &c. Editor of 'Epochs of American History,' &c., &c. Crown 8vo. 6s.

Hearn.—THE GOVERNMENT OF ENGLAND: its Structure and its Development. By W. EDWARD HEARN. 8vo., 16s.

Historic Towns.—Edited by E. A. FREEMAN, D.C.L., and Rev. WILLIAM HUNT, M.A. With Maps and Plans. Crown 8vo., 3s. 6d. each.

BRISTOL. By the Rev. W. HUNT.
CARLISLE. By MANDELL CREIGHTON, D.D., Bishop of Peterborough.
CINQUE PORTS. By MONTAGU BURROWS.
COLCHESTER. By Rev. E. L. CUTTS.
EXETER. By E. A. FREEMAN.
LONDON. By Rev. W. J. LOFTIE.
OXFORD. By Rev. C. W. BOASE.
WINCHESTER. By Rev. G. W. KITCHIN, D.D.
YORK. By Rev. JAMES RAINE.
NEW YORK. By THEODORE ROOSEVELT.
BOSTON (U.S.) By HENRY CABOT LODGE.

Horley.—SEFTON: A DESCRIPTIVE AND HISTORICAL ACCOUNT. Comprising the Collected Notes and Researches of the late Rev. ENGELBERT HORLEY, M.A., Rector 1871-1883. By W. D. CARÖE, M.A., and E. J. A. GORDON. With 17 Plates and 32 Illustrations in the Text. Royal 8vo., 31s. 6d.

Joyce.—A SHORT HISTORY OF IRELAND, from the Earliest Times to 1608. By P. W. JOYCE, LL.D. Crown 8vo., 10s. 6d.

Lang.—ST. ANDREWS. By ANDREW LANG. With 8 Plates and 24 Illustrations in the Text by T. HODGE. 8vo., 15s. net.

Lecky.—Works by WILLIAM EDWARD HARTPOLE LECKY.

HISTORY OF ENGLAND IN THE EIGHTEENTH CENTURY.
Library Edition. 8 vols. 8vo., £7 4s.
Cabinet Edition. ENGLAND. 7 vols. Crown 8vo., 6s. each. IRELAND. 5 vols. Crown 8vo., 6s. each.

HISTORY OF EUROPEAN MORALS FROM AUGUSTUS TO CHARLEMAGNE. 2 vols. Crown 8vo., 16s.

HISTORY OF THE RISE AND INFLUENCE OF THE SPIRIT OF RATIONALISM IN EUROPE. 2 vols. Crown 8vo., 16s.

THE EMPIRE: its Value and its Growth. An Inaugural Address delivered at the Imperial Institute, November 20, 1893, under the Presidency of H.R.H. the Prince of Wales. Crown 8vo. 1s. 6d.

History, Politics, Polity, and Political Memoirs—*continued.*

Macaulay.—Works by LORD MACAULAY.

COMPLETE WORKS OF LORD MACAULAY.

Cabinet Edition. 16 vols. Post 8vo., £4 16.

Library Edition. 8 vols. 8vo., £5 5s.

HISTORY OF ENGLAND FROM THE AC-CESSION OF JAMES THE SECOND.

Popular Edition. 2 vols. Cr. 8vo., 5s.
Student's Edition. 2 vols. Cr. 8vo., 12s.
People's Edition. 4 vols. Cr. 8vo., 16s.
Cabinet Edition. 8 vols. Post 8vo., 48s.
Library Edition. 5 vols. 8vo., £4.

CRITICAL AND HISTORICAL ESSAYS, WITH LAYS OF ANCIENT ROME, in 1 volume.

Popular Edition. Crown 8vo., 2s. 6d.
Authorised Edition. Crown 8vo., 2s. 6d., or 3s. 6d., gilt edges.
Silver Library Edition. Cr. 8vo., 3s. 6d.

CRITICAL AND HISTORICAL ESSAYS.

Student's Edition. 1 volume. Cr. 8vo., 6s.
People's Edition. 2 vols. Cr. 8vo., 8s.
Trevelyan Edition. 2 vols. Cr. 8vo., 9s.
Cabinet Edition. 4 vols. Post 8vo., 24s.
Library Edition. 3 vols. 8vo., 36s.

ESSAYS which may be had separately price 6d. each sewed, 1s. each cloth.

Addison and Walpole.
Frederick the Great.
Croker's Boswell's Johnson.
Hallam's Constitutional History.
Warren Hastings. (3d. sewed, 6d. cloth).
The Earl of Chatham (Two Essays).
Ranke and Gladstone.
Milton and Machiavelli.
Lord Bacon.
Lord Clive.
Lord Byron, and The Comic Dramatists of the Restoration.

SPEECHES. Crown 8vo., 3s. 6d.

MISCELLANEOUS WRITINGS

People's Edition. 1 vol. Crown 8vo., 4s. 6d.
Library Edition. 2 vols. 8vo., 21s.

MISCELLANEOUS WRITINGS AND SPEECHES.

Popular Edition. Crown 8vo., 2s. 6d.
Student's Edition. Crown 8vo., 6s.
Cabinet Edition. Including Indian Penal Code, Lays of Ancient Rome, and Miscellaneous Poems. 4 vols. Post 8vo., 24s.

SELECTIONS FROM THE WRITINGS OF LORD MACAULAY. Edited, with Occasional Notes, by the Right Hon. Sir G. O. Trevelyan, Bart. Crown 8vo., 6s.

May.—THE CONSTITUTIONAL HISTORY OF ENGLAND since the Accession of George III. 1760-1870. By Sir THOMAS ERSKINE MAY, K.C.B. (Lord Farnborough). 3 vols. Crown 8vo., 18s.

Merivale.—Works by the Very Rev. CHARLES MERIVALE, Dean of Ely.

HISTORY OF THE ROMANS UNDER THE EMPIRE.

Cabinet Edition. 8 vols. Cr. 8vo., 48s.
Silver Library Edition. 8 vols. Crown 8vo., 3s. 6d. each.

THE FALL OF THE ROMAN REPUBLIC: a Short History of the Last Century of the Commonwealth. 12mo., 7s. 6d.

O'Brien.—IRISH IDEAS. REPRINTED ADDRESSES. By WILLIAM O'BRIEN, M.P. Cr. 8vo. 2s. 6d.

Parkes.—FIFTY YEARS IN THE MAKING OF AUSTRALIAN HISTORY. By Sir HENRY PARKES, G.C.M.G. With 2 Portraits (1854 and 1892). 2 vols. vo., 32s.

Prendergast.—IRELAND FROM THE RESTORATION TO THE REVOLUTION, 1660-1690. By JOHN P. PRENDERGAST, Author of 'The Cromwellian Settlement in Ireland'. 8vo., 5s.

Round.—GEOFFREY DE MANDEVILLE: a Study of the Anarchy. By J. H. ROUND, M.A. 8vo., 16s.

Seebohm.—THE ENGLISH VILLAGE COMMUNITY Examined in its Relations to the Manorial and Tribal Systems, &c. By FREDERIC SEEBOHM. With 13 Maps and Plates. 8vo., 16s.

Sheppard.—MEMORIALS OF ST. JAMES'S PALACE. By the Rev. EDGAR SHEPPARD, M.A., SubDean of the Chapel Royal. With Illustrations. *[In the Press.*

Smith.—CARTHAGE AND THE CARTHAGINIANS. By R. BOSWORTH SMITH, M.A., Assistant Master in Harrow School. With Maps, Plans, &c. Crown 8vo., 3s. 6d.

Stephens.—PAROCHIAL SELF-GOVERNMENT IN RURAL DISTRICTS: Argument and Plan. By HENRY C. STEPHENS, M.P. 4to., 12s. 6d. Popular Edition, crown 8vo, 1s.

Stephens.—A HISTORY OF THE FRENCH REVOLUTION. By H. MORSE STEPHENS, Balliol College, Oxford. 3 vols. 8vo. Vols. I. and II. 18s. each.

Stubbs.—HISTORY OF THE UNIVERSITY OF DUBLIN, from its Foundation to the End of the Eighteenth Century. By J. W. STUBBS. 8vo., 12s. 6d.

History, Politics, Polity, and Political Memoirs—*continued.*

Sutherland.—THE HISTORY OF AUS-TRALIA AND NEW ZEALAND, from 1606 to 1890. By ALEXANDER SUTHERLAND, M.A., and GEORGE SUTHERLAND, M.A. Crown 8vo., 2s. 6d.

Thompson.—POLITICS IN A DEMOCRACY: an Essay. By DANIEL GREENLEAF THOMPSON. Crown 8vo., 5s.

Todd.—PARLIAMENTARY GOVERNMENT IN THE BRITISH COLONIES. By ALPHEUS TODD, LL.D. 8vo.

Tupper.—OUR INDIAN PROTECTORATE: an Introduction to the Study of the Relations between the British Government and its Indian Feudatories. By CHARLES LEWIS TUPPER, Indian Civil Service. 8vo., 16s.

Wakeman and Hassall.—ESSAYS INTRO-DUCTORY TO THE STUDY OF ENGLISH CON-STITUTIONAL HISTORY. By Resident Members of the University of Oxford. Edited by HENRY OFFLEY WAKEMAN, M.A., and ARTHUR HASSALL, M.A. Crown 8vo., 6s.

Walpole.—Works by SPENCER WALPOLE.

HISTORY OF ENGLAND FROM THE CON-CLUSION OF THE GREAT WAR IN 1815 TO 1858. 6 vols. Crown 8vo., 6s. each.

THE LAND OF HOME RULE: being an Account of the History and Institutions of the Isle of Man. Crown 8vo., 6s.

Wylie.—HISTORY OF ENGLAND UNDER HENRY IV. By JAMES HAMILTON WYLIE, M.A., one of H. M. Inspectors of Schools. 3 vols. Vol. I., 1399-1404. Crown 8vo., 10s. 6d. Vol. II. Vol. III. [*In preparation.*

Biography, Personal Memoirs, &c.

Armstrong.—THE LIFE AND LETTERS OF EDMUND J. ARMSTRONG. Edited by G. F. ARMSTRONG. Fcp. 8vo., 7s. 6d.

Bacon.—THE LETTERS AND LIFE OF FRANCIS BACON, INCLUDING ALL HIS OC-CASIONAL WORKS. Edited by JAMES SPED-DING. 7 vols. 8vo., £4 4s.

Bagehot.—BIOGRAPHICAL STUDIES. By WALTER BAGEHOT. 8vo., 12s.

Boyd.—TWENTY-FIVE YEARS OF ST ANDREWS, 1865-1890. By A. K. H. BOYD, D.D., LL.D., Author of 'Recreations of a Country Parson,' &c. 2 vols. 8vo. Vol. I. 12s. Vol. II. 15s.

Carlyle.—THOMAS CARLYLE: a History of his Life. By J. A. FROUDE.
1795-1835. 2 vols. Crown 8vo., 7s.
1834-1881. 2 vols. Crown 8vo., 7s.

Fabert.—ABRAHAM FABERT: Governor of Sedan and Marshal of France. His Life and Times, 1599-1662. By GEORGE HOOPER, Author of 'Waterloo,' 'Wellington,' &c. With a Portrait. 8vo., 10s. 6d.

Fox.—THE EARLY HISTORY OF CHARLES JAMES FOX. By the Right Hon. Sir G. O. TREVELYAN, Bart.
Library Edition. 8vo., 18s.
Cabinet Edition. Crown 8vo., 6s.

Hamilton.—LIFE OF SIR WILLIAM HAMILTON. By R. P. GRAVES. 3 vols. 15s. each.
ADDENDUM TO THE LIFE OF SIR WM. ROWAN HAMILTON, LL.D., D.C.L. 8vo., 6d. sewed.

Hassall.—THE NARRATIVE OF A BUSY LIFE: an Autobiography. By ARTHUR HILL HASSALL, M.D. 8vo., 5s.

Havelock.—MEMOIRS OF SIR HENRY HAVELOCK, K.C.B. By JOHN CLARK MARSHMAN. Crown 8vo., 3s. 6d.

Macaulay.—THE LIFE AND LETTERS OF LORD MACAULAY. By the Right Hon. Sir G. O. TREVELYAN, Bart.
Popular Edition. 1 volume. Cr. 8vo., 2s. 6d.
Student's Edition. 1 volume. Cr. 8vo., 6s.
Cabinet Edition. 2 vols. Post 8vo., 12s.
Library Edition. 2 vols. 8vo., 36s.

Marbot.—THE MEMOIRS OF THE BARON DE MARBOT. Translated from the French by ARTHUR JOHN BUTLER, M.A. Crown 8vo., 7s. 6d.

Montrose.—DEEDS OF MONTROSE: THE MEMOIRS OF JAMES, MARQUIS OF MONTROSE, 1639-1650. By the Rev. GEORGE WISHART, D.D., (Bishop of Edinburgh, 1662-1671). Translated, with Introduction, Notes, &c., and the original Latin (Part II. now first published), by the Rev. ALEXANDER MUR-DOCH, F.S.A., (Scot.) Canon of St. Mary's Cathedral, Edinburgh, Editor and Translater of the Grameid MS. and H. F. MORELAND SIMPSON, M.A. (Cantab.) F.S.A. (Scot.) Fettes College. 4to., 36s. net.

Seebohm.—THE OXFORD REFORMERS—JOHN COLET, ERASMUS AND THOMAS MORE: a History of their Fellow-Work. By FRED-ERIC SEEBOHM. 8vo., 14s.

Biography, Personal Memoirs, &c.—*continued.*

Shakespeare.—OUTLINES OF THE LIFE OF SHAKESPEARE. By J. O. HALLIWELL-PHILLIPPS. With numerous Illustrations and Fac-similes. 2 vols. Royal 8vo., £1 1s.

Shakespeare's TRUE LIFE. By JAMES WALTER. With 500 Illustrations by GERALD E. MOIRA. Imp. 8vo., 21s.

Sherbrooke.—LIFE AND LETTERS OF THE RIGHT HON. ROBERT LOWE, VISCOUNT SHERBROOKE. G.C.B., together with a Memoir of .iis Kinsman, Sir JOHN COAPE SHERBROOKE, G.C.B. By A. PATCHETT MARTIN. With 5 Portraits. 2 vols. 8vo., 36s.

Stephen. — ESSAYS IN ECCLESIASTICAL BIOGRAPHY. By Sir JAMES STEPHEN. Crown 8vo., 7s. 6d.

Verney. — MEMOIRS OF THE VERNEY FAMILY DURING THE CIVIL WAR. Compiled from the Letters and Illustrated by the Portraits at Claydon House, Bucks. By FRANCES PARTHENOPE VERNEY. With a Preface by S. R. GARDINER, M.A., LL.D. With 38 Portraits, Woodcuts and Fac-simile. 2 vols. Royal 8vo., 42s.

Wagner.—WAGNER AS I KNEW HIM. By FERDINAND PRAEGER. Crown 8vo., 7s. 6d.

Walford.—TWELVE ENGLISH AUTHORESSES. By L. B. WALFORD, Author of 'Mischief of Monica,' &c. With Portrait of Hannah More. Crown 8vo., 4s. 6d.

Wellington.—LIFE OF THE DUKE OF WELLINGTON. By the Rev. G. R. GLEIG, M.A. Crown 8vo., 3s. 6d.

Wordsworth. — Works by CHARLES WORDSWORTH, D.C.L., late Bishop of St. Andrews.

ANNALS OF MY EARLY LIFE, 1806-1846. 8vo., 15s.

ANNALS OF MY LIFE, 1847-1856. 8vo. 10s. 6d.

Travel and Adventure, the Colonies, &c.

Arnold.—SEAS AND LANDS. By Sir ED-WIN ARNOLD, K.C.I.E., Author of 'The Light of the World,' &c. Reprinted letters from the 'Daily Telegraph'. With 71 Illustrations. Crown 8vo., 7s. 6d.

AUSTRALIA AS IT IS, or, Facts and Features, Sketches and Incidents of Australia and Australian Life, with Notices of New Zealand. By A CLERGYMAN, thirteen years resident in the interior of New South Wales, Crown 8vo., 5s.

Baker.—Works by Sir SAMUEL WHITE BAKER.

EIGHT YEARS IN CEYLON. With 6 Illustrations. Crown 8vo., 3s. 6d.

THE RIFLE AND THE HOUND IN CEYLON. 6 Illustrations. Crown 8vo., 3s. 6d.

Bent.—Works by J. THEODORE BENT, F.S.A., F.R.G.S.

THE RUINED CITIES OF MASHONALAND: being a Record of Excavation and Exploration in 1891. With a Chapter on the Orientation and Mensuration of the Temples. By R. M. W. SWAN. With Map, 13 Plates, and 104 Illustrations in the Text. Crown 8vo., 7s. 6d.

THE SACRED CITY OF THE ETHIOPIANS: being a Record of Travel and Research in Abyssinia in 1893. With 8 Plates and 65 Illustrations in the Text. 8vo., 18s.

Brassey.—Works by the late LADY BRASEY.

THE LAST VOYAGE TO INDIA AND AUSTRALIA IN THE 'SUNBEAM.' With Charts and Maps, and 40 Illustrations in Monotone, and nearly 200 Illustrations in the Text 8vo., 21s.

A VOYAGE IN THE 'SUNBEAM'; OUR HOME ON THE OCEAN FOR ELEVEN MONTHS.
Library Edition. With 8 Maps and Charts, and 118 Illustrations. 8vo. 21s.
Cabinet Edition. With Map and 66 Illustrations. Crown 8vo., 7s. 6d.
Silver Library Edition. With 66 Illustrations. Crown 8vo., 3s. 6d.
Popular Edition. With 60 Illustrations. 4to., 6d. sewed, 1s. cloth.
School Edition. With 37 Illustrations. Fcp., 2s. cloth, or 3s. white parchment.

SUNSHINE AND STORM IN THE EAST.
Library Edition. With 2 Maps and 141 Illustrations. 8vo., 21s.
Cabinet Edition. With 2 Maps and 114 Illustrations. Crown 8vo., 7s. 6d.
Popular Edition. With 103 Illustrations. 4to., 6d. sewed, 1s. cloth.

IN THE TRADES, THE TROPICS, AND THE 'ROARING FORTIES'.
Cabinet Edition. With Map and 220 Illustrations. Crown 8vo., 7s. 6d.
Popular Edition. With 183 Illustrations. 4to., 6d. sewed, 1s. cloth.

THREE VOYAGES IN THE 'SUNBEAM'.
Popular Edition. With 346 Illustrations. 4to., 2s. 6d.

Travel and Adventure, the Colonies, &c.—*continued.*

Curzon.—PERSIA AND THE PERSIAN QUESTION. With 9 Maps, 96 Illustrations, Appendices, and an Index. By the Hon. GEORGE N. CURZON, M.P., late Fellow of All Souls College, Oxford. 2 vols. 8vo., 42s.

Froude.—Works by JAMES A. FROUDE.

OCEANA : or England and her Colonies. With 9 Illustrations. Crown 8vo., 2s. boards, 2s. 6d. cloth.

THE ENGLISH IN THE WEST INDIES: or, the Bow of Ulysses. With 9 Illustrations. Crown 8vo., 2s. boards, 2s. 6d. cloth.

Howard.—LIFE WITH TRANS-SIBERIAN SAVAGES. By B. DOUGLAS HOWARD, M.A. Crown 8vo., 6s.

Howitt.—VISITS TO REMARKABLE PLACES. Old Halls, Battle-Fields, Scenes, illustrative of Striking Passages in English History and Poetry. By WILLIAM HOWITT. With 80 Illustrations. Crown 8vo., 3s. 6d.

Knight.—Works by E. F. KNIGHT, author of the Cruise of the ' Falcon '.

THE CRUISE OF THE 'ALERTE': the narrative of a Search for Treasure on the Desert Island of Trinidad. With 2 Maps and 23 Illustrations. Crown 8vo., 3s. 6d.

WHERE THREE EMPIRES MEET: a Narrative of Recent Travel in Kashmir, Western Tibet, Baltistan, Ladak, Gilgit, and the adjoining Countries. With a Map and 54 Illustrations. Cr. 8vo., 7s. 6d.

Lees and Clutterbuck.—B. C. 1887 : A RAMBLE IN BRITISH COLUMBIA. By J. A. LEES and W. J. CLUTTERBUCK, Authors of ' Three in Norway '. With Map and 75 Illustrations. Crown 8vo., 3s. 6d.

Nansen.—Works by Dr. FRIDTJOF NANSEN.

THE FIRST CROSSING OF GREENLAND. With numerous Illustrations and a Map. Crown 8vo., 7s. 6d.

ESKIMO LIFE. Translated by WILLIAM ARCHER. With 31 Illustrations. 8vo., 16s.

Peary.—MY ARCTIC JOURNAL : a Year among Ice-Fields and Eskimos. By JOSEPHINE DIEBITSCH-PEARY. With an Account of the Great White Journey across Greenland. By ROBERT E. PEARY, Civil Engineer, U.S. Navy. With 19 Plates, 3 Sketch Maps, and 44 Illustrations in the Text. 8vo., 12s.

Pratt.—TO THE SNOWS OF TIBET THROUGH CHINA. By A. E. PRATT, F.R.G.S. With 33 Illustrations and a Map. 8vo., 18s.

Riley.—ATHOS : or, the Mountain of the Monks. By ATHELSTAN RILEY, M.A. With Map and 29 Illustrations. 8vo., 21s.

Rockhill.—THE LAND OF THE LAMAS: Notes of a Journey through China, Mongolia, and Tibet. By WILLIAM WOODVILLE ROCKHILL. With 2 Maps and 61 Illustrations. 8vo., 15s.

Stephens.—MADOC : An Essay on the Discovery of America, by MADOC AP OWEN GWYNEDD, in the Twelfth Century. By THOMAS STEPHENS. Edited by LLYWARCH REYNOLDS, B.A. Oxon. 8vo., 7s. 6d.

THREE IN NORWAY. By Two of Them. With a Map and 59 Illustrations. Crown 8vo., 2s. boards, 2s. 6d. cloth.

Von Höhnel.—DISCOVERY OF LAKES RUDOLF and STEFANIE : A Narrative of Count SAMUEL TELEKI's Exploring and Hunting Expedition in Eastern Equatorial Africa in 1887 and 1888. By Lieutenant LUDWIG VON HÖHNEL. Translated by NANCY BELL (N. D'Anvers). With 179 Illustrations and 5 Coloured Maps. 2 vols. 8vo., 42s.

Whishaw.—OUT OF DOORS IN TSARLAND : a Record of the Seeings and Doings of a Wanderer in Russia. By FRED. J. WHISHAW. Crown 8vo., 7s. 6d.

Wolff.—Works by HENRY W. WOLFF.

RAMBLES IN THE BLACK FOREST. Crown 8vo., 7s. 6d.

THE WATERING PLACES OF THE VOSGES. Crown 8vo., 4s. 6d.

THE COUNTRY OF THE VOSGES. With a Map. 8vo., 12s.

Sport and Pastime.

Campbell-Walker.—THE CORRECT CARD: or, How to Play at Whist; a Whist Catechism. By Major A. CAMPBELL-WALKER, F.R.G.S. Fcp. 8vo., 2s. 6d.

DEAD SHOT (THE): or, Sportsman's Complete Guide. Being a Treatise on the Use of the Gun, with Rudimentary and Finishing Lessons on the Art of Shooting Game of all kinds, also Game Driving, Wild-Fowl and Pigeon Shooting, Dog Breaking, etc. By MARKSMAN. Crown 8vo., 10s. 6d.

Sport and Pastime—*continued.*

THE BADMINTON LIBRARY.

Edited by the DUKE of BEAUFORT, K.G., assisted by ALFRED E. T. WATSON.

ATHLETICS AND FOOTBALL. By MONTAGUE SHEARMAN. With 51 Illustrations. Crown 8vo., 10s. 6d.

BIG GAME SHOOTING. By C. PHILLIPPS-WOLLEY, F. C. SELOUS, W. G. LITTLEDALE, Colonel PERCY, FRED. JACKSON, Major H. PERCY, W. C. OSWELL, Sir HENRY POTTINGER, Bart., and the EARL OF KILMOREY. With Contributions by other Writers. With Illustrations by CHARLES WHYMPER and others. 2 vols. Crown 8vo., 10s. 6d. each. [*In the press.*]

BOATING. By W. B. WOODGATE. With an Introduction by the Rev. EDMOND WARRE, D.D., and a Chapter on 'Rowing at Eton,' by R. HARVEY MASON. With 49 Illustrations. Cr. 8vo., 10s. 6d.

COURSING AND FALCONRY. By HARDING COX and the Hon. GERALD LASCELLES. With 76 Illustrations. Cr. 8vo., 10s. 6d.

CRICKET. By A. G. STEEL and the Hon. R. H. LYTTELTON. With Contributions by ANDREW LANG, R. A. H. MITCHELL, W. G. GRACE, and F. GALE. With 64 Illustrations. Crown 8vo., 10s. 6d.

CYCLING. By VISCOUNT BURY (Earl of Albemarle), K.C.M.G., and G. LACY HILLIER. With 89 Illustrations. Crown 8vo., 10s. 6d.

DRIVING. By the DUKE OF BEAUFORT. With 65 Illustrations. Crown 8vo., 10s. 6d.

FENCING. BOXING, AND WRESTLING. By WALTER H. POLLOCK, F. C. GROVE, C. PREVOST, E. B. MITCHELL, and WALTER ARMSTRONG. With 42 Illustrations. Crown 8vo., 10s. 6d.

FISHING. By H. CHOLMONDELEY-PENNELL. With Contributions by the MARQUIS OF EXETER, HENRY R. FRANCIS, Major JOHN P. TRAHERNE, FREDERIC M. HALFORD, G. CHRISTOPHER DAVIES, R. B. MARSTON, &c.

Vol. I. Salmon, Trout, and Grayling. With 158 Illustrations. Crown 8vo., 10s. 6d.

Vol. II. Pike and other Coarse Fish. With 133 Illustrations. Crown 8vo., 10s. 6d.

GOLF. By HORACE G. HUTCHINSON, the Rt. Hon. A. J. BALFOUR, M.P., Sir W. G. SIMPSON, Bart., LORD WELLWOOD, H. S. C. EVERARD, ANDREW LANG, and other Writers. With 89 Illustrations. Crown 8vo., 10s. 6d.

HUNTING. By the DUKE OF BEAUFORT, K.G., and MOWBRAY MORRIS. With Contributions by the EARL OF SUFFOLK AND BERKSHIRE, Rev. E. W. L. DAVIES, DIGBY COLLINS, and ALFRED E. T. WATSON. With 53 Illustrations. Crown 8vo., 10s. 6d.

MOUNTAINEERING. By C. T. DENT, Sir F. POLLOCK, Bart., W. M. CONWAY, DOUGLAS FRESHFIELD, C. E. MATHEWS, C. PILKINGTON, and other Writers. With 108 Illustrations. Crown 8vo., 10s. 6d.

RACING AND STEEPLE-CHASING. By the EARL OF SUFFOLK AND BERKSHIRE and W. G. CRAVEN. With a Contribution by the Hon. F. LAWLEY. *Steeple-chasing:* By ARTHUR COVENTRY and ALFRED E. T. WATSON. With 58 Illustrations. Crown 8vo., 10s. 6d.

RIDING AND POLO. By Captain ROBERT WEIR, J. MORAY BROWN, the DUKE OF BEAUFORT, K.G., the EARL OF SUFFOLK AND BERKSHIRE, &c. With 59 Illustrations. Crown 8vo., 10s. 6d.

SHOOTING. By LORD WALSINGHAM and Sir RALPH PAYNE-GALLWEY, Bart. With Contributions by LORD LOVAT, LORD CHARLES LENNOX KERR, the Hon. G. LASCELLES, and A. J. STUART-WORTLEY.

Vol. I. Field and Covert. With 105 Illustrations. Crown 8vo., 10s. 6d.

Vol. II. Moor and Marsh. With 65 Illustrations. Crown 8vo., 10s. 6d.

SKATING, CURLING, TOBOGGANING, AND OTHER ICE SPORTS. By J. M. HEATHCOTE, C. G. TEBBUTT, T. MAXWELL WITHAM, the Rev. JOHN KERR, ORMOND HAKE, and Colonel BUCK. With 284 Illustrations. Crown 8vo., 10s. 6d.

SWIMMING. By ARCHIBALD SINCLAIR and WILLIAM HENRY, Hon. Secs. of the Life Saving Society. With 119 Illustrations. Crown 8vo., 10s. 6d.

TENNIS, LAWN TENNIS, RACKETS AND FIVES. By J. M. and C. G. HEATHCOTE, E. O. PLEYDELL-BOUVERIE and A. C. AINGER. With Contributions by the Hon. A. LYTTELTON, W. C. MARSHALL, Miss L. DOD, H. W. W. WILBERFORCE, H. F. LAWFORD, &c. With 79 Illustrations. Cr. 8vo., 10s. 6d.

YACHTING. By the EARL OF PEMBROKE, the MARQUIS OF DUFFERIN AND AVA, the EARL OF ONSLOW, LORD BRASSEY, Lieut.-Col. BUCKNILL, LEWIS HERRESHOFF, G. L. WATSON, E. F. KNIGHT, Rev. G. L. BLAKE, R.N., and G. C. DAVIES. With Illustrations by R. T. PRITCHETT, and from Photographs. 2 vols. [*In the press.*]

Sport and Pastime—*continued.*

FUR AND FEATHER SERIES.

Edited by A. E. T. WATSON.

THE PARTRIDGE. Natural History, by the Rev. H. A. MACPHERSON; Shooting, by A. J. STUART-WORTLEY; Cookery, by GEORGE SAINTSBURY. With 11 full-page Illustrations and Vignette by A. THORBURN, A. J. STUART-WORTLEY, and C. WHYMPER, and 15 Diagrams in the Text by A. J. STUART-WORTLEY. Crown 8vo., 5s.

THE GROUSE. By A. J. STUART-WORTLEY, the Rev. H. A. MACPHERSON, and GEORGE SAINTSBURY. [*In preparation.*

THE PHEASANT. By A. J. STUART-WORTLEY, the Rev. H. A. MACPHERSON, and A. J. INNES SHAND. [*In preparation.*

THE HARE AND THE RABBIT. By the Hon. GERALD LASCELLES, etc. [*In preparation.*

WILDFOWL. By the Hon. JOHN SCOTT-MONTAGU, M.P., etc. Illustrated by A. J. STUART-WORTLEY, A. THORBURN, and others. [*In preparation.*

Falkener.—GAMES, ANCIENT AND ORIENTAL, AND HOW TO PLAY THEM. By EDWARD FALKENER. With numerous Photographs, Diagrams, &c. 8vo., 21s.

Ford.—THE THEORY AND PRACTICE OF ARCHERY. By HORACE FORD. New Edition, thoroughly Revised and Re-written by W. BUTT, M.A. With a Preface by C. J. LONGMAN, M.A. 8vo., 14s.

Francis.—A BOOK ON ANGLING: or, Treatise on the Art of Fishing in every Branch; including full Illustrated List of Salmon Flies. By FRANCIS FRANCIS. With Portrait and Coloured Plates. Crown 8vo., 15s.

Hawker.—THE DIARY OF COLONEL PETER HAWKER, Author of 'Instructions to Young Sportsmen.' With an Introduction by Sir RALPH PAYNE-GALLWEY, Bart. 2 vols. 8vo., 32s.

Hopkins.—FISHING REMINISCENCES. By Major F. P. HOPKINS. With Illustrations. Crown 8vo., 6s. 6d.

Lang.—ANGLING SKETCHES. By ANDREW LANG. With 20 Illustrations by W. G. BURN MURDOCH. Crown 8vo., 7s. 6d.

Longman. — CHESS OPENINGS. By FREDERICK W. LONGMAN. Fcp. 8vo., 2s. 6d.

Payne-Gallwey.—Works by Sir RALPH PAYNE-GALLWEY, Bart.

LETTERS TO YOUNG SHOOTERS (First Series). On the Choice and use of a Gun. With Illustrations. Crown 8vo., 7s. 6d.

LETTERS TO YOUNG SHOOTERS. (Second Series). On the Production, Preservation, and Killing of Game. With Directions in Shooting Wood-Pigeons and Breaking-in Retrievers. With a Portrait of the Author, and 103 Illustrations. Crown 8vo., 12s. 6d.

Pole.—THE THEORY OF THE MODERN SCIENTIFIC GAME OF WHIST. By W. POLE, F.R.S. Fcp. 8vo., 2s. 6d.

Proctor.—Works by RICHARD A. PROCTOR. HOW TO PLAY WHIST: WITH THE LAWS AND ETIQUETTE OF WHIST. Cr. 8vo., 3s. 6d. HOME WHIST: an Easy Guide to Correct Play. 16mo., 1s.

Ronalds.—THE FLY-FISHER'S ENTOMOLOGY. By ALFRED RONALDS. With coloured Representations of the Natural and Artificial Insect. With 20 coloured Plates. 8vo., 14s.

Wilcocks.—THE SEA FISHERMAN: Comprising the Chief Methods of Hook and Line Fishing in the British and other Seas, and Remarks on Nets, Boats, and Boating. By J. C. WILCOCKS. Illustrated. Cr 8vo., 6s.

Mental, Moral, and Political Philosophy.

LOGIC, RHETORIC, PSYCHOLOGY, ETC.

Abbott.—THE ELEMENTS OF LOGIC. By T. K. ABBOTT, B.D. 12mo., 3s.

Aristotle.—Works by.
THE POLITICS: G. Bekker's Greek Text of Books I., III., IV. (VII.), with an English Translation by W. E. BOLLAND, M.A.; and short Introductory Essays by A. LANG, M.A. Crown 8vo., 7s. 6d.

Aristotle.—Works by—*continued.*

THE POLITICS: Introductory Essays. By ANDREW LANG (from Bolland and Lang's 'Politics'). Crown 8vo., 2s. 6d.

THE ETHICS: Greek Text, Illustrated with Essay and Notes. By Sir ALEXANDER GRANT, Bart. 2 vols. 8vo., 32s.

Mental, Moral and Political Philosophy—*continued.*

Aristotle.—Works by—*continued.*

THE NICOMACHEAN ETHICS: Newly Translated into English. By ROBERT WILLIAMS. Crown 8vo., 7s. 6d.

AN INTRODUCTION TO ARISTOTLE'S ETHICS. Books I.-IV. (Book X. c. vi.-ix. in an Appendix). With a continuous Analysis and Notes. Intended for the use of Beginners and Junior Students. By the Rev. EDWARD MOORE, D.D., Principal of St. Edmund Hall, and late Fellow and Tutor of Queen's College, Oxford. Crown 8vo. 10s. 6d.

Bacon.—Works by FRANCIS BACON.

COMPLETE WORKS. Edited by R. L. ELLIS, JAMES SPEDDING and D. D. HEATH. 7 vols. 8vo., £3 13s. 6d.

LETTERS AND LIFE, including all his occasional Works. Edited by JAMES SPEDDING. 7 vols. 8vo., £4 4s.

THE ESSAYS: with Annotations. By RICHARD WHATELY, D.D. 8vo., 10s. 6d.

Bain.—Works by ALEXANDER BAIN, LL.D.

MENTAL SCIENCE. Crown 8vo. 6s. 6d.
MORAL SCIENCE. Crown 8vo., 4s. 6d.
The two works as above can be had in one volume, price 10s. 6d.
SENSES AND THE INTELLECT. 8vo., 15s.
EMOTIONS AND THE WILL. 8vo., 15s.
LOGIC, DEDUCTIVE AND INDUCTIVE. Part I. 4s. Part II. 6s. 6d.
PRACTICAL ESSAYS. Crown 8vo., 3s.

Bray.—Works by CHARLES BRAY.

THE PHILOSOPHY OF NECESSITY: or Law in Mind as in Matter. Cr. 8vo,, 5s.

THE EDUCATION OF THE FEELINGS: a Moral System for Schools. Cr. 8vo., 2s. 6d.

Bray.—ELEMENTS OF MORALITY, in Easy Lessons for Home and School Teaching. By Mrs. CHARLES BRAY. Cr. 8vo., 1s. 6d.

Crozier.—CIVILISATION AND PROGRESS. By JOHN BEATTIE CROZIER, M.D. With New Preface. More fully explaining the nature of the New Organon used in the solution of its problems. 8vo., 14s.

Davidson.—THE LOGIC OF DEFINITION, Explained and Applied. By WILLIAM L. DAVIDSON, M.A. Crown 8vo., 6s.

Green.—THE WORKS OF THOMAS HILL GREEN. Edited by R. L. NETTLESHIP.
Vols. I. and II. Philosophical Works. 8vo., 16s. each.
Vol. III. Miscellanies. With Index to the three Volumes, and Memoir. 8vo., 21s.

Hearn.—THE ARYAN HOUSEHOLD: its Structure and its Development. An Introduction to Comparative Jurisprudence. By W. EDWARD HEARN. 8vo., 16s.

Hodgson.—Works by SHADWORTH H. HODGSON.

TIME AND SPACE: a Metaphysical Essay. 8vo., 16s.

THE THEORY OF PRACTICE: an Ethical Inquiry. 2 vols. 8vo., 24s.

THE PHILOSOPHY OF REFLECTION. 2 vols. 8vo., 21s.

Hume.—THE PHILOSOPHICAL WORKS OF DAVID HUME. Edited by T. H. GREEN and T. H. GROSE. 4 vols. 8vo., 56s. Or separately, Essays. 2 vols. 28s. Treatise of Human Nature. 2 vols. 28s.

Johnstone.—A SHORT INTRODUCTION TO THE STUDY OF LOGIC. By LAURENCE JOHNSTONE. With Questions. Cr. 8vo., 2s. 6d.

Jones.—AN INTRODUCTION TO GENERAL LOGIC. By E. E. CONSTANCE JONES. Cr. 8vo., 4s. 6d.

Justinian.—THE INSTITUTES OF JUSTINIAN: Latin Text, chiefly that of Huschke, with English Introduction, Translation, Notes, and Summary. By THOMAS C. SANDARS, M.A. 8vo., 18s.

Kant.—Works by IMMANUEL KANT.

CRITIQUE OF PRACTICAL REASON, AND OTHER WORKS ON THE THEORY OF ETHICS. Translated by T. K. ABBOTT, B.D. With Memoir. 8vo., 12s. 6d.

INTRODUCTION TO LOGIC, AND HIS ESSAY ON THE MISTAKEN SUBTILTY OF THE FOUR FIGURES. Translated by T. K. ABBOTT. 8vo., 6s.

Killick.—HANDBOOK TO MILL'S SYSTEM OF LOGIC. By Rev. A. H. KILLICK, M.A. Crown 8vo., 3s. 6d.

Ladd.—Works by G. T. LADD.

ELEMENTS OF PHYSIOLOGICAL PSYCHOLOGY. 8vo., 21s.

OUTLINES OF PHYSIOLGGICAL PSYCHOLOGY. A Text-book of Mental Science for Academies and Colleges. 8vo., 12s.

Lewes.—THE HISTORY OF PHILOSOPHY, from Thales to Comte. By GEORGE HENRY LEWES. 2 vols. 8vo., 32s.

Max Müller.—Works by F. MAX MÜLLER.

THE SCIENCE OF THOUGHT. 8vo., 21s.

THREE INTRODUCTORY LECTURES ON THE SCIENCE OF THOUGHT. 8vo., 2s. 6d.

Mental, Moral and Political Philosophy—*continued.*

Mill.—ANALYSIS OF THE PHENOMENA OF THE HUMAN MIND. By JAMES MILL. 2 vols. 8vo., 28s.

Mill.—Works by JOHN STUART MILL.
A SYSTEM OF LOGIC. Crown 8vo., 3s. 6d.
ON LIBERTY. Crown 8vo., 1s. 4d.
ON REPRESENTATIVE GOVERNMENT. Crown 8vo., 2s.
UTILITARIANISM. 8vo., 5s.
EXAMINATION OF SIR WILLIAM HAMILTON'S PHILOSOPHY. 8vo., 16s.
NATURE, THE UTILITY OF RELIGION, AND THEISM. Three Essays. 8vo., 5s.

Monck.—INTRODUCTION TO LOGIC. By W. H. S. MONCK. Crown 8vo., 5s.

Ribot.—THE PSYCHOLOGY OF ATTENTION. By TH. RIBOT. Crown 8vo., 3s.

Sidgwick.—DISTINCTION: and the Criticism of Belief. By ALFRED SIDGWICK. Crown 8vo., 6s.

Stock.—DEDUCTIVE LOGIC. By ST. GEORGE STOCK. Fcp. 8vo., 3s. 6d.

Sully.—Works by JAMES SULLY.
THE HUMAN MIND: a Text-book of Psychology. 2 vols. 8vo., 21s.
OUTLINES OF PSYCHOLOGY. 8vo., 9s.
THE TEACHER'S HANDBOOK OF PSYCHOLOGY. Crown 8vo., 5s.

Swinburne.—PICTURE LOGIC: an Attempt to Popularise the Science of Reasoning. By ALFRED JAMES SWINBURNE, M.A. With 23 Woodcuts. Post 8vo., 5s.

Thompson.—Works by DANIEL GREENLEAF THOMPSON.
THE PROBLEM OF EVIL: an Introduction to the Practical Sciences. 8vo., 10s. 6d.
A SYSTEM OF PSYCHOLOGY. 2 vols. 8vo., 36s.
THE RELIGIOUS SENTIMENTS OF THE HUMAN MIND. 8vo., 7s. 6d.
SOCIAL PROGRESS: an Essay. 8vo., 7s. 6d.
THE PHILOSOPHY OF FICTION IN LITERATURE: an Essay. Crown 8vo., 6s.

Thomson.—OUTLINES OF THE NECESSARY LAWS OF THOUGHT: a Treatise on Pure and Applied Logic. By WILLIAM THOMSON, D.D., formerly Lord Archbishop of York. Post 8vo., 6s.

Webb.—THE VEIL OF ISIS: a Series of Essays on Idealism. By T. E. WEBB. 8vo., 10s. 6d.

Whately.—Works by R. WHATELY, D.D.
BACON'S ESSAYS. With Annotation. By R. WHATELY. 8vo. 10s. 6d.
ELEMENTS OF LOGIC. Cr. 8vo., 4s. 6d.
ELEMENTS OF RHETORIC. Crown 8vo., 4s. 6d.
LESSONS ON REASONING. Fcp. 8vo., 1s. 6d.

Zeller.—Works by Dr. EDWARD ZELLER, Professor in the University of Berlin.
HISTORY OF ECLECTICISM IN GREEK PHILOSOPHY. Translated by SARAH F. ALLEYNE. Crown 8vo., 10s. 6d.
THE STOICS, EPICUREANS, AND SCEPTICS. Translated by the Rev. O. J. REICHEL, M.A. Crown 8vo., 15s.
OUTLINES OF THE HISTORY OF GREEK PHILOSOPHY. Translated by SARAH F. ALLEYNE and EVELYN ABBOTT. Crown 8vo., 10s. 6d.
PLATO AND THE OLDER ACADEMY. Translated by SARAH F. ALLEYNE and ALFRED GOODWIN, B.A. Crown 8vo., 18s.
SOCRATES AND THE SOCRATIC SCHOOLS. Translated by the Rev. O. J. REICHEL, M.A. Crown 8vo., 10s. 6d.
THE PRE-SOCRATIC SCHOOLS: a History of Greek Philosophy from the Earliest Period to the time of Socrates. Translated by SARAH F. ALLEYNE. 2 vols. Crown 8vo., 30s.

MANUALS OF CATHOLIC PHILOSOPHY.
(Stonyhurst Series).

A MANUAL OF POLITICAL ECONOMY. By C. S. DEVAS, M.A. Crown 8vo., 6s. 6d.

FIRST PRINCIPLES OF KNOWLEDGE. By JOHN RICKABY, S.J. Crown 8vo., 5s.

GENERAL METAPHYSICS. By JOHN RICKABY, S.J. Crown 8vo., 5s.

LOGIC. By RICHARD F. CLARKE, S.J. Crown 8vo., 5s.

MORAL PHILOSOPHY (ETHICS AND NATURAL LAW. By JOSEPH RICKABY, S.J. Crown 8vo., 5s.

NATURAL THEOLOGY. By BERNARD BOEDDER, S.J. Crown 8vo., 6s. 6d.

PSYCHOLOGY. By MICHAEL MAHER, S.J. Crown 8vo., 6s. 6d.

History and Science of Language, &c.

Davidson.—LEADING AND IMPORTANT ENGLISH WORDS: Explained and Exemplified. By WILLIAM L. DAVIDSON, M.A. Fcp. 8vo., 3s. 6d.

Farrar.—LANGUAGE AND LANGUAGES: By F. W. FARRAR, D.D., F.R.S. Crown 8vo., 6s.

Graham.—ENGLISH SYNONYMS, Classified and Explained: with Practical Exercises. By G. F. GRAHAM. Fcp. 8vo., 6s.

Max Müller.—Works by F. MAX MÜLLER. SELECTED ESSAYS ON LANGUAGE, MYTHOLOGY, AND RELIGION. 2 vols. Crown 8vo., 16s.

THE SCIENCE OF LANGUAGE, Founded on Lectures delivered at the Royal Institution in 1861 and 1863. 2 vols. Crown 8vo., 21s.

BIOGRAPHIES OF WORDS, AND THE HOME OF THE ARYAS. Crown 8vo., 7s. 6d.

Max Müller.—Works by F. MAX MÜLLER —*continued.*

THREE LECTURES ON THE SCIENCE OF LANGUAGE, AND ITS PLACE IN GENERAL EDUCATION, delivered at Oxford, 1889. Crown 8vo., 3s.

Roget.—THESAURUS OF ENGLISH WORDS AND PHRASES. Classified and Arranged so as to Facilitate the Expression of Ideas and assist in Literary Composition. By PETER MARK ROGET, M.D., F.R.S. Recomposed throughout, enlarged and improved, partly from the Author's Notes, and with a full Index, by the Author's Son, JOHN LEWIS ROGET. Crown 8vo. 10s. 6d.

Whately.—ENGLISH SYNONYMS. By E. JANE WHATELY. Fcp. 8vo., 3s.

Political Economy and Economics.

Ashley.—ENGLISH ECONOMIC HISTORY AND THEORY. By W. J. ASHLEY, M.A. Crown 8vo., Part I., 5s. Part II. 10s. 6d.

Bagehot.—ECONOMIC STUDIES. By WALTER BAGEHOT. 8vo., 10s. 6d.

Barnett.—PRACTICABLE SOCIALISM: Essays on Social Reform. By the Rev. S. A. and Mrs. BARNETT.

Brassey.—PAPERS AND ADDRESSES ON WORK AND WAGES. By Lord BRASSEY.

Crump.—AN INVESTIGATION INTO THE CAUSES OF THE GREAT FALL IN PRICES which took place coincidently with the Demonetisation of Silver by Germany. By ARTHUR CRUMP. 8vo., 6s.

Devas.—A MANUAL OF POLITICAL ECONOMY. By C. S. DEVAS, M.A. Crown 8vo., 6s. 6d. (*Manuals of Catholic Philosophy.*)

Dowell.—A HISTORY OF TAXATION AND TAXES IN ENGLAND, from the Earliest Times to the Year 1885. By STEPHEN DOWELL, (4 vols. 8vo.) Vols. I. and II. The History of Taxation, 21s. Vols. III. and IV. The History of Taxes, 21s.

Jordan.—THE STANDARD OF VALUE. By WILLIAM LEIGHTON JORDAN. 8vo., 6s.

Leslie.—ESSAYS IN POLITICAL ECONOMY. By T. E. CLIFFE LESLIE. 8vo., 10s. 6d.

Macleod.—Works by HENRY DUNNING MACLEOD, M.A.

THE ELEMENTS OF BANKING. Crown 8vo., 3s. 6d.

THE THEORY AND PRACTICE OF BANKING. Vol. I. 8vo., 12s. Vol. II. 14s.

THE THEORY OF CREDIT. 8vo. Vol. I. 10s. net. Vol. II., Part I., 4s. 6d. Vol. II. Part II., 10s. 6d.

Meath.—PROSPERITY OR PAUPERISM? Physical, Industrial, and Technical Training. By the EARL OF MEATH. 8vo., 5s.

Mill.—POLITICAL ECONOMY. By JOHN STUART MILL.

Silver Library Edition. Crown 8vo., 3s. 6d. Library Edition. 2 vols. 8vo., 30s.

Shirres.—AN ANALYSIS OF THE IDEAS OF ECONOMICS. By L. P. SHIRRES, B.A., sometime Finance Under-Secretary of the Government of Bengal. Crown 8vo., 6s.

Symes.—POLITICAL ECONOMY: a Short Text-book of Political Economy. With Problems for Solution, and Hints for Supplementary Reading. By Professor J. E. SYMES, M.A., of University College, Nottingham. Crown 8vo., 2s. 6d.

Toynbee.—LECTURES ON THE INDUSTRIAL REVOLUTION OF THE 18th CENTURY IN ENGLAND. By ARNOLD TOYNBEE. 8vo., 10s. 6d.

Wilson. — Works by A. J. WILSON. Chiefly reprinted from *The Investors' Review.*

PRACTICAL HINTS TO SMALL INVESTORS. Crown 8vo., 1s.

PLAIN ADVICE ABOUT LIFE INSURANCE. Crown 8vo., 1s.

Wolff.—PEOPLE'S BANKS: a Record of Social and Economic Success. By HENRY W. WOLFF. 8vo., 7s. 6d.

Evolution, Anthropology, &c.

Clodd.—THE STORY OF CREATION: a Plain Account of Evolution. By EDWARD CLODD. With 77 Illustrations. Crown 8vo., 3s. 6d.

Huth.—THE MARRIAGE OF NEAR KIN, considered with Respect to the Law of Nations, the Result of Experience, and the Teachings of Biology. By ALFRED HENRY HUTH. Royal 8vo., 7s. 6d.

Lang.—CUSTOM AND MYTH: Studies of Early Usage and Belief. By ANDREW LANG, M.A. With 15 Illustrations. Crown 8vo., 3s. 6d.

Lubbock.—THE ORIGIN OF CIVILISATION and the Primitive Condition of Man. By Sir J. LUBBOCK, Bart., M.P. With 5 Plates and 20 Illustrations in the Text. 8vo., 18s.

Romanes. — Works by GEORGE JOHN ROMANES, M.A., LL.D., F.R.S.

DARWIN, AND AFTER DARWIN: an Exposition of the Darwinian Theory, and a Discussion on Post-Darwinian Questions. Part I. The Darwinian Theory. With Portrait of Darwin and 125 Illustrations. Crown 8vo., 10s. 6d.

AN EXAMINATION OF WEISMANNISM. Crown 8vo., 6s.

Classical Literature and Translations, &c.

Abbott.—HELLENICA. A Collection of Essays on Greek Poetry, Philosophy, History, and Religion. Edited by EVELYN ABBOTT, M.A., LL.D. 8vo., 16s.

Æschylus.—EUMENIDES OF ÆSCHYLUS. With Metrical English Translation. By J. F. DAVIES. 8vo., 7s.

Aristophanes. — THE ACHARNIANS OF ARISTOPHANES, translated into English Verse. By R. Y. TYRRELL. Crown 8vo., 1s.

Becker.—Works by Professor BECKER.

GALLUS : or, Roman Scenes in the Time of Augustus. Illustrated. Post 8vo., 7s. 6d.

CHARICLES : or, Illustrations of the Private Life of the Ancient Greeks. Illustrated. Post 8vo., 7s. 6d.

Cicero.—CICERO'S CORRESPONDENCE. By R. Y. TYRRELL. Vols. I., II., III., 8vo., each 12s.

Clerke.—FAMILIAR STUDIES IN HOMER. By AGNES M. CLERKE. Crown 8vo., 7s. 6d.

Farnell.—GREEK LYRIC POETRY: a Complete Collection of the Surviving Passages from the Greek Song-Writing. Arranged with Prefatory Articles, Introductory Matter and Commentary. By GEORGE S. FARNELL, M.A. With 5 Plates. 8vo., 16s.

Harrison.—MYTHS OF THE ODYSSEY IN ART AND LITERATURE. By JANE E. HARRISON. Illustrated with Outline Drawings. 8vo., 18s.

Lang.—HOMER AND THE EPIC. By ANDREW LANG. Crown 8vo., 9s. net.

Mackail.—SELECT EPIGRAMS FROM THE GREEK ANTHOLOGY. By J. W. MACKAIL, Fellow of Balliol College, Oxford. Edited with a Revised Text, Introduction, Translation, and Notes. 8vo., 16s.

Plato.—PARMENIDES OF PLATO, Text, with Introduction, Analysis, &c. By T. MAGUIRE. 8vo., 7s. 6d.

Rich.—A DICTIONARY OF ROMAN AND GREEK ANTIQUITIES. By A. RICH, B.A. With 2000 Woodcuts. Crown 8vo., 7s. 6d.

Sophocles.—Translated into English Verse. By ROBERT WHITELAW, M.A., Assistant Master in Rugby School; late Fellow of Trinity College, Cambridge. Crown 8vo., 8s. 6d.

Tyrrell.—TRANSLATIONS INTO GREEK AND LATIN VERSE. Edited by R. Y. TYRRELL. 8vo., 6s.

Virgil.—THE ÆNEID OF VIRGIL. Translated into English Verse by JOHN CONINGTON. Crown 8vo., 6s.

THE POEMS OF VIRGIL. Translated into English Prose by JOHN CONINGTON. Crown 8vo., 6s.

THE ÆNEID OF VIRGIL, freely translated into English Blank Verse. By W. J. THORNHILL. Crown 8vo., 7s. 6d.

THE ÆNEID OF VIRGIL. Books I. to VI. Translated into English Verse by JAMES RHOADES. Crown 8vo., 5s.

Wilkins.—THE GROWTH OF THE HOMERIC POEMS. By G. WILKINS. 8vo., 6s.

Poetry and the Drama.

Allingham.—Works by WILLIAM ALLINGHAM.

IRISH SONGS AND POEMS. With Frontis- of the Waterfall of Asaroe. Fcp. 8vo., 6s.

LAURENCE BLOOMFIELD. With Portrait of the Author. Fcp. 8vo., 3s. 6d.

FLOWER PIECES; DAY AND NIGHT SONGS; BALLADS. With 2 Designs by D. G. ROSSETTI. Fcp. 8vo., 6s.; large paper edition, 12s.

LIFE AND PHANTASY: with Frontispiece by Sir J. E. MILLAIS, Bart., and Design by ARTHUR HUGHES. Fcp. 8vo., 6s.; large paper edition, 12s.

THOUGHT AND WORD, AND ASHBY MANOR: a Play. With Portrait of the Author (1865), and four Theatrical Scenes drawn by Mr. Allingham. Fcp. 8vo., 6s.; large paper edition, 12s.

BLACKBERRIES. Imperial 16mo., 6s.

Sets of the above 6 vols. may be had in uniform Half-parchment binding, price 30s.

Armstrong.—Works by G. F. SAVAGE-ARMSTRONG.

POEMS: Lyrical and Dramatic. Fcp. 8vo., 6s.

KING SAUL. (The Tragedy of Israel, Part I.) Fcp. 8vo., 5s.

KING DAVID. (The Tragedy of Israel, Part II.) Fcp. 8vo., 6s.

KING SOLOMON. (The Tragedy of Israel, Part III.) Fcp. 8vo., 6s.

UGONE: a Tragedy. Fcp. 8vo., 6s.

A GARLAND FROM GREECE: Poems. Fcp. 8vo., 7s. 6d.

STORIES OF WICKLOW: Poems. Fcp. 8vo., 7s. 6d.

MEPHISTOPHELES IN BROADCLOTH: a Satire. Fcp. 8vo., 4s.

ONE IN THE INFINITE: a Poem. Crown 8vo., 7s. 6d.

Armstrong.—THE POETICAL WORKS OF EDMUND J. ARMSTRONG. Fcp. 8vo., 5s.

Arnold.—Works by Sir EDWIN ARNOLD, K.C.I.E., Author of ' The Light of Asia,' &c.

THE LIGHT OF THE WORLD: or the Great Consummation. A Poem. Crown 8vo., 7s. 6d. net.

Presentation Edition. With 14 Illustrations by W. HOLMAN HUNT, 4to., 20s. net.

POTIPHAR'S WIFE, and other Poems. Crown 8vo., 5s. net.

ADZUMA: or the Japanese Wife. A Play. Crown 8vo., 6s. 6d. net.

Barrow.—THE SEVEN CITIES OF THE DEAD, and other Poems. By Sir JOHN CROKER BARROW, Bart. Fcp. 8vo., 5s.

Bell.—Works by Mrs. HUGH BELL.

CHAMBER COMEDIES: a Collection of Plays and Monologues for the Drawing Room. Crown 8vo., 6s.

NURSERY COMEDIES: Twelve Tiny Plays for Children. Fcp. 8vo., 1s. 6d.

Björnsen.—PASTOR SANG: A PLAY. By BJÖRNSTJERNE BJÖRNSEN. Translated by WILLIAM WILSON. Crown 8vo., 5s.

Dante.—LA COMMEDIA DI DANTE. A New Text, carefully Revised with the aid of the most recent Editions and Collations. Small 8vo., 6s.

Goethe.

FAUST, Part I., the German Text, with Introduction and Notes. By ALBERT M. SELSS, Ph.D., M.A. Crown 8vo., 5s.

FAUST. Translated, with Notes. By T. E. WEBB. 8vo., 12s. 6d.

FAUST. The First Part. A New Translation, chiefly in Blank Verse; with Introduction and Notes. By JAMES ADEY BIRDS. Crown 8vo., 6s.

FAUST. The Second Part. A New Translation in Verse. By JAMES ADEY BIRDS. Crown 8vo., 6s.

Ingelow.—Works by JEAN INGELOW.

POETICAL WORKS. 2 vols. Fcp. 8vo., 12s.

LYRICAL AND OTHER POEMS. Selected from the Writings of JEAN INGELOW. Fcp. 8vo., 2s. 6d. cloth plain, 3s. cloth gilt.

Lang.—Works by ANDREW LANG.

GRASS OF PARNASSUS. Fcp. 8vo., 2s. 6d. net.

BALLADS OF BOOKS. Edited by ANDREW LANG. Fcp. 8vo., 6s.

THE BLUE POETRY BOOK. Edited by ANDREW LANG. With 12 Plates and 88 Illustrations in the Text by H. J. FORD and LANCELOT SPEED. Crown 8vo., 6s.

Special Edition, printed on India paper. With Notes, but without Illustrations. Crown 8vo., 7s. 6d.

Lecky.—POEMS. By W. E. H. LECKY. Fcp. 8vo., 5s.

Leyton.—Works by FRANK LEYTON.

THE SHADOWS OF THE LAKE, and other Poems. Crown 8vo., 7s. 6d. Cheap Edition. Crown 8vo., 3s. 6d.

SKELETON LEAVES: Poems. Crown 8vo. 6s.

2

Poetry and the Drama—*continued.*

Lytton.—Works by THE EARL OF LYTTON (OWEN MEREDITH).
MARAH. Fcp. 8vo., 6s. 6d.
KING POPPY: a Fantasia. With 1 Plate and Design on Title-Page by ED. BURNE-JONES, A.R.A. Crown 8vo., 10s. 6d.
THE WANDERER. Crown 8vo., 10s. 6d.
LUCILE. Crown 8vo., 10s. 6d.
SELECTIONS FROM POETICAL WORKS. Crown 8vo., 10s. 6d.

Macaulay.—LAYS OF ANCIENT ROME, &c. By Lord MACAULAY.
Illustrated by G. SCHARF. Fcp. 4to., 10s. 6d.
——————————— Bijou Edition. 18mo., 2s. 6d. gilt top.
——————————— Popular Edition. Fcp. 4to., 6d. sewed, 1s. cloth.
Illustrated by J. R. WEGUELIN. Crown 8vo , 3s. 6d.
Annotated Edition. Fcp. 8vo., 1s. sewed, 1s. 6d. cloth.

Nesbit.—LAYS AND LEGENDS. By E. NESBIT (Mrs. HUBERT BLAND). First Series. Crown 8vo., 3s. 6d. Second Series. With Portrait. Crown 8vo., 5s.

Piatt.—AN ENCHANTED CASTLE, AND OTHER POEMS: Pictures, Portraits, and People in Ireland. By SARAH PIATT Crown 8vo. 3s. 6d.

Piatt.—WORKS BY JOHN JAMES PIATT.
IDYLS AND LYRICS OF THE OHIO VALLEY. Crown 8vo., 5s.
LITTLE NEW WORLD IDYLS. Cr. 8vo. 5s.

Rhoades.—TERESA AND OTHER POEMS. By JAMES RHOADES. Crown 8vo., 3s. 6d.

Riley.—Works by JAMES WHITCOMB RILEY.
OLD FASHIONED ROSES: Poems. 12mo., 5s.
POEMS: Here at Home. Fcp. 8vo., 6s. *net.*

Roberts.—SONGS OF THE COMMON DAY AND AVE! An Ode for the Shelley Centenary. By CHARLES G. D. ROBERTS. Cr. 8vo., 3s. 6d.

Shakespeare. — BOWDLER'S FAMILY SHAKESPEARE. With 36 Woodcuts. 1 vol. 8vo., 14s. Or in 6 vols. Fcp. 8vo., 21s.
THE SHAKESPEARE BIRTHDAY BOOK. By MARY F. DUNBAR. 32mo., 1s. 6d. Drawing Room Edition, with Photographs. Fcp. 8vo., 10s. 6d.

Stevenson. — A CHILD'S GARDEN OF Verses. By ROBERT LOUIS STEVENSON. Small Fcp. 8vo., 5s.

Works of Fiction, Humour, &c.

ATELIER (THE) DU LYS: or, an Art Student in the Reign of Terror. Crown 8vo., 2s. 6d.

BY THE SAME AUTHOR.

MADEMOISELLE MORI: a Tale of Modern Rome. Crown 8vo., 2s. 6d.

THAT CHILD. With Illustrations by GORDON BROWNE. Crown 8vo., 2s. 6d.

UNDER A CLOUD. Crown 8vo., 2s. 6d.

THE FIDDLER OF LUGAU. With Illustrations by W. RALSTON, Crown 8vo., 2s. 6d.

A CHILD OF THE REVOLUTION. With Illustrations by C. J. STANILAND. Crown 8vo., 2s. 6d.

HESTER'S VENTURE. Cr. 8vo., 2s. 6d.

IN THE OLDEN TIME: a Tale of the Peasant War in Germany. Cr.8vo.,2s.6d.

THE YOUNGER SISTER. Crown 8vo., 2s. 6d.

Anstey.—Works by F. ANSTEY, Author of 'Vice Versa '.

THE BLACK POODLE, and other Stories. Crown 8vo., 2s. boards, 2s. 6d. cloth.

VOCES POPULI. Reprinted from 'Punch'. First Series. With 20 Illust. by J. BERNARD PARTRIDGE. Fcp. 4to., 5s. Second Series. With 25 Illust. by J. BERNARD PARTRIDGE. Fcp. 4to., 6s.

THE TRAVELLING COMPANIONS. Reprinted from 'Punch'. With 25 Illust. by J. BERNARD PARTRIDGE. Post 4to., 5s.

THE MAN FROM BLANKLEY'S: a Story in Scenes, and other Sketches. With 24 Illustrations by J. BERNARD PARTRIDGE. Fcp. 4to., 6s.

Baker.—BY THE WESTERN SEA. By JAMES BAKER, Author of 'John Westacott'. Crown 8vo., 3s. 6d.

Works of Fiction, Humour, &c.—*continued.*

Beaconsfield.—Works by the Earl of BEACONSFIELD.

NOVELS AND TALES. Cheap Edition. Complete in 11 vols. Cr. 8vo., 1s. 6d. each.

Vivian Grey.	Henrietta Temple.
The Young Duke, &c.	Venetia. Tancred.
Alroy, Ixion, &c.	Coningsby. Sybil.
Contarini Fleming,&c.	Lothair. Endymion.

NOVELS AND TALES. The Hughenden Edition. With 2 Portraits and 11 Vignettes. 11 vols. Crown 8vo., 42s.

Comyn.—ATHERSTONE PRIORY: a Tale. By L. N. COMYN. Crown 8vo., 2s. 6d.

Deland.—Works by MARGARET DELAND, Author of 'John Ward'.

THE STORY OF A CHILD. Cr. 8vo., 5s.

MR. TOMMY DOVE, and other Stories. Crown 8vo. 6s.

Dougall.—Works by L. DOUGALL.

BEGGARS ALL Crown 8vo., 3s. 6d.

WHAT NECESSITY KNOWS. 3 vols. Crown 8vo., 25s. 6d.

Doyle.—Works by A. CONAN DOYLE.

MICAH CLARKE: A Tale of Monmouth's Rebellion. With Frontispiece and Vignette. Cr. 8vo., 3s. 6d.

THE CAPTAIN OF THE POLESTAR, and other Tales. Cr. 8vo., 3s. 6d.

THE REFUGEES: A Tale of Two Continents. Cr. 8vo., 6s.

Farrar.—DARKNESS AND DAWN: or, Scenes in the Days of Nero. An Historic Tale. By Archdeacon FARRAR. Cr. 8vo., 7s. 6d.

Froude.—THE TWO CHIEFS OF DUNBOY: an Irish Romance of the Last Century. by J. A. FROUDE. Cr. 8vo., 3s. 6d.

Haggard.—Works by H. RIDER HAGGARD.

SHE. With 32 Illustrations by M. GREIFFENHAGEN and C. H. M. KERR. Cr. 8vo., 3s. 6d.

ALLAN QUATERMAIN. With 31 Illustrations by C. H. M. KERR. Cr. 8vo., 3s. 6d.

MAIWA'S REVENGE: or, The War of the Little Hand. Cr. 8vo., 1s. boards, 1s. 6d. cloth.

Haggard.—Works by H. RIDER HAGGARD. —*continued.*

COLONEL QUARITCH, V.C. Cr. 8vo. 3s. 6d.

CLEOPATRA. With 29 Full-page Illustrations by M. GREIFFENHAGEN and R. CATON WOODVILLE. Crown 8vo., 3s. 6d.

BEATRICE. Cr. 8vo., 3s. 6d.

ERIC BRIGHTEYES. With 17 Plates and 34 Illustrations in the Text by LANCELOT SPEED. Cr. 8vo., 3s. 6d.

NADA THE LILY. With 23 Illustrations by C. H. M. KERR. Cr. 8vo., 6s.

MONTEZUMA'S DAUGHTER. With 24 Illustrations by M. GREIFFENHAGEN. Crown 8vo., 6s.

Haggard and Lang.—THE WORLD'S DESIRE. By H. RIDER HAGGARD and ANDREW LANG. Cr. 8vo. 6s.

Harte.—IN THE CARQUINEZ WOODS and other stories. By BRET HARTE. Cr. 8vo., 3s. 6d.

KEITH DERAMORE: a Novel. By the Author of 'Miss Molly'. Cr. 8vo., 6s.

Lyall.—THE AUTOBIOGRAPHY OF A SLANDER. By EDNA LYALL, Author of 'Donovan,' &c. Fcp. 8vo., 1s. sewed.

Presentation Edition. With 20 Illustrations by LANCELOT SPEED. Crown 8vo., 5s.

Melville.—Works by G. J. WHYTE MELVILLE.

The Gladiators.	Holmby House.
The Interpreter.	Kate Coventry.
Good for Nothing.	Digby Grand.
The Queen's Maries.	General Bounce.

Cr. 8vo., 1s. 6d. each.

Oliphant.—Works by Mrs. OLIPHANT.

MADAM. Cr. 8vo., 1s. 6d.

IN TRUST. Cr. 8vo., 1s. 6d.

Parr.—CAN THIS BE LOVE? By Mrs. PARR, Author of 'Dorothy Fox'. Crown 8vo. 6s.

Works of Fiction, Humour, &c.—*continued.*

Payn.—Works by JAMES PAYN.

THE LUCK OF THE DARRELLS. Cr. 8vo., 1s. 6d.

THICKER THAN WATER. Cr. 8vo., 1s. 6d.

Phillipps-Wolley.—SNAP: a Legend of the Lone Mountain. By C. PHILLIPPS-WOLLEY. With 13 Illustrations by H. G. WILLINK. Cr. 8vo., 3s. 6d.

Robertson.—THE KIDNAPPED SQUATTER, and other Australian Tales. By A. ROBERTSON. Cr. 8vo., 6s.

Sewell.—Works by ELIZABETH M. SEWELL.

A Glimpse of the World.	Amy Herbert.
Laneton Parsonage.	Cleve Hall.
Margaret Percival.	Gertrude.
Katharine Ashton.	Home Life.
The Earl's Daughter.	After Life.
The Experience of Life.	Ursula. Ivors.

Cr. 8vo., 1s. 6d. each cloth plain. 2s. 6d. each cloth extra, gilt edges.

Stevenson.—Works by ROBERT LOUIS STEVENSON.

STRANGE CASE OF DR. JEKYLL AND MR. HYDE. Fcp. 8vo., 1s. sewed. 1s. 6d. cloth.

THE DYNAMITER. Fcp. 8vo., 1s. sewed, 1s. 6d. cloth.

Stevenson and Osbourne.—THE WRONG BOX. By ROBERT LOUIS STEVENSON and LLOYD OSBOURNE. Cr. 8vo., 3s. 6d.

Sturgis.—AFTER TWENTY YEARS, and other Stories. By JULIAN STURGIS. Cr. 8vo., 6s.

Suttner.—LAY DOWN YOUR ARMS (*Die Waffen Nieder*): The Autobiography of Martha Tilling. By BERTHA VON SUTTNER. Translated by T. HOLMES. Cr. 8vo., 7s. 6d.

Thompson.—A MORAL DILEMMA: a Novel. By ANNIE THOMPSON. Crown 8vo., 6s.

Tirebuck.—Works by WILLIAM TIREBUCK.

DORRIE. Crown 8vo. 6s.

SWEETHEART GWEN. Crown 8vo., 6s.

Trollope.—Works by ANTHONY TROLLOPE.

THE WARDEN. Cr. 8vo., 1s. 6d.

BARCHESTER TOWERS. Cr. 8vo., 1s. 6d.

Walford.—Works by L. B. WALFORD, Author of 'Mr. Smith'.

THE MISCHIEF OF MONICA: a Novel. Cr. 8vo., 2s. 6d.

THE ONE GOOD GUEST: a Story. Cr. 8vo., 2s. 6d.

West.—HALF-HOURS WITH THE MILLIONAIRES: Showing how much harder it is to spend a million than to make it. Edited by B. B. WEST. Cr. 8vo., 6s.

Weyman.—Works by STANLEY J. WEYMAN.

THE HOUSE OF THE WOLF: a Romance. Cr. 8vo., 3s. 6d.

A GENTLEMAN OF FRANCE. 3 vols. Cr. 8vo. 25s. 6d.

Popular Science (Natural History, &c.).

Butler.—OUR HOUSEHOLD INSECTS. An Account of the Insect-Pests found in Dwelling-Houses. By EDWARD A. BUTLER, B.A., B.Sc. (Lond.). With 113 Illustrations. Crown 8vo., 6s.

Furneaux.—THE OUTDOOR WORLD; or The Young Collector's Handbook. By W. FURNEAUX, F.R.G.S. With 18 Plates, 16 of which are coloured, and 549 Illustrations in the Text. Crown 8vo., 7s. 6d.

Hartwig.—Works by Dr. GEORGE HARTWIG.

THE SEA AND ITS LIVING WONDERS With 12 Plates and 303 Woodcuts. 8vo., 7s. net.

THE TROPICAL WORLD. With 8 Plates and 172 Woodcuts. 8vo., 7s. net.

THE POLAR WORLD. With 3 Maps, 8 Plates and 85 Woodcuts. 8vo., 7s. net.

Popular Science (Natural History, &c.)—*continued.*

Hartwig.—Works by Dr. George Hartwig—*continued.*

The Subterranean World. With 3 Maps and 80 Woodcuts. 8vo., 7s. net.

The Aerial World. With Map, 8 Plates and 60 Woodcuts. 8vo., 7s. net.

Heroes of the Polar World. 19 Illustrations. Cr. 8vo., 2s.

Wonders of the Tropical Forests. 40 Illustrations. Cr. 8vo., 2s.

Workers under the Ground. 29 Illustrations. Cr. 8vo., 2s.

Marvels Over our Heads. 29 Illustrations. Cr. 8vo., 2s.

Sea Monsters and Sea Birds. 75 Illustrations. Cr. 8vo., 2s. 6d.

Denizens of the Deep. 117 Illustrations. Cr. 8vo., 2s. 6d.

Volcanoes and Earthquakes. 30 Illustrations. Cr. 8vo., 2s. 6d.

Wild Animals of the Tropics. 66 Illustrations. Cr. 8vo., 3s. 6d.

Helmholtz. — Popular Lectures on Scientific Subjects. By Hermann von Helmholtz. With 68 Woodcuts. 2 vols. Cr. 8vo., 3s. 6d. each.

Lydekker.—Phases of Animal Life, Past and Present. By. R. Lydekker, B.A. With 82 Illustrations. Cr. 8vo., 6s.

Proctor.—Works by Richard A. Proctor.

Light Science for Leisure Hours. Familiar Essays on Scientific Subjects. 3 vols. Cr. 8vo., 5s. each.

Chance and Luck: a Discussion of the Laws of Luck, Coincidence, Wagers, Lotteries and the Fallacies of Gambling, &c. Cr. 8vo., 2s. boards. 2s. 6d. cloth.

Rough Ways made Smooth. Familiar Essays on Scientific Subjects. Cr. 8vo., 5s. Silver Library Edition. Cr. 8vo., 3s. 6d.

Pleasant Ways in Science. Cr. 8vo., 5s. Silver Library Edition. Cr. 8vo., 3s. 6d.

The Great Pyramid, Observatory, Tomb and Temple. With Illustrations. Cr. 8vo., 5s.

Nature Studies. By R. A. Proctor, Grant Allen, A. Wilson, T. Foster and E. Clodd. Cr. 8vo., 5s. Silver Library Edition. Crown 8vo., 3s. 6d.

Proctor.—Works by Richard A. Proctor. —*continued.*

Leisure Readings. By R. A. Proctor, E. Clodd, A. Wilson, T. Foster and A. C. Ranyard. Cr. 8vo., 5s.

Stanley.—A Familiar History of Birds. By E. Stanley, D.D., formerly Bishop of Norwich. With Illustrations. Cr. 8vo., 3s. 6d.

Wood.—Works by the Rev. J. G. Wood.

Homes without Hands: a Description of the Habitation of Animals, classed according to the Principle of Construction. With 140 Illustrations. 8vo., 7s., net.

Insects at Home: a Popular Account of British Insects, their Structure, Habits and Transformations. With 700 Illustrations. 8vo., 7s. net.

Insects Abroad: a Popular Account of Foreign Insects, their Structure, Habits and Transformations. With 600 Illustrations. 8vo., 7s. net.

Bible Animals: a Description of every Living Creatures mentioned in the Scriptures. With 112 Illustrations. 8vo., 7s. net.

Petland Revisited. With 33 Illustrations. Cr. 8vo., 3s. 6d.

Out of Doors; a Selection of Original Articles on Practical Natural History. With 11 Illustrations. Cr. 8vo., 3s. 6d.

Strange Dwellings: a Description of the Habitations of Animals, abridged from 'Homes without Hands'. With 60 Illustrations. Cr. 8vo., 3s. 6d.

Bird Life of the Bible. 32 Illustrations. Cr. 8vo., 3s. 6d.

Wonderful Nests. 30 Illustrations. Cr. 8vo., 3s. 6d.

Homes under the Ground. 28 Illustrations. Cr. 8vo., 3s. 6d.

Wild Animals of the Bible. 29 Illustrations. Cr. 8vo., 3s. 6d.

Domestic Animals of the Bible. 23 Illustrations. Cr. 8vo., 3s. 6d.

The Branch Builders. 28 Illustrations. Cr. 8vo., 2s. 6d.

Social Habitations and Parasitic Nests. 18 Illustrations. Cr. 8vo., 2s.

Works of Reference.

Maunder's (Samuel) Treasuries.

BIOGRAPHICAL TREASURY. With Supplement brought down to 1889. By Rev. JAMES WOOD. Fcp. 8vo., 6s.

TREASURY OF NATURAL HISTORY: or, Popular Dictionary of Zoology. With 900 Woodcuts. Fcp. 8vo., 6s.

TREASURY OF GEOGRAPHY, Physical, Historical, Descriptive, and Political. With 7 Maps and 16 Plates. Fcp. 8vo., 6s.

THE TREASURY OF BIBLE KNOWLEDGE. By the Rev. J. AYRE, M.A. With 5 Maps, 15 Plates, and 300 Woodcuts. Fcp. 8vo., 6s.

HISTORICAL TREASURY: Outlines of Universal History, Separate Histories of all Nations. Fcp. 8vo., 6s.

TREASURY OF KNOWLEDGE AND LIBRARY OF REFERENCE. Comprising an English Dictionary and Grammar, Universal Gazeteer, Classical Dictionary, Chronology, Law Dictionary, &c. Fcp. 8vo.. 6s.

Maunder's (Samuel) Treasuries--*continued.*

SCIENTIFIC AND LITERARY TREASURY. Fcp. 8vo., 6s.

THE TREASURY OF BOTANY. Edited by J. LINDLEY, F.R.S., and T. MOORE, F.L.S. With 274 Woodcuts and 20 Steel Plates. 2 vols. Fcp. 8vo., 12s.

Roget.—THESAURUS OF ENGLISH WORDS AND PHRASES. Classified and Arranged so as to Facilitate the Expression of Ideas and assist in Literary Composition. By PETER MARK ROGET, M.D., F.R.S. Recomposed throughout, enlarged and improved, partly from the Author's Notes, and with a full Index, by the Author's Son, JOHN LEWIS ROGET. Crown 8vo., 10s. 6d.

Willich.—POPULAR TABLES for giving information for ascertaining the value of Lifehold, Leasehold, and Church Property, the Public Funds, &c. By CHARLES M. WILLICH. Edited by H. BENCE JONES. Crown 8vo., 10s. 6d.

Children's Books.

Crake.—Works by Rev. A. D. CRAKE.

EDWY THE FAIR ; or, The First Chronicle of Æscendune. Crown 8vo., 2s. 6d.

ALFGAR THE DANE : or, the Second Chronicle of Æscendune. Cr. 8vo. 2s. 6d.

THE RIVAL HEIRS : being the Third and Last Chronicle of Æscendune. Cr. 8vo., 2s. 6d.

THE HOUSE OF WALDERNE. A Tale of the Cloister and the Forest in the Days of the Barons' Wars. Crown 8vo., 2s. 6d.

BRIAN FITZ-COUNT. A Story of Wallingford Castle and Dorchester Abbey. Cr. 8vo., 2s. 6d.

Ingelow.—VERY YOUNG, and QUITE ANOTHER STORY. Two Stories. By JEAN INGELOW. Crown 8vo., 2s. 6d.

Lang.—Works edited by ANDREW LANG.

THE BLUE FAIRY BOOK. With 8 Plates and 130 Illustrations in the Text by H. J. FORD and G. P. JACOMB HOOD. Crown 8vo., 6s.

THE RED FAIRY BOOK. With 4 Plates and 96 Illustrations in the Text by H. J. FORD and LANCELOT SPEED. Crown 8vo., 6s.

Lang.—Works edited by ANDREW LANG. —*continued.*

THE GREEN FAIRY BOOK. With 11 Plates and 88 Illustrations in the Text by H. J. FORD and L. BOGLE. Crown 8vo., 6s.

THE BLUE POETRY BOOK. With 12 Plates and 88 Illustrations in the Text by H. J. FORD and LANCELOT SPEED. Cr. 8vo., 6s.

THE BLUE POETRY BOOK. School Edition, without Illustrations. Fcp. 8vo., 2s. 6d.

THE TRUE STORY BOOK. With 8 Plates and 58 Illustrations in the Text, by H. J. FORD, LUCIEN DAVIS, C. H. M. KERR, LANCELOT SPEED, and LOCKHART BOGLE. Cr. 8vo., 6s.

Meade.—Works by L. T. MEADE.

DADDY'S BOY. With Illustrations. Crown 8vo., 3s. 6d.

DEB AND THE DUCHESS. With Illustrations by M. E. EDWARDS. Crown 8vo., 3s. 6d.

THE BERESFORD PRIZE. With Illustrations by M. E. EDWARDS. Crown 8vo., 5s.

Children's Books—*continued.*

Molesworth.—Works by Mrs. MOLES-WORTH.

SILVERTHORNS. Illustrated. Crown 8vo., 5s.

THE PALACE IN THE GARDEN. Illustrated. Crown 8vo., 5s.

THE THIRD MISS ST. QUENTIN. Crown 8vo., 2s. 6d.

NEIGHBOURS. Illustrated. Crown 8vo., 6s.

THE STORY OF A SPRING MORNING, &c. Illustrated. Crown 8vo., 2s. 6d.

Reader.—VOICES FROM FLOWER-LAND: a Birthday Book and Language of Flowers. By EMILY E. READER. Illustrated by ADA BROOKE. Royal 16mo., cloth, 2s. 6d.; vegetable vellum, 3s. 6d.

Stevenson.—Works by ROBERT LOUIS STEVENSON.

A CHILD'S GARDEN OF VERSES. Small Fcp. 8vo., 5s.

A CHILD'S GARLAND OF SONGS, Gathered from 'A Child's Garden of Verses'. Set to Music by C. VILLIERS STANFORD, Mus. Doc. 4to., 2s. sewed; 3s. 6d., cloth gilt.

The Silver Library.

CROWN 8vo. 3s. 6d. EACH VOLUME.

Baker's (Sir S. W.) Eight Years in Ceylon. With 6 Illustrations. 3s. 6d.

Baker's (Sir S. W.) Rifle and Hound in Ceylon. With 6 Illustrations. 3s. 6d.

Baring-Gould's (Rev. S.) Curious Myths of the Middle Ages. 3s. 6d.

Baring-Gould's (Rev. S.) Origin and Development of Religious Belief. 2 vols. 3s. 6d. each.

Brassey's (Lady) A Voyage in the 'Sunbeam'. With 66 Illustrations. 3s. 6d.

Clodd's (E.) Story of Creation: a Plain Account of Evolution. With 77 Illustrations. 3s. 6d.

Conybeare (Rev. W. J.) and Howson's (Very Rev. J. S.) Life and Epistles of St. Paul. 46 Illustrations. 3s. 6d.

Dougall's (L.) Beggars All: a Novel. 3s. 6d.

Doyle's (A. Conan) Micah Clarke. A Tale of Monmouth's Rebellion. 3s. 6d.

Doyle's (A. Conan) The Captain of the Polestar, and other Tales. 3s. 6d.

Froude's (J. A.) Short Studies on Great Subjects. 4 vols. 3s. 6d. each.

Froude's (J. A.) Cæsar: a Sketch. 3s. 6d.

Froude's (J. A.) Thomas Carlyle: a History of his Life.
1795-1835. 2 vols. 7s.
1834-1881. 2 vols. 7s.

Froude's (J. A.) The Two Chiefs of Dunboy: an Irish Romance of the Last Century. 3s. 6d.

Froude's (J. A.) The History of England, from the Fall of Wolsey to the Defeat of the Spanish Armada. 12 vols. 3s. 6d. each.

Gleig's (Rev. G. R.) Life of the Duke of Wellington. With Portrait. 3s. 6d.

Haggard's (H. R.) She: A History of Adventure. 32 Illustrations. 3s. 6d.

Haggard's (H. R.) Allan Quatermain. With 20 Illustrations. 3s. 6d.

Haggard's (H. R.) Colonel Quaritch, V.C.: a Tale of Country Life. 3s. 6d.

Haggard's (H. R.) Cleopatra. With 29 Full page Illustrations. 3s. 6d.

Haggard's (H. R.) Eric Brighteyes. With 51 Illustrations. 3s. 6d.

Haggard's (H. R.) Beatrice. 3s. 6d.

Harte's (Bret) In the Carquinez Woods and other Stories. 3s. 6d.

Helmholtz's (Hermann von) Popular Lectures on Scientific Subjects. With 68 Woodcuts. 2 vols. 3s. 6d. each.

Howitt's (W.) Visits to Remarkable Places. 80 Illustrations. 3s. 6d.

Jefferies' (R.) The Story of My Heart: My Autobiography. With Portrait. 3s. 6d.

Jefferies' (R.) Field and Hedgerow. Last Essays of. With Portrait. 3s. 6d.

Jefferies' (R.) Red Deer. With 17 Illustrations by J. CHARLTON and H. TUNALY. 3s. 6d.

Jefferies' (R.) Wood Magic: a Fable. With Frontispiece and Vignette by E. V. B. 3s. 6d.

Jefferies (R.) The Toilers of the Field. With Portrait from the Bust in Salisbury Cathedral. 3s. 6d.

Knight's (E. F.) The Cruise of the 'Alerte': the Narrative of a Search for Treasure on the Desert Island of Trinidad. With 2 Maps and 23 Illustrations. 3s. 6d.

Lang's (A.) Custom and Myth: Studies of Early Usage and Belief. 3s. 6d.

Lees (J. A.) and Clutterbuck's (W. J.) B. C. 1887, A Ramble in British Columbia. With Maps and 75 Illustrations. 3s. 6d.

Macaulay's (Lord) Essays and Lays of Ancient Rome. With Portrait and Illustration. 3s. 6d.

Macleod's (H. D.) The Elements of Banking. 3s. 6d.

The Silver Library—*continued.*

Marshman's (J. C.) Memoirs of Sir Henry Havelock. 3s. 6d.

Max Müller's (F.) India, what can it teach us? 3s. 6d.

Max Müller's (F.) Introduction to the Science of Religion. 3s. 6d.

Merivale's (Dean) History of the Romans under the Empire. 8 vols. 3s. 6d. each.

Mill's (J. S.) Principles of Political Economy. 3s. 6d.

Mill's (J. S.) System of Logic. 3s. 6d.

Milner's (Geo.) Country Pleasures: the Chronicle of a Year chiefly in a Garden. 3s. 6d.

Newman's (Cardinal) Apologia Pro Vitâ Sua. 3s. 6d.

Newman's (Cardinal) Historical Sketches. 3 vols. 3s. 6d. each.

Newman's (Cardinal) Callista: a Tale of the Third Century. 3s. 6d.

Newman's (Cardinal) Loss and Gain: a Tale. 3s. 6d.

Newman's (Cardinal) Essays, Critical and Historical. 2 vols. 7s.

Newman's (Cardinal) An Essay on the Development of Christian Doctrine. 3s. 6d.

Newman's (Cardinal) The Arians of the Fourth Century. 3s. 6d.

Newman's (Cardinal) Verses on Various Occasions. 3s. 6d.

Newman's (Cardinal) The Present Position of Catholics in England. 3s. 6d.

Newman's (Cardinal) Parochial and Plain Sermons. 8 vols. 3s. 6d. each.

Newman's (Cardinal) Selection, adapted to the Seasons of the Ecclesiastical Year, from the 'Parochial and Plain Sermons'. 3s. 6d.

Newman's (Cardinal) Sermons bearing upon Subjects of the Day. 3s. 6d.

Newman's (Cardinal) Difficulties felt by Anglicans in Catholic Teaching Considered. 2 vols. 3s. 6d. each.

Newman's (Cardinal) The Idea of a University Defined and Illustrated. 3s. 6d.

Newman's (Cardinal) Biblical and Ecclesiastical Miracles. 3s. 6d.

Newman's (Cardinal) Discussions and Arguments on Various Subjects. 3s. 6d.

Newman's (Cardinal) Grammar of Assent. 3s. 6d.

Newman's (Cardinal) Fifteen Sermons Preached before the University of Oxford. 3s. 6d.

Newman's (Cardinal) Lectures on the Doctrine of Justification. 3s. 6d.

Newman's (Cardinal) Sermons on Various Occasions. 3s. 6d.

Newman's (Cardinal) The Via Media of the Anglican Church, illustrated in Lectures, &c. 2 vols. 3s. 6d. each.

Newman's (Cardinal) Discourses to Mixed Congregations. 3s. 6d.

Phillipps-Wolley's (C.) Snap: a Legend of the Lone Mountain. With 13 Illustrations. 3s. 6d.

Proctor's (R. A.) The Orbs Around Us: Essays on the Moon and Planets, Meteors and Comets, the Sun and Coloured Pairs of Suns. 3s. 6d.

Proctor's (R. A.) The Expanse of Heaven: Essays on the Wonders of the Firmament. 3s. 6d.

Proctor's (R. A.) Other Worlds than Ours. 3s. 6d.

Proctor's (R. A.) Rough Ways made Smooth. 3s. 6d.

Proctor's (R. A.) Pleasant Ways in Science. 3s. 6d.

Proctor's (R. A.) Myths and Marvels of Astronomy. 3s. 6d.

Proctor's (R. A.) Nature Studies. 3s. 6d.

Smith (R. Bosworth) Carthage and the Carthaginians. With Maps, Plans, &c. 3s. 6d.

Stanley's (Bishop) Familiar History of Birds. 160 Illustrations. 3s. 6d.

Stevenson (R. L.) and Osbourne's (Ll.) The Wrong Box. 3s. 6d.

Weyman's (Stanley J.) The House of the Wolf: a Romance. 3s. 6d.

Wood's (Rev. J. G.) Petland Revisited. With 33 Illustrations. 3s. 6d.

Wood's (Rev. J. G.) Strange Dwellings. With 60 Illustrations. 3s. 6d.

Wood's (Rev. J. G.) Out of Doors. 11 Illustrations. 3s. 6d.

Cookery, Domestic Management, etc.

Acton.—MODERN COOKERY. By ELIZA ACTON. With 150 Woodcuts. Fcp. 8vo., 4s. 6d.

Bull.—Works by THOMAS BULL, M.D.

HINTS TO MOTHERS ON THE MANAGEMENT OF THEIR HEALTH DURING THE PERIOD OF PREGNANCY. Fcp. 8vo., 1s. 6d.

THE MATERNAL MANAGEMENT OF CHILDREN IN HEALTH AND DISEASE. Fcp. 8vo., 1s. 6d.

De Salis.—Works by Mrs. DE SALIS.

CAKES AND CONFECTIONS À LA MODE. Fcp. 8vo., 1s. 6d.

DOGS; A Manual for Amateurs. Fcp. 8vo.

DRESSED GAME AND POULTRY À LA MODE. Fcp. 8vo., 1s. 6d.

DRESSED VEGETABLES À LA MODE. Fcp. 8vo., 1s. 6d.

DRINKS À LA MODE. Fcp. 8vo., 1s. 6d.

ENTRÉES À LA MODE. Fcp. 8vo., 1s. 6d.

Cookery and Domestic Management—*continued.*

De Salis.—Works by Mrs. DE SALIS—*cont.*

FLORAL DECORATIONS. Suggestions and Descriptions. Fcp. 8vo., 1s. 6d.

NEW-LAID EGGS: Hints for Amateur Poultry Rearers. Fcp. 8vo., 1s. 6d.

OYSTERS À LA MODE. Fcp. 8vo., 1s. 6d.

PUDDINGS, AND PASTRY À LA MODE. Fcp. 8vo., 1s. 6d.

SAVOURIES À LA MODE. Fcp. 8vo., 1s. 6d.

SOUPS AND DRESSED FISH À LA MODE. Fcp. 8vo., 1s. 6d.

SWEETS AND SUPPER DISHES À LA MODE. Fcp. 8vo., 1s. 6d.

TEMPTING DISHES FOR SMALL INCOMES. Fcp. 8vo., 1s. 6d.

WRINKLES AND NOTIONS FOR EVERY HOUSEHOLD. Crown 8vo., 1s. 6d.

Harrison.—COOKERY FOR BUSY LIVES AND SMALL INCOMES. By MARY HARRISON. Crown 8vo., 1s.

Lear.—MAIGRE COOKERY. By H. L. SIDNEY LEAR. 16mo., 2s.

Poole.—COOKERY FOR THE DIABETIC. By W. H. and Mrs. POOLE. With Preface by Dr. PAVY. Fcp. 8vo., 2s. 6d.

Walker.—A HANDBOOK FOR MOTHERS: being Simple Hints to Women on the Management of their Health during Pregnancy and Confinement, together with Plain Directions as to the Care of Infants. By JANE H. WALKER, L.R.C.P. and L.M., L.R.C.S. and M.D. (Brux). Crown 8vo., 2s. 6d.

Miscellaneous and Critical Works.

Allingham.—VARIETIES IN PROSE. By WILLIAM ALLINGHAM. 3 vols. Crown 8vo., 18s. (Vols. 1 and 2, Rambles, by PATRICIUS WALKER. Vol. 3, Irish Sketches, etc.)

Armstrong.—ESSAYS AND SKETCHES. By EDMUND J. ARMSTRONG. Fcp. 8vo., 5s.

Bagehot.—LITERARY STUDIES. By WALTER BAGEHOT. 2 vols. 8vo., 28s.

Baring-Gould.—CURIOUS MYTHS OF THE MIDDLE AGES. By Rev. S. BARING-GOULD. Crown 8vo., 3s. 6d.

Battye.—PICTURES IN PROSE OF NATURE, WILD SPORT, AND HUMBLE LIFE. By AUBYN TREVOR BATTYE, B.A.

Boyd ('A. K. H. B.').—Works by A. K. H. BOYD, D.D., LL.D.

AUTUMN HOLIDAYS OF A COUNTRY PARSON. Crown 8vo., 3s. 6d.

COMMONPLACE PHILOSOPHER. Crown 8vo., 3s. 6d.

CRITICAL ESSAYS OF A COUNTRY PARSON. Crown 8vo., 3s. 6d.

EAST COAST DAYS AND MEMORIES. Crown 8vo., 3s. 6d.

LANDSCAPES, CHURCHES AND MORALITIES. Crown 8vo., 3s. 6d.

LEISURE HOURS IN TOWN. Crown 8vo., 3s. 6d.

LESSONS OF MIDDLE AGE. Crown 8vo., 3s. 6d.

OUR LITTLE LIFE. Two Series. Cr. 8vo., 3s. 6d. each.

OUR HOMELY COMEDY: AND TRAGEDY Crown 8vo., 3s. 6d.

RECREATIONS OF A COUNTRY PARSON. Three Series. Crown 8vo., 3s. 6d. each. Also First Series. Popular Ed. 8vo., 6d.

Butler.—Works by SAMUEL BUTLER.

Op. 1. EREWHON. Cr. 8vo., 5s.

Op. 2. THE FAIR HAVEN. A Work in Defence of the Miraculous Element in our Lord's Ministry. Cr. 8vo., 7s. 6d.

Op. 3. LIFE AND HABIT. An Essay after a Completer View of Evolution. Cr. 8vo., 7s. 6d.

Op. 4. EVOLUTION, OLD AND NEW. Cr. 8vo., 10s. 6d.

Op. 5. UNCONSCIOUS MEMORY. Cr. 8vo., 7s. 6d.

Op. 6. ALPS AND SANCTUARIES OF PIEDMONT AND CANTON TICINO. Illustrated. Pott 4to., 10s. 6d.

Op. 7. SELECTIONS FROM OPS. 1-6. With Remarks on Mr. ROMANES' 'Mental Evolution in Animals'. Cr. 8vo., 7s. 6d.

Op. 8. LUCK, OR CUNNING, AS THE MAIN MEANS OF ORGANIC MODIFICATION? Cr. 8vo., 7s. 6d.

Op. 9. EX VOTO. An Account of the Sacro Monte or New Jerusalem at Varallo-Sesia. 10s. 6d.

HOLBEIN'S 'LA DANSE'. A Note on a Drawing called 'La Danse'. 3s.

Halliwell-Phillipps.—A CALENDAR OF THE HALLIWELL-PHILLIPPS' COLLECTION OF SHAKESPEAREAN RARITIES. Enlarged by ERNEST E. BAKER, F.S.A. 8vo., 10s. 6d.

Hodgson.—OUTCAST ESSAYS AND VERSE TRANSLATIONS. By H. SHADWORTH HODGSON. Crown 8vo., 8s. 6d.

Miscellaneous and Critical Works — *continued.*

Hullah.—Works by JOHN HULLAH, LL.D.
COURSE OF LECTURES ON THE HISTORY OF MODERN MUSIC. 8vo., 8s. 6d.
COURSE OF LECTURES ON THE TRANSITION PERIOD OF MUSICAL HISTORY. 8vo., 10s. 6d.

James.—MINING ROYALTIES: their Practical Operation and Effect. By CHARLES ASHWORTH JAMES, of Lincoln's Inn, Barrister-at-Law. Fcp. 4to., 5s.

Jefferies.—Works by RICHARD JEFFERIES.
FIELD AND HEDGEROW: last Essays. With Portrait. Crown 8vo., 3s. 6d.
THE STORY OF MY HEART: my Autobiography. With Portrait and New Preface by C. J. LONGMAN. Crown 8vo., 3s. 6d.
RED DEER. With 17 Illustrations by J. CHARLTON and H. TUNALY. Crown 8vo., 3s. 6d.
THE TOILERS OF THE FIELD. With Portrait· from the Bust in Salisbury Cathedral. Crown 8vo., 3s. 6d.
WOOD MAGIC: a Fable. With Frontispiece and Vignette by E. V. B. Crown 8vo., 3s. 6d.

Jewsbury.—SELECTIONS FROM THE LETTERS OF GERALDINE ENDSOR JEWSBURY TO JANE WELSH CARLYLE. Edited by Mrs. ALEXANDER IRELAND. 8vo., 16s.

Johnson.—THE PATENTEE'S MANUAL: a Treatise on the Law and Practice of Letters Patent. By J. & J. H. JOHNSON, Patent Agents, &c. 8vo., 10s. 6d.

Lang.—Works by ANDREW LANG.
LETTERS TO DEAD AUTHORS. Fcp. 8vo., 2s. 6d. net.
BOOKS AND BOOKMEN. With 2 Coloured Plates and 17 Illustrations. Fcp. 8vo., 2s. 6d. net.
OLD FRIENDS. Fcp. 8vo., 2s. 6d. net.
LETTERS ON LITERATURE. Fcp. 8vo., 2s. 6d. net.

Macfarren.—LECTURES ON HARMONY. By Sir GEORGE A. MACFARREN. 8vo., 12s.

Max Müller.—Works by F. MAX MÜLLER.
HIBBERT LECTURES ON THE ORIGIN AND GROWTH OF RELIGION, as illustrated by the Religions of India. Crown 8vo., 7s. 6d.
INTRODUCTION TO THE SCIENCE OF RELIGION: Four Lectures delivered at the Royal Institution. Crown 8vo., 3s. 6d.
NATURAL RELIGION. The Gifford Lectures, 1888. Crown 8vo., 10s. 6d.
PHYSICAL RELIGION. The Gifford Lectures, 1890. Crown 8vo., 10s. 6d.

Max Müller.—Works by F. MAX MÜLLER.
—*continued.*
ANTHROPOLOGICAL RELIGION. The Gifford Lectures, 1891. Cr. 8vo., 10s. 6d.
THEOSOPHY OR PSYCHOLOGICAL RELIGION. The Gifford Lectures, 1892. Crown 8vo., 10s. 6d.
INDIA: WHAT CAN IT TEACH US? Cr. 8vo., 3s. 6d.

Mendelssohn.—THE LETTERS OF FELIX MENDELSSOHN. Translated by Lady WALLACE. 2 vols. Cr. 8vo., 10s.

Milner.—Works by GEORGE MILNER.
COUNTRY PLEASURES: the Chronicle of a Year chiefly in a Garden. Cr. 8vo., 3s. 6d.
STUDIES OF NATURE ON THE COAST OF ARRAN. With Illustrations by W. NOEL JOHNSON.

Perring.—HARD KNOTS IN SHAKESPEARE. By Sir PHILIP PERRING, Bart. 8vo., 7s. 6d.

Proctor.—Works by RICHARD A. PROCTOR.
STRENGTH AND HAPPINESS. With 9 Illustrations. Crown 8vo., 5s.
STRENGTH: How to get Strong and keep Strong, with Chapters on Rowing and Swimming, Fat, Age, and the Waist. With 9 Illustrations. Crown 8vo., 2s.

Richardson.—NATIONAL HEALTH. A Review of the Works of Sir Edwin Chadwick, K.C.B. By Sir B. W. RICHARDSON, M.D. Cr., 4s. 6d.

Roget.—A HISTORY OF THE 'OLD WATER-COLOUR' SOCIETY (now the Royal Society of Painters in Water-Colours). By JOHN LEWIS ROGET. 2 vols. Royal 8vo., 42s.

Rossetti.—A SHADOW OF DANTE: being an Essay towards studying Himself, his World and his Pilgrimage. By MARIA FRANCESCA ROSSETTI. With Illustrations and with designs on cover by DANTE GABRIEL ROSSETTI. Cr. 8vo., 10s. 6d.

Southey.—CORRESPONDENCE WITH CAROLINE BOWLES. By ROBERT SOUTHEY. Edited by E. DOWDEN. 8vo., 14s.

Wallaschek.—PRIMITIVE MUSIC: an Inquiry into the Origin and Development of Music, Songs, Instruments, Dances, and Pantomimes of Savage Races. By RICHARD WALLASCHEK. With Musical Examples. 8vo., 12s. 6d.

West.—WILLS, AND HOW NOT TO MAKE THEM. With a Selection of Leading Cases. By B. B. WEST, Author of "Half-Hours with the Millionaires". Fcp. 8vo., 2s. 6d.